The Director's Cut

'Hadn't we better call the police?'

'Or tell the hotel. Or . . .'

'Don't be stupid!' Hodgson's voice was harsher than hers. 'You'd better go back to the hotel. Or your car.' He was barring her way, as if she was about to go up and give the animal the kiss of life. Or scream and summon the RSPCA.

'But we can't just leave it.'

'It's just been left for me.' Hodgson's voice was loud and bitter.

'What?' Kate swayed a little, the fresh night air cutting through her alcoholic bravado. 'What are you talking about?'

'The dog's been left for me. It's a warning.'

Also by Lis Howell

After the Break

About the author

Lis Howell was born and educated in Liverpool and has worked in television for many years. After starting at BBC radio in Leeds, she became a TV reporter, presenter and producer, then Head of News at Border TV, going on to be managing editor of Sky News. She was the shortlived first Director of Programmes for GMTV, served for a short time after that as a producer on 'Good Morning with Anne and Nick' and is now Director of Programmes for UK Living, the cable and satellite channel.

The Director's Cut

Lis Howell

CORONET BOOKS
Hodder and Stoughton

First published in Great Britain in 1996 by Hodder and Stoughton
A division of Hodder Headline PLC
First published in paperback in 1996 by Hodder and Stoughton
A Coronet Paperback

10 9 8 7 6 5 4 3 2 1

A CIP catalogue record for this title is available from the British
Library
ISBN 0-340-64908-9

Typeset by Avon Dataset Ltd, Bidford-on-Avon, Warks

Printed and bound in Great Britain by
Cox & Wyman, Reading, Berks

Hodder and Stoughton
A division of Hodder Headline PLC
338 Euston Road
London NW1 3BH

For everyone who loves Cumbria

Thanks to David Lloyd,
Carol Bedford and Janice Newbury

Chapter One

It threatened to be a chilly night on the coast. The clang of a farm gate faded, until all that was left was the soft sucking of the sea, scrunching backwards and forwards over the pebbles and licking with the dishwater slaps of a flat, bleak west coast tide. The cold was cut by the harsh, sad cry of oyster-catchers and the occasional disembodied challenge of gulls.

The wheelchair, one wheel already buckled, squeaked over the rutted path to the shoreline. The woman's voice rose, a wittering whine, lost against the screeching metal and increased anxiety of the birds. Her hands lifted and fluttered like little claws scrabbling at the sky.

Suddenly the chair was pushed forward towards the sea. It rolled slowly over the mud and pebbles then lurched and stopped, tilted and crippled, on the stony beach. The old woman's skeletal body slumped. Her hands scrabbled at the wheels but they were stuck fast. Her cries grew louder and more frantic in the emptiness, like the hysterical oyster-catchers scrambling on thin legs along the mud flat before taking off in a cloud. Then she was left alone to the circling gulls.

* * *

The plane was on time, and Kate Wilkinson was propelled with the other passengers up the stairs and along the glass corridor, towards the brightness of the lounge at Newcastle Airport. She had always wanted to be met by a chauffeur with a card bearing her name, ready to sweep her off to a waiting limo and this time, to her delight, one had been promised. She had to admit she had been surprised. Chauffeur driven cars did not seem in keeping with independent TV companies on location in the wild North of England. She certainly wasn't complaining, although she was amused to find she felt rather embarrassed.

But she needn't have, because there was no-one waiting for her. She looked again, feeling increasingly uncomfortable. It was like making a second-rate début on to a stage. The audience on the other side of the glass stared back at her, uninterested. As she watched, the faces broke into smiles – for other people. If the film director hadn't organised the car as he'd promised, what would she do? She couldn't imagine hailing a taxi and calmly saying, 'Take me to West Cumbria; it's only ninety miles.'

She walked through the automatic doors and stood there, mesmerised by the other welcomes. The Sunday afternoon flight from Heathrow had hardly been full, and most people on board had looked as if they were coming home, unlike Kate. She felt a quiver of panic. She didn't know a soul and she was bound for the other side of Britain.

She sat down, then stood up again, undecided, before approaching the two remaining drivers who still stood there with cards bearing illegible names.

'Excuse me,' she said awkwardly.

'Why, flower? What've you done?' sniggered one of the men.

2

She grinned. 'Has anyone been looking for a Miss Wilkinson?'

'Nae such luck,' said another, making her laugh before scampering after a woman whose plastic hair and wheeled luggage looked far more compatible with a chauffeur driven car.

In a minute, she thought, she would tackle the new mobile phone she had rented, but the thought was discouraging. The other option was to wait, but there was something especially isolating about being abandoned at an airport. Airports were bubbles on the froth of towns, miles from the local bustle of train and bus stations. Kate saw her reflection in the glass panel, caught the look of disguised desperation on her own face, her mussed auburn hair out of shape like a woolly hat over one eye, her shoulder dragged down by the wretched bag she had heaved from Heathrow, and her nice bright floaty scarf lying drooped like a dead bird over her crumpled linen jacket. She was cold too. She sat down again, looked around twitchily, then fumbled with her briefcase. It flew open, scattering bits of paper.

Not very smart, Kate thought. For a horrible moment she suffered traveller's terror . . . where was that essential document? But of course the letter was there, hiding under the newspaper, and Kate felt relief as sharp as a headache.

Rural Rides Revisited was not a well known company, and Kate had been surprised by their smart vellum paper and glossy brochure. But they had a track record – and money, clearly. So where was the chauffeur? Kate re-read the letter. It said that film director Andy de Salas's PA would arrange a driver to meet her at the airport '. . . so you'll have no worries on that score. And if we have a problem

arranging a driver on a Sunday, I'll be there myself!' de
Salas had finished with a flourish.

Perhaps that was the answer. Had she missed him? What
did Andy de Salas look like? Kate had worked with plenty
of film directors before, though never on a project quite
like this. She imagined him to be about forty-five, running
a little bit to seed, in an Aran sweater or something suitably
folksy, with faded jeans or baggy cords. However well-
heeled, the owner of an independent television production
company called Rural Rides Revisited was bound to have a
look of being hand knitted. She glanced around. No-one
answering that description was anywhere in the vicinity.
In fact, no-one was in the vicinity at all.

Kate shivered. At Heathrow there were always residual
crowds, but here the flight came in, the people
disembarked, they met their families and they went. She
felt like the last person left on earth. She focused on her
papers instead of the emptiness. It had all seemed so clear
and organised, three hundred miles away

'Rural Rides Revisited is making a unique film about rural
crafts in North West Cumbria,' de Salas had written. 'We
originally approached Lady Marshall of Skirlbeck Woollen
Mill, who has helped us organise the project. We expect to
receive financial support from the North West Cumbria
Tourist Centre's video budget. The Tourist Centre is run
by Paul Pym, an ex TV man himself. And we believe the
film will find a slot on at least one TV network. At present,
though, it is a risk venture, like so many independent
productions these days. But Rural Rides Revisited is well
used to risks. Other projects that have paid off have
included the Lindisfarne dolphin film "Grace's Darlings"
for Channel Four and the much acclaimed film about the

Scottish Borders, "Uncommon Riding".'

Uncommon set-up, thought Kate. Or perhaps not, in these days of spare TV talent chasing rare opportunities. Kate had become involved in the project through her friend Liz Jones, a producer with two young children who worked part time. Liz, a bubbly type whose dizzy manner hid a sharp organisational brain, had met Andy de Salas at a TV conference. A few months later, he had contacted Liz in desperation. His partner in the business, who was also his executive producer, had injured his leg badly on a Lakeland crag while 'recce-ing' an outdoor pursuits centre for the film leaving Andy de Salas with a crisis. Liz had spoken to Kate on his behalf, asking her friend to step in, and the offer had come at just the right moment. The current affairs programme Kate was working on for a cable TV channel had completed one series successfully and was due to go into its second run the next month. Kate had been left with four weeks of unpaid holiday. After just one phone call from de Salas's harassed PA, she had arranged to join Rural Rides for a fortnight to help out.

Kate sighed. Opposite her was a plate glass window and beyond that the dark merging of runway and rain. The chance to escape had been very convenient, for other reasons too. Kate's personal situation was unusual, but it had never posed a problem before. But now her love life seemed as grounded as the fat, immobile jet outside the window, after two years of flying high. She had made John, her partner, promise to visit her in the middle of the shoot for a quiet weekend. In asking him to join her, miles from anyone they knew and far from the pressure of his work, she hoped they might find time to talk things through.

Thinking of him, on impulse she fumbled in her case

and took out the mobile phone that had been organised for her by Andy de Salas's assistant, the efficient sounding June who had been Kate's contact at Rural Rides. Kate had hardly ever used a mobile phone, and remembered what had happened to Liz when as a proud new working mum, she had mastered the technology, only to be viewed with contempt by a train carriage full of inter-city businessmen when she used it to ask, 'Has Thomas finished his eggie weggie then?'

Gingerly, Kate punched a number. There was of course no reply. John must have had to do Evensong. When Kate had first met him, the Reverend John Maple was a demoralised, unhappy man who had taken religious orders, but who believed he had failed as a parish priest. He was twelve years older than Kate, but despite the fact that she had no religious leanings, they had fallen deeply in love, and he had cherished her common sense and cheerfulness. However, in the last year he had edged back more and more into conventional church work, and become increasingly busy and distant from her. Now he was assisting in a seedy South London parish where one of his friends, the melodramatic Anglo-Catholic Father Marcus, was getting over the nervous breakdown John had himself so narrowly avoided.

So Kate was feeling increasingly marginalised. She had made no secret of the fact that she couldn't share John's faith, but that didn't mean she had no intellect. Yet John refused to talk to her about anything, especially his beliefs. He was either out, doing parish work, or he studiously avoided even discussing anything of significance with her in case they rowed. Even so, sitting alone at Newcastle airport, she missed him with a physical ache.

She was suddenly stopped, in the familiar act of torturing herself, by one of the most handsome young men she had ever seen dripping rain on to her briefcase.

'Kate Wilkinson, I presume?'

With his opening words the charmer before her had neatly engineered a greeting without an apology. Kate gaped at him.

'I'm Andy de Salas. Good journey? I should imagine so. Now, can we get all your stuff together. Dear me, rather a lot of bits and pieces, aren't there? OK, follow me.'

Feeling completely clumsy, Kate bundled everything together, and trundled behind him, clutching the miscellaneous receipts, business cards and last minute lists that threatened to splay out of her grasp on to the floor. In her left hand she suddenly noticed an envelope with a number and a note scrawled in John Maple's strong, spiky writing. 'George Goff' it said, with a Cumbria telephone number underneath. 'Meant to mention him. Good bloke. Reliable. Would love to meet you. We could see him at the weekend. Ring him as soon as you arrive.' *Ring him as soon as you arrive?* What was John thinking of? That wasn't the plan at all. Kate had wanted them to be alone together the next weekend, unhindered by John's endless commitments. She looked round for a litter bin.

'I suppose you're wondering what kept me.' She could hardly hear de Salas's voice as he swept before her, his full length Barbour crackling and his casually flung white knitted scarf streaming behind him. 'Well, we had a meeting this afternoon about tomorrow's shoot at the woollen mill at Skirlbeck, and Lady Marshall persuaded us to stay for lunch. So I didn't get away as fast as I hoped. I was sure you wouldn't mind.' He turned, and smiled a melting smile, and went on, 'Now we just need to get you out of the airport and into the car, and then I'll have a chance to go through things with you. Oh, look, I'm really sorry about that bag. You *do* seem to be struggling. Let me give you a hand!' His brown eyes crinkled and with a boyish flick of his thick dark hair he grabbed her shoulder bag as if it was a mere shopping holdall and strode ahead.

The airport car park was bleak and wet, and Kate prepared herself for a trek to de Salas's car. But he had ignored the rules, and his low slung Porsche was waiting like a tame alligator at the pavement's edge. He opened the door with the click of a remote control and flung her luggage into the back whilst indicating that she should lower herself into the leather seat next to him.

He paid jauntily at the booth, then with sudden speed veered out of the car park. Surreptitiously, she gripped the edge of the seat. As he sped round the corner, almost immediately leaving the lights of the airport behind, she found she hardly had time to exchange pleasantries before he began a long discourse on country life and how he and his film company were the guardians of its reality.

'You see, Kate, what is so key about Rural Rides is our commitment to regional Britain. That's our role, and that's why people want to buy our product. And we don't restrict ourselves to postcard scenes of course . . . we're not the Landscape Channel – absolutely not. What we do, is look at country life as it really is, warts and all, although of course the warts are a lot fewer than in a place like London.' His tone implied horror at the carbuncles on the capital.

'Yes,' Kate murmured, thinking suddenly that she had forgotten to pack any Tampax . . . But this hardly seemed

8

the moment to ask if there was a handy Eight til Late store nearby. Andy de Salas was now well into his stride.

'The film we're making is about North West Cumbria. Not the prettiest place in Britain, and it suffers from being on the edge of the immaculate Lake District, but it has its own post industrial grandeur.'

Wow! But Kate limited herself to saying conversationally, 'Of course,' and stopped, watching the blackness out of the window as if de Salas was speeding her down a tunnel. Then oncoming headlights swept across them, and to her surprise she saw the tension on his face. It alarmed her.

How much did she really know about where she was going and what she was doing? The previous day, in a rare moment together, she and John had taken out the road atlas of Britain and studied the map. John Maple was from one of the Pennine textile towns, and as a child he had gone on trips to the Lake District, which had meant taking two buses and then the railway crawling like a scar over the backbone of England. It had left him with a deep affection not just for the Lakes but also for the remote strip of shore beyond. Dotted with industries needing sea or seclusion, it had progressed from ugly pits through steel and timber, to chemicals and nuclear reprocessing. Kate imagined the area was having an identity crisis. Not picturesque like the mountainous hinterland, nor famous for character like other northern manufacturing areas, it was a fascinating example of the blend of a rural and an industrial way of life.

De Salas's silky voice in the dark seemed at odds with the taut face she had just glimpsed. He said smoothly, 'Our film is about the fact that country crafts are being revived in this area, and the return to a more traditional way of life, thanks to some local people who have had the foresight to encourage this.'

'Mmm,' said Kate. 'And presumably you've now got a transmission slot on BBC or Channel Four . . . or maybe Border TV?'

Andy took a bend so sharply Kate felt she had to come up for air.

'Not yet,' he said. 'A lot of that sort of work was done by my partner, Ben Lowe. To be honest, I spend most of my time making the local contacts. Ben's the visionary, and he usually sells the ideas to the networks.'

'And Ben's in the Cumberland Infirmary with a crushed leg?'

'Quite so.'

There was a moment's silence. Kate reconsidered the little she really knew about Andy de Salas. Liz had kept quiet about his stunning looks and his youth, which surprised Kate who was used to her friend discussing every aspect of any new man she met from his brains to his bottom. She had said that de Salas was from a wealthy background, and had sunk his own money into the company. But Kate had assumed they were talking about a man well into his forties. Now, realising de Salas was much younger, she felt slight qualms. She tried to recall the names of Rural Rides Revisited's other staff and their titles in the blurb de Salas's PA had sent her. She had heard of Ben Lowe who had been named with de Salas on the headed paper, and had assumed Ben was the second in command and de Salas the boss. Now she wondered.

'And you've made a lot of programmes?' she queried gently.

'Well, the two most well known were the one about the

dolphins – Ben my partner did a marvellous job – and the Scottish riders one, which we sold to America.'

'And you directed those? Or was that – Ben?'

'Oh . . . a joint effort.' Oh dear, Kate thought, does that mean he's as green as he looks?

'Here we are,' de Salas went on. He accelerated the car up a sudden steep bend off the dual carriageway. Kate frowned a little. He was driving with immense bravado.

'We're leaving the A69 now and making for Hadrian's Wall. It's the back road, really, the route the locals use. It's one of the most fabulous roads in England . . . well, England and Scotland in a sense. Pity it's such a foul night, but it's atmospheric, isn't it? Can you imagine the Roman legions, far away from home, tramping through this bleak and cold country?'

Not at this speed, Kate thought. The Porsche was slicing through the night, up gradients that she had forgotten existed after six uninterrupted months in London. The car seemed to hiccough over a hump before de Salas accelerated at a crazed angle. Then, thankfully, there was a stretch of unbending road ahead – the remains of the Roman route, she hoped, longing for it to go on, straight and safe – and out of the window she suddenly saw the lighter darkness of the sky stretching above a dense, rocky horizon.

'Where's the Wall?' she asked, trying to keep cool.

De Salas took his left hand off the wheel, to her horror. 'There,' he said gesturing vaguely to the right. Then she saw it too, the clear line of something unnaturally square and straight in the wild landscape. It made her shiver. All that effort, to wall something out! Surely a few Picts in wolfskins hardly merited *that*? She wondered if perhaps

11

the Wall had really been built against something even darker, and then allowed herself to shiver off the stupid thought.

'It's pretty powerful,' she said.

'Yes, absolutely. Hey, are you cold?'

'Not really.'

'Fine.'

It was as if he suddenly felt no more need to charm her. His mood had tensed. Kate wondered what she had said. De Salas was concentrating more determinedly now, not so much on showing off as on fighting the road beneath them. At the same time he carried on talking, but less smoothly. He was still emphasising the splendour of the scenery as they raced over the hill tops, but Kate was hardly taking it in. His driving scared her and she was becoming increasingly anxious to find out just how long the journey was going to last.

'Sorry to interrupt, er, Andy, but where are we staying?'

'Ah, yes,' Andy seemed to have to drag himself back to practicalities. 'Well, June and I are at Summerlake Hall, near Bassenthwaite. It's marvellous. We've heard Lord Archer stays there.'

'And me?'

'Well, that's the problem. Of course, there are B&B places close by . . .'

'You mean I'm not booked in?'

'Look,' he said with strained patience, 'it's one of the best hotels in the Lakes and we're hoping that a room will come free for you within a couple of days. But just at the moment they're full. June is looking out for somewhere else for you, but what with getting involved with Lady Marshall this afternoon, we're a little bit behind schedule.

Anyway, if you come with me to the Summerlake, I'm sure June will have booked you in for dinner, and she's bound to have found you somewhere nice in the village.'

The car took a bend on two wheels. Kate gritted her teeth and went on, 'But if the film's set in North West Cumbria, why are you staying in the Lakes?'

'It's only fifteen miles away.'

Kate began to feel irritated now, as well as worried about his driving, which was becoming increasingly erratic. She had heard of the Summerlake Hall Hotel, she thought distantly. It was one of those top class hotels that occasionally offered the prize of 'a superb luxury weekend for two' on radio quiz shows. It was a beautiful place, obviously, but at odds with de Salas's protestations of commitment to the region he was filming, and certainly way beyond the budget of an average TV project, she was sure. Still, if he had his own money . . .

The Roman road began to kink again. They careered round a hairpin bend on the black scalp of the world. To take her mind off the alarm she felt, Kate said hoarsely, 'So how many locations are there in the film?'

'Four or five, depending on time. There's the woollen mill, the barn converted to a tea shop, the Rough Diamonds jewellery workshop, the aromatherapy collective, and possibly the sailing school, though that isn't really what I wanted.'

'Wrong sort of craft?'

But de Salas wasn't amused. She sensed him glancing at her, but she turned to look out of the window, not wishing either to irritate him further or distract him from his driving. After a pause she added in a conciliatory tone, 'Who's voicing the film?'

'We've been trying for Joanna Lumley or Melvyn Bragg. It has to be a person with the right sensitivity.'

Of course, thought Kate, wondering what on earth would make this film good enough for any major 'voice' to get involved. She still couldn't see quite what the idea was, other than a long self-congratulatory list of small business ventures. She wondered if the film's theme had become fractured along with Ben Lowe's femur. He certainly seemed to have provided the credibility for Rural Rides' other projects.

'So you want views of the mill, a sit down interview with this Lady Whatsername, and then vox pops with the workers?'

'Er, no, not vox pops. I think we'll talk to whichever one of the workers Lady Marshall suggests.' Kate raised one eyebrow, a wasted gesture in the dark.

Again, a light from a roadside cottage caught his face, and she saw now that there were tiny beads of perspiration along his upper lip. Was she upsetting him? She found the only way she could cope with the speed of the car was to look down at her knees and try to continue a conversation. She redoubled her efforts to sound interested, wondering as she did so just how she was going to pull the film together into something more than a tourist puff.

'So on day two it's . . . a tea shop? Just a tea shop?'

'Yes.' De Salas was suddenly quieter, but fiercely quiet, so she could almost hear his annoyance. Kate was at a loss to know why he was so agitated. She was just about to speak when de Salas's hands slipped on the steering wheel so the car swerved into the middle of the road. He said, 'Oh shit!' and she saw him wipe the sweat from his palms on his cotton trousers, one hand at a time, the car veering each time he did it. She was becoming seriously scared. She ploughed on, gabbling frantically.

'And then an aromatherapy centre. That sounds rather good. But what about some of the things that really do generate money and jobs? You mentioned the sailing school . . .'

She stopped to grab her seat belt. De Salas was driving crazily through the night on a switchback of hills that leapt and rippled beneath them. Kate gasped involuntarily. He knows the road, she told herself; don't be stupid, he knows what he's doing. She tried again to speak, having to moisten her dry lips with her tongue. Her voice sounded tight and far more excitable than she meant it to.

'I mean,' she went on, feeling the back of her throat and her whole windpipe contract as the car ricocheted round a corner, 'what about something like the tourist industry . . . are you looking at that? I read that the Tourist Centre is backing you.'

'Yes, they certainly are. At least they better bloody had be,' snarled de Salas. 'But that's not the point. The film's not about tourism. It's about the real countryside. We don't want superficial elements. Lady Marshall would be horrified.'

The car seemed to jump off the road. Kate could have sworn all four wheels left the ground. She wanted to say, 'Isn't tourism as much part of the real countryside now as growing cabbages?' but the strain in de Salas's voice warned her off. As the car slewed across the greasy surface, she spoke in a voice high with anxiety.

'But what about catering, then? There must be a small local hotel we could feature, perhaps on the coast . . .'

At that moment they seemed to plunge downhill. Kate

could see the glow of a large, comforting pub at the bottom of the dip and her first thought was: thank God, back to the bright lights! But suddenly the pub went off centre, and the sensation was one of falling, because the lights lurched madly to one side. She felt the pressure of the seat belt cutting into her, then her head was flung from one side to the other, out of control, leaving her quite literally unable to catch her breath even to scream. De Salas was yelling, 'Oh fucking hell, fucking *fucking* hell!' and she saw his hands leave the wheel, as the wet thwacking crash of the car hitting some sort of vegetation told her they were off the road. The car swayed, crashed into the verge again, and hit something underneath so hard Kate thought the base of her spine was about to come through her mouth. Within seconds it was over and her bones were settling back, though her whole body tingled with the sense of bruises just missed. The Porsche had stopped, tilted crazily, but still intact.

'My God,' she breathed. 'Are you all right?'

De Salas was hunched over the wheel but she could see he was fine. She began to formulate something, anything, to say.

'We seem to have survived that,' she tried gently, though she knew she was shaking from shock.

To her horror, de Salas turned on her, spitting with rage.

'Get out! *Get out!*' he screamed. 'Get out of my fucking car!'

For a moment Kate wondered if he thought the Porsche was about to catch fire; then she realised his fury was completely personal.

'Get out! Take your fucking bag and go. Just leave me! I'll sort this out. I'll sort this out, d'you hear me?' He breathed a little more evenly. 'There's a pub up there. Go and get yourself a taxi. Just get out and go away.'

Kate realised he was near hysteria. All right, she thought, if that's how he feels – shaken herself, as much by his reaction as by the accident, she tried the door of the car. It swung open lazily and gently hit a gorse bush. The light came on and revealed de Salas with his head in his hands. She forced her bag out of the back seat, and lurched round the back of the Porsche, slamming the door behind her.

She wasn't sure whether her stagger to the pub was the result of shock or the genuine difficulty of navigating her feet along the pitted roadside to the door. Inside it was quiet, with just a few regulars dotted round the bar, the soft ping of a gaming machine and the drone of the telly. They all looked at her, but with a sort of passive interest.

'Phone?' she said.

'Aye, in t'corner. Were you in that car that's just come to grief?' said the barman. 'We 'eard the noise and Sam there 'ad a look but he reckoned you were right. It's allus happening on that bend.' He nodded wisely.

'Yes, thanks. My . . . colleague's sorting it out. But I need a taxi to . . .' She couldn't remember where the Summerlake Hall Hotel actually was. The barman interrupted to say, ' . . . there's Ted's Taxis in Haltwistle, probably your best bet. I'll ring him for you, lass. If you need the public phone it's over there like I said. Going to Carlisle, are you?'

'I think so . . . I'm not . . . I don't really . . .' Kate staggered towards the public phone box, then remembered her mobile. She stood there, dazed and wondering what to do. The thought of getting a taxi to Summerlake Hall, and waiting for de Salas after what had happened appalled her. She wanted to get as far away from him and his explosive

17

arrogance as possible. Only then could she work out what to do next.

Tentatively she pushed John's numbers, hoping just to hear his voice. The phone rang in the flat, but of course he wasn't there. She felt desperately alone. Then her hand felt in the pocket of her jacket and found the telephone number she had meant to throw away. Goff. George Goff. John's reliable bloke. Well, she'd find out just how reliable. She fished out the phone again and punched the numbers.

'Hello.' The voice was old and trembled slightly. 'St John's Vicarage, Reverend George Goff speaking.'

Oh God, she thought, not another vicar!

In the smoky atmosphere of Ted's taxi, Kate sat back against the worn upholstery and shut her eyes. Ted seemed in complete control, and he was monosyllabic too, which was just what she needed.

Kate had always avoided John's clerical colleagues, especially the volatile Father Marcus who had recently been absorbing so much of John's time. The moment she had realised George Goff was a priest she had expected some censorious old patriarch to tell her how silly she had been, getting herself stuck in the middle of nowhere. Instead he had been wonderful, capable and uncomplaining. He had arranged to meet her in Carlisle.

'Are we nearly there?' she asked the cab driver.

'Just in Brampton now, lass. Not far to go.'

She realised that thinking about vicars had taken her mind off the week ahead. Just as she allowed herself to worry over how she was going to get out of the job and back to London, the tinny ringing of the mobile phone sent her into a panic.

'Hello?'

'Kate? Kate Wilkinson?'

'Yes.'

'Thank goodness I've got you! It's June Ridley here, you know, Andy de Salas's PA. I've just had a call from Andy to say how sorry he is.'

'Yes?' said Kate shortly.

'Poor Andy! He said driving conditions were terrible. He seems to think he was rather rude to you, but he says he was very shaken! He's got someone to look at the car and it's fine, so he's on his way over. He went back to the pub for you but you'd left, so he called me to sort it out. Are you OK?'

'Yes, I'm fine.' No thanks to de Salas, she thought.

'Do you know where to meet us?' June asked. But Kate didn't feel like chatting about arrangements as if de Salas's outrageous behaviour had never happened.

'I know you're at the Summerlake Hall Hotel, June, but I'm afraid after what's happened I need time to reconsider. Andy de Salas behaved very weirdly. Not only that, I understand the company hasn't even booked me in at a hotel. If you haven't made proper arrangements for me, I shall make my own.'

In actual fact, Kate had no idea where she would be staying. She had left it to George Goff, who had offered to organise a hotel for her.

'Oh dear,' June Ridley sounded highly agitated. 'I'm sorry about all this, but really, you must understand that someone as talented as Andy gets very harassed by these things . . .'

'Harassed! How do you think *I* feel? I don't care how talented he is, he's behaved very badly tonight. This isn't a very good start.' The world of media was full of strange and temperamental people, but Kate felt her tolerance of the artist had been stretched to the limit.

'No, of course, oh dear . . .' June said again. 'But Andy is really very nice. Road accidents, however minor, can be very upsetting. Oh, I hope this doesn't mean you're thinking of leaving us . . .' Her voice rose, as if she was controlling tears, and her obvious distress made Kate feel slightly awkward. Rural Rides was clearly in a mess, and de Salas must have been under a great deal of strain. She thought of her obligation to Liz Jones too. Her friend clearly rated de Salas.

'All right, June, I hear what you say. Look, if you need me, you can get me on the mobile phone. Don't worry, I won't storm off back to London. Yet. Where is Andy planning to start tomorrow?'

'Lady Marshall's woollen mill in Skirlbeck.'

'OK. I'll meet you, all of you, at the woollen mill at eight o'clock in the morning for a planning meeting.'

'Lady Marshall won't be open . . .'

'We can talk in the cars.'

'But eight o'clock! Well, I don't know if Andy . . .'

'Look, Andy de Salas is going to have to sharpen up his act, stress or no stress. If he wants a producer on this ill-thought-out venture, then he's going to have to learn to treat me as one. The whole project seems to me to need a great deal more effort than has been lavished on it so far. But I am not wasting time discussing it tonight after the journey I've had. OK?'

'Oh dear. OK,' said June unhappily.

The phone went dead.

'Carlisle station, love,' said the taxi driver.

Two hours later, in the lounge of one of the cosiest hotels she had ever come across Kate stretched her legs in front of a roaring fire sipping malt whisky appreciatively. She had wolfed down home-made soup followed by shepherd's pie, and felt relaxed at last. Opposite her an elderly clergyman, complete with dog collar, beamed back at her.

'You look better,' George Goff said approvingly. 'Plenty of colour in your face now.'

Kate had arrived at the Skirlbeck Bridge Hotel to be ushered into a pretty room with pink flowered wallpaper and thick velvet curtains, the view over the dark shoreline promising to be glorious in the morning. She had heard the sound of the sea and smelt the salt as she walked up the gravel path, and from her window she could see the blink of a lighthouse and make out the silhouette of the village.

After showering and changing, and polishing off a plate of hot food under the kindly gaze of the Reverend Goff, she was beginning to feel as if the whole ghastly enterprise might not be so bad. The after dinner drink was even more welcome. The only drawback now was that John still hadn't been at home when she had called him in London.

'It's a delightful place, this. I'm really glad I thought to phone them for you. Bit of luck really,' George Goff said. 'It's run by two brothers, Terry and Bill.' He leaned forward conspiratorially. 'Neither of them are married, and they've been very much dominated by their old mother who's rather a nasty piece of work, between you and me. The sons are a mite eccentric, but I've never asked ... either them or myself for that matter ... quite what the set-up is. I try not to pry into people's sexuality, you know.'

He leaned back in his comfy armchair. Kate tried not to

look surprised, but couldn't help glancing round as if she was trying to catch sight of the strange siblings.

'Oh, they're not here,' said George, quick as a flash. 'On a Sunday night their mother goes to play cards with her cronies. She needs a lot of looking after, but on Sundays the boys are off the leash. So they usually go to the Spiritualists' meeting in Workington.' He laughed at Kate's face. 'Up here we have to embrace everybody into the parish, you know. The Robinson boys at least find their amusement in something harmless.' He frowned a little.

'What do you mean? I would hardly have thought sex and drugs and rock 'n' roll had made big inroads into Skirlbeck.'

'Wouldn't you? You'd be surprised, my dear.'

'But surely, in a peaceful environment like this . . . ?'

George Goff looked at her with gentle irritation. 'Yes, it's very peaceful. Just the occasional family murder, and of course, child abuse is something we're all used to hearing about. The incidence of mental illness is also very high, and alcoholism can be quite a nightmare for people in remote villages, but the visitors don't notice – they think it's peaceful enough. And if your husband's left you and you've only the children for company and the nearest neighbour is half a mile away, that's very peaceful too.'

'But surely it can't be as bad as in the city?'

'Oh, we have our own particular, less glamorous evils.'

'Like what?'

'Frustration. Cruelty. And bullying.'

'All kids have to expect that a bit, don't they?'

'Oh, I don't mean *children*; I mean adults.'

'Adults?'

'Yes. Imagine what it's like living in a community of two

22

or three hundred people at most. A few families, perhaps the richest or the roughest, predominate, and if you don't get on with them your life isn't worth living. Other people have far more power over you in a village than in the relative anonymity of the town. Have you never thought of that?'

'Well . . . no.'

'Look at a village like Skirlbeck. One post office, one school, one church . . . all run by the same people. Here, thank God, it's decent people. Largely.' His face darkened, and for the first time that evening, he seemed to forget about Kate and stare into the fire. Then he seemed to physically pull himself together in his chair, and made an effort to smile at her and start again. 'And tomorrow, Kate, you're filming at the woollen mill with the formidable Lady Marshall?'

'That's right. She sounds quite forceful.'

George laughed: 'Well, Celia Marshall's probably bitten off more than she can chew with her opposition to the theme park.'

'Sorry?'

'The theme park. It's the brain child of one of our local councillors. Malcolm Hodgson. Don't you know about it?'

'No. But it sounds interesting. A bit of controversy would make this film a lot more exciting.'

George smiled. 'Perhaps. One of the businesses on the coast has offered to put up the money to make a small industrial theme park – you know, experience the bad old days with the help of holograms and lightshows!' Kate laughed. 'But you mustn't underestimate local politics. Celia Marshall and several others hate the idea. There isn't room for two tourist attractions and Lady Marshall could see the area accommodating rather a nice extension of her

woolweaving business . . . but far be it from me to gossip.'
He laughed genially at himself, then went on, 'I should be
going. I'm so glad you're safe and well now, my dear, and
I've been delighted to help. Now you're all set? And you've
organised a taxi for tomorrow morning?'

'Yes, thank you, George. In fact, I can't thank you enough.'

She walked with him to the door of the hotel and they
paused on the threshold. Outside the soft, damp, salty air
of the coast lapped round them. George put out his hand
to shake hers, and on impulse she leaned forward instead
to kiss him on the cheek. As her lips touched his pleasant,
slightly wrinkled face, she felt him flinch. For a moment
she thought it was because of her, and then with surprise
she felt the grip of the elderly man's hand on her arm. He
was frozen in the doorway, his eyes staring down the lane.
At the end of the gravel drive, Kate saw three men pass,
with a dog on a lead. They were mumbling softly and she
saw the flash of a torch and heard the odd word and some
laughter. George relaxed his grip, but still stood there,
immobile.

'George, are you OK?' In the pool of light from the porch
lamp, he looked like an old man now, and Kate suddenly
felt guilty for dragging him out.

'Yes,' he said with a new trace of weariness.

'And will you be around later this week?'

'Not till next weekend, my dear. My wife Eileen and I
are away on a spiritual retreat this week. She's gone on
ahead. We need it, you know.' He paused again, and she
seemed to see his shoulders stoop. 'There *is* a lot of evil in
the country, Kate.' Far away, a dog barked and the sound
made the old man shudder. Kate patted him on the arm.

'Safe journey.'

24

'Thank you, m'dear.' And he walked slowly to his car.

Waving him off, Kate wondered what had upset him. But she wanted to hurry inside and get up to her room and try John one more time on the phone. This time she was lucky, catching him before he went to bed, but once she had got him, she found the situation strained. He listened as she told him about the nightmare trip with de Salas, but he seemed to feel she should take it in her stride, and sounded preoccupied until she explained about George's help. Then he livened up, telling Kate he had met George at theological college, when George had been a tutor and John a mature student.

'He's a marvellous chap. Very unusual. And his wife is very different too. You'll enjoy meeting them, Kate.' But Kate said nothing. She was still hoping they would get their weekend alone together, and she recalled George Goff saying that he and his wife were going away on a retreat. Good.

John did not sound as if he was missing her. She wanted to hear need in his voice, not cheerful acceptance of the fact that she was hundreds of miles away. But at least he confirmed that he would be coming up to join her at the weekend. 'I'm quite looking forward to it, especially if we can meet up with George and Eileen,' he said. There was a little silence before he rang off.

The conversation made her feel lower than ever. What was wrong between them? Only a few hours earlier, she had been waiting for John to give her a lift to Heathrow. He arrived back late from yet another parish visit to Marcus, hurtling through the door with seconds to spare.

'I'm sorry, Kate, the car's outside.' He sounded weary, as if she were another duty.

She disguised her hurt as vexation. 'Why are you late?'

'Marcus was having another crisis about women priests. I needed to talk him through it.'

'Marcus and his crises! If you ask me, he sounds like a spiritual fascist!' Kate had grabbed her case and pushed John to the door. 'I hope you told him this time that he should come to terms with the twentieth century.' But John was striding on ahead to open the car.

'Hey, John, don't cop out just because we're leaving.' Kate slammed the front door and ran down to join him. She plonked herself into the passenger seat, eyes bright with interest, alert with the hope this was something they could discuss. 'I mean, I know I'm not one of your faithful, but everyone has views on women priests, don't they? It's surely just a question of basic equality.'

'Kate, with all due respect it's not that simple.'

'What? Can't I have a view on it? Or don't you want to talk about it?'

'Well, not really. I'm trying to drive, and I've got to think about what I'm going to do tonight. Marcus really isn't up to taking Evensong and it looks as if I'm going to have to do an impromptu sermon. I know you'll understand. I need to get my thoughts together.'

He had kissed her goodbye at the airport in a desultory way, and as she had passed into the departure lounge she had felt lonelier than almost ever before.

Now, reviewing all the events of a very strange day, she needed comfort, like a hot water bottle or a cup of tea. It was only just past eleven o'clock. She tiptoed across the silent corridor to the carved oak stairs leading down to the bar. On the landing, Kate smelt the outdoor tang of the sea, and felt the cold that lingered from a recently opened door. There was almost a mist around the dark broad shoulder she could see in the hallway, and something made her stop there, one hand on the bannisters.

The shoulder shifted as the man moved forward into full view, to reveal the black and white chequered hat band of a police officer. Coming to greet him were two small, blondish men, just like cherubic schoolboys – except that their faces were pursed with horror.

Kate heard the last words.

' . . . sorry to break it to you like this . . .'

The group melted into the bar. Kate stood, listening to the muffled sounds. But one sentence was very clear.

'The wheelchair had tipped on to the beach; she'd been dead some time.'

There was the sound of a cry, and then male sobbing. Horrified, Kate tiptoed back to her bedroom and shut the door.

Chapter Two

In London, John Maple couldn't sleep. He had promised himself an early night, but the left hand side of the bed where Kate slept was ruffled not with her body but with his restlessness. He put on his glasses to look at the bedside clock, ruefully remembering the time when he hadn't been shortsighted. He was older than Kate, and it had never bothered him before.

But he was bothered by it now. He knew he wasn't sleeping because their telephone call had been so cool. He was scared of telling Kate how much he missed her in case she felt pressurised. He found it so hard to believe that she could be in love with a middle-aged priest that he was terrified of alienating her. Her quick brain and quicker temper alarmed him sometimes. And he couldn't deny that sometimes he grew irritable, and was frightened when they talked about their relationship, in case she tried to compete with his faith. Deep down, he knew there were issues they disagreed on, issues where his generation had very different views from hers, and where they had to struggle to find common ground. It was hard to explain, to someone with a liberal background in the media, that women priests and homosexuality and abortion and euthanasia could be difficult concepts to argue. He wanted desperately not to raise them.

It was only half past midnight. He thought about the intellectual struggle he felt over living with Kate without being married. He knew it would soon become a matter for his bishop, and that there might be a deadline. This was the first time he had considered that they might not make it. He wanted to speak to her so much his hand twitched near the phone, but reasoned that the last thing she wanted was to be pestered when she probably needed a good night's sleep.

Then the phone rang out and he grabbed it. But it was only Father Marcus, agonising about gay bishops. John sighed, and resigned himself to listening.

In Cumbria, Kate jolted upright. She had woken herself by calling out. In her dream she had seen the sweat on de Salas's lips and his palms slipping on the steering wheel. She was literally shaking. She tried to remember the reality. Had de Salas really been driving like a mad man? Or had her subconscious turned a bad journey into the world's worst trip? She went over it again. He could obviously handle the Porsche, as she had seen when he had first used it to stalk the steep country roads in the dark. It was only later that his speed and skill had become manic.

She had to get a grip on herself. Shaking in the night was not her style. She told herself that however neurotic de Salas had seemed, she had come to no harm. She thought of what his PA had said, and of her obligation to Liz Jones. She would have to stick with the project, at least for that day. And, thank goodness, she had a haven at

Skirlbeck Bridge. Or had she? Something else was undermining her sleep.

Of course. It was the undigested memory of the policeman and the two strange-looking little men, glimpsed last night from the hotel landing. There had obviously been an accident. Last night Kate had reasoned that there was nothing she could do to help, so she had crept away. But the sound of male sobbing had lurked in her dreams.

Perhaps that morning she would find out more. There was bound to be some chit-chat among the hotel staff. But she didn't feel a bit like getting up. Despite everything, she was physically very comfortable. The room was just the right temperature, with a cosy glow from the lamp and the pink wallpaper. She had already associated the Skirlbeck Bridge Hotel with security. There was no doubt that the fresh smell of polish, good food and sea air gave her a sense of love, care and exhilaration reminiscent of childhood holidays.

Eventually she sat up, climbed out of the big bed, and walked to the window, feeling the fibres of the woolly carpet on her toes. It was a beautiful autumn day, a golden October in the making, with a high blue sky over a grey-blue sea and, in the distance on the Scottish shore, one clearly-drawn mountain running down to a misty dwindling series of rocky outcrops on the horizon.

She bathed and dressed, then she put her head round the door. When she listened, she could hear no signs of life at all from anywhere in the hotel. Usually in these places there was the throb of activity somewhere, and the slight tang of something fried or toasted well before the official breakfast.

Kate crept downstairs, tiptoeing for no good reason

except that the place was deserted. She glanced at her watch again. There was the sound of a car coming up the drive. She saw through the big Victorian bay window of the dining room that her taxi was early, but the front door was still bolted. Struggling to open it, she wondered if the noise would bring someone to investigate, but there was no sound. Whatever had happened to immobilise the hotel was obviously serious. On the step was an untouched crate with six milk bottles, and a pile of slightly damp newspapers, the smell of fresh newsprint rising in the cold, fresh morning air.

Kate glanced up to the strip of blue horizon. A gull cried, and somewhere in the distance a car door slammed and someone called out a friendly greeting and laughed, the sound coming in through the clean air like the clink of ice cubes.

It was simple and beautiful and in one of those arbitrary moments of raw appreciation, Kate felt deeply glad to be there, whatever. She lifted her head and took a deep breath which left her nostrils smarting. She smiled at the taxi driver and said brightly: 'I'm Kate Wilkinson. Are you here for me?' He was, of course. And he smiled back, and winked. Her spirits rose. 'You'd better take me to the Skirlbeck Woollen Mill, please.'

'Michael.' The breathless sound of Celia Marshall reached her husband before the sight of her tubular body, dressed as usual in a handwoven swathe of mud-coloured wool.

'Mmm?' He was drinking his tea very slowly out of one of the large, chipped stoneware cups which Celia told him gave an air of Provençal charm to the breakfast room. It was at the back of the house, just up the steps from the gloomy kitchen where the woman who came in every day to do everything, was clattering over breakfast and listening intently to the radio. Sir Michael Marshall preferred television, though he told himself it was because he was keen on new technology. He congratulated himself on keeping ahead of the game although he was getting on. He had even been thinking of getting a satellite dish.

'Michael! It's unbelievable! We've just heard it on Radio Cumbria on the eight o'clock news. Jean Robinson has been found dead!'

'Really?' Sir Michael was interested now. Even at this time in the morning, as his brain coughed and stumbled into reality, he could appreciate that for someone's death to be mentioned on the radio meant it was unusual. But Jean Robinson couldn't be dead! She was the sort of creaking gate that would last for ever. Usually the death of one of his contemporaries filled him with new energy . . . but Jean, so crippled and yet so strong, had been a symbol of spirit! He had known her for a good many years, before the accident which had started her decline into disability, and there had been a time, forty years before, when he had rather fancied her mischievous little face, fringed by black curls, combined with her rather devilish attitude. Not that it would have done to get involved with someone from the village, of course.

'Yes, really, Michael. And the strange thing is that they found the body on the beach!'

'On the beach? Don't be ridiculous, Cee, Jean Robinson couldn't walk as far as her own front door.'

'No, they found her wheelchair on the shore. It looks as if she'd wheeled herself down there, goodness knows why. And the chair must have jammed and then tipped up and

she fell out and that was that. What a horrible way to die!'
Celia's usually pink and confident features were screwed
up in horror at the tragedy. Sir Michael was mildly
surprised. He had suspected his wife of disliking Jean
Robinson because she commanded far too much influence
in the area, and would have expected her death to give
Celia a dramatic thrill.

'Good heavens.' There was nothing he could add. He
saw himself as a person who took time to reflect, unlike
his wife with her whirlwind energy. But he was already
relapsing back into his dream world, in which he was a
key member of the West Cumbrian elite.

His father had been an eminent North Lancashire
manufacturer, and Michael had spent all his teenage
holidays on the Solway coast nearly half a century earlier.
Then he had inherited the family business, but he had put
most of his modest energy into local politics. He had been
bought out by a huge national concern long before his
sixties but his subsequent knighthood had set the seal on
his middle age, and meant the end of any meaningful work.
Early retirement to an estate in Cumbria had suited his
view of himself, but he was lazy rather than unintelligent
so he knew his mental alignment needed to be with new
technology and progress rather than with the landed gentry.
So he imagined himself to be a captain of modern industry,
retired, and preserved this fantasy by assuming it to be
true when talking to his aged and wealthy friends who
had bought battlements or bungalows along the coast
with the bunce of the eighties. His ambition was to be
on the board of Border Television, and to talk
knowledgeably with respectful young men in front of
banks of fabulous machines. It was quite the opposite of

his wife's concern with all things folksy.

He was aware suddenly that the telephone was ringing. It was unlikely to be anybody local sharing the news about Jean Robinson. The Marshalls saw themselves as county rather than country people, and they tried to mix with county types. Their 'friends' – usually people with whom Michael had shared his public school vacations half a century previously – would not be interested in the death of a wheelchair bound harridan from the village, however saucy she had once been.

'Phone, Cee darling.'

'I know, I know. I'm just going.'

She was back before he realised.

'Oh, Michael, you won't believe it. That was the film director on the phone. Today we were supposed to be filming the mill for the programme we're hoping to get on Border . . .' Sir Michael's ears pricked up '. . . and that awful Councillor Hodgson has turned up at the mill shop with Carruthers from the farm in protest.'

'Protest?'

'To stop us expanding!'

Celia Marshall bustled away. Ten minutes later her Ford Escort Cabriolet was seen throbbing down to the mill shop.

Councillor Malcolm Hodgson did not like the Marshalls. However, he tried not to let that affect his judgement, although he was unsure of the wisdom of arriving in person at the mill shop with the aggressive Will Carruthers from the farm across the road. But there was no doubt that if Lady Marshall's woollen mill was extended, then there would be no hope for the industry theme park which had applied for planning permission only yards away. There was a limit to what the country roads could stand. Councillor Hodgson had nothing against the Skirlbeck Mill as such, but he was passionately in favour of the theme park, which was his brainchild.

He believed it would reflect the area's real heritage, attract tourists – particularly Americans and Canadians whose ancestors had left the area in droves – complement and contrast with the huge Sellafield Exhibition just down the coast, provide scores of jobs at least whilst being built, and swell the local coffers. Celia Marshall made similar claims for the mill, but Hodgson privately believed it would employ fifteen people at most, and only swell her ego.

Will Carruthers was not so altruistic. He just didn't want the bloody Marshalls building a ruddy great mill and car park right opposite his milking parlour. But he and Hodgson had formed an alliance, despite the fact that Hodgson had an even bigger farm, with a manager, several miles away on the prettier Lakeland side of the fells. Hodgson's family had made their money out of tourist cottages, and Carruthers had always thought of him as posh. Hodgson, a graduate, forty-five, divorced, and with a local reputation as a roué, was finding his role of man of the people rather novel. But he was devoted to the area. His son was at agricultural college. His daughter was at university. His wife had finally divorced him and left the farm to live with a male teacher she had worked with, and he was on his own. Now he was single, his adventures with women seemed somehow more complicated and less satisfying, and the council was becoming more and more important to him. He was aware of the complex local social structure which placed him one rung below Sir Michael Marshall and one rung above Will Carruthers, and he thought it was bollocks. But it couldn't be ignored.

There were three cars parked outside the mill shop, a converted outbuilding next to the mill itself. It still looked sleepy and folksy and had a crooked sign saying 'Closed' propped up against its window. One of the cars was a Porsche. And there was a Volvo estate full of metal boxes. The third was a local taxi. As Hodgson watched, a woman climbed out of the cab, and slammed the door. She looked furious. She strode with long legs towards the edge of the car park and kicked one of Celia Marshall's white painted boulders with a deft display of feeling. Hodgson was immediately struck by her slim ankles and the fact that she wore leggings and a big fluffy jumper instead of the ubiquitous middle class Barbour. Hodgson wouldn't have admitted it, but the truth was that he had exhausted the available talent in the compact circle in which he moved, and the sight of a new woman, about his own age, and clearly of a lively disposition, immediately interested him. She didn't even need to be particularly attractive, and Kate Wilkinson would not have put herself in that category. But as she turned to walk back, Kate lifted her arms to brush the short, thick auburn hair away from her face, caught Hodgson's glance and grinned, realising he had witnessed her display of temper. Her smile was genuinely appealing to him. With the assurance that here was a familiar game he hadn't played for a while he walked towards her.

'Hello. I'm Councillor Malcolm Hodgson,' he said, stretching out his hand.

'Councillor,' she replied, in a deeper voice than he had expected, with a southern accent that both annoyed and attracted him. But Kate was thinking: oh God, another damn smoothie! Wasn't Cumbria supposed to be full of salt-of-the-earth whippet fanciers and horny-handed tons of soil . . . sorry, sons of toil? Although nothing had been as she expected it so far.

Including that morning's re-introduction to Andy de Salas. He had looked smaller and less menacing, clambering out of his Porsche with June in tow. He had walked over to join her in the taxi, followed by his worried PA, and taken control as if nothing had happened the night before. June had given Kate a pleading look as if to say: please don't mention it. Kate was completely shattered by his audacity. If it hadn't been for June's agonised glances, Kate would have thought that it really had all been a nightmare. It was unbelievable. Kate was tempted to say, 'Don't you owe me an apology?' but one look at June stopped her. De Salas reminded her more and more of an arrogant schoolboy, showing off to hide his insecurity. After five minutes of listening to his instructions, she had felt so irritated she had to get out of the cab.

She looked again at the older man in front of her. He was bulky, wearing the baggy cords and huge sweater of a countryman, with a weatherbeaten, fleshily attractive face. But it was his accent, with its unusual lilt, yet tone of authority, which made her refocus. Not such a smoothie, then.

'You're involved with the filming?'

'I'm the producer, yes.' On location, casually dressed, she was always prepared to be taken for a production secretary but Hodgson didn't look surprised.

'I'm glad we've met.'

'Why?'

Hodgson raised his eyebrow. He liked her directness, even though at that very moment Kate was kicking herself

or being rude. Kate was aware she was sounding southern
and haughty and dismissive, all the things she didn't want
to be. Suddenly a sharp shout made both their heads turn.

'Kate? Can you come here, please?'

It was de Salas. Kate raised one eyebrow to show
Hodgson she wasn't keen on being summoned. He smiled
conspiratorially and she smiled back. It was a humorous,
grown-up smile which by comparison made de Salas look
like the nervous, volatile boy he really was.

Kate walked slowly back to where de Salas was scooping
gravel with the side of his perfect, unscuffed Timberland
boot. He was looking at the ground. Almost out of the corner
of his mouth he said, 'That chap Hodgson has made a lot
of enemies in this area. Lady Marshall is one, and Paul
Pym who runs the Tourist Centre is another. They can't
stand him. And we need both of them if we're going to get
his programme made.'

As if on cue, Kate heard a scrunch of wheels, and the
Ford Cabriolet came hurtling into the car park, appearing
to open its door and disgorge its small stout driver almost
before stopping.

'Lady Marshall!' de Salas called out as he hurried over.
He did not stop to introduce Kate. Perhaps as well, she
thought, as the sound of Celia Marshall's strident voice
followed her back to the cab. As she opened the cab door,
Kate turned back to see an excitable altercation between
Lady Marshall and Will Carruthers, with Hodgson and de
Salas standing at the side, eyeing each other like suspicious
seconds in a duel of words.

Inside Kate's taxi, June Ridley was hunched in the
corner. Despite the PA's swift movement Kate had caught
her with her hand clutched to the side of her head in an

attitude of weary desperation, and although she straightened up ineffectually, she knew Kate had seen her distress. Half pleading, half annoyed, June said, 'I'm sorry about Andy. But he really is goodhearted. I hope you understand.'

'I'm afraid I don't, to be honest. He doesn't make it easy.'

'No. No, I can see that. But he's very committed to this film. It's his first venture without Ben and he's very uptight. I realised after I spoke to you last night that we hadn't been as organised or as welcoming as we should have been. But it's been very awkward.'

'Awkward? June, this is a mess! I appreciate your problems. But de Salas behaved like a monster.'

'I'm sorry. But you must realise Andy's an excitable character. When you get to know him better, you'll see how talented he is.'

'Really? Do you know he could have killed me? He drove over here like a madman.'

'Yes. I realise the bump must have been his fault. But he's been under such a lot of strain lately. This isn't an easy project to pull together. Without Ben . . .'

'June, I'm the producer now. And I'm certainly not the enemy. It's of no benefit to me if this film is a disorganised, ill-thought-out shambles. I didn't come here and expect to get paid for holding the clapperboard. My name will go on the end of this, and I want to give you value in return for my pay cheque.' She meant this to be a casual remark but June Ridley's head came up sharply. Kate picked up on it at once.

'Is money the problem? Is that why you're both so stressed?'

June turned to look away. Then she said, 'I think the

world of Andy – we all do – but you're right. If you're going to be the producer, you should know. This film is proving almost impossible to fund.'

'Then why did Rural Rides want to make it?'

'It mattered a lot to Andy. He desperately wanted to make his film. And we'd had a few successes so Ben went along with it. Andy did secure some money . . .' She paused, and Kate waited, ' . . . but it wasn't very much.' June Ridley was clearly embarassed.

'You mean there are no real funds at all? Does Ben know?' Kate suddenly had visions of dinner at the Summerlake Hall Hotel and felt a degree of cynicism.

'Ben thinks things are fine. There's no point worrying him. And of course there's money. Some money.' June tried to snap, but the effort was betrayed by the anxious way she glanced around. 'Andy is wealthy in his own right and has money of his own. We are absolutely confident the rest will be forthcoming.' The company line sounded tired.

'But it's not in the bank right now?'

'No. But please . . .'

Kate heard the scrunching of feet on the gravel. De Salas was coming back. Kate knew at once what June meant: please don't rock the boat, put up with his moods, and please, please, don't mention the funding. Kate found it hard to resist the other woman's pleading. She looked out of the window herself, seeing the crisp skyline, and the varying velvety shades of moss and russet. When she turned back, June was looking straight at her, and her eyes were crinkled like contour lines on a Lakeland Ordnance Survey map. Kate nodded just perceptibly, and June unclenched her knotted arms. No, I won't rock the boat, thought Kate. This isn't my gig, and they hired me as a good, jobbing producer, so that's what I'll be.

In fact, the morning's filming worked better than she had any right to hope. Celia Marshall seemed enlivened by the row with campaigning farmer Will Carruthers and did a usable interview. Kate kept it short. To her surprise Andy de Salas listened to her suggestions once or twice, and allowed her, as the producer, to ask the questions while he organised the shots. The scenes of the woollen mill were surprisingly atmospheric in a sepia sort of way and Kate found herself surprised by de Salas's talent.

At lunchtime de Salas was called to the phone and Kate breathed a sigh of relief, and concentrated on whether to drink or munch the gelatinous blobs of instant soup from the mill shop microwave.

When she had finished, she strolled over to speak to the crew, eating their sandwiches outside in the fresh air. 'He's calmed down a bit,' said the cameraman, nodding towards the office where de Salas was on the phone. 'Nervy bloke. You never know when he'll blow. Raving one minute, oily the next . . . Look, he's a changed man now!'

He was right. When de Salas came back from the phone, he was beaming expansively, as cool and confident as he had been at the airport. Something had completely restored his sense of well-being.

'Kate.' De Salas was smiling as if meeting her for the first time, the tensions of the last twenty-four hours miraculously dissolved. 'Tonight, I wonder if you'd be free to join us for dinner over at Summerlake Hall?'

'Me? Really? Well . . .' Kate felt some conciliation was necessary, for June's sake, but she was still wary. 'Anything special?'

'Yes it is, rather. We have a guest. Paul Pym, director of the North West Cumbria Tourist Centre. He wants to meet the whole team for a meal.' De Salas paused, as if for applause. Kate was aware that this was some sort of coup, but she wasn't sure what. Over his shoulder she saw that June looked as if she was going to faint with relief. Paul Pym. The esteemed ex TV man with a budget for local videos who was supposed to provide the rest of the money, according to the letter Kate had been reading at the airport. De Salas was gazing at her with just enough genuine concern that she might say no, to make her say yes.

'OK, fine. I'll be there.'

De Salas's smirk became a genuine smile of appreciation. To her astonishment he said: 'Thanks Kate. We need you. I'm really grateful.'

In the afternoon break Kate took the chance to do two sensible things. The first was to arrange for a hire car to be delivered from the Skirlbeck Garage. It took some organising, but she was determined. The second was to tell June a joke as they drank scalding tea. The joke was quite simple, and Kate wasn't sure it would work.

'A lady rings up a house and a little boy answers in a whisper. The lady says, "Where's your mum, dear?"

The boy says, "She's busy."

"Well, your dad then."

"He's busy."

"Any other adult?"

"There's a policeman."

"Can I talk to him?"

"He's busy."

"Who else?"

43

"A fireman."

"Can I speak to him?"

"He's busy too."

"So there's your mum, your dad, a policeman and a fireman, and they're all busy?"

"Yes." '

It was only at this point Kate was sure she had June's full attention for the punchline. 'So the lady said, "What are they all doing?"

And the little boy whispered, "Looking for ME!" ' '

Kate held her breath, and June smiled. Then she actually laughed out loud, not at Kate's joke but in sympathy with her effort, and squeezed Kate's arm.

The hire car arrived at half past five, with all the complications of delivery and transport back for the driver. When Kate went back into the mill, the crew was packing up to go.

'See you at Summerlake Hall,' June said anxiously. 'I've booked us a table. Paul Pym and his deputy are meeting us for drinks at eight, with dinner at eight thirty. I'm glad you're going to be there.'

Kate needed to go back to her own hotel to change. She had deferred speculating about the Skirlbeck Bridge Hotel whilst she was working, but now that the first day of the shoot was over, she felt a little apprehensive about going back. She tried starting the hired car and kangaroo-hopped across the gravel before getting it right. Driving at dusk was always worst and she crawled along the lanes, unsure that she was on course until she could see the coastline. The hotel, double fronted, with symmetrical bay windows flanking an arched entrance, poked up on the skyline to her right, its gable end silhouetted. There was a muted glow from the windows, and Kate noticed that the sign was no longer lit up on the dark roadside.

The massive front doors were open, leading into the narrow Victorian hallway, with a doorway to the right into the dining room, and to the left into the bar. She walked forward nervously. There was no sign of any staff, and no light in the dining room. But on her left, there was the smudgy glow of a table lamp glancing off the optic bottles behind the burnished bar, and the flicker of flames. She was adjusting to the gloom when she heard a voice say softly, 'Hello,' and then another voice echoing it. She had been looking straight ahead at the mesmerising firelight and had missed the two little men who were there, one polishing glasses, the other decanting some warm, Christmas-smelling liquid into a cut-glass bottle. They looked like busy gnomes of some indeterminate age between thirty-five and fifty, and small enough to fit snugly behind the little bar like toys.

'Hi,' she said, wondering what tone to take.

'You're Miss Wilkinson, aren't you?' said one voice.

'We missed you last night because we were out,' continued the other. The accent was gentle, lilting, like a cross between Irish and Geordie, going up at the end of sentences.

'Yes.'

'You came with the vicar. The Reverend Goff. He phoned us about you. That makes all the difference, of course . . .' It was the smaller man who spoke. The other was slightly bigger, with cruder, more mobile features. The first man stopped, looking at her in a pleading way but the second, bigger man went straight on as if they were the same voice, like someone rescuing an actor who had dried.

' . . . and the other guests had to be asked to leave of course, just two commercial travellers and a couple touring, it's not really a busy time, but even so, we couldn't handle them. We've given the staff a few days off, out of respect. But *you*, well, we promised Reverend Goff . . .'

The first speaker had regained his nerve and went on smoothly, ' . . . so we have to keep our promise. Especially in the circumstances . . .'

'Yes.' She couldn't be sure any more which man was talking because their voices were so quiet. They passed the conversation from one to the other with the ease and instinct of a born double act. Of course. Twins. Then the first man opened the bar hatch and came through, hand outstretched.

'I'm Bill Robinson and this is my brother Terry. We're usually more welcoming . . .'

'It's something we pride ourselves on . . .'

'But in the circumstances . . .' he said again. He stood looking at her.

'Yes?'

The smaller brother rushed in, 'Don't get in a fret, Bill. It'll be all right, Miss Wilkinson. We'll be back to normal in just a few days . . . after the funeral.'

'Funeral?'

'Yes.' The bigger brother looked at her as if amazed at having to spell it out. 'Mother's funeral.'

'Your mother? Oh, my goodness.' Kate had adopted their old-fashioned way of speaking. 'I'm very, very sorry. Look, if you want me to go . . . I mean, I really don't want to add to your problems. You must be so upset . . .'

'We are,' said Bill, his voice breaking with emotion. 'It's the first time we've ever let our guests down.'

* * *

In the car an hour later, driving with some nervousness over the terrifying dark roads inland to dinner at the other, posher hotel, Kate found herself wanting to smile. The two men had ushered her to her room with a continual antiphonal chorus leading to one refrain . . . if she gave them a chance to get over all the fuss and shock, she would see what Skirlbeck Bridge hospitality was really like. She had finally asked, 'Your mother . . . what happened?' and had been told in voices of assumed solemnity that there had been a nasty accident. Their mother had gone for a breath of fresh air and trapped her wheelchair on the beach.

'She must have blacked out, and then of course her heart went. She wouldn't have had her tablets with her.' 'No, she'd have left them at Ada's.' 'Yes, you see, mother could be rather difficult and she told Ada she was sick of Ada's cheating at pontoon, and she was going out for a bit of air.' 'And she must have wheeled herself to the beach and got stuck.'

Kate had not been concentrating too much on the details, although the horror of a wheelchair trapped on the cold and lonely shore made her shiver. She had the impression that the dead woman's two sons were strangely unaffected, despite their careful conversation. The twins ran the hotel themselves with minimal staff, none of whom lived in, and the hotel was now temporarily closed. But Kate was sure they had asked the other guests to leave because of the arrangements for the huge local funeral they were planning, not because they were prostrate with sorrow. Now their concern was the catering for this major event . . . that and making sure the Reverend George Goff's friend was made welcome. Her local connection made her an entirely different class of guest.

47

And she had warmed to Bill and Terry. They had been in a frenzy of curiosity and excitement when she had said she was going to the glamorous Summerlake Hall for dinner, and had asked for a complete report. 'We won't wait up . . .' Bill had said. 'Not in the circumstances,' said Terry yet again. 'But we'll want a full description of the whole meal in the morning.' And they had both giggled in a way that was grotesque but harmless, embracing Kate in a caterers' conspiracy. It was the nearest she had come to feeling at ease since she had kissed the weary Reverend George Goff goodnight.

The Summerlake Hall Hotel was magnificent. On the wooded rhododendron clustered hillside, it shone like a liner on the waves of the fells, huge and bright, even the tasteful green and gold sign discreetly lit in a reverent halo. Around it, even in the dark of night, Kate could sense the huge flank of Skiddaw to the left and the lesser mountains crumbling to the right, while the soft, mysterious waters of Bassenthwaite Lake lay in a great still pool below. The hotel itself was awash with light. It was floodlit from the lush sculptured garden, and sparkling from the inside with the crystal gemshine of chandeliers.

Kate felt as if she was in a film as she clattered up the stone flagged steps to the front door, where a uniformed flunkey swung it open for her and smiled ingratiatingly, trained to be oblivious to the creases in her little black number. She felt reasonably well dressed. It was such a relief not to have to look attractive. For a 'work' dinner, smartness was the key. No cleavage, no jewellery other than her understated pearls – a Christmas present from John which had taken her completely by surprise and which she always felt were his good luck message every time she had to survive this sort of event. As she walked over the black and white tiles she heard her name called from the lounge on the left. It was de Salas, leaning of course on the marble mantelpiece, dressed in a beautiful grey cashmere suit, with three others in the overstuffed chairs grouped round him. June looked tired and still tense, but certainly smarter in a navy two piece.

'Let me introduce you,' de Salas said smoothly. 'I'd like you to meet Paul Pym and his assistant. Paul . . . Kate Wilkinson.' Kate looked at the imposing middle-aged man who was rising to his feet like a racehorse, heavy but still fluid and classy. Large, handsome, with a quiet quiff of rich silvery hair and dark eyebrows, a prominent jaw and good white teeth, his size alone seemed to put him on another level, and Kate, not a small woman, found herself missing his face and smiling stupidly at his dark silk tie when he stood up. He smiled back, literally above her head in a sophisticated and distracted way, as if his pleasure in meeting her was only tempered by mild irritation at finding his glass empty. Beside him a smaller man, plumper and slightly balding, was beaming and twitching a little, as if desperate to say something clever.

'Mrs Producer,' the small man chirruped, 'or should it be Ms Producer? Hard to know these days. You must be thrilled to get a lovely young lady like this on the case, de Salas.' Kate seethed behind the social hypocrisy of her smile. The assistant, whose name appeared to be Roy something, seemed a nudge-nudge wink-wink merchant in a different class from Pym, but Pym's tolerant little nod explained their relationship: the big man and his jester. As they sat down the greasy Roy was saying, 'You work in satellite TV, I hear? Lots of Aussies in satellite TV. Of course they're all nice guys but not great on small talk. You've heard the Aussie description of foreplay? "Brace yourself, Sheila." ' Kate smiled, but she knew her face betrayed her boredom with the old joke, and her assessment of the assistant as a fool.

'Another drink before we go in?' De Salas was absorbed in the smooth running of the party, and was already signalling the waiter. Pym looked approvingly at him.

'Good idea.' His voice was light and pleasant and unmistakably Oxbridge. Kate was surprised. She had deduced that Pym was an imposing man but she had expected someone who sounded more like Councillor Hodgson . . . middle class but definitely local. She ordered a sherry to express solidarity with June who seemed less uptight, but who was definitely not daring to risk anything by contributing.

'And you've joined Rural Rides to pull things together now Ben is out of action?' Pym inclined towards Kate, smiling. She thought he seemed rather nice, in a patronising sort of way, the sort of way you would expect from an eminent man of his age.

'Yes, I've had a break from my series for cable, and I . . .'

'Your drink, sir, madam . . .' the barman was at Andy's elbow. Kate took her amontillado and continued. 'I took the chance to . . .'

'And you feel confident, de Salas?' Pym had cut right across Kate's reply, distracted by the arrival of his glass into forgetting she had been speaking. She was left in mid-word, hearing the conversation move on without her. Kate caught June's eye and raised her eyebrow slightly. Terrified, June looked down quickly into her glass.

It was probably that incident which made Kate drink

more than usual over dinner. June was too inhibited to make anything other than a few conversational curtseys, and it was clear that Kate was expected to say little, agree with the men, and at most to mention a few examples of her own competence to support de Salas's choice.

She was also under the impression that a little eyelash fluttering would not go amiss, if the perspiring, boozy Roy's heavyhanded references to 'this delightful young lady who's helping you' were anything to go by. As Kate considered herself neither young nor a lady, the whole thing was laughable on one level and sickening on another. It became clear over the game soup and smoked salmon mousse that the one thing she was not to do was venture any opinions, despite the fact that the conversation quickly moved on to the wider issues of 'new media', in which she was more experienced than any of them. At one point, alarmed by the sound of her own voice for the first time in fifteen minutes, she heard her words die away as she attempted to join in the talk about the future of television. She had suggested that 'new media' – the world of cable and satellite TV – had widened the skill base of the professionals. She always put these points in a gentle way because her contemporaries in television were often touchy on the subjects of Sky and the cable industry. But even with this experience, she was taken aback by the force of Paul Pym's response.

'Oh, come on. With all due respect, most of this cable stuff is pretty grim. I mean, tacky repeats, American rubbish, low grade programming.' Kate was baffled by the strength of his feelings. Why should the boss of a Tourist Centre feel so aggressive about cable TV? Careful not to satisfy him by overreacting, and reminding herself that they had all drunk several glasses of claret, she said gently, 'Well, it is a developing medium.'

She caught the servile glance the assistant threw at Pym. He said, 'Of course, Paul was a freelance TV producer himself, in news and current affairs. He feels things have really gone downhill in the last few years. Isn't that right, Paul?'

'Oh really?' Kate was trying to stay pleasant. TV was littered with middle-aged casualties who felt the changes in the nineties had dealt them a duff hand, and the press relations and corporate affairs industries were swollen with the diaspora of elderly prophets deprived of the promised land. Now they'd become Jeremiahs, each with their own brand of bitterness. Kate could see where Pym was coming from. But that explained rather than excused his bad manners. Even so, she tried again.

'Then Paul, you probably know one of my friends. Felix Smart. He used to run a current affairs department, but he's consulting now and making an awful lot of money. Worth every penny, they say. And of course, if you've worked in news, you must know of Chrissia Cohen. Hasn't she done brilliantly getting that job at Channel Four?'

There was a short, strained silence. Then Pym said, 'I never had much time for Felix Smart,' signalling the wine waiter with his right hand as if parrying Kate's remarks. 'And the lady? I don't think I've ever heard of her.'

Chrissia Cohen was commissioning editor in the new Channel Four news features department, and Kate was sure that anyone who had worked in news would know her, by reputation at least. If Paul Pym didn't admit to knowing Chrissia he was either less familiar with the world of TV than he pretended, or deeply prejudiced against people, possibly women in particular, who were doing well.

'But you must know Chrissia. Everyone does. And where did you train?'

'Paul worked down south. At LondonVision in the seventies,' Roy the assistant said, in quiet triumph.

'Really, Paul!' Kate was genuinely surprised. 'What a coincidence. You must have been there just before my time!' Pym looked up from his lamb. The chances of meeting a LondonVision executive north of Watford were slim, and he tensed at once.

Kate went on, 'What an amazing coincidence. I was head of features at LondonVision a few years ago.' She did not tell him she had left, demoralised and disillusioned, and had had to repair her career. She sensed him waiting, wary and suspicious, neither smiling nor ready to exchange shared friends.

'Did you know . . .' She carefully reeled off the name of four major LV executives from the past, all of whom had names she could neatly turn into chummy diminutives – Ricky, Sid, Sir Freddie – Kate had known none of them other than as wafts of cigar smoke in the lift, but she could see Pym was shifting unhappily in his designer suit.

She was certain she had discovered a fraud. She was sure now that Pym was one of the people from the fringes of the media who claim an intimate knowledge of TV in order to impress minions like his gullible deputy. Kate could play that game as well as anyone. She heard herself becoming garrulous, rabbiting about the people she knew and their successes in TV news, concentrating on the women, watching Pym's discomfort. She really did flutter her eyelashes when she said, 'And what programmes did you make?'

She was ninety-nine percent sure that all he could say was a few local news bulletins twenty years before. She sat back ready to bask in a short-term, pointless triumph. He looked at her coolly. There was a short, charged silence. Then he murmured quietly, ' "Inside Scope".'

Even as he said it she felt it had been dragged out of him, but that didn't help. Kate could only say, 'Oh.' She was genuinely astonished, winded by surprise. Her embarrassment was covered by the assistant, fork with a chunk of bleeding meat halfway to his lips, who splashed it down in his gravy and said, 'What? Really, Paul? I remember that programme. You've never mentioned that before.'

'Inside Scope' had been one of the flagship current affairs programmes of the seventies. Watched by a tiny minority but feared by all in power, it had been relentlessly excellent until, with characteristic style, it axed itself before running out of steam.

But Kate was *sure* that if Pym had really worked on 'Inside Scope', he would have known Chrissia Cohen! And she was convinced that if what he said were true, he would have been bound to have had more respect for her friend Felix Smart, a past master at news documentaries. And if he were that talented, for God's sake, he would surely still be in a job in TV! Most of the 'Inside Scope' team, now in their fifties, were running the media industry. She was speechless, but unless Pym was a barefaced liar, there was no real reason to doubt him, and nothing she could say. She had lost. Crushingly. Pym did not elaborate about 'Inside Scope'. Instead he took his revenge differently.

'Yes. You seem to know a lot of girls in the business, er . . . Kate. I rather think the positive discrimination fad will be out of fashion shortly. So many very average people promoted for political reasons. Not that some of the ladies aren't quite good, of course. Don't get me wrong. Infotainment, chat shows, that sort of thing. Now what about the future of Rural Rides, de Salas? With all this work, no doubt you and Ben will be looking for a good man soon?'

The put-down was obvious and Kate sat there looking at her sorbet and wondering how she could have been so foolish. The assistant wiped the grease from round his little shiny mouth and whispered in a loud aside to Kate, 'Have you heard the one about why women need legs? To get them from the bedroom to the kitchen,' then sniggered. Pym tut-tutted playfully at him, then went on suggesting suitable 'men' de Salas should contact. After a moment, reminded she was still there, Pym turned to Kate as if he was charmingly trying to make amends and said, 'I see Anneka Rice is producing too, these days. I always rather fancied her. Beautiful bottom.'

'Is that how you rate women in TV?' Kate knew she was rising to the bait, but she couldn't stop herself. She was aware of June's panic and de Salas's fear, and that made her worse.

The assistant's red face leered at her across the starched white cloth.

'Now don't burn your bra, young lady,' he said. 'Not without my help.'

'Excuse me,' said Kate, and staggered to the Ladies. Predictably, the face she saw in the mirror was harsh and aggressive, with red blotches on the cheeks and neck and a snarl to the tight, raw mouth.

'Why are you so stupid? Why can't you just take it?' she said to her reflection which grimaced drunkenly back at her. The velour padded door swished open and June's wretched, distorted face peeked around, as stiff with anxiety as the crumpled pink towel Kate was clutching.

'Kate . . .' she said, desperately.

'I'm not coming back,' Kate answered, 'so don't ask me. What do you think their next little titbit will be? The joke about the difference between women and toilets: toilets don't follow you around after you've used them? Or the one about the useless flesh around the vagina: you've guessed it – a woman? Or how do you give a woman an orgasm: who cares?' They were all jokes that had been repeated to Kate in great good humour by the guys in the sales department, and Kate knew all the jokes were reversible. But now they seemed to be part of the macho heritage which men like Pym transmitted through a freemasonry to the nice young lads Kate had to work with.

'You're part of it, June,' Kate knew she was being nasty, but she was deeply hurt and angry. She pushed past June and out, clattering with her one pair of high heeled shoes on the parquet of the dining room, past two obsequious waiters who had the amused look of regularly needing to make way for hysterical women. She was seeing hostility everywhere. 'You're drunk, calm down,' a little voice inside was saying, immediately drowned by the louder chorus of hundreds in her head screaming, 'The bastards!'

She raced over the tiles and into the cool night air, with the speed and clarity of the drinker who knows it and perceives everything with fierce intensity. She could hear her shoes like Mah Jong tiles, clacking down almost faster than thought. Obsessed with keeping upright, she hurtled between the rows of vehicles and then stood perplexed. She'd reached the end of the car park. The hire car. What the hell did it look like? And was she really fit to drive? She was suddenly alone, away from the bank of lights. Her furious footsteps stopped, slightly ahead of her brain.

Then she saw the man. He was lurching back from the shadowy borders of the garden and she guessed he had been violently ill. He clutched his stomach and she thought she could smell the acrid sick stench on the air. The smell was making her reel a little herself. It seemed strong even for vomit. She was still too dazed to feel fear, but she knew she should be frightened.

Then the man stopped. He looked up and saw her, and she was frozen with drunken indecision, and a faint sense of recognition. Hesitantly, he said, 'Oh . . . it's you.' Within seconds she realised who it was and grasped back her social graces, twisting John's string of pearls in an automatic gesture like getting a grip on herself.

'Councillor Hodgson.'

'Yes,' he said, and then lurched a little again.

'Hello.' She paused. He seemed in a worse state than she was, but she knew intuitively he wasn't drunk. 'Are you all right?'

He moved sideways towards the Range Rover parked at the end of the row, and leaned, gasping, on the driver's door. Kate had been standing in the middle of the tarmac. Now she turned towards him instinctively, but he called out harshly, in real panic, 'No. No, don't come near here.'

'What?' Kate was bemused. He seemed to be trying to kick away a matted piece of fabric by the front right wheel of the car. She wondered why a filthy car rug should be upsetting him. The smell made her wonder if he had vomited on it. She tried to see over his shoulder.

'No!' he snapped again. As she moved forward and focused, she saw that it wasn't a rug. It seemed to have a head, horribly distorted, with one bulbous eye twisted skywards. It was grotesque and fascinating. It took her several seconds to make out that it was some sort of terribly mangled animal. She opened her mouth but shut it sharply. She was not going to show horror at whatever disgusting rural mess this was.

'What the hell is that?' Her voice sounded super southern, brisk and businesslike. Yet Hodgson, the countryman, was bent double with nausea. She tried to understand what he was saying.

'It's a dead dog,' he said.

'*What?*'

'It's a dead dog.'

He retched slightly.

How nasty. Ugh. She was mesmerised trying to make sense of the twisted bundle in front of them, but wrenched her eyes back to him. He was resting his head on the window now, and taking deep breaths. She was surprised he was so clearly affected. Her words were slightly blurred, but she was sure she was talking common sense.

'Well, hadn't we better call the police? Or tell the hotel. Or . . .' the thought was inevitable even though the thing had obviously been dead a while, ' . . . have you run it over?'

'Don't be stupid!' Hodgson's voice was harsher than hers. 'You'd better go back to the hotel. Or your car.' He was barring her way, as if she was about to go up and give the animal the kiss of life. Or scream and summon the RSPCA.

'But we can't just leave it.'

'It's just been left for me.' Hodgson's voice was loud and bitter.

'What?' Kate swayed a little, the fresh night air cutting through her alcoholic bravado. 'What are you talking about?'

'The dog's been left for me. It's a warning.'

'A warning. I don't understand . . .'

'Look, it doesn't matter. I was just shocked. You'd better get back to your car.'

'My car.' Kate looked round hopelessly, and stumbled a little.

'Christ!' Hodgson looked her up and down and seemed to regain his composure. 'You're in no state to drive anywhere.' Her inebriation was forcing him back to normality. 'Look, I'll give you a lift.'

Kate hated the phrase 'pull yourself together', but she tried it, physically gathering up her arms and legs which seemed to have drifted away from her. She gestured, flapping at the dead dog. 'And what about that?'

'We'll leave it. I dare say they'll take it away now it's served its purpose. They won't want anyone else to see it.'

'Take it away? Who? I don't understand.'

'It's too difficult to explain.'

'Why?' The word reminded him of the straightforward way she had opted out of the flirtation game that morning. He looked at her. She looked back, slightly drunk and more than slightly aggressive, but the challenge in her eyes made him gather his thoughts.

'All right,' he said. 'I'll tell you. But you need a lift. Get in.'

As she did so, she saw Paul Pym on the terraced steps of the hotel. As Hodgson backed the Range Rover speedily out of the car park and turned right to negotiate the long, sweeping drive, Kate looked left out of the passenger window. It was only feet away from the bright, glitzy doorway. Framed there, for an instant she caught Pym's sneering glance. Behind him, de Salas was scowling with the face she remembered from her nightmare.

Chapter Three

Kate felt safe in Malcolm Hodgson's Range Rover. It was several feet higher off the ground than de Salas's Porsche, and Hodgson drove steadily. There was a comfortable smell of leather and warm woolly clothing. She leaned back against the worn seat and shut her eyes for a moment, seeing nothing but black behind them and breathing with deep relief at not having to cope with the hire car on the country roads in the pitch dark night. For two or three minutes, she thought: I'm fine. She had her nausea at bay, then one signal from her stomach changed her mind. She burped into the silence, words and wind mixed up.

'I think I'm going to be sick.'

'That'll even the score. Hang on while I pull over.' She had absolute faith he would do so, and he did, seconds before it was too late. She opened the door and jumped out in one movement. She could smell the fresh Lakeland air, a mixture of wetness, bracken and woodsmoke, and then all she knew was the pounding head and the vile release of throwing up. In the dark she wasn't even sure where it landed, except not on her shoes, but whichever damp mossy part of Cumbria she had chosen accepted what she threw at it and within thirty seconds she could lift up her head and smell fresh air again. Walking back to the car she was almost lightheaded. She opened the passenger door and climbed back in.

'That's better,' she beamed at Malcolm Hodgson in relief.

'God, you smell like a hamster cage. But at least that makes two of us. What brought that on?'

'Oh, probably . . .' She paused.

'Something you ate?' They both laughed. Without saying anything he indicated left, into the forecourt of a low whitewashed pub, with the obligatory tubs of brown headed roses waving in the autumn night wind.

'Coffee?'

'What time is it?' Her voice sounded cool and ungracious, precisely because she was desperately grateful. She wondered whether, if she made a good impression on this man, it would somehow absolve her from her ill-judged behaviour with the other men that evening. In the calm of Hodgson's car she felt acute embarrassment for letting Paul Pym tweak her sensitivities so effectively. And worse, she felt a stab of pain at the thought that she had been rude to poor June.

Hodgson looked at his watch and then at her, with a friendly, open acceptance which made her grin back, and feel normal again. Did I do the right thing, or the wrong thing at dinner? she wondered. Would Hodgson be a good judge? The idea of coffee and warmth and someone who would listen made her long to be inside.

'Ten to eleven,' he said.

'OK. But I've got to be back at Skirlbeck by twelve. That's late enough for me.'

'No problem. But I reckon we could both do with a hot drink. To tell you the truth I'm still rather shaky at the wheel.' After the pomposity of Pym and the slimy Roy, his acknowledgement of weakness delighted her.

'Of course. I should have thought of that. I'd love a coffee too. And I'm really grateful.'

He'd been parking as she spoke, and he pulled on the handbrake, leaned across to unfasten his seat belt, and smiled at her. The smile was real. He was glad she was there and it showed. She smiled back.

'Did you say you were staying at the Skirlbeck Bridge Hotel?'

'Yes.'

'But I'm surprised to hear they're still open after what happened.'

'You mean the old lady?' Kate was already talking like an insider. It was a seductive feeling.

'Yes. An appalling tragedy. Not that she wasn't a bad old bitch, of course.'

They'd reached the pub door. Kate stopped and looked at him in surprise, but he was looking ahead, grimly. He'd sounded very local and very shrewd with that one remark, and though she was mildly shocked at his bluntness, she knew, from her one conversation with Bill and Terry, her browbeaten sons, that he was right about Jean Robinson.

'So I gather. But in what way?'

'Oh, she was into everything. School governor, parish councillor, purveyor of liquor after hours, manipulator of the council, repository of all the gossip, particularly the salacious sort. And worst of all, local bully.'

His words reminded her of the conversation with the Reverend George Goff, a hundred years ago.

'I see,' she said thoughtfully.

He steered her inside, taking her elbow in an objective

way which gave her an uneasy feeling of pleasure, and guiding her through the low ceilinged bar area into a little snug at the back where there was an upright settle and an oak table under black beams, all dimly lit. Here too there was a fire, not the large handpicked logs of the Summerlake Hall but a gas flame effect, yet to her surprise and annoyance with her own gullibility it certainly worked. She had a strange feeling of going back in time. The pub was obviously eighteenth century even if the fire wasn't, but the sensation of hospitality from the elements outside struck more forcibly than in many buildings of equivalent age in London.

'Margaret will get us some coffees, if I ask nicely,' said Hodgson. A plump girl in a white blouse, black skirt and frilly pinny had materialised in the doorway. She nodded and disappeared.

'Sit down,' said Hodgson, and Kate slid along the polished wood seat. He sat beside her, rather than opposite, staring into the organised flames.

Kate leaned her elbows on the table and dropped her head into them. She had that feeling of delicate well-being that comes after vomiting up everything and was frightened any sudden movement would bring back the nausea. Through her fingers she saw the fire's glow and, slowly, she lost her goosepimples.

'I've had a bloody awful evening,' she said.

'Snap. I've been to a dinner for a retiring education officer. What were you doing there?'

'Oh, sucking up to one of our film director's local worthies. You probably know him. Everyone knows everyone round here.'

'Yes, they do. There's nothing wrong with that.'

'No, except that everyone has a view on everyone else.'
She remembered her flat in South West London and the
freedom of not knowing or caring who lived three doors
away. It had always seemed a bad thing before, but now
she wasn't so sure. Funny, how the lack of space bred more
privacy than the open country.

'Who was it?' asked Hodgson, with confident nosiness.

'Chap called Pym. Paul Pym. Know him?'

Hodgson turned away abruptly to take the tray of coffee
from the girl, who handed it over deftly. 'Do you mind if I
turn the fire out, Mr Hodgson? It'll stay warm for about
another half an hour.'

'Fine,' said Hodgson absently. The girl fiddled at the
grate and then slipped away. He seemed to be taking a
long time straightening out the cups and saucers.

'Yes, I do know Pym,' Hodgson sighed. 'But I wouldn't
say we were the best of friends.' He paused and looked at
the declining flames.

'Go on.' Kate wanted to know as much as she could now.
The row with Pym was turning her from a spectator to a
participant. She was becoming fascinated by these rural
manoeuvres. Malcolm turned to her, and seemed to take
the measure of her face. She knew her eyes were bloodshot,
her makeup non existent, her hair tousled and that her
breath smelt. But Hodgson saw someone genuinely
interested, without the greed for power which motivated
so many of his local friends and acquaintances when anyone
else trembled on the brink of a confidence.

'We don't get on because I've been having an affair with
his secretary.'

It was a bald statement and not what Kate had expected
to hear. She felt a jolt of irrational disappointment, and her

65

eyebrows raising. But her mind was already determinedly moving on from Malcolm's confession to Paul Pym's involvement. Why should it matter to Paul Pym if someone was bonking his secretary? Surely if that was what the woman wanted . . .

'Oh, come on!' Kate smiled. 'I mean, why would that upset him? Unless he fancied her too?'

'Pym? God no, he's whiter than white in that department, and anyway I can't see him even considering a situation which might allow Mrs Pym to get away with the BMW.'

Kate grinned. 'Well, then, why was he bothered?'

'Gallantry, I suppose.'

Kate nodded. That fitted with the patronising manner she had experienced that evening. 'Gallantry, and territorialism I should think,' she added. 'After all, a lot of men think their secretaries belong to them. It's nothing to do with sex and everything to do with property.'

'Right! Gets us back to the BMW.'

They both chuckled. What am I doing, Kate thought, laughing companionably with an obvious philanderer, in a strange pub in the middle of nowhere?

Hodgson said: 'I can see you're not surprised. Perhaps you've already heard about my reputation . . .' Kate didn't correct him. ' . . . and it's a small world here. Anyway, Pym didn't like what was going on and he warned me off. Quite rightly, I suppose, except that it spurred me on. You know how it is.' Kate was about to say archly that no, she didn't, but honesty prevailed and she nodded over her coffee cup.

'And what did your girlfriend think in all this?'

'Ex-girlfriend. To be honest I think she was flattered that Pym noticed. That's what's so interesting.'

'What do you mean?'

'Well, everyone wants his attention. He's actually too big for the job he's doing. There's no doubt he's genuinely a very talented operator and the Tourist Centre has fairly blossomed since he took it on. But to be honest, it isn't really crucial to the local economy and they don't have all that much money to spend, yet Paul Pym always seems to be the man whom people want to impress. He's got presence, I suppose, and a sort of southern superiority. And whatever people say, they're all suckers for a posh accent up here.' He shrugged.

'I know exactly what you mean.' Kate was interested. 'That's just what has happened with us. My director and his PA have spent a fortune tonight sucking up to Paul Pym for the sake of a few grand which they could probably get from Border or Channel Four if they stopped toadying and just made a decent film. But Pym was acting as if he was the Heritage Minister. And he brought another chap along to set the scene. Like a second rate courtier. His assistant.'

'That creep! Right up Pym's arse. God, I don't know how Pym manages to get hold of these people . . .'

'He attracts them, I suppose. Anyway, the people I'm up here working for seem to feel they can't do without Pym's money.'

'Really?' Hodgson sounded mildly contemptuous.

'That's right. Apparently the Tourist Centre has some cash to spend on a video of the area, and our director was relying on getting it. Except that I've probably gone and blown it.' She felt the cold realisation of just how she had behaved dawning like a wet grey hangover and shivered. What an idiot she had been.

She paid Hodgson back for his confidence by telling him about the farcical dinner. It was a cross between self-justification and confession, but Hodgson's friendly support bolstered her. He laughed at her story of how she thought she was going to put Pym in his place, only to be wrongfooted herself, and snorted sympathetically when she repeated the assistant's crass remarks. She hadn't credited Hodgson with being understanding – but then of course, she reminded herself, there were some people who were naturally fair-minded.

'You should have said that women have legs to get them from the kitchen to the boardroom!'

'Ha ha. It's always easy afterwards, isn't it? I hate people who tell you what you *should* have said.' But she didn't hate Hodgson. Quite the opposite.

They paused to drink the hot black liquid and Kate felt the warmth go down her throat and straight into her cold feet. It was headier than alcohol.

'So where does the dead dog fit in?' she said lightly.

Hodgson visibly shuddered, so the cup rattled in the saucer. He put his head down.

'I'm sorry,' said Kate. 'Look, if you don't want to tell me . . .'

'Well, it's a night for telling, isn't it. And I said I would. But you mustn't think people in this area are bad, if I do tell you. I mean . . .' He stopped and Kate was reminded of June, writhing about where her loyalties lay.

'Of course I won't make that sort of judgement,' Kate said stoutly. 'Anyway, so far the mystery is probably sounding worse than it is.' She laughed, but this time he did not join in.

'I doubt it,' he said.

She waited for him to go on. At the back of her mind she was still bemused by the way a dead dog could upset this big, confident countryman who was sitting, head down, deep in thought. She could tell he was working out what to say, and it was a struggle for him to start. Then he looked up.

'Look, I don't know if you know much about lads. Teenage lads, that is?'

Kate was at a loss. She was about to say that she knew nothing at all, but she wanted to help the embarrassed Hodgson along. The only young man she really knew was John's son. For reasons she didn't want to examine, she stopped herself saying, 'My boyfriend's son . . .' and tried instead to think of some generalisation.

'Teenage lads? You mean completely disgusting and then all self-righteous . . . sort of crude one minute and caring the next?'

'Yes!' Hodgson's face relaxed. 'That's exactly it. Telling jokes about dead babies and then crying over the Jamie Bulger case . . .'

'Or having their eyebrows pierced and then helping old ladies across the road . . .'

'Yes! You see what I mean, don't you?' Kate nodded, unsure where this was going. Almost in relief, Hodgson was talking faster now.

'Of course, they're not all that sort of mixture. Some are just brutal bastards and that's really why the trouble happened.'

'Go on.'

'My lad Alan is just eighteen. And he thinks . . . thought . . . he was tough.' Kate listened as Hodgson talked, clenching and unclenching his fists. What had happened had obviously struck at all his notions of masculinity and what it was for.

'He came home from college this summer full of himself. Yes, he'd had his ear pierced, and he'd obviously had his first taste of a lot of drink. He'd been on a trip to Amsterdam and hitch-hiked to Glasgow, and stayed with some dirty New Age types down south, and done quite a bit. And there was a crude edge to him that I thought was just showing off. He was all right for a few days, then he started going into the towns, Workington and Whitehaven, Cockermouth once or twice, and coming back pretty drunk. And not just drunk. With a sort of glint . . .'

'Drugs?' Kate felt this was going to be the predictable story, but Hodgson looked up at her in surprise.

'Oh no, not drugs.' He shook his head in irritation. 'No, not drugs. He was high on something else. He finally told me because he couldn't keep it to himself. He even thought I might approve. Through one of the pubs, he'd got involved in a group who were setting up dogfights.' He paused. 'Do you know what I mean?'

'Well, sort of.' Memories of RSPCA videos loomed at the back of Kate's mind, but she couldn't feel any real disgust, certainly nothing like the sort of sensation which was tautening Hodgson's face and making him twist his coffee cup so the liquid sloshed up the sides.

'Dogfights. What they do is have two fighting dogs, dogs bred for it, and they feed them raw meat, starve them, excite them God knows how . . .' he paused again and she looked back, getting a sense now of his horror ' . . . and then they throw them at each other in a ring and bet on which dog will tear out the other's throat first.'

'Nasty. But there's always been that sort of thing in the country, hasn't there?'

'For Christ's sake! This isn't some sort of rural sport.

This is an illegal organised form of sadism. We're not talking about a fox getting a fair run or even something as "nasty", as you call it, as hare coursing. This makes badger baiting look like a kids' game. The dogs kill each other under the excited eyes of people who get their kicks from animals tearing each other limb from limb.'

'Sick,' said Kate. Then she remembered the warm woolly smell in the back of the car, the smell of live collie dog, and took the risk of adding, 'But it's 'cos it's dogs, isn't it, that it upsets you so much?'

'Yes. It is because it's dogs. We've been brought up with dogs here. And for Alan, it was worse.'

'Worse?'

'Yes.' She could tell by his voice that he had never told anyone before, but had thought about it a lot. The words were well chosen but strained.

'He started to feel sick when the dogs were fighting. He hadn't realised what it was like to watch animals die like that. And he was frightened by the . . . well . . .' He looked at Kate, ' . . . the sexual lust that was there. He said you could see they had erections, some of the men. I think what started to upset Alan was that he felt the same way at first and then one of the dogs had its eye scratched out, and Alan realised they really were going to die. I think until then he'd thought it was sort of like a tough version of "The Gladiators".'

'But it was the real thing?'

'Yeah. Then apparently one of the dogs got . . . finished off . . . faster than the men wanted. So they . . .' he choked slightly. It was as if this bit had never been put into words, but had just been a sick film in his head. 'They had an old collie bitch with one of them. She was blind in one eye.

71

What you might think was a faithful working dog. Alan said she was with one of the men on the fringe of it. An old farmer we both know. And two of the lads from the front took the dog and threw her into the ring. And they all watched and cheered as the fighting dog savaged her. It tore her face off.'

Kate waited, trying to imagine what he had told her.

'And your son?'

'My son. My son found he was crying and trying to get out. My son was a wimp.'

'But his reaction was the right one, wasn't it?'

'Of course it was. But he was in a terrible state when he got home. They'd put him up against a wall and told him that he wasn't a man, and that he should get a grip and they . . . they took him and pushed his head over the edge of the barrier and made him look into that collie's dying eyes, what was left of them. Thank God he was staying with me, not his mother. He could never have told her. They tipped him out of a van at the top of our track and he stumbled home.'

'And what did you do? Ring the police?'

'Oh, I agree, that would have been sensible. But I got Al to bed that night, and when he woke I was going to get him organised and take him down to Cockermouth. But . . .'

'Yes?'

'In the morning, there was blood everywhere. Smeared over the front door and the barn. And the collie's body was in the path. I tried to get rid of it before Alan saw it, but of course, he'd woken up and put his head out of the window for air and there was the little body in the path. The bastards must have come back.'

'But you know who they are?'

'Alan knows who they are. He won't say any more. The only person he told me about was Flint, the old farmer with the dog they killed, and I can't see him being behind all this. Apparently there were quite a few people caught up on the fringes, possibly several who felt like Alan but weren't young enough or stupid enough to show it. But no-one is talking. Alan was certainly too terrified to mention anyone else. And he was a wreck. He wouldn't go out of the house.'

'What did you do?'

'This was in late July. I couldn't leave the farm myself. We let a lot of holiday property in summer and there are the caravans and catering businesses too, so I persuaded Alan to go to Greece with his cousins from Manchester. I ended up paying for them, but I thought the change would be good for him.'

'And was he OK?'

'Yeah, seemed to be. He didn't come back home though. He went to his mum's until the end of August and then – all credit to him – got himself a temporary job at a supermarket near her. We've never spoken about it since.'

Kate could understand the unspoken pact between father and son never to dredge this up. She thought of John and his son, who had never really discussed the divorce and the crisis this had meant for John as a clergyman, never mind what it must have meant for the child.

'So why another dead dog tonight?'

'Because it's half term.'

'What?'

'Half term. Alan's back from college. What the bastards don't know is that he's only passing through the area. He's too damn scared to stay here. But someone must have seen him over the weekend. I don't know how, he hardly left the farm until I put him on the train south last night to his mother's. It makes me fucking furious because these swine are ruining things between me and my son. Alan doesn't want to come home; I'm tied to the farm and can't go anywhere else; and all the time I know these sadists are carrying on with this. Every time I see a pup, or stop to chat with a neighbour with the dogs round our heels, I don't know if they're the same people who get their pleasures that way. And I don't know what they're going to do next to keep us in line.'

'But why would they leave the . . . body . . . here?'

'Most embarrassing place, I suppose. Or maybe there's another one in my yard. God, I don't know what makes these bastards tick.'

'Did you know these sort of fights happened before your son got involved?'

'Yes, I suppose I did, vaguely. But it didn't mean anything to me. It probably doesn't mean that much to you. But anyway, now you know, for what it's worth.'

She had the impression he had expected that telling her would cause some sort of catharsis which hadn't happened. Her coffee was cold.

'You're in a hell of a dilemma,' she said softly.

He looked round at her, almost surprised. 'Yes, I am, aren't I? I expected you to say something brisk and sensible, like "go to the police anyway" or "sell up and move away" or "forget about it, it's only dogs". But you're right, I am in a hell of a dilemma. I'm glad you see that.'

Kate breathed out quietly with relief. She had managed to say the right thing through sheer lack of anything positive to say. What Hodgson had needed to hear was not a solution, but the acknowledgement that he was in a mess. Now, it wouldn't be unmanly for him to admit it to himself.

'I owe you dinner for listening,' he said, then saw the surprise on her face and mistook it for distaste. 'Really, just to talk about West Cumbria. It's a marvellous place and I'd love to tell you about it. I don't want you to get the wrong idea . . .' he laughed, ' . . . either about the area, or about me!'

Kate's eyes slipped to his big hands cradling the thin china cups. For a moment she imagined what it would be like to feel them round her waist. She told herself not to be ridiculous. She was aware of a feeling of mild confusion. She wanted Malcolm to find her attractive, even though she sensed that in his own way he was paying her the greatest compliment he could by not putting her in the commodity class.

But he was saying, 'Oh well, I suppose my reputation precedes me . . .'

'No, not at all!'

'Listen, we've nearly thrown up over each other so a little misunderstanding over my motives is nothing!'

'Oh, I realised you weren't chatting me up,' Kate said defensively, suddenly aware of her tired, lined face, smeared makeup and dishevelled hair. Not to mention the very unsexy way she had vomited into the hedgerow.

'Chatting you up?' Malcolm was smiling at her. 'No, this was a real conversation.' She laughed, flattered and slightly disappointed at the same time. He went on, 'I'll tell you one thing . . .' he was rummaging through his pockets now, clearly looking for his wallet. 'You've made me feel better. You're so right. It's no good me pretending I haven't got a problem and then waking up in the night dreaming of dead dogs. But I doubt there'll be one waiting for me at home. They usually only kill one a session.'

Suddenly the horror of it hit Kate. 'God, you're right! It's awful!'

'Now, you promised me you wouldn't let it spoil the place for you. Remember that. It's a bloody good area to live in. Come on, anyway, we'd better pay up and go.'

He called for the girl who had served them but there was no reply. So they strolled through into the silent bar, and he shouted 'Margaret?' once or twice.

'Let's leave some change?' Kate suggested.

'Yes, we could do that, but I like to make sure I pay properly when I pop in like this. Anyway . . .' he rooted through his big waxed anorak pocket, and then through his tweed jacket, ' . . . I've only got my credit cards.'

'And I've not got any money on me either. There weren't any cash points on the trees between Summerlake and Skirlbeck.'

They both looked round again, but there was no-one in sight. The bar was polished and clear, the tables gleamed and it was clearly closed for the night.

'Looks like they've gone to bed.' Kate was surprised. It seemed a strange way to behave with customers in the place. She went on, 'I suppose we'll have to leave it . . . and come back.'

'Good idea.' He smiled at her. 'I'm probably just being a bit Northern and punctilious about the money anyway. But I never like to presume, even though I own the place.'

'What?'

He smiled and shrugged.

'Did I hear you correctly?'

In reply, he opened the heavy wooden front door so she

had no option but to walk through, out into the cooling night. He slammed it behind them and anything she could have said would have been snatched by the wind. As she caught his glance he was laughing and she was totally charmed. She was still smiling as he started the engine.

Ten minutes later he turned off the short cut only a local driver would know, and dropped her at the Skirlbeck Bridge Hotel. As she undid her seat belt, swivelling awkwardly to get out, yet happily aware that inches of her legs were showing, she heard him say, 'I'll call you tomorrow.'

For a moment Kate was tempted to say 'Why?' again with her usual directness. But as she turned to reply, Malcolm Hodgson leant from behind the steering wheel and with gentle precision kissed her on the side of her face. It was a gesture as innocent yet sensual as the nuzzle of a kitten, and Kate felt the damp impression of his lips like an ice burn.

'Thanks,' he said softly. 'I really enjoyed talking to you. Shall we do it again soon?'

'Oh yes,' she said, hearing the unsophisticated enthusiasm in her voice before she could catch it. He laughed, and the excitement of the sound followed her up the steps and into the little hotel.

The next morning was dank with stained clouds draped over the charcoal mound in the distance, which was just a poor blotched copy of the Scottish mountain etched on the horizon the day before. The sea was like dirty bathwater and the cry of the birds was sad. But the Skirlbeck Bridge Hotel smelt of hot crispy bacon and lightly browned toast, and Kate lay dozing, reviewing the night before with moods swinging between self-revulsion, self-congratulation, and fear that de Salas would have every right to put her on the next plane home. Had she stuck up for herself and her sex? Or had she perpetuated a myth and behaved boorishly too? And yet underlying all this worry was a feeling of excitement. She touched her cheek where Malcolm Hodgson had kissed her. It had surely been just a friendly gesture, the sort of thing media luvvies did every day? But then he wasn't a media luvvy . . .

There was a tentative tap at the door followed by a hesitant voice saying, 'Hello? May I come in?' and the enticing clink of cups.

Kate straightened her nightie, feeling that whilst her body was hardly likely to inflame one of the Robinsons (or anyone else that morning, she thought morosely, looking at her blotchy skin) her hosts would appreciate modest behaviour, and called, 'Of course.'

Bill Robinson pushed the door open, saying diffidently, 'Tea? Or we'll go back for coffee if you'd prefer?'

'How nice of you! Tea will be fine.'

'Lovely! Now, don't get up, I don't want to embarrass you. It was a bit of a risk coming up unannounced but you seemed like the sort of person who would appreciate it. And we don't want you to find us inhospitable.'

'Absolutely not!'

'And how was the Summerlake? It's been done up again in the last year. You're the first person we know who's been over there since.' Bill was looking at her intensely, and she remembered the twins' eagerness for a report on the sumptuous establishment fifteen miles away. Their fascination was a mixture of professional interest and absurd competitiveness. Bill wanted to hear it was fabulous . . . but perhaps not that fabulous.

'Gorgeous.'

He sighed voluptuously, but with a hint of a hope for criticism. 'Yes?'

'Unbelievable.' She knew she was hitting the right buttons. She sipped the hot liquid which insulated her against the outdoors. The view from the window was growing fuzzier with encroaching mist and rain.

'Yes, it was marvellous. Better than anything in London.' Kate had learnt during other trips to the north that this qualification was a prerequisite. And in the case of the Summerlake it was true. The sculptured terraced gardens down to the lake would have been turned into three rows of Georgian townhouses in most parts of the capital.

'Aah . . .' Bill Robinson sighed with satisfaction, then waited, as if a choice titbit was still to come.

'But it was rather too grand, I thought.' Kate watched him relax happily. 'It lacked real warmth, and to be honest it was a bit too overdone to be really tasteful. One flunkey too many, if you know what I mean.'

'Yes, yes, I do, I think I do.' Bill was happily into gossip mode now. 'And what was the company like?' Kate groaned. 'Well, I'm afraid I made a mess of that. My boss was entertaining a man called Paul Pym, from the Tourist Centre. But I put my foot in it. I took a bit of a dislike to him . . .'

'You did? We know him, but not well. He's often on Radio Cumbria. Quite a big wheel. What didn't you like about him?'

'Well, to be honest, I thought he was a patronising windbag and I virtually told him so.'

'Good for you. I have to say Terry and I find that type rather overpowering. Not that it would do to let on.'

'That it wouldn't.' Terry Robinson was peeping round the door. 'All right if I come in too? Quite a party isn't it?'

'And who else was there?' Bill still looked greedy for news.

'Well, he wasn't actually part of our group but . . .' she wondered why she had an urge to mention Hodgson. The thought of him was warm and tingling, and the avid need of the brothers for interesting chit-chat tempted her to be indiscreet. 'Er, another person I met was Malcolm Hodgson. Councillor Hodgson.'

'Ooh!' Terry looked cagily at Bill. 'We rather like him, don't we, Bill?'

'Yes, we certainly do. Mother wasn't keen, but I have to say on the occasions we've met him, he's been charming. Very nice.' She thought she caught him glancing in warning at his brother, but couldn't be sure. The twins were not camp, but she suspected that because they had each other and had always been a twosome, they had developed mannerisms which might otherwise have led them to be ostracised.

'Malcolm Hodgson. A handsome man.' Terry was giggling and Bill added gruffly, 'Good councillor as well. Bit too outspoken, though.'

'True.' Terry was nodding. 'You have to watch what you say round here. People can be touchy.'

'You said it.' Kate remembered de Salas. 'Listen,' she went on. 'I've got a hell of a day ahead, so I'll have to get up. What time's breakfast?'

'As soon as you want it.'

'We'll both disappear now and make sure it's ready the moment you come downstairs.'

'Great. I'll have a bath, and then I *must* ring my boyfriend. And my friend Liz.' Not before time, Kate thought to herself.

She would relish a chat with Liz about de Salas, even if she had burnt her boats the night before.

A few minutes later she could hear the phone ringing in Liz's untidy little Hammersmith house. She smiled to herself at the thought of five-year-old Lily, Liz's 'big girl', racing round to get ready for 'real school', with her brother Thomas clamouring for his sports kit or something similar, and Liz and her husband presiding over near panic. Yet at the same time, Liz Jones was virtually Kate's best friend, and she knew she wouldn't begrudge her the moment for a quick chat.

'Hello?' It was Liz's husband Steve at the other end.

'Hi, Steve. It's Kate. Can I talk to Liz?'

'No you can't!' He sounded grumpy as hell, and Kate, even though she knew Steve was not given to wasting charm, felt his brusqueness bristling down the phone. 'OK. Is she in the loo or something? I'll ring back . . .'

'No, she isn't in the bloody loo. She's not bloody here.'

'Sorry?'

'She's not here, Kate. I thought you might know where she is better than I do.'

'What?'

'She's at another of her bleeding conferences. I thought this was one you were at too.'

'No, I'm in the Lake District, filming.'

'Oh, well, I can't help you then. Anyway, she's a damn sight more likely to tell you what she's doing than to tell me these days.'

Kate was silent. He sounded too crabby for a reasonable conversation.

'Stop that, Lily!' Steve was shouting. 'For Christ's sake, don't touch that milk bottle . . .'

'I'll let you go,' Kate said weakly.

'Fine. If she bothers to call me I'll tell her you rang.' And he put the phone down. Kate sat on the edge of her bed, looking at the handset before she replaced it thoughtfully. Liz usually mentioned what she was doing, and she and Kate talked once a week at least. Kate had been aware that Steve was 'going through a difficult patch'. 'A touch of the Victorian fathers,' Liz had said laughingly. Kate had laughed with her. It had not seemed like a crisis.

She dressed and went downstairs, hugging herself against the damp air that seemed to be seeping through every joint of the house.

'Come in to the warmth,' said Bill Robinson expansively, at the dining room threshold. 'And what would you like, madame? Full Cumbrian breakfast, or just tea and toast, or kippers, freshly brought over on the Manx steam packet?'

'Oh, the works,' said Kate cheerily. The dining room was delightful. They had laid a table for her in the bay window with a sea view and even this morning, it had an air of a British holiday with all the fresh air and good food you could dream of. A little glass vase held some Michaelmas daisies and a spray of fuchsias, and there were fresh pats of butter on a china dish, and home-made jam in a ramekin. Terry was ready with tea in a brown china pot, and Bill left them to go and 'dish up' as he put it. Somewhere, in the kitchen at the back, Kate heard the phone ring.

'Excuse me,' said Terry with exaggerated politeness, making her giggle. Whilst he was answering it, Bill reappeared with bacon, egg, tomatoes and mushrooms. He hovered again as she started to eat, and Kate felt for a moment the same sensation she'd had as an only child at

Christmas when the whole family had leaned over her to get the vicarious pleasure of seeing her opening presents.

Then she was aware he had turned away and was hurrying, arms outstretched and flailing a fish slice, towards his brother. Terry was standing, his face as pale as porridge, in the kitchen doorway. They bent to whisper together, the first time since she had met them, Kate realised, when she had been excluded. Absurdly, Terry was holding a tiny silver toast rack, like a little bell he had forgotten to ring. The toast lurched dangerously, but he was too involved in what he was saying to notice.

'Terry, the toast!' she said.

'Oh, yes, of course,' he cried, misunderstanding her. 'So sorry. Here it is.'

'No. I just didn't want you to drop it!'

'Well, we shouldn't have started talking like that. So rude,' said Bill.

'And so unlike us,' said Terry in a voice of deep depression.

'What's the problem? Anything I can do?'

'No, really . . .' The two men stood uncomfortably looking at her. Then Terry blurted, 'It really isn't anything to do with you . . .'

'Oh dear, Terry, that does sound rude. That isn't what he meant, Kate . . .'

To her horror, Terry's lower lip started to quiver, and he turned away from her.

'It's about mother. That was the third one.'

'The third what?'

'The third person to say they can't come to the funeral.'

'Oh, I'm sorry to hear that.'

'Sorry!' Terry Robinson's voice rose to a cry. 'Mother

83

had her flaws – we all do – but not even the regulars from the Castle Arms are making the effort. She deserves better than this.' And he flounced back towards the kitchen. His brother fluttered after him.

Kate ate the rest of her breakfast in silence, then went out with Bill who had quietly returned and kindly offered to take her back to the Summerlake Hall Hotel to pick up the hire car.

'Don't be upset by Terry,' Bill said, once they were a few miles down the road. 'But Tom Flint giving backword about the funeral has really hurt his feelings. The trouble is, Kate, that mother had a lot of enemies.'

She certainly seemed to have, Kate thought. And it struck her again as strange that Jean Robinson should have died on the shore. There was no evidence the woman was a great nature lover. But for this morning, Kate put her speculation to the back of her mind, and tried to concentrate on how she was going to face Andy de Salas.

Except that every time her mind took a rest, she saw the crumpled body of the dead dog, and Malcolm's Hodgson's hands clenched around his coffee cup.

Chapter Four

It was half past ten that morning before Kate remembered she hadn't phoned John as she had promised. She made a mental note to try and ring him at lunchtime to apologise. She had been too worried about catching Liz on the phone, and then too pre-occupied with the Robinson twins and most of all, she had been concerned about facing de Salas after the debacle at dinner, and flustered at having to navigate her way to the location. It was a workshop for some very chunky and fearsomely expensive rustic jewellery which looked as if it was made of human remains.

June was waiting for her, standing alone.

'Where's Andy?' Kate asked anxiously. She noticed that the crew were unloading the car a few yards down the road.

'Not here. He's rather the worse for wear this morning. The food at the Summerlake can be very rich.' Kate could hardly hide her relief.

June led her into the premises, where a large, noisy man with a very Scottish accent was chivvying his wife as she tried to drape a set of bronzed knee caps over a velvet plinth. He turned to grin toothily at them and offer a 'wee corrffee' in the kitchenette next door. June accepted graciously. She had obviously 'recce-ed' the place and seemed in complete control. Kate perched her bottom on the bench.

'To be honest, I thought you might be asking me to pack up this morning, rather than take over.'

'What? Because you felt ill and left the dinner early?'

'You know it wasn't like that, June.'

June shrugged noncommittally, 'There's nothing like a good discussion. That's what Paul Pym said.'

'Really? I thought he was doing his best to override me rather than have a good discussion.'

'Oh, that isn't entirely fair. Perhaps you're overreacting?'

Kate had been accused of that before, and the suggestion usually goaded her into more of the same, but June was smiling nervously at her, and she knew the PA only wanted to make peace. June went on, 'You really shouldn't worry about it, Kate. Anyway, once dinner was over it was still relatively early and we were all asked back to Paul's house. He's got a magnificent Georgian farmhouse, you know, like something out of Barbara Cartland, complete with fanlight over the front door and marble fireplaces and an elegant hall, and even a billiard room! It would cost half a million down south, in Manchester, I mean. Paul Pym is very well thought of locally. He's a churchwarden and a local historian. Quite the lord of the manor type. Anyway, Andy had an awful lot to drink, but it was well worth it because Paul Pym virtually promised us the Tourist Centre's video. He seemed very impressed with Andy's synopsis.'

'But what about the row? Didn't it bother either of you, the way he went on about cable TV being rubbish, and women in TV getting preferential treatment?'

'Oh, it was all in fun. After you'd gone they had a little laugh about it. I did worry slightly at the time if it might have turned Paul Pym against us. But he didn't seem a *petty* man.'

Kate felt a shudder of irritation, but bit her lip.

'So de Salas has to rely on me today just because he has a hangover?'

'Well, you did a good job yesterday, and I made sure he realised it!'

'He wasn't exactly fulsome in his praise last night! He and your friend Mr Pym treated me like dirt.'

'Oh, Kate! It wasn't as bad as that. Anyway, it didn't do us any harm. Paul Pym didn't seem to mind at all.' June looked tolerantly over her cup, and Kate bridled.

'And so the guys had a good chat, and agreed that it was just a little spat, and everything was OK.'

'Kate, we have to live and let live. And most important, the film needs this Tourist Centre money. If anything were to go seriously wrong at Rural Rides, I've got my family to think of . . .'

Kate had the grace to blush guiltily. How could she have been so insensitive as to let her pride threaten another woman's pay?

'You're right. I'm sorry. Perhaps I behaved badly. I'm glad it doesn't seem to have mattered. And I understand your worry about the funds. Look, why don't I put my money where my big mouth is and ring Chrissia Cohen at Channel Four? Maybe we *could* try to see if they might be interested. A commission from them, even for a low prestige slot . . .'

'Would you, Kate? That would be absolutely marvellous for Andy!'

'Of course.' But as she said it Kate worried that she was promising more than she could deliver. 'What time will he turn up?'

'Oh, he won't be here at all today.' June looked uncomfortable now, and shifted away along the workbench. 'He's got to meet someone at the airport.'

Kate felt a moment's panic.

'Really? Who?'

'It's just a personal friend.'

'Thank goodness for that. I thought you meant another producer! Well, then, I'll definitely call Chrissia this lunchtime so I can find out where we stand with Channel Four while Andy is out of the way.'

'Thanks, Kate. Any extra funding would be a godsend.' June hesitated. 'Paul *was* marvellous. But he didn't actually promise anything definite.' She frowned again, so Kate patted her arm in sympathy.

'We'll find something, June. Just think how brilliant it would be if you got the Tourist Centre money *and* a Channel Four commission.'

And so, when the lunchbreak came, Kate again forgot to phone John Maple.

By then it had become a blowy day with the platinum clouds punctuated by falling leaves. The sheets on the washing line in the garden next door to the workshop were cracking like sails. Kate had left the stifling atmosphere of the jeweller's soldering bench, intending to take a breath of air. Instead the air took her breath away, and she gasped as the gusts exploded down from the fellside. She walked to the top of the yard and looked down over the slatey town, wondering how she was going to follow up the call she had just made. She couldn't quite believe she had been put through so easily to Channel Four's chrome and glass bastion in Victoria.

She had suspected it was a mistake even as she was doing it. Chrissia's voice had said brightly, 'This is Chrissia Cohen. I'm not in the office just now . . .' (Kate had started talking before realising it was voice mail, so she felt foolish) . . . but if you would like to speak to someone personally, then my stand-in commissioning editor, Hugh Ruscroft, is on . . .' Kate quickly jotted the number down, and rang it before she had time to give up. As it was connecting she was thinking, Ruscroft . . . Ruscroft . . . how do I know that name? When the soft voice answered she was none the wiser.

'Hugh Ruscroft? My name's Kate Wilkinson. I'm an ex-colleague of Chris's from LondonVision, and I also know Felix Smart, who can vouch for me . . .' She heard herself burbling pleasantries until he cut in.

'And now you've set up as an independent producer and you think you have a programme idea we might want to commission?' He sounded tolerant, but very tired, as if he had heard it all before, which he probably had.

'Well, not me exactly . . .'

'I see. Well, perhaps you could jot it down for us. I really would appreciate seeing any submission in writing.' Kate knew she was losing his interest. Behind her she could hear the jeweller handgrinding a large femur shaped piece of metal.

'Is Chrissia not there? When will she be back?'

'I'm afraid she's in hospital. Nothing too serious, before you ask, but it was rather sudden and she will be away for several weeks.'

'Oh dear. Poor Chrissia.' Kate waited for a suitable few seconds, her mind racing to work out how long she need pause sympathetically before Hugh Ruscroft was tempted to put down the phone with a murmured goodbye. 'Look,' she rushed on, 'I'm not in a position to write something out for you. But I really think you'll be interested – and we're making the film anyway, so we don't need development money.'

Did she feel Hugh Ruscroft's breath becoming slightly warmer down the phone?

'And you're Kate Wilkinson? Felix Smart's friend?'

'Yes, that's right.'

'Actually, I think we may have met before. You left LondonVision and went off to work at Northern TV for a while? And now you're with cable?'

'Yes, that's me. I'm just taking a break from my regular job to freelance for a friend.'

This sounds weaker and weaker, she thought desperately.

'Well, tell me the outline,' he said dutifully. Kate began to explain Andy's thesis, about how country crafts were reviving an area of the north west where the marriage between industry and agriculture had spawned an almost Victorian mixture of rural and urban cultures.

'You know,' she could hear herself saying desperately, 'like the railway in Middlemarch. Or the mining and farming in Lawrence's Nottinghamshire.'

'But I rather think Nottingham is still like that,' Ruscroft said reasonably.

'Yes, but . . .'

'But what?'

'Our film will show how the rural elements are the ones to which we return for real regeneration.' I don't believe that, she thought to herself . . .

'Well, Kate, it's nice to talk to you but I really do think

we'll need to see a treatment written out before we can even consider talking further . . .'

Kate realised she was losing him. In a moment of inspiration and desperation she heard herself say:

'And then, of course, there's the cruelty and violence of rural life which has to be overcome . . .'

'I beg your pardon?'

'The black side of it all . . .'

She could hear Ruscroft's sharp intake of breath sucking back up the phone line. Gotcha, she thought. Here was something that might tempt him.

'We do have evidence that hand in hand with this rural revival some of the cruellest of the old seventeenth century customs are being revived too.'

'Really? What sort of thing?'

Kate paused, listening to hear if his interest was growing or dying. It was becoming charged.

'Look, I'm not in a position to talk more fully.' She glanced around. She was sure June had gone with the camera crew for a sandwich at the pub and the jeweller, with visor and tools, seemed out of earshot. Even so, Kate was frightened she had gone too far.

But at that moment she had the ear of a Channel Four commissioning editor, albeit an acting one, and she had known producers who would have held a party to celebrate less. She wasn't prepared to let go on the grounds of a small matter like de Salas's vision, and her own lack of evidence. But if Malcolm Hodgson would co-operate . . .

'I could come to London if you could find time to see me,' she said on the spur of the moment.

'Well . . .' Ruscroft sounded doubtful again. 'I do have a window for fifteen minutes at eleven thirty on Friday. But I have to say we would need an awful lot more information.'

'I'll be there,' said Kate quickly.

'Well, all right then. You did say cruelty and violence, didn't you?'

'Oh, yes,' said Kate. In buckets if you want it. Of course there was de Salas to persuade, but hard as that seemed it was surely worth a try if a Channel Four commission was in the offing?

'Well,' Ruscroft said tentatively, reserving his position after his rush of qualified enthusiasm. 'Maybe there'll be something interesting there. I've only got fifteen minutes, though.'

'No problem. I look forward to meeting you.'

And then she had gone out into the yard, knowing that shortly she would have to tackle a grumpy crew to explain that the director wasn't coming back in the afternoon either. But at least they still had a producer.

Just beyond Kate's horizon, over the ridge beyond the grey-scaled town roofs, the sharp rock outlines of the western Lake District slowly started to decline into the shaly, muddy slopes to the sea. High Scar Farm was tucked into a last bony elbow of the fells. It wasn't a pretty farm. But it belonged to Will Carruther's godfather Tom Flint, and to Will it had always been mucky perhaps, and messy, but a good working business.

From where he and his cowman were trudging, it looked like a scrap yard. Even from the front, where the once commanding doorway looked out over the windy hills, there were the scars, not of neglect or dereliction, but of thrift. The thick grime round the door frame revealed it hadn't been opened for twenty years. There was a piece of hardboard usefully covering a crack in the thick wood and at the nicely proportioned windows, thin net curtains stretched across the panes like taut layers of crinkled elderly skin, essential to hide the works within, but ugly.

The farm was Victorian, but built in the Georgian style that had meant money and status to the first Flint. It had only taken two generations for the rest of the family to grow out of his need to establish himself. They knew they had always been there and did not give a tuppeny ha'penny damn for panelling and portals. An outsider would have thought that here was a farm on the edge of extinction. Carruthers knew better. The family had bags of money and no taste, and Will felt that was the right way to be, not like Councillor Malcolm Hodgson with his poncy potted trees by his smooth front step, and his neat little cottages with their trellised roses.

They had reached the broken gate with its scabby bright blue paint, leading into the yard. The barn, with its corrugated iron roof and piles of trussed hay, brooded over rusting rib cages of old machinery. A man like Malcolm Hodgson would have painted them black and filled them with geraniums, thought Will Carruthers. The tractor was parked at an angle in a puddle of deep brown rainbowed cow urine, and two scraggy tabby cats pattered past. Their new confidence led Will's eyes to a sad, neglected plywood kennel with a chain trailing pathetically to nowhere. Blotches of damp lifted the surface off the wood. A shallow metal dish stood beside it, empty.

'He nivver got another dog then, eh?' the cowman remarked, following Will's glance.

'Nay. Not since Fly.'

'Bad sign that.'

'Aye.'

As always, the back door was ajar, and Will stooped automatically as he went in, taking his cap off and shaking his head. He automatically went to put his cap on the peg next to his godfather's, but Tom's cap was not there. Strange, he thought. Tom always came home for his dinner, and always put his cap on the peg before going through to the kitchen and sitting down.

'Tom?' There was no answer. Will heard his wellies scraping on the uneven flags of the dark, damp passage leading to the warmth of Tom and Mary's kitchen. He felt the smelly overcoats on the pegs on the wall brush against him and heard, somewhere in the house, the sound of the telly with the lunchtime news. But there was no other, more usual sound, no 'Howdo' from Tom or 'Come in, lad' from Mary, greetings Will had heard so often from childhood that he could hardly identify what was missing from the scene. And there was a horrible smell, a smell totally unlike the dank coats on the wall, or the latent smell of frying and baking, the good smells of a farm. It was a smell like cooking meat, burning meat, with a sickly fetid unfamiliarity. Yet it wasn't unfamiliar to a farmer. It was just in the wrong place.

Will stopped. It was the first time he had stopped in the passageway in thirty years. His cowman, less sensitive – though Will would never have stooped to describing himself that way – bumped into Will's back.

'Owt t'matter?'

'Canst smell it?'

'Aye. What's on t' stove?'

'God knows, but it's bad.'

The two men shuffled forward. Very slowly, without thinking about his dread, Will Carruthers nudged the ridged planks of the rough kitchen door, hearing the latch clatter as it swung open. In front of him he saw normality, the old-fashioned kitchen cupboards with their thick rime of paint, the stone sink, Mary Flint's few bits of plants in margarine tubs on the windowsill, the calendar from the tractor company on the wall with dates marked in biro. He turned as he would always have done to his left, to where Tom was sitting at the kitchen table, feet in his wellingtons sprawled out to one side, and his matted jacket as always on the back of the chair.

But this time Tom's shotgun was wedged against the seat of his chair, between his legs, and what was left of his head. There was a great bloodied mass on the wall behind him, strange in the way it stuck out like something growing there, the force with which it had hit the pale green gloss paint keeping it sprawled like a huge, shiny red and white tumour. But the mess had spattered right through the kitchen. And where the Aga warmed the house day and night, more of Tom Flint's brain was burning on the hotplate.

Kate walked over to where the cameraman was grumpily setting up his tripod. That morning they had taken shots of the jeweller at work at his bench, and of his wife tastefully displaying bits of the grotesque but fascinating metalwork on smooth pads of grey velvet. Kate had begun by feeling irritated with the chatty Scotsman, Kenny the jeweller, and repelled by his work. Now, though, she could see its novelty, especially if you wanted to go out with something that looked like a sheep's skull dangling from your collar bone. But she had seen weirder things on highly stylish creatures posturing around Knightsbridge, and wondered ruefully if that was really the attraction. She imagined the gilded children of the metropolis wanting to look like Nordic deities, and the local girls in the villages giving their eye teeth for pseudo-Cartier.

At the end of the afternoon she helped the female sound assistant pack up the kit. The assistant wore skin-tight stretch black trousers over the figure of an Olympic gymnast, and her cropped blonde hair turned her young face into the features of a sexy but petulant pixie. To make conversation Kate said genially, 'Well, tomorrow should run rather more smoothly, seeing we'll have our director back.'

'Don't bank on it,' the girl murmured grimly.

'I'm sorry?'

'I said don't bank on it. Last time his girlfriend . . . or, should I say, lady friend, arrived on the scene, we didn't see de Salas for three days. Mind you, that was only when we did the recce. Perhaps he'll be a bit more serious now.'

'What do you mean, his lady friend?'

'Oh, that's who Mr Smartarse de Salas has gone to pick up. It's just like last time. *She* . . .' the girl pointed disparagingly at June, ' . . . went all coy about him going to the airport, and the next thing he breezed by with this mystery woman in the front of the car. No introductions to us, no nothing. There's something funny about it.' She spoke with all the intolerance of someone whose emotional life was sorted out. Kate looked down involuntarily at the broad gold band of servitude on the girl's ring finger, and then over to the greying cameraman, his hair still combed forward seventies style, and his little pot belly straining over his jeans. 'Jerry had left his first wife when he met me,' snapped the sound assistant defensively. She turned her back on Kate.

As she and June walked companionably to the parked cars, Kate murmured, 'I hope Andy is feeling better. I know we managed reasonably well, but I think Jerry's assistant feels he should be here.'

June looked away, and changed the subject. 'We'll meet at the new wholefood tea shop tomorrow morning?'

'Yes, unless you can cook up something better.' It was a pitiful joke but it made June smile, to show she appreciated the effort.

'And you really think we may have a chance with Channel Four?'

'Who knows? But it's worth a try. Goodnight.'

'Goodnight, Kate. And thanks.'

Kate had a bit of trouble manoeuvring the hire car out of the small town. She had to concentrate on the sheer operational problem of trying to drive in the twilight and cope with the unfamiliar procedures for full and dipped beams. It was just too late when she realised she had been filtered to go east rather than west, but she couldn't see a way to turn back. Finally, she took a risk, heading across country down a lane that seemed like a canyon between high banks of hedges. She had to squeeze over twice to avoid other cars. The third time the oncoming vehicle slid into her lights almost before she could react. She braked sharply, and turned to back up to the last gateway. As she was doing so, she realised that the car in front had the outline of de Salas's Porsche. What a coincidence, she thought . . . immediately followed by the mischievous idea that this would be her chance to see the mystery woman. The thought amused her. Contrary to the rules of the road, she backed across the lane into an opening on her right, so de Salas would have to pass with his passenger side next to her. He obviously had no idea who was in the anonymous little car she had hired. The Porsche took three seconds to glide by in the dusk, with the woman in the passenger seat barely visible.

But Kate knew her. She had the certainty that comes instantly, before the brain can really register, and while the conflicting contexts war like two photographs exposed, one over the other. Yet the moment after the recognition it was all painfully obvious. Kate felt hurt and, worse still, stupid. What sort of friend was she, if Liz Jones couldn't even confide in her the truth about her relationship with Andy de Salas? The Porsche accelerated away up the lane, leaving Kate sitting there, stunned.

Then she had to drive on. There was nothing she could do about what she had seen. She would need to contact Liz at some point, and she was sure that Liz would explain. But what could this mean about de Salas? If Liz cared for him, could he be unbalanced as she suspected, or was it just artistic temperament out of control? She remembered the journey from hell over the Pennines and shuddered. What are you doing, Liz? she asked the windscreen in front of her, only to realise that darkness had fallen and she had no idea where she was.

Mechanically she turned left at the end of the lane because it felt sensible, and then found herself on a better road, but one which meandered hopelessly until she had no sense of where she was at all. It was growing darker and she glanced at her watch. The road offered no useful lay-bys. She was completely lost. Then she remembered her mobile phone and in desperation pulled up on the tiny grass verge. She parked the car with its left side in a thick hedge of something bushy. She fumbled in her handbag, found the phone and breathed audibly with relief when she pressed a button at random and the lights came on. She cleared the little screen, forced herself to think clearly, and dialled the Skirlbeck Bridge Hotel. There was the whining sound of dead frustration – a long single note. Then she remembered she should ring the whole code, and scrabbled in her bag for the card the Robinsons had given her. The whole number was there. She dialled again.

'Bill! Thank goodness. It's Kate. I'm lost. All I can see are hedges, and fields.' Laboriously, she tried to tell him how she had got to where she was.

'Oh dear. Sounds like you might be on the way to *Pen*rith.' He stressed the first syllable so that for a moment Kate felt more confused than ever. '*Pen*rith? Oh, Pen*rith*. That's miles away!'

'Now don't panic, Miss Wilkinson. I only said you were on the way there. Have you passed any houses?'

'Houses? There've been no signs of civilisation for the last ten miles!'

'Really? But you said there were hedges and fields.'

Kate sighed. Civilisation meant something quite different to Bill. 'Yes, well, those.'

'So you must be near a farm.'

'Must I?'

It was Bill's turn to sigh.

'Now, Kate, listen. Drive very slowly along until you see a farmhouse. You've probably already passed a few without realising it. Can you keep talking . . . or at least keep the phone handy?'

'OK.' She started the car and drove at snail's pace, the phone cradled between her chin and her shoulder.

'Oh, yes, you're right, Bill. Here we are.' There was a gate now, on her left. By it was a tatty wooden sign which read: 'Gillfoot Farm'.

'I seem to have found "Gillfoot Farm".'

'Pardon?'

Kate realised she had made it sound like a town in Surrey and repeated the name, imitating the sharp consonants of the twins' accents.

'Gill – foot. Gillfoot Farm.'

'Oh, yes.' Bill was immediately back in control. 'That's a bit of luck. That's Thompson's farm. I know exactly where you are now. Anyone would have helped you, but Robert and Margaret Thompson are particularly nice. Just turn in there. By the time you get up the track, I'll have phoned them to say you'll be coming. And then I'll drive over to bring you back here.'

'But I don't have a clue about these Thompson people. They won't want me just arriving like that.'

'Why ever not? I may have got it wrong but I think Margaret is one of our second cousins. On the Robinson side.'

Well, that explains everything, thought Kate, who was deeply confused.

'So is everyone around here related to everyone else?'

'Well, not everyone. But a lot of people. Anyway, get yourself up there. Margaret'll make you a cuppa.'

'Well, thanks. But I don't know about just turning up . . .'

Bill had rung off.

Kate bumped the car up the lane, nervously negotiating the grassy strip in the middle, which looked like wet carpet in the headlights. She was tense and irritated. She had enough to think about that evening, without having to make conversation with people who would surely not want her turning up on their doorstep, on a dark night, in the middle of nowhere. And Kate knew nothing about farms. She had visions of childhood books, of having to navigate through a crowded farmyard full of disturbed hens and ducks and pigs and dogs. And what about bulls? One thing she did know was that coloured pictures of farms never communicated the ghastly stench. She had once had to film at a Home Counties dairy and yoghurt business, as lush and cushioned as this farm seemed to be bleak and exposed. But it had taken a day to get over the after-tang of the acrid cowsheds.

Then suddenly the lane turned and she was in front of the farm itself. Her headlights lit up another of the square, Georgian style houses she had seen from the road. This one had gleaming paintwork and a neat ivy trained along the front, with the two large sash windows showing looped back curtains and the outline of deep panelled shutters. She stood, irresolute, by the side of the car, and heard a woman calling, 'Yoohoo? Hello?' She turned to see a plump, bustling figure at the side of the house, wearing some sort of overall and clumpy wellingtons. A housekeeper? Or some sort of farm worker?

'Hello?' Kate said cautiously.

'Well, come in,' said the woman. Kate looked round baffled.

'This way, round't back. Get a move on, it's cold out here.' Rubbing her hands, the woman turned and barrelled back to where a five-bar gate at the rear left corner of the house was swinging. She stood by it as Kate followed through into what she immediately realised was the real working yard of the farm. Three dogs, too well-trained to bark or go for the crotch like so many of their overfamiliar townie cousins, padded around her, curious rather than suspicious. It was all as neat as a freshly-scoured hospital ward, and Kate was aware of a sharpish smell that meant animals and chemicals but it was somehow antiseptic rather than sickening. To her left, in an open barn, piles of hay were stacked as evenly as well-combed flaxen hair, and to her right, low sheds with swinging lightbulbs seemed to house warm, sweet smelling creatures she couldn't quite see.

'I wus just finishing t'calves' feed when Bill rang,' said the woman. She went towards the sheds to pick up a pail, and Kate saw four melted chocolate eyes catch the light as the calves peeped over the stall at her.

'They're lovely,' she said.

'Aye, we've done well this time. Come on in then, lass.'

She followed the woman through the bare back-door of the big house, and almost immediately into a bright kitchen, lit by an unfashionable but hugely effective neon strip. Two men sat at a scrubbed table in front of a stove where gingham tea towels hung from a rail steaming slightly, and a large flat bottomed kettle buzzed and spluttered.

'Well, tek a seat lass. This is Bob, and our son Clifford.'

''Owdo,' said the younger of the two men. 'And what are you up here for?'

'I'm staying at the Skirlbeck Bridge Hotel because I'm working on a film, and I was stupid enough to have lost my way back from today's location. We were filming a local jeweller. It's all about the new cottage industries setting up. It's being made by a company called Rural Rides. Have you heard about it?'

'Oh, aye,' the old farmer nodded, completely uninterested. But his son said, 'That's right. You were over at yon woollen mill, yesterday?'

'Yes.'

'Aye, you remember, Faither? Will Carruthers went to have it out with them. Lady Bountiful wants to extend the barn and Will says the traffic will cause chaos at milking time.'

'Aye.' The old man nodded wisely, still sublimely unconcerned. But Clifford was leaning forward, taut with interest like one of the lean dogs outside, friendly, but not effusive.

'There's a lot of folk think this film will only show half the story.'

'Really?' Kate felt it come out as 'rairlly?' and shivered with embarrassment.

'Aye. I mean, how many jobs have these businesses really brought up here? A ruddy handful, if you'll excuse my French. And half of them are offcomers. Not that I've anything against them . . .' he winked beguilingly at Kate and she laughed back, ' . . . but it doesn't mean much really. No, we need something like this theme park place Malcolm Hod'son talks about.'

'So you know . . . Councillor Hodgson?'

'Of course we do. Everyone does, don't they, Mother?'

'That's right, Cliff.' His mother was bustling away in a big stripped-pine cupboard by the sink. Kate was at a loss about what to say. The reference to Malcolm Hodgson had startled her, and as if waiting for Mrs Thompson to continue, she distracted herself with her surroundings.

The kitchen was a wonderful blend of the old and new. It was like a genuine version of something from Country Life magazine. It held a clever combination of whatever was originally fitted that could be stripped to the pine and polished, and new units. There was an Aga, a microwave, a massive dishwasher, a huge fridge freezer, a mixer, some stainless steel pans and a Le Creuset dish on the drainer, a gorgeous row of gleaming copper pots on a low pine shelf, and next to them the latest in stainless steel implements. This is it, thought Kate, glancing back at the old farmer, placid in his own wooden-winged chair, and his son, bright as a button – the core of country living. She remembered the joke about how to get a beautiful British lawn. You prepare the ground, use the best grass seed, tend it and keep the birds off and then roll it for four hundred years! She couldn't imagine Mrs Thompson ever needing to pop down to Patel's for a pair of tights and a bottle of wine.

As if on cue a small glass of glowing pale amber liquid was put in front of her.

'Sup up,' said the old man in his curious high voice.

'Aye.' Mrs Thompson had sat down. 'Malcolm Hodgson's grandmother was a Hetherington. Not the Carlisle Hetheringtons, the Wigton Hetheringtons. And my mother's grandma was a Hetherington, so we must be related.' She beamed at Kate, looking ten years younger when she smiled. Kate reckoned she was about sixty, but her husband was a few years older. Cliff was early thirties, she thought. A younger son? The only son? Was he married? Would he inherit the farm? Either the atmosphere or the ginger wine was making her think differently. A week ago she would never have mentally trespassed on other people's family lives.

But here, she thought, it's no sin to want to know. Everybody knows everything about everybody. Everybody's related. There are feuds and rows and jealousies and evil, George Goff had made that clear. But wasn't that how life should be? Not in a box in London, communicating by cellnets and dependent on the media? She sipped more wine and smiled back at Margaret.

'Aye, well, Malcolm's got a good business. He's made a real go of that farm, and turning the buildings into holiday cottages was very bright.'

'He was always clever, Mam. Like me.' Cliff winked at Kate again, and his mother smiled fondly at him.

'Well, I hope when you get round to getting married you aren't clever enough to see your wife tek off with another man, Clifford. Not that she wasn't sorely tried.' Margaret Thompson looked at Kate as if Kate would know all about it. And I want to, thought Kate. I've become completely caught up in this.

'I have heard.' She tried to look conspiratorially at Margaret. 'But I don't really know what happened.'

'Oh, she were a lovely lass, Susan Hodgson. A good teacher too. But Malcolm always had someone else on the go. Not that he wasn't discreet and there's worse than him. But there was allus someone.' The wine made Kate warm and tolerant, and perhaps understanding too. She looked again round the womblike security of the farm kitchen. It was gloriously cosy.

'What Malcolm needs . . .' Margaret went on, ' . . . is someone as smart as he is and a bit more worldly than Susan.' She looked at Kate shrewdly, making her want to change the subject.

'And I understand you were related to the twins' mother, Jean Robinson?'

To her surprise Mrs Thompson curled her lip and

hitched her bosom up before putting her elbows on the table and leaning forward.

'Not to *her*. To her husband,' she said. 'My father was Sam Robinson's cousin. And we always did what we could for the twins. Sam had no more sense than yon kettle, and was less use. That's probably why he married her.'

'So she was the business brains?'

'Huh, if you can call it that. They nivver had two pennies to rub togither that Sam made. He helped on a milk round, as a lad, but he spent more time going dancing in Whitehaven than working. Then he got her into trouble. Though I would *say*...' she leaned forward and frowned darkly, '... it was the other way round.'

'So how did they manage for money?' I'm getting good at this, thought Kate, leaning forward herself.

'Her father lent them a few bob. Or should I say, gave – I can't see Sam ever paying anyone back. But Jean was allus a worker, I'll say that for her. And she looked after those twins like they were dolls. She used to work part time in the shop, and cleaning at the Skirlbeck Bridge. It was owned by offcomers then, not local people. The twins went to catering college at Workington. Anyway, Sam died years ago, and then seventeen years ago Jean had her accident.'

'Accident?'

'Oh, yes, didn't you know? She had to go over to Newcastle for something and she was in a bad smash. We never knew the details because it happened over that way. On the Military Road.' Kate nodded, remembering her smash with de Salas. It was obviously a blackspot.

'And what happened then?'

'Well, no-one really knew, but Jean collapsed. She'd

always had a weak heart – rheumatic fever you know.' Kate nodded, as if she was knowledgeable about health lore. 'But from then on she was in a wheelchair. Likely as not she must have got some compensation, though we never heard much about it, because after the accident she could afford someone to wait on her hand and foot *and* she led those twins a dance. I think they'd have gone on to Manchester or London but she wouldn't have it. I know Bill tried to get away; he talked to us about it and he would have taken Terry, they've always been close. But she wouldn't let him go. Then a few years later, the old woman that owned the Skirlbeck died. We were all surprised, you know, when Jean Robinson bought the hotel, but she must have had money from the accident.'

'And that's the story?'

'Some of it.' The son, Clifford, wasn't smiling any more. 'She was a bad old bitch, our cousin Jean.'

His use of the same phrase as Hodgson made the words more emphatic to Kate. His mother tutted, but didn't correct him. Clifford got up and prowled around the kitchen and the unspoken allusions hung between them. Then he suddenly turned. 'And if you ask me, the odd couple are better off without her!'

'Now, Clifford . . .'

'You know that's what I think, Mam. There's a lot of good in Bill and Terry Robinson and they can't help what they are. I just hope they get over all this fuss and get on with their lives. I don't think it matters how the old woman died. It's a good thing she's gone. They deserve a chance.' To Kate's surprise, his elderly father nodded in agreement.

'Aye, well,' the old farmer said after a moment. 'Back to

work, Clifford. I want to go up to the byre before we sit down for the night.'

'Hadn't you better ring Sally?' Mrs Thompson was smiling again now. 'That's Clifford's girlfriend. Sally Dodd. He always rings her when she's driving back from work. She finishes late on a Tuesday.'

' 'Appen I will.' To Kate's chagrin, Cliff pulled a mobile phone out of his breast pocket.

'I hope she gets here before one of the Robinson twins comes to pick you up. I bet she'd love to meet you. She's a lecturer in . . . whatsit . . . broadcast studies at Carlisle College.'

That is *it*, Kate thought: I will never make assumptions again.

'More home-made ginger wine?' Margaret Thompson had the bottle, with its neat handwritten label, poised temptingly above Kate's glass. 'Leave the car,' she went on. 'Clifford'll drive it back to you tomorrow.'

'Really? Would he?'

'Aye. No problem. Good, here's Sally now.'

Kate heard the sound of a car in the yard, and the joyous yelp of restrained ecstasy as the dogs were patted. Sally's shoes clip-clipped along the stone flagged passageway and she brought a rush of cold damp air in with her. She was a pretty woman in her late twenties with sleek light brown hair and rosy cheeks. But there the resemblance to the picture book farmer's wife ended. Sally was wearing a navy suit Kate would trade her car for, stockings like shimmering starlight and a cashmere jumper of the subtlest shade of pink which highlighted her figure as if it had been coated in blushing cream. The rest of the family were as riveted as Kate, not by her appearance, by what she was saying.

'Hi, everyone. It's a cold night out there. Sorry I'm late, but I popped in at Mam's on the way here. And you'll never guess what I heard. Old Tom Flint's shot himself!'

Chapter Five

'Well, it's hard to explain really how the place gets to you, but it's different.'

'What do you mean, Kate, different?'

Kate could hear the tone of restrained irritation in John Maple's voice. But she knew he had every right to be annoyed.

An hour earlier, she had been collected by Bill Robinson from the cosiness of Gillfoot Farm where the Thompson's had plied her with ginger wine until she felt she was walking in an amber glow. Bill had brought her back to the Skirlbeck Bridge Hotel, chatting about family connections and relatives long dead, which should have bored Kate but which instead lured her deeper into this new country.

It was now seven o'clock and when the phone had rung in her bedroom she had answered it absently, thinking it would be one of the twins telling her dinner was ready. Kate had been thinking about Gillfoot Farm, and trying desperately to remember where she had heard the name Flint before, Tom Flint, so it had taken her at least ten seconds to realise that it was John on the line.

She had meant to tell him all about seeing Liz Jones with Andy de Salas. Kate knew that John would be surprised and interested. He was fond of Liz, with her slightly dizzy air. But somehow the phone call refused to move on from a tetchy start.

'I'm sorry I haven't had a chance to call, John, the place is just so absorbing. It's not like any assignment I've had before. Everybody's more involved, more so than anywhere else I've been. I ended up at a farmhouse out in the wilds tonight. It was a real eye opener. I've been on the go since I got here . . .'

'Listen, Kate, I don't mind whether you phone or not. Seriously. I'm a grown up and I don't need reassurance every five minutes, so it's not that which bothers me.'

The echo of superiority was creeping into John's voice. Kate suspected it might be his form of defence but it irritated her nonetheless. Pity, she thought, he might be a little more human and a little less perfect if he did need the odd bit of reassurance like the rest of us. She loved John least when he was being mature and condescending.

'So what *is* bothering you then?' she said snappily, focusing back on the conversation. She was hoping he would say something like 'the pain of separation' but he didn't.

'What's bothering me, Kate, is that you said you would phone this morning, and I told Father Marcus that I couldn't be at early communion, just so I could take your call. Then you didn't ring. It's OK to mess *me* around, but I ended up letting someone else down.'

'All right, I'm sorry.' There was a silence which worried her. 'Really, John, I am. I should have thought of that. And I do miss you.'

'And I miss you. You know that.' He made it sound like something he said because he was a decent man.

'Say it again. With feeling.'

'I miss you.'

'Do you really?'

She heard his sharp intake of irritation.

'Kate, you're starting to badger me. I have to go now because we have a service at eight tonight. I'll call *you* tomorrow. OK?'

'OK,' she said in a leaden voice and put the phone down. She felt as if she had been kicked in the chest. John could sometimes distance her with just a tone of voice which left her feeling guilty for being argumentative or irritating. The result was usually to make her worse or to leave her feeling panicky at the thought of his ebbing affection. This time he had seemed coolest of all, and when she had felt insecure, he had told her not to *badger* him. Well, he could go to hell, except, of course, she'd be there already! She pummelled the pillow.

The phone rang through again to her room, and she leapt to get it. It *had* to be John phoning back to apologise. 'Call for you,' said Terry in a rather sickly 'ooh aah' tone of voice.

'Hello?' She was breathless, already smiling down the phone for him, waiting for John to say, 'Katy, I'm sorry, I shouldn't have been so crabby; I realise you're under pressure . . .' when a male voice said, 'Kate Wilkinson? Malcolm Hodgson here. Have you eaten?'

She gasped, incapable of coherent speech.

'No . . . yes . . . well, I'm just going downstairs for dinner. The twins have cooked for me . . .'

'Oh, don't worry, I wouldn't ring at this time of night to take you out. We'll do that tomorrow if you like. No, I just thought I'd come round for a drink but I don't want to

intrude if you think Bill and Terry Robinson aren't up to
it?'

'Oh, well . . . I'm sure they'd love to see you.' Kate felt
ridiculously flustered.

'Good.'

She made an attempt to rally. 'By the way, today I met
some people who know you.'

'Everyone knows me. Tell me later. I'll see you at – what?
About nine thirty?'

'Er, yes, great. I'll tell the twins you're coming.'

She sprang off the bed and into the shower. It took ten
minutes to dry her hair and get into a pair of slacks and a
bright jumper. The jumper was long and fluffy and hid the
new bulges on her hips. But the fresh air had brought colour
to her face and the soft water made her hair lustrous. Not
so bad, she thought. She put her gold studs in her ears,
and reached reflexively for John's pearls. Then she thought:
no . . . and let them trickle back into the box.

Dinner was, of course, delicious and the twins talked
throughout about the plans for their mother's funeral. They
even relaxed enough to start calling it 'the do'. At about
nine forty, when Kate had gone through to the bar for her
coffee, the bell rang and Terry went skittishly off to open
the door. He was, he confessed, 'all of a doodah' because
she had told him Malcolm Hodgson was calling, and even
Bill had an air of restrained excitement.

Malcolm was more handsome than Kate remembered,
standing in the doorway, taking off his waxed jacket and
handing it to Bill who had the look of an acolyte in a trance.
Underneath he wore a tracksuit top and a pair of loose
cotton trousers and Kate was acutely aware of his forearms

because the sleeves were slightly rolled up. He had an expensive chunky watch and a salt and pepper coating of fine hair down to his wrists. Fortunately Bill and Terry were so disconcerted that Kate's embarrassment seemed minor by comparison. He came into the bar and stood, about a head taller than the twins, looking down at Kate.

'Hi,' she said, surprisingly shy.

'Hi,' he replied, and grinned, and turned to where the Robinsons were fussing over his drink.

'We're going to be so busy this week,' cooed Terry. 'We'll need a few more bottles of this!'

'And will you be coming to the funeral, Councillor Hodgson?' Kate said. It was meant to be a light remark, but it froze them all. For a minute Kate thought the liquor was going to go on pouring into the glass while Bill stood motionless and Terry, all prepared with the cut glass water jug, stood like a ludicrous garden gnome, pitcher in hand, waiting for Malcolm to speak.

'Thanks, Bill.' Then Malcolm turned to look at Kate. 'No, I don't think so,' he said evenly.

'Oh, I'm sorry.' What she had meant as a light remark seemed more loaded than she could have imagined, until she remembered Terry's distress that morning. 'It's just that I assumed after talking to Margaret Thompson at Gillfoot that you were all related, you know, branches of one family.'

Then Hodgson diffused things by laughing at her. He gave her a sexy, lopsided smile with full eye contact so that her stomach knotted, and he sank down into the armchair opposite her. 'Well, there hasn't been much family feeling between us, other than bad feeling. But I came over here to put that behind us. I'd like to buy you all a drink. Especially you, Bill and Terry. You've had a hell of a week. Come over and join us. I have to say . . .' he looked around, ' . . . it's a great place you've got here.' And he laughed.

'You mean you've never been here before?' Kate was astonished.

'Nope,' said Hodgson, and twinkled with amusement in the direction of Bill who now breathed out with visible relief. The older twin turned away behind the bar and busied himself with a bottle of bright blue liquor, then smiled and came over with the lurid drink in his hand, and the air of making a speech.

'We're very, very thrilled you're here now,' he said to Malcolm. 'We know why you never came before and much as we . . . loved . . . Mother, we have to say we didn't always agree with her likes and dislikes.'

'No, indeed,' said Terry, and he rushed on before Bill could throw him his usual restraining glance. 'We know there are folk who aren't exactly grieving over Mam, but at least *you've* come to see us. We appreciate that.'

'The late Mrs Robinson and I didn't get on,' said Hodgson to Kate. 'That's why it was a great excuse for me, you being here, to come and give my condolences to Bill and Terry. If I'd asked them direct, they might have felt they should say no, if that was what they thought their mother would have wanted. But I was sure that if a guest invited me to the place, they'd hardly refuse.'

So much for her theory that he couldn't stay away from her. Even so, Kate was aware of Hodgson's warm smile and the fact that when her big mouth had got in the way, he had been there to close it for her. The idea made her think of kissing him. She was alarmed by her own reactions and she concentrated on her coffee cup and the point that he had just made.

So why didn't he and Jean Robinson get on? Kate was burning to ask. Terry and Bill sipped their cocktails reflectively.

'Mother did have a lot of feuds,' sighed Bill. 'But she really took against Councillor Hodgson. We always thought she went a bit too far though,' he whispered, as if his dead mother could hear him.

'Why was that?' Kate asked.

Hodgson said, again in a measured way, 'I don't think Mrs Robinson approved of my reputation. She once . . . er . . . brought it up with me. She thought that if she followed her conscience and mentioned my extra-mural activities to my wife, it might help her with a licence extension she was after. I told her I didn't think it would make any difference. That was a couple of years ago. Recently we fell out about my theme park scheme. Mrs Robinson hated that.'

'She did indeed,' said Bill. 'And she'd have got it stopped, you know that. She was absolutely determined.'

'So she was in league with Lady Marshall?' asked Kate cautiously.

'Good Lord, no.' Bill looked quite shocked. 'She didn't bother with people like her. Oh no, Mother was talking to a lot of folk.'

'But why was she so against it?'

'Because she didn't want them knocking down bits of the village to build it. Like the old barn,' said Terry.

'And because,' said Bill, 'they hadn't asked her to be a consultant on the plans, and Mother was involved in everything near Skirlbeck.'

'Quite so,' Malcolm Hodgson murmured. 'A consultancy

would have been worth a fee, of course.' There was a meaningful silence.

Kate watched him. Hodgson was leaning back in the chair now, at ease. She wondered if he had organised the whole visit to lobby the twins. If Bill and his brother were prepared to ignore their mother's objections, then Hodgson would have cleared another obstacle, however small, in the way of his theme park scheme. She was fairly sure that Hodgson guessed how flattered the twins were about his visit . . . and how susceptible they were to his masculinity.

Bill finally spoke, his cool, organised, older-brother manner coming to the fore.

'Well, thank you for bothering to come and see us, Councillor Hodgson.'

'Call me Malcolm. How do you feel about the theme park?'

Bill beamed. 'Malcolm. I think we've got enough to do just keeping the hotel going, without getting involved in that sort of row. Mother enjoyed all the scrapping. We don't. We just want to run the hotel and keep our customers happy. As long as the Skirlbeck Bridge is doing well . . .'

Malcolm said casually: 'Of course, lots of visitors to the theme park will want to stay and eat in the area.'

Terry eyes lit up. 'Bill, that could be great for us! We could do theme park specials . . .'

'Yes. I think we'd like that.'

'I'm sure some sort of arrangement could be made.' Hodgson and Bill looked each other in the eye, then both relaxed.

Malcolm turned back to Kate. 'Well, I dare say this is all very parochial to you, Kate, but it's the lifeblood of Skirlbeck.' He tossed back his whisky in a casual way that alarmed Kate slightly, and Terry leapt up to give him a refill which he didn't refuse. When Terry came back he put a glass in front of her too. The ginger wine at the Thompsons, a glass of red at dinner, and now another whisky. Yet the warm feeling of just smelling the liquor was hard to beat. And it all seemed so right, here by the log fire with the sound of the waves in the background. The sound seemed to remind Bill of something too.

'We'll just fill the dishwasher,' he said.

'Yes, back in a minute,' Terry intoned. She felt rather than saw the twins get up and make for the kitchen and was suddenly, painfully, aware she was alone with Hodgson. He leaned forward so she could smell the whisky on his breath and feel the heat from his body.

'Interesting point, that,' he said.

'What?' She found it hard to speak, frightened her voice would emerge as a silly squeak or a southern, supercilious drawl.

'What you said about families.'

'The cross connections? Yes. It struck me tonight at Gillfoot with the Thompsons. The family links . . . and the fact everyone knows and values them seems remarkable to someone from South West London!'

'Aye, yes. But "value" isn't always the word I would use!'

'I'm sorry?' Kate looked at his brooding face.

'Oh, people like you always assume neighbourliness and family feeling are sweet supportive things. But it isn't always like that. Don't sentimentalise it.'

'What do you mean?' He looked back at her with a twist to his full lips.

'Think about it. Sometimes it can be murder in families!'

She thought he had made a joke till she saw the intensity

in his eyes. And then she was aware that Bill Robinson had not followed his brother into the kitchen but was standing in the doorway, behind Malcolm Hodgson, a look of fear on his face.

Sally Dodd edged away from Cliff, heaved her beautifully rounded bottom to the edge of the bed and sat up, her neat little breasts with the nipples still erect silhouetted against the uncurtained window of the bungalow. Then she stood up and looked out, confident that for miles around there was no-one who could see in. Acres of grey-green fields were bleached in the moonlight, almost a washed out colour version of themselves. Clifford Thompson, son and heir of the Thompsons of Gillfoot, watched her, thinking how gorgeous she looked with her long straight back parting perfectly at the base of her spine and each buttock rising like a dimpled pudding with the cleft in between just tight enough to give his hand a squeeze.

'You've got a lovely bum,' he said sleepily.

'I know.' Sally's voice was sharper, not the sort of post coital creaminess he was used to.

'What's up, Sal? Didn't you like doing it that way?'

'Yes, as long as you don't put me in the cow diary. You know, Sally to the bull October 23rd.'

Cliff laughed. 'It's about time you went into calf.'

'Well, I'm not coming off the pill till the wedding. Don't think you can road test me and then send me to the knackers' if there's anything wrong with my reproductive tract.'

'Sal! That isn't very nice.'

'Well, that's the way it used to be, isn't it? Get her pregnant before you commit yourself to make sure there'll be a son to run the farm?'

'Oh, come on, Sally. If we can't have children we can always adopt a little lad.'

'There you are, you see! A little lad! What about adopting a little lass, eh?'

'All right, all right, a little lass; as long as she can drive a tractor, I don't care. I don't have any hang ups about having a son. Look at Sarah Little, or Mary Routledge, or Sandra Parker. All bloody good women farmers. And I suppose Mary Flint will just carry on until she retires . . .'

Sally came and sat on the edge of the bed. 'I don't think so, Cliff.'

'Oh, is that what's upsetting you? Old Tom Flint?'

'Yes.' Sally pulled the duvet round her, so that Cliff had to grab some of it back, laughing, to cover the fact he was starting another erection when she wanted to talk, his big penis flapping as he struggled for the cover. Sally glanced at it. 'I'll come back to bed in a minute. But listen, Cliff. Everyone's saying that Tom has been miserable for a couple of months. And Mary's in a terrible state. They're saying she'll have to go to Garlands.' Garlands was the psychiatric hospital in Carlisle. 'She's not going to be in any condition to run the farm. Folk are saying she has no idea why Tom did such a thing. I mean the farm was running well. He had no money worries.'

There were times when Sally's accent was even stronger than Cliff's, despite her daily exposure to the students at Carlisle. Cliff knew it meant she was really upset.

'Why do you think he did it, Cliff?'

'What, killed himself?

'Yes.'

'I don't know.'

'Haven't you got any ideas?'

121

'No. Come in here, Sally, and get some ideas about this.'

'You don't sound as if you care about Tom Flint. I mean, he was a neighbour, Cliffie.'

'Well, it's nowt to do with us.'

'What do you mean? What happens to farmers round here is *always* to do with us. What's wrong?'

'Nothing's wrong.'

'Cliff, is there something you're not telling me?'

'Stop going on, Sally.'

'A minute ago you were laughing. Now you've got a face like a wet weekend. What is it?'

'I'm OK. Come back into bed.'

'Cliff, you've never lied to me. I believe that. Now tell me what's wrong.'

'Nothing.'

Sally twisted quickly at the edge of the bed and tweaked the duvet up. Cliff lay there, exposed. But his penis was as soft as an uncooked sausage.

'Cliff.' Sally's voice was fierce with determination. 'Now I know there's something up. Or not, obviously. So I think you'd better tell me what's upsetting *you* about old Tom Flint.'

That night, at the same time, Kate too was looking out at the full moon, but she could see its light in an unbroken ribbon on the glassy surface of the Solway Firth. It was so quietly beautiful she tried to concentrate on the scenery to give her mind a rest. She had been to fabulous places and had seen far more dramatic coastlines. But the eerie emptiness of the Solway, its muddy isolation and its facility for revealing more shades of grey than she had ever thought existed, was exercising a fascination. Even the moonlight had a steely quality about it which she could never remember seeing before. She tiptoed back from the window to her bed and snuggled in.

Malcolm Hodgson had not lingered very long after talking to the twins. She had walked with him to the door. Terry and Bill were safe in the kitchen, doing something arcane to a huge piece of ham, ready for the big day. Malcolm had said, 'Think about it,' for the second time. He meant the conversation they had just had, which was reeling round her mind. But he meant something else too. He had leaned forward and taken her hand. His was dry and warm, and very large. Her own hand felt like a mouse curled up in it. Then he had leaned forward and brushed her lips with his, just the softest of touches. He had smelt of damp wool, standard deodorant, and a hint of sweat.

'Dinner tomorrow?'

'Oh, thank you, but I ought to eat here.'

'Why? Tell the twins you're out. Ask for a key.'

She nodded, her eyes wide. A key. So he expected her to be out late, did he? Well, he shouldn't make assumptions. But she knew that even if he didn't, she would . . .

'Goodnight,' he said suddenly, loudly, and strode out to his Range Rover.

'Goodnight,' she'd whispered back, and went back into the house.

And here she was. In bed, unable to sleep, feeling the trickles of arousal and the anger brought on by guilt, and at the same time wondering about all the bits of information that flew round her head like a poltergeist on speed. Liz Jones and de Salas. How could she do it . . . and more to the point, how could she do it without telling Kate? Then John and his tetchiness on the phone.

And Malcolm Hodgson and his neat manipulation of the twins – was it a form of local sleaze: don't get in the way of the theme park and a nice fat catering contract will come your way? Or worse, a blatant exploitation of their susceptibility to his charm? But no man who was a real shit would put his head in his hands and shudder over the horror of a dog fight, would he?

So why had Malcolm come to the Skirlbeck? As much as any desire to sweet-talk the Robinsons it also had to be because of the sexual attraction she felt growing. She didn't want to have to make a decision about that.

And there were other things to think about. She mentally exhausted the subject of Andy de Salas and Liz Jones and resolved to get hold of Liz and tackle her about it in the morning. Now her imagination was rambling over these other strange Cumbrian affairs as if her mind had been let loose on the fells, unsure where the marshes ended and the clear vistas began. She got out of bed, opened the window and let the freezing cold air blow through. It was so icy that within seconds she was banging down the sash and feeling suitably chilled. So what about the dead farmer Tom Flint? After his remark about families, Malcolm had said, 'There's been another death today, Kate.'

Kate had nodded. 'Tom Flint.'

'How did you know?'

Kate was no longer making small talk. 'It's a long story. I got lost and ended up at a farm owned by some people called Thompson . . .'

'Well, that cuts it down to about three dozen places in Cumbria. Which Thompsons?'

'Margaret. And I think the husband was Bob. And the son was called . . .'

'Cliff. I'm related to them. My mother was . . .'

'I know, a Wigton Hetherington . . .'

'Well done.'

'I'm getting better at all this. Which brings me to Tom Flint. He was the farmer you talked about, wasn't he?'

'Which farmer?'

'The farmer whose dog was savaged at the fight.'

'Yes, that's right. I wasn't sure you'd remember.'

He was silent for a moment.

'You were going to say, Malcolm . . .'

'Kate, I told you about the dogfights because I was upset, and also because I didn't know how much you'd seen or what you'd make of it. I suppose I didn't want you running round telling everybody in your carrying southern voice of authority that you'd seen me sicking up over a dead dog's body.'

'Well, thanks. I thought you'd chosen to confide in me.'

'Well, that too, of course, and now I know you, I'm sure you wouldn't go blethering. But the situation has changed.' His forehead was furrowed with worry. 'I'm bothered that I've told you too much . . .'

'Why?'

'Because it's got nastier.'

'You mean because this man Flint has shot himself?'

'They *say* he did it himself . . .'

She remembered ' . . . families can be murder . . .'

'Malcolm, what do you mean?'

'Oh, for Christ's sake, Kate, I don't know!' Hodgson had stood up and started to prowl round. He plunged his hands in his pockets, pulling the trousers tight across his bottom and even though she was intrigued by what he was saying, Kate missed the real implication by staring at the powerful muscles in his buttocks. He was a very attractive man. He swivelled to face her, almost catching her out. Of course he couldn't know what she was thinking ...

Then the kitchen door swung open to usher in a little procession. The twins were bearing more coffee, and scones with brandy butter.

'You have to have brandy butter at funerals and we'd like you to try our first batch,' cried Terry joyfully.

'But Terry, at this time of night? I'll get indigestion,' and worse, Kate thought, feeling the lumps of her hips under her jumper and wondering what Malcolm would make of them if he held her. She thought he might be the sort of man to say 'Love handles. I like women with flesh on them' but she couldn't be sure, and anyway, the fantasy of being loved because of your flab, not despite it, was one which would never come true. She blinked back to reality.

'Please, do try one,' crooned Terry. So she did.

It was only when he and his brother had disappeared back to the kitchen to bone the ham that Malcolm had leaned forward and with the very tip of his tongue, licked a crumb of scone and brandy butter from the side of her mouth. The shock of it burnt her cheek. 'Think about it,' he had said, again.

And here she was, thinking about it. And thinking about more than she ever wanted to ... She went back to concentrating on facts.

When Malcolm had made his remark about murder, he had clearly been talking about Tom Flint. But she had seen what Malcolm hadn't, the silhouette of Bill Robinson in the kitchen doorway, riveted. She thought of the twins, still up now, in the kitchen, in their element, boning ham, and pounding butter and demerara sugar for the biggest local event there had been for years, Jean Robinson's funeral. She thought about what Clifford Thompson had said: 'I'm glad the old bitch is dead. I don't care who did it.'

Why had the word murder stopped Bill in his tracks? Why were they treating this funeral like a sort of celebration? Bill and Terry were free now, like they never had been. They could even entertain their mother's enemies in the hotel, and flirt gently with handsome men like Hodgson. Their lives had been transformed, and no-one in the community begrudged them that.

So had Mrs Robinson been murdered? And by her sons?

Kate tossed and turned in bed, knowing she had drunk too much. She dreamed about a wheelchair on the shore, and in it was John Maple, who laughed at her saying he was in love with Liz Jones. She woke flushed and agitated, and got up to open the window again, but minutes later had to close out the cold sea breeze. She lay still then, and tried to work out what she could do to make sense of all the strange things that were happening. If she didn't get a grip she would imagine everyone she had come across since Sunday night was in some way crazed. She forced herself to think of the nice, normal people she had met. The Reverend George Goff and Sally Dodd, Cliff Thompson's girlfriend. Kate had spoken to Sally for only a few minutes, but there had been something sensible and pleasant and vaguely humorous about her which had impressed Kate. Sally reminded Kate of a younger, northern, more carefree version of Liz Jones. She had mentioned a party of students who would love a talk on cable TV, and she had also suggested meeting Kate for a drink to show her some of the local atmosphere. There was something reassuring about Sally Dodd.

And Malcolm Hodgson too was surely a good guy. But she couldn't afford to think of him in the middle of the night. John Maple, she thought, whatever has gone wrong, I do love you. She tried to remember the desperate passion of their early meetings, but could only see herself as a damaged person who had leaned too much on a man who no longer needed her. Kate had been a TV executive at LondonVision in the late eighties, a surprise success story, confident, unpushy, sure of her place in the meritocracy, until she had fallen foul of the ambitions of a man she had been stupid enough to sleep with as well as work for. He had been far too clever to sack her when he moved on to a better bet, but had sidelined her until the humiliation had driven her away from the company where she had been most of her working life. She had gone north and found work and renewed confidence, and John Maple, and everything had seemed so good until now, when that sick feeling of being pushed sideways was bubbling up again.

She crept out of bed to rummage in her briefcase for a book to read. Nestling in her papers was the scrap of envelope with Reverend George Goff's address scrawled on the back. The innocent little note aroused all sorts of feelings – relief that she had been able to contact George when she needed him and gratitude that his calming influence and local pride had kept her in Skirlbeck, along with irritation with herself for being dependent, nevertheless, on one of John's friends. And beneath all that was a sadness for the loneliness she and John felt as a couple. She tried to imagine George Goff's wife, and thought of a comfortable and comforting elderly lady with white hair who would fight every good fight at her husband's side until death parted them. The image emphasised her isolation. Absently, she turned the scrap of envelope over. There was a printed, cursive address along the top of the flap. To her surprise, she realised it was the logo and address of an anti-abortion organisation. Kate looked at it numbly. In all her irritation about John Maple's refusal to argue with her, she had never really considered that they might be passionately opposed on something fundamental. Kate was a firm believer in a woman's right to choose. What if John was not? Surely that was a major issue they should discuss? But it was another controversy he had never let them face.

She knew it shouldn't matter, except that to her, now, in the middle of the night, it did. All the anger she felt for being marginalised in his life boiled up, so she slammed the briefcase lid down, and kicked it under the bed. Then she crawled back into bed, and thought of Malcolm Hodgson in deliberate defiance.

Within minutes she felt the tingling of another wave of desire, and was tempted to bring herself to a climax and get it over with. But she would feel both guilty and unsatisfied if she did that. And a naughty little voice at the back of her mind suggested that she wait for the real thing. But which was the real thing? John's pre-occupied lovemaking, or the novelty of Malcolm Hodgson's lust?

And lust has a mind of its own. Kate knew now that she would have to find a complete distraction or give in to it. A nice cup of tea? The thought made her smile, but it might work. There were tea things in the cupboard, but she hated the UHT milk. Surely the twins wouldn't mind if she crept downstairs for some real milk? She knew that her suspicion of them would not go away, but she was sure that whatever they had done to their ghastly old mother, they would never do anything to a guest at the Skirlbeck Bridge Hotel. She put her feet into her slippers and shuffled to the door.

The hotel was one of those places which was as reassuring in the dark as in the full light of day. A lamp burned on the landing, and the moonlight through the fanlight and the bay windows of the open dining room lit up the hall carpet. She could hear the faint hum of the fridge in the big kitchen, and the tick of the clock. She pattered down the stairs, through the bar, and put the light on in the passageway.

The kitchen was a picture of cleanliness and order. The big ham was covered by muslin and still gave off its warm cooked smell. Trust the Robinsons not to put it in the fridge until it had properly cooled down. The breakfast pans were laid out – frying pan, saucepan, poacher, and her early morning tray was on the workbench, all ready for seven thirty.

Kate opened the fridge door and took out the milk bottle, then poured some into a cup and turned to go back upstairs. She turned off the light and padded through the bar. Then of course, it all went wrong. It had to, she thought, even as her slippers with their smooth soles started to slip on the staircarpet. The last tread had come lose, and she stumbled, dropping the cup which hit the thick carpet pile and bounced without breaking, spilling the milk all over the stairs. Fortunately she had hardly made any noise, but there was the mess to consider.

She crept back along the landing, not turning to her own room, but to the communal bathroom with the big airing cupboard which she had visited when she put her damp jacket in there to dry. She guessed the twins' room must be at the end of the corridor, and for the first time, she wondered where Mrs Robinson had slept. There were no adaptations in the house for a disabled person. Pattering towards the bathroom, she saw that the light was on in the room next door. Not really thinking about it, she went past on tiptoe. It seemed important not to let the twins know she had got up in the night for milk. They would blame themselves for not providing absolutely everything for her.

And then she heard that sound again. The sound of a man sobbing that she had heard the first night at the hotel. This time was different. Kate felt she knew the twins well enough to do something, and she couldn't bear the thought of eavesdropping.

'Hello?' she said calmly. 'Are you OK?'

The door opened, and Bill stood there, in striped pyjamas and a sort of ridiculous Noel Coward silky dressing gown. She almost wondered where his cravat was. But it wasn't a comical scene. Behind him, in exactly the same outfit, Kate could see Terry sitting on a big old-fashioned bed, with hundreds of papers and several fat note books spread out in front of him. It was Terry who was crying, in big childish gulps.

'Can I do anything?' Kate said lamely.

Bill was coming forward now, and he put his hand on her arm.

'Oh, Kate, we're sorry we disturbed you.'

'No, you didn't, really. Look is there anything I can do? Make you tea or anything?'

'No, really . . .' Bill was trying to shut the door behind him, but Terry said, 'No, Bill, I don't mind Kate seeing me cry. I miss Mam and I can't help it!'

Kate waited. Either they would include her, or she would just say goodnight and go to bed, and then lie there, restless, wondering what this latest development meant.

'You need your sleep,' she said to Bill. 'You've got the funeral in three days' time.'

'If the post mortem shows Mam just died of a heart attack on the beach.'

'What do you mean?'

'If we tell you, you must promise not to tell anyone,' Bill said.

'Of course.'

He ushered her in and signalled her to sit on the bed. She found herself in a messy, powder pink bedroom with heavy old-fashioned furniture at odds with the tasteless ornaments on every surface. The smell of unused clothes and sickly patent medicines hung in an undispersed cloud. The room was unlike any of the other scrupulously clean and rurally tasteful rooms in the hotel.

'Your mother's room?' she asked. Bill nodded.

'And these are her papers,' he said. 'We never expected to find things like this. Not as much as this.' He held up a roll of premium bonds, a bunch of share certificates, and a cluster of legal looking documents that meant nothing to Kate. But she noticed that, on the headed paper, the Skirlbeck Bridge Hotel was described as a partnership, with three directors, Jean, Terry and Bill Robinson.

Bill showed her a small building society book. In it, she saw, were large monthly payments.

'So what's that?'

'We don't know.' Bill shook his head. 'But people were paying her money for something. One . . . transaction . . . I knew about. But there were more. Things that meant big payments. But we don't know what.'

'Something to do with the business?' Kate asked hopelessly.

'The business?' Bill was looking at her almost with affection despite his misery, as if her innocence somehow cheered him, while behind him Terry said nothing, but sobbed like a child with a broken toy. 'You didn't know Mother! These payments aren't anything to do with a business, other than a bloody funny business!'

'What do you mean?'

'Don't say anything, Bill,' Terry's voice came shrilly from inside the fusty bedroom.

'Now, Terry.' Bill's big brother manner seemed to give him back his confidence. 'Kate is part of this for us . . . don't you understand?'

'I think I do,' Kate said softly, trying to be reassuring. 'Whenever you remember this awful week, I'll be part of your memories even though I'm not part of your family!'

'That's it!' Bill breathed. 'It's almost as if you belong in Skirlbeck, just for a few days.'

Crazy as it was, in that horrid cluttered bedroom, smelling of old clothes and spilt cheap medicaments, Kate experienced something like pride, in a quick shiver which passed. 'So can I do anything to help?'

'I don't think anyone can.' Bill was looking fretful again.

'Except say nothing,' Terry breathed. 'You see, Kate, what this means is . . .'

'Someone . . . more than one person . . . was paying Mother,' Bill whispered. 'So they might have wanted her . . .'

'Dead!' Terry's voice rose again in the strange twisted crying of a grown up man-child.

Kate was fiercely aware of two things. One was that her

suspicion about the twins was completely wrong. However much they were now set free, she could not imagine them deliberately and cruelly abandoning their mother to die. But she also realised that however innocent *they* might be of murdering Mrs Jean Robinson, they were convinced someone else had done it. Terry was still crying, and Bill was holding him like a father with a child. 'Mam,' Terry was calling out, 'Mam, Mam.' But the look she saw on Bill's face held more grievance than grief, a deep and bitter grievance that made Kate shudder as she silently left them together.

Chapter Six

Sir Michael Marshall had turned what had been known as the gun room at Skirlbeck House into his personal office, and that Wednesday morning, he sat dreamily in front of his rolltop desk, reading a magazine about video equipment. He seemed unaware of the contrast, as he lolled in his battered old chair, sopping up the warmth from the ancient electric fire he had plugged in to the old round pin socket on the wall. His obsession with technology rarely led to buying it. One of his wife's greatest trials was his meanness, combined with his irritating habit of lecturing her about digital superhighways, computers and camcorders whilst showing no inclination to spend money on something as advanced as a microwave oven. Celia Marshall knew her husband lived in a dream world, but she didn't. She needed funds for her mill project, but getting money out of Michael was wellnigh impossible.

'Mikey?' He heard her calling before she bustled into the room, and he sighed. 'Mikey? I want to talk to you. It's about the mill. I've decided we should spend a little bit of our own cash on it. Invest a little of the profit. As you know, it actually made money this summer but I want to put more in to get more out. When we get the extension passed, I want the showroom to be properly decorated. I thought we should get someone over from Newcastle. Or even up from London!'

'Cee! You must be mad. We can't afford that kind of thing.'

'Oh, can't we, Mikey? Are you sure?' Wheedling, Celia Marshall put her hand on her husband's shoulder. It was the first time they had deliberately touched since his birthday kiss in July.

'Really, Cee, now that you fancy yourself as a businesswoman . . .' he made it sound like a circus act, '. . . you should know that's a ridiculous suggestion. We just don't have the money.'

'Why is it ridiculous, Mikey?' Times of dispute were few and far between in the Marshall household, simply because they had evolved a formula for not communicating about anything even vaguely contentious.

'Because, Celia, interest rates are not what they were when I retired, because we are on a fixed income, and because the woollen mill is only a hobby.' He barked the last word at her. Even if the mill had made them a million a month, Sir Michael would have treated it as a little sideline of his wife's. His anger usually shut her up, even if she then flounced off and did what she wanted anyway, but on the subject of money Sir Michael would not be brooked.

This time, however, Celia stood her ground. She grew even pinker and more vibrant. But Sir Michael was undaunted. He was in charge, and he cut across her high pitched argument.

'Do be quiet Celia. That's all there is to say on the subject.'

'But, Michael, we do have a little more money at our disposal.'

'What on earth do you mean?'

'Look.'

Lady Celia put a bank statement in front of him. He could tell she was nervous, but he was distracted from wondering why, by the sum of money at the bottom of the page.

'Good Lord, Celia. I had no idea. It must have been a wonderful season!'

His wife looked slightly embarrassed, and he was aware again of how edgy she had been recently.

'Well, I understand now, Cee darling, things are looking better than I thought. But should we really be pouring money into the mill?'

'Pouring money into the mill! I think you should remember it's the mill that earns me my car, pays for the domestic help, and keeps me in clothes.' Unfortunately, that was true, thought Sir Michael, looking at her grey sack suit.

'But, Celia, this might well be an unnecessary embellishment . . . '

'But it's what I want.' For a minute he thought she was going to stamp her surprisingly small but forceful feet.

'Just because you want it, Celia, doesn't mean it's the right thing to do. I have to look at the estate as a whole. However, if you insist, I'll think about it.'

'Think about it? Michael, that really is too much. We need to spend on refurbishment and extending. You have no idea what I've had to do . . .' She stopped suddenly, and stood blinking at him, reminding him of the gauche young woman in heavy shoes and equally shapeless tweeds of forty years before. For a moment he was slightly concerned, and tempted to ask her why she was biting her lip, her arms akimbo and her knuckles white. But she had turned away from him. And he let his eyes stray back to the glossy advertisements in his magazine. Perhaps with the surprise money the mill had brought in, he would one day be able to afford one of the new digital TV receivers. When he looked up again, his wife had gone.

Five miles away, in the pretty little wholefood tea shop, Kate pushed her plate of carrot cake away. Only the damp russet brown edges were left. She had not really wanted it, but once it was in front of her she had succumbed. Succrumbed even! She giggled. She felt slightly lighthearted with lack of sleep and surfeit of thought. She glanced to where Andy de Salas was showing Jerry the camera positions for the next shots. The dinner party with Paul Pym had not been mentioned, and seemed light years away. With luck, de Salas would be pre-occupied for the next ten minutes, and Kate would be able to sneak out to the car.

She had decided to put Malcolm Hodgson and the Skirlbeck Bridge Hotel to the back of her mind. The issue which was likely to affect her working day was the relationship between Andy de Salas and Liz Jones, and it was that she needed to think about.

This morning, she was determined to find a way to contact Liz. So far the shoot had gone well, professionally speaking. It was busy, which helped. The atmosphere was strained, but not to breaking, and the tension between Kate and the director had lost its heat, though not its threat.

De Salas had nodded absently at her when they arrived to set up, and it had been June who had talked her through the running order. She too was quiet, and it seemed to Kate that they were pussyfooting around as if de Salas *was* a sleeping baby. Kate had wondered about bringing up the subject of Paul Pym and his views, not to mention her call to Channel Four, but felt unusually restrained. Part of her reticence came from being distracted by the thought of Liz Jones in de Salas's bed.

Kate had been best friends with Liz for fifteen years or more. For years, Kate had always assumed that she was the one more prone to sexual crises. She looked wonderingly at de Salas. He was desperately handsome, so handsome that Kate could never in a million years find him sexy. She wondered if perhaps she liked her men plain enough to be grateful! But it wasn't that. Beautiful men always seemed smug to Kate and smugness for any reason was death to attraction. She had assumed her friend would feel the same. Kate had always trusted Liz's judgement. There had to be a reason for her attachment to de Salas. Liz could be comical, but never silly.

Kate watched de Salas's small round bottom, long thin legs and shock of black hair. She noticed that he had his hands in his pockets. The flamboyant gestures and the loud voice of the previous days had gone. His movements had become slow and almost languid but his eyes were ringed and dark, not with the sleeplessness Kate associated with lust, but with a lack of peace. Yet de Salas was easier to work with. He showed off less, and concentrated more. He was taking pains, at this point, to get the lighting in the pine and chintz tea-room just right.

Kate smiled her thanks at the cheerful woman who had served her the free sample of carrot cake, and scooted out through the back door to where the cars were parked. Despite her hurry she caught sight of the lace-frilled sea to her right, and the great padded velour clouds to her left.

Even a townie could tell a storm was on the way. The fretful wind picked up a few leaves and played with them before moving on, gaining force like a children's gang picking up followers and moving skittishly down the valley.

She opened the door of her car and groped for the mobile phone. It took less than three minutes to get the number of the Summerlake Hall Hotel from directory enquiries, and then ring the hotel. A strenuously smart voice answered and Kate said, 'Could you put me through to Mr de Salas's room?'

She felt her heart was pounding as if it was she who was involved in an affair rather than her friend.

The phone was ringing. One ring. Two rings. Would Liz be there? In Kate's experience few things were harder to ignore than a ringing phone. Four rings. Five rings. Then the phone was lifted, but nothing happened.

'Is that you, Liz? It's Kate.' Pause. 'It's me, Kate.'

There was further silence, then a sound as if the phone was being moved.

'Don't put the phone down, Liz. Please. I know it's not the chambermaid because she would have said so by now. Talk to me, Liz. It is you, isn't it? Tell you what, you pretend to be anonymous and I'll pretend to be an agony aunt. Now tell me your problem, lovey . . .'

A giggle. 'Oh, Kate . . .' Liz's voice sounded soft and weary, then she panicked. 'How did you know? Does anyone else?'

'Relax, Liz, it was pure coincidence. I got lost driving back to my hotel yesterday and passed you in de Salas's car.' A thought occurred to her. 'Hey, is that why de Salas couldn't get me a room in the Summerlake . . . because he was expecting to entertain you there?'

'No! I only decided to turn up on the spur of the moment after . . . oh, never mind. I suppose you think I'm a bitch?' There was a tone of defiant expectancy.

'Of course I don't. I'm mad with envy and curiosity.' Well, curiosity.

'Oh, Kate, thank God. I thought you'd be all quiet and sorry and sensible.'

'Judgemental? Me?'

'Well, these days you aren't renowned for keeping your opinions to yourself.'

'No? Well, in this case I want to hear all about it first, and the jury's out. I suppose you're lying there in a pink negligee, eating chocolates and ringing room service. Getting fat is your moral dilemma, never mind your marriage! Anyway, I need your help, Liz.'

Kate had calculated that asking her friend's help would work far better than any questioning.

'You do?' Liz's voice brightened.

'Yep. There's something about this set-up which bothers me and I want you to enlighten me. I bet you don't have time to talk today, do you? I suppose Andy will be dashing back at lunchtime for a little something to keep him going . . . or do I mean coming?'

'For Christ's sake, Kate, in the circumstances! Don't be juvenile!' It crossed Kate's mind to ask what the circumstances actually were, but Liz was saying, 'He *is* going to come back for half an hour.'

'What about later then? Can you tie the silken sheets together and lower them out of the window, and escape for an hour at about six thirty? I'll have you back by seven thirty, because I have a dinner date myself.' If Malcolm rings. And if I want to go. And if it's the right thing to do . . .

'Of course I can. I'm not a hostage. I'll leave Andy a note, but I *must* be back soon after him.' Liz's anxiety made her sound, if not a prisoner, like a voluntary inmate at some authoritarian institution. Kate wondered if she should make some cheery remark about de Salas's bum, the way she and Liz used to joke about most of the handsome young men they met, but Kate sensed that although she had broken the ice, the freeze could set in again at any time. Liz had never seemed so strained.

'I'll see you at six thirty.' She fixed the venue.

'I'll get a taxi there. And Kate?'

'Yes?'

'Don't say anything to Andy.'

'As if I would!' The one thing Kate wanted to avoid was tangling with any more of Andy de Salas's neuroses.

At six thirty Kate was sitting in the bar of the pub where Malcolm Hodgson had taken her. It was deserted, except for the barman and a farmer and there was hardly a ripple of interest when a taxi drew up and deposited Liz outside. She was ten minutes late, and came in waving scarves and handbags, talking before she was through the door, and Kate at once realised what Malcolm Hodgson had meant by the strong carrying voice of the south.

'Kate, so lovely to see you.' Liz was bestowing the famous media kiss, a regulation one inch away from the face, in the vague direction of Kate's nose.

'For God's sake keep your voice down,' Kate whispered. 'This is a pub in Cumberland, not Black's Club. And it's only me, you idiot. You're acting like something out of This is Your Life.'

Liz slumped into the chair opposite. 'All right, there's

no need to be snide. I haven't been out of the hotel all day and I feel like shit.'

'We'd better have a drink.'

'Too right!'

'For goodness sake, keep your voice down, Liz.'

'OK, OK, you'll just have to forgive me if I haven't absorbed the local ambience. I'm from Stevenage, and all this is a bit alien to me.'

'Just remember that you can't do anything here without people knowing. The Summerlake isn't the Heathrow Hilton, and from what I've worked out, everyone in the area is related, so I wouldn't put it past the smart reception- ist at your hotel to be reverting to type and phoning her second cousin on the farm about you right now!'

'You're joking!'

'Yes, but only just. This place is not like anywhere else. I'll give you my insights into rural life later. Now I'm going to the bar. You look as if you need a drink.' For someone who had been in bed all day, and who was having a torrid affair with a younger man, Liz looked dreadful. Again, it was not the worn and cheery tiredness of passion, but a pale, drained look which combined with Liz's strained conviviality to give Kate a stomach wrenching sense of sympathy. Liz looked ill. Kate wondered for a moment what was really the matter, but Liz made a desperate effort to smile so Kate left her to settle down until she came back from the bar with two schooners.

'Here we are. Anyway, what I really want to know about is – what's going on with you?'

'You said you needed my help?'

'I do. But I'd like you to confide in me first. I'm really sad you haven't already.'

'How could I, Kate? You might have tried to stop me. It's all right for you, with your sexy vicar. Now you're all sorted out, you could easily turn round and tell me I should be grateful for what I've got. On top of that, John's friendly with Steve too. If I told you, and you told John, would John tell Steve? He might even feel he had to – sanctity of marriage and all that.'

Kate was hurt. 'That's not fair, Liz. I would never tell anyone, if you talked to me in confidence. And even if John found out, he wouldn't blab to your husband. You don't have to tell all, but if you want to, I'd like to hear. And then you can help me. I'm obviously completely wrong, but I just can't get on with Andy. I just don't understand what he wants from this film.'

It was the right way to get to the truth. Kate could see the colour and animation coming back to Liz's stiff, pale face as she spoke.

'Andy's incredibly talented.'

'Very possibly. But he's not very organised.'

Liz nodded regretfully. 'True. But visually, he's gifted. I met him at a tedious conference. There was no real reason why I should have been at the conference,' Liz said, 'but that was part of the whole problem.'

The problem was that Liz had what so many people wanted, but sussed it wasn't of any real substance. Yes, there was the husband, the lovely children and the jobshare as a TV producer which so many women would have killed for. But Liz knew the job was a front. She was employed at LondonVision, the company where Kate had been head of features before she had been demoted. But times had changed and Liz was part of the caring nineties package and a jobshare had been set up between her and a male producer, who also wanted time off for childcare. It was a personnel officer's dream. The trouble was, that having been lucky enough to get the jobshare, Liz was expected to sit back and cruise. The last thing anybody had expected was that she would actually want to take part in the full running of – and the status of running – her department. Like all part timers Liz suspected she was doing more, and being respected less, than any of her colleagues.

'How could you have been so naive?' Kate chortled, to Liz's annoyance. 'Christ, Lizzie, it's hard enough being treated as an equal when you work *twice* as long as them, never mind when you're only there three days a week.'

'Two and a half, actually. And it's a jobshare, not part time.'

'Oh come on, what's the difference? And don't give me the company line for God's sake! Look what that did for you.'

Liz shrugged, and went on to describe how she had nagged and whinged her way out of her reputation for solid, uncomplaining work, and into a role as the departmental troublemaker. It had distressed her, but slowly a few higher profile things had come her way, amongst which was 'Marketing the Country' at the Savoy Hotel.

'You're kidding!' Kate had laughed aloud. 'Who in daytime programming would want to go to a conference like that?'

'I would, for a start. When you're starved of stimulation, anything will do.'

'And what sort of stimulus did you have in mind?'

'That came later. Seriously, Kate, I just wanted to go to something which broadened my mind.'

'OK, Liz, so you got to a few minor conferences which,

let's face it, had nothing to do with LondonVision. But where does de Salas come into this?' And that was where Liz had taken a deep gulp of her second schooner of sherry, and had told Kate how she felt about her marriage.

Liz described what she called household harassment. Her husband Steve, she said, had started soon after Tom was born, to monitor what she was doing. 'It was almost as if I wasn't fit to look after children,' she said. He had been as openly supportive as anyone could wish, encouraging Liz to go back to work and telling everyone how proud he was of her. But at home, the vicious little checklist had started. 'He would follow me round the house to see whether I cut the bread and folded the tea towel the way he liked. He complained about the wash cycle I used in the machine; if I put things in on ten, he would stop the machine and put them on five. He'd say that I was working part time, so I had time to get things right. It was his way of asserting himself. He made me feel so guilty I took on more and more of the housework and childcare. In the end I realised I was more worried about Steve's reaction than about the domestic issues themselves, and as a result I was working twice as hard. Once, when she was three, Lily fell off a friend's trike and I had to take her to the West Middlesex Hospital for stitches. I sat in the Casualty Department and when they took Lily behind the curtain and left me, I started to howl. Really cry. The woman next to me thought it was relief because Lily was out of my hands and in the hands of professionals, but it was really because I was terrified of telling Steve. I knew he'd blame me for not watching her. For months after that, I hardly let the kids out of my sight when I was home. I never wound down between the office and the living room. I'd have given my eyeteeth to sit and listen to the football results and fill in my coupon, which was my dad's reward for a working week . . .'

Kate nodded. She had been married too, but not for very long. Graham, her husband, had gone to work in the Middle East as a film producer, after losing his job at a LondonVision shakeup in the eighties. Kate had been promoted while he was away, and afterwards things had never been right. Kate tried to imagine what it would have been like if she and Graham had had children. She had become pregnant, but had lost the baby. Once, ten years before that, she'd had an abortion, but she tried not to think about it. After the miscarriage, she had never conceived again, and she did not expect to have children now. But she could understand what Liz was saying.

Liz stopped to whimper with self-pity and wipe her nose on a piece of toilet roll which had the cream fluffy fullness of something from the en-suite bathroom of the Summerlake Hall Hotel. And that's where Liz is staying, Kate reminded herself. However bad Liz's life was, she was the one who was cheating . . .

'I stayed faithful to Steve for years. Believe me, Kate, I wanted to be a good wife. Oh, don't look at me like that! I know you're thinking perhaps that was only because I didn't get any offers! And you're right. The first offer I got, I said yes to. I was at a conference on new programming initiatives, with a useless token seminar on enablement for women producers. It was the first thing they sent me to. And I met him.'

'Who? De Salas?'

'No! Andy wasn't the first. No, it all started last year. You were so wrapped up with the vicar that you were the last person I could confide in. It was . . .' Liz leaned forward and whispered the name of an elder statesman in TV.

'You're joking!'

'No, I'm not. He was there to give the keynote speech. On the new initiatives of course, not on the women producers.' She giggled snuffily.

'Good grief! What was it like?'

'The speech?'

'No, you idiot.'

'You mean in bed? Oh, he was a sweet old womaniser. I mean, he obviously picked someone up at every conference he went to. He was years older than me, but you'd just found blissful happiness with John, who is older than you, and I thought perhaps an older man would be the answer. You know, at least he'd be an understandable old sexist, not a hypocrite like Steve. And it was OK.'

'You . . . enjoyed it?'

'Yeah, at least I managed a frisson. The earth didn't move, but the bed shook a bit. He wasn't that attractive when he took his expensive suits off – skin like those tired freckly peaches we used to get in the LV canteen, and a belly. I mean, Steve isn't skinny, but an elderly stomach sags more.' She and Kate were laughing out loud now, Kate more in sympathy than with humour. 'Oh and Kate, he kept his socks on because he said he had poor circulation! Can you imagine a fifty-five-year-old woman even daring to imagine seducing a man my age, and keeping her socks on? I tell you, any theories you have about equality just get exploded!'

'But were you repulsed?'

'Repulsed? No, I was bloody relieved! I didn't have to hold my stomach in! It was a damn sight better than worrying about having bags under your eyes or stretch marks. He thought I was lovely. I could have done it again with him except . . .'

'Except?'

'Well, we did actually have a conversation. And he told me he thought adultery was more acceptable in men than women!'

'No! So who does he think all these men should do it with, then?'

'Presumably a few 'bad women' who act like flypaper to keep the rest clean! And I didn't fancy a life covered in flies. Anyway after him, I ricocheted straight into the arms of randy Ronald, the floor manager at LondonVision. You remember him? Always joshing. He'd chatted me up for years – it was almost a joke – so I called his bluff, and discovered it *was* a joke after all. We had to do it, once I took him seriously, and it was a case of a good flirtation being ruined by reality. It was a disaster.'

'And then?'

Liz went quiet and sat up straight in the pub's armchair. 'And then I met Andy. And I decided I would pursue him. After Mr Important, and then the mad floor manager, I thought that next time, what I wanted was a handsome young man, and as no-one would ever know, I was going to do what men did, and pick one up. And if I got rejected, I'd do what men do, and ask another. So I saw Andy at the bar, and I went over and chatted him up.'

'And it worked.'

'Not exactly. He didn't know I was flirting. He's a very serious person. I realised as soon as we started to talk that he was insecure.'

'Was that part of the attraction?'

'What?'

'Oh, never mind; tell me what happened.'

'Well, it took months for us to get it together. By the time we went to bed, Ben had already had his accident and Andy had come to me for help. I got you for him *and* got him introductions to all sorts of people including the man who runs the Tourist Centre in North West Cumbria.'

'Paul Pym?'

'That's right. I never knew him, but Felix gave me his name. And then Andy and I became deeply involved. I knew it wouldn't just be a friendship.' She paused, almost sadly, and played with the beer mat, twisting it under the slim sherry glass so the schooner spun round on the dark oak table.

'Well, I suppose that explains why Andy was so suspicious of me, for a start. He must have been hyper-sensitive to you and me being friends.'

'I suppose so. But he was desperate when Ben was injured. I just had to get him someone who could pull the film out of the shit. It was pure luck that you were available. And Andy seems to think you've managed it.'

'Does he? I've hardly done anything, except upset that Pym man the night before last.'

'Yes, Andy told me about that, but he said Pym just laughed about it after you'd gone. Andy says June Ridley likes having you on the shoot, and so does he. You make him think straight. He's so . . . volatile.'

'You can say that again.' It crossed Kate's mind to tell Liz about her journey from Newcastle in de Salas's Porsche, but the sense of strain in her friend's face put her off. 'I can see what you mean about him being visually talented, though.'

Liz's face lit up. 'Yes, isn't he . . . ?'

'But Liz, where is he getting the money from for this film?'

'Well, Paul Pym's contributing, isn't he? And surely they'll get a commission, even if it's just from Border TV?'

'I don't think you can be that sure.'

'Oh, come on, Kate. Andy knows what he's doing. And he really needs to make this film.'

And if Andy needs something, you suspend judgement and supply him, Kate thought. She had always found Liz's unconditional care for her children admirable but exhausting. Perhaps it was explained in part by Steve's constant criticisms. Or perhaps Liz needed to be needed and now her children had been replaced by this new cuckoo whose demands appeared to come first.

'Do you love him, Liz?'

'Yes.' Liz jutted her chin forward. Kate realised that this time, she couldn't say, 'And does he wear socks?' and have a laugh.

'And Steve? And Lily and Tom?'

'Oh God, Kate, don't talk to me about children.' Liz put her head in her hands. 'If you only knew . . .'

'Knew what?'

'Oh, nothing. I'm sorry. I'm a bit emotional on the subject. But it was a fair question. After what I've just done, I ache for my kids. I know now I can't possibly leave them. It doesn't matter for a few days at the moment. I know Steve has days off owing to him, and he can damn well use them up. He's talking about taking them on holiday for half term – that's next week. I think he should anyway.'

'And give you time for Andy?'

'Yes. Why not?' said Liz defensively. 'But in the future I

can't possibly do without my children. We have to sort this out. But, Kate, please don't think I'm bad. One day on the radio I heard a remake of one of those classic songs that came out when we were teenagers, full of hope and sex and guts, and I thought: Christ, I'm going back there, cellulite like cauliflowers and all. I want fun and variety and self-respect and sexuality. The big female turn-on is being desired, you know, and Steve used to fuck me as if he was doing me a favour. And when I made my bid for freedom I found I liked it. I expected to be a disaster like Anna Karenina, or knowing me, someone sad and whinging from a magazine advice column. But I found I *liked* putting it about again. And the kids didn't know; if I'd been at a flower arranging class it would have made the same difference to them . . .'

'Very exotic flowers!'

'Yeah. All stem!'

Kate smiled. 'And then Andy came along?'

'Yes. And I wanted him so much, Kate. It was over with Steve.'

And if that's how Liz feels, shouldn't I examine myself a lot more carefully, Kate thought? Liz had left her abruptly, the pained, thin-skinned look coming over her face again as she got up to go. She kissed Kate with feeling, clinging to her friend for a few seconds, and swaying in a way that made Kate fear she was going to faint. For a moment Kate wondered what else was wrong. Liz seemed so brittle and ill. Then Liz had left, hurrying back to the cab which had been waiting outside. Whatever Liz's problems, money wasn't one of them.

When Kate arrived back at the Skirlbeck there was a message from Malcolm Hodgson, saying he would call for her at eight, to take her to dinner as promised. She had refused to think about the possibility during the day, but now she felt her stomach turn with excitement. To calm it, she asked if John Maple had called. But there was no message. She felt it was an omen.

It was seven fifty and she was standing in front of the mirror, inspecting herself. She might never look any better than she did that night. She had no children, no husband, not much of a career ... and no guilt? How could she, only two years after falling in love with John, be staring in the glass, assessing whether she could really attract another man? Yet attracting him was only half of it. Hodgson attracted her in return. She thought of Liz's remark about Steve fucking her as a favour. It was crude but it had the ring of truth. With John she had begun to feel it was a duty. She wanted someone who wanted her.

Half an hour later, her nervousness seemed like vanity. Malcolm arrived, pleasant but businesslike, and the twins had poured them a drink before they left as if they were a long established, unremarkable couple. It hardly seemed like a sexually charged, exciting evening. She clambered into Malcolm's Range Rover and said nothing as he turned the key in the engine. It spluttered and dried up. He turned it again. Nothing happened.

'Bloody leads. One of them's loose.'

'Big problem?'

'No, not really. It'll just take me a minute.'

'Look, Malcolm, why not take my car?'

'Your car?'

'Yes. I hired it from Skirlbeck Garage.'

'Is it insured for me?'

'No, but that doesn't matter, does it?'

153

The idea that she might drive had not occurred to him. Hodgson was used to his Range Rover being another pair of legs, allowing him to stride around his territory. He grunted. They climbed out of the Range Rover and walked across the car park to her little Renault. Malcolm seemed to make heavy weather of getting his bulk into the passenger seat.

'OK.' Kate heard her voice sounding bright and helpful, like a pre-school TV presenter. 'Where do we go?'

It wasn't easy to drive to Hodgson's instructions. He knew the way so well he kept forgetting to tell her where to turn on the winding country roads, and at least twice she had to make three-point-turns to get them back on course.

'It looked stormy today,' Kate volunteered.

'Yes. But it hasn't broken yet, even over the fells. I daresay it'll catch up with us later.'

He said no more apart from clipped instructions. Kate had to concentrate hard. Finally she realised they were aiming for a low black and white building, lit by carriage lamps, in a dark velvety fold of hills which sheltered a more gentle wooded valley than the bleak shoreline Kate was growing to know.

'It's called "The String at Rest," Hodgson said. 'It's an old pack horse stopping-off place, one of the nicest country pubs in Britain, on the old drovers' route north. The trouble is, we've taken so long to get here they may have abandoned our booking.'

He was impatient while she parked, then climbed out of the car and strode ahead of her into the pub. By the time Kate had sorted out the Renault, and followed him inside, he was already deep in conversation. Kate joined him just as he was discussing some aged relative's heart condition with the landlady. Reluctantly he tore himself away. Kate tried to smile. 'Someone else you're related to? I'm learning you never know who's connected to whom up here.'

And just as she was about to launch into small talk Hodgson paused and looked up, his face breaking into his first genuine smile of the evening, but it wasn't for Kate. 'Here's a couple of blokes I really must speak to. Get yourself a drink, Kate – oh sorry, you can't of course, if you're driving. But I will, if you don't mind. Just excuse me a minute . . .'

'Malcolm,' she said, rather proud now of her carrying, southern voice. 'Why not introduce me to your friends?'

She could see the embarrassment, the hunching of shoulders into the ill-fitting jackets. Hodgson looked at her as if she was mad, but she stood there, pretending someone had tried to snub her in the Groucho Club in Dean Street, Soho W1. She wouldn't let it happen there, so why let it happen here? 'Just some lads . . .' Hodgson made to elbow her back to the table, but Kate held out her hand to the group.

'Kate Wilkinson, TV producer. How are you?' The men sheepishly stretched out their dry, calloused hands. 'Will Carruthers, howdo.' 'Billy Dixon.' 'Ian Graham, evening.'

'Nice to meet you. Shall we go and order now, Malcolm?' She wondered what he would do. He could turn his back on her, or tell her to go and wait for him.

But Hodgson had style. He raised his glass to her, and said, 'Of course. I'm looking forward to this,' and walked in front of her so she could be sure he wasn't signalling his amusement to 'the lads' behind her back. When they sat down he said, more in curiosity than anger, 'Why did you do that?'

'Because I'm not here to be ignored.'

'By God!' He looked at her with laughter now. I really fancy you.'

She laughed back. She had known it was true, but it was cheering to hear it.

'I fancy you too,' she said, to her own surprise, and knew then she had crossed a boundary, for both of them. Malcolm's eyes opened wide at her remark.

'Good job, isn't it?' she said in a challenge to his raised eyebrows, as the landlady appeared at their elbows.

It was a lovely meal, homemade soup, chicken casserole, cheese. But it was hardly intimate, and throughout Kate was aware of the men at the bar, who occasionally broke ranks to come over to speak to Malcolm, along with several other diners who stopped to say hello.

'I had no idea it would be so busy. But then, it's auction day in Carlisle. Oh, excuse me Kate, there's someone I have to wave to . . .'

It reminded Kate of being out with a minor TV presenter, the sort of good-natured person who felt obliged to speak to all the fans, as opposed to the megastar in London who conspired with a sophisticated public to ignore the tiny nuances of recognition.

While they had coffee Kate let her attention wander over the open log fire, the black beams and the shiny brasses. It had not been the sort of dinner she was expecting, but it had its own charm. The public nature of it, which had stopped them discussing Tom Flint or the Robinsons or the theme park, made it a light and cheerful evening. She liked the sound of Hodgson's accent, broader now he was relaxed, though she understood only one word in three as he talked heatedly with the people he had known all his life. Part of her liked cutting a dash too, being southern and different. But most of all she felt there was something embracing about the warmth and the cosiness, the fact Malcolm was so at home here, yet wanted to be with her. She was surprised not to feel excluded. For a moment, she almost felt she belonged . . .

Which was bloody stupid. As if realising it, she suddenly sat upright, and Malcolm got to his feet, making for the bar to pay.

The other people had gone. She watched detachedly as Malcolm paid the bill. And then he turned and came towards her, and the dilemma was there as surely as if he had plunged his hands between her thighs. I've had no drink, she thought. I've hardly thought about flirting, and we haven't talked about sex. I've had about as much warmup as a frozen burger. So why, as he walks towards me, do I want, suddenly, to slip back and lie along this bench and pull him on top of me?

Malcolm put out his hand, gently. She responded tentatively with her own, and he pulled her up from the chair. He had her jacket in his other hand, holding it as if it were a feathery shawl, not a bulky Marks and Spencer's all-wool blazer. She felt overwhelmed by the size of him as he smiled down at her.

'Thanks for being so good about tonight,' he said. 'I never realised we would see so many people.'

'I didn't mind. In fact, it made me feel at home. Much nicer than being spirited off to a candlelit meal for two.'

'That was what you expected, wasn't it? The starter pack seduction kit?'

'Except you're not a starter.'

'And this isn't a seduction.'

'No?'

'No. Because you wouldn't be seduced, would you? You'd only do it if you really wanted to . . .'

Of course that was what he should think. It made her sound so pulled together, so mentally and emotionally sure of herself. But it wasn't the truth. The truth was that she was committed to John Maple, but attracted to Malcolm Hodgson: and if only he *would* seduce her how much easier it would be.

They walked to the car through the dank loaded air, without touching. The fact that she was driving made everything straightforward. She felt every movement was heavy with disappointment as she fastened her seat belt. She made the odd bright remark as they drove along. And then suddenly she thought: what the hell, I *do* want him . . .

'Kate, you should turn left here, and then immediately right . . . oh shit, that was it. Can you back up?'

'Hang on, I should be able to.' In the dark she chugged the little Renault at snail's pace backwards down the lane.

'Where are we, Malcolm?'

'I'm not sure. Oh, bloody hell, it's starting to rain. It's been threatening this all day.'

The rain was in plump bursting drops, each one seeming charged as they splatted on the windscreen. Then there was a flash of lightning which made Kate start and gasp.

'Keep your nerve, Kate; you need to back up further.'

'OK.' She was twisted in the seat now, hardly touching the accelerator and willing the car to crawl backwards down the lane. Then she heard Malcolm say, 'Oh shit,' again, and she edged the car to the side of the road, and pulled on the handbrake.

'What's wrong?'

'Nothing. Except that you've just backed past the turnoff and we seem to be in someone's gateway.' He laughed. 'Now you can have your evil way with me.'

Kate felt her hands trembling.

'Malcolm, this isn't the right time . . .'

'No time's the right time . . .'

But he had started now to stroke her leg. With the ease of a man who knew what he was doing, she felt his fingers slip under the hem of her skirt. She couldn't help but open her legs so he could slip his hand between her knees.

He turned in his seat and leaned his right hand heavily on her thigh, swivelling so his left leg was pinning her to the seat, and his left hand moved slowly, lazily under her jumper. He was so big she could drop her head into his shoulder, and see nothing but the darkness of his jacket. His hand moved up, over the top of her skirt, towards her breasts. She couldn't say stop, because she didn't want him to, and Kate had never been the sort of person to say no when she meant yes. Now she wanted the car to be a little separate bubble, so she need think of no other world except the one in which his hand was going to move on and up.

It did, creeping under the wool so that the first time he touched her flesh, the band between waistband and bosom which should have been uninteresting fizzed like a new erogenous zone. His hand moved in a circular stroking movement over her diaphragm as if even her most boring stretch of skin was electric.

Then, slowly, his right hand still braced on her thigh, his left hand found the curve of her bra cup and moved slowly upwards to cuddle her breasts, until only the stretched lace was left, impenetrable, between him and her left nipple. It was so erect she felt it bursting out like a hot pebble in sand, desperate to escape from the tautness of her bra. She knew that this *was* sex, whatever he said, but the feeling of doing it, without doing it, had a delight all its own. Malcolm was a practised expert, and although she felt she should despise him for it, she had to admit that his gentle, circular stroking technique made her breath come quicker and the skin of her bosom feel hot.

There was surely no harm in this? And anyway, it felt so good. Her chest rose up to him with the intake of her breath as she gasped. She knew he was going to try and undress her, but she was inert with curiosity and desire. She wanted him to, but she didn't want to think that she did.

Then, instead of roughly pushing up her bra so the tight elastic caught and squashed her, which would have made her wince, and feel cross, and slap him away, she felt his huge hands roving round to her back to unhook her in one practised movement. Even as she was thinking, 'It won't work, you smooth bastard,' the fastening tightened under his touch and then sprang open, so her breasts fell gratefully from their lacy binding into his warm rough hands, regardless of any intelligent reservations she might have. The sensation of freedom from the tightness of her bra was intox-icating; she seemed to grow into the hot, dry, slightly calloused palm. He moved his thumb and forefinger around her nipple with the gentlest squeeze. It made her groan and push herself towards him, so that with one huge hand he could fondle both breasts, one areola in the fork of his finger and thumb, the other stroked by his fingertips. It was almost like a tiny orgasm in itself and she knew she was leaning forward to force her nipples against his fingers and rub them there. 'Oh God, Malcolm!' she breathed.

And then another flash of lightning bleached through her closed eyelids and she was aware that Malcolm had stopped moving.

'What is it?' Suddenly the melting sticky irresistible passion was no more than flopping boobs and a twist of much-washed greying nylon. Malcolm was staring ahead.

'Did you see them?'

'What?'

The lightning came again and Kate gasped. On the horizon were men, silhouetted as they came over the hill. Once she had seen them, she could hear them, their loud drunken voices, the plodding of the boots in the wet earth, the heaving breathing and odd yelp of dogs.

Dogs.

'Oh, God,' she whispered. 'What is it?'

'I don't know. Keep quiet.' She knew they were coming closer. Then a torch beam shone like a vicious intrusion into the car on her side, and the vehicle slowly shook as the men surrounded it. For a moment Kate thought the shoving would stop as the crowd in the narrow lane passed by. But then the rocking took up a rhythm and she realised the car was being pushed backwards and forwards, more and more violently.

Suddenly Malcolm leaned forward.

'Fuck this!' he snarled. 'I'm getting out to find out what's going on. I don't like this one bit!'

He opened the door with such force the movement stopped, and Kate could see through the opening at least three men in boots and weatherproof jackets jump

161

backwards. Malcolm was yelling, 'Hey! What's going on here?' and then Kate heard some calling, and the fast deep voice of another man, his accent so heavy she had no idea what he was saying.

Hodgson got back in the car, soaking wet. He brought with him the smell of rain and animals.

'Get this fucking car into reverse and get out of here,' he said. Kate jammed the gear lever home and then started the engine so the car jumped backwards. She knew her driving was going to pieces. As the car careered down the track, she was aware of men scattering to either side.

'Right, turn here. Now rev up and get moving.'

'You knew where we were all along?'

'I had a good idea. Bloody good thing too. Did you see what they had with them?'

'No.'

'Two enormous pit bulls.'

'Did you know those men?'

'No, they sounded like Geordies. But there were a few more, lurking. I bet they were locals. If I'd been in the Range Rover they'd never have touched us . . .'

The rain was hammering now on the car window. Hunched forward Kate could hardly see where she was going. The lights of the little car were as weak as a child's nightlight and the windscreen wipers seemed so burdened with the weight of the rain they could hardly labour to wipe the glass. Hodgson was silent except to say 'Left here' or 'Right'. Kate drove like a mole, by feel rather than sight, aiming always for the ring of light that looked like the end of a tunnel but which was really the tiny area illuminated by her headlamps in the total, saturating, curtain of rain. They seemed to rise over a crest and for a moment she thought she saw a strip of lighter darkness in the distance as if it might be calm out at sea.

And then, with an abrupt change of heart, the rain lost its force, and eased off tetchily into an ordinary shower, taking away the drama and the passion. Kate turned left, then right, and found the shoreline and the road she now knew, which led them back to Skirlbeck.

When she pulled up in the hotel car park, Hodgson said, 'Don't tell anyone about those men. You don't know what they could do to you.' Kate nodded. He looked at her, but said nothing more, opening the door of her little car with a force that rocked it in a hideous reminder of the mob in the lane, before he heaved himself out and walked away through the drizzle. Kate leant her head momentarily on the steering wheel, then sat up, shaking before struggling weakly out of the driving seat. Her legs buckled slightly as she made for the hotel, fumbling with the big outside door key with wet, stumpy, unresponsive fingers, before stumbling inside.

On the stairs, feeling the twisted pull of her unhooked bra, she remembered the passion she had felt and how it had disappeared instantly at the sight of the silhouettes on the ridge of the hill. Now she was aware that she was shaking. She had felt bad, just for a few seconds, in the car. But her sin, if it was a sin at all, was as nothing compared to the sense of evil she had felt on the outside, rocking the car to get in.

Chapter Seven

The house was mid Victorian, encrusted with towers and pinnacles. It was painted as white as an iced cake, with select pieces of lacy plasterwork outlined in black, but however pretty it might have been in bright sunshine, it looked gloomy silhouetted against the rain heavy sky.

The North West Cumbria Tourist Centre was an independent organisation. It was funded by grants from the local council, plus donations from the few remaining thriving businesses in the area, and a major legacy from a deceased local worthy who had made money in the thirties, outlived his times, and bequeathed his Gothic villa to the development of the tourist trade.

Yet again, it was not what Kate had expected. She had imagined something neater, so was surprised by this mansion perched on a hill over one of West Cumbria's smallest towns. Still, when standing in the windswept grounds it was possible to look down on the eighteenth century streets as they nudged each other into the sea, and imagine for a moment that you were in one of the grey toned etchings of old west coast ports which the twins hung in the Skirlbeck Bridge dining room.

Kate was chilly, waiting in the car park.

Approaching winter seemed to have soaked into her marrow from the night before. She felt desperate to escape both from the guilty heat of Hodgson's hands on her breasts, and the horror that had turned them both cold. She shivered compulsively and wrapped her jacket around her. That morning she had woken with half-formed dreams and fully-fledged dread brawling in her brain, and a determination to get back to London as soon as possible had won. After all, she reasoned, she had to get to Channel Four to see Ruscroft early the next day. If she could have left Skirlbeck there and then, she would have done. But at eight thirty am, she was outside the Tourist Centre on the outskirts of the town because Andy de Salas had changed the venue for the last two days of the week's filming. He had planned to be at an aromatherapy centre, but his need to schmooze Paul Pym had led to an expedient re-organisation of the itinerary.

This was going to be difficult, Kate thought, grimacing and shivering. She had not seen Pym since striding out of that terrible dinner party. Pym was shaking Andy by the hand, cheerily, and patting June on the arm. Then it was Jerry the cameraman's turn to be hailed as a jolly good chap – Pym was good at making the workers feel important – and the female sound assistant received a warm smile. Then Pym said, 'Kate, how nice to see you this morning. And I'm so sorry that you had to dash away before we finished dinner on Monday. I enjoyed chatting to you. It's always good to have one's preconceptions challenged.' Kate felt her eyes widening. 'Come along inside.' Over Pym's shoulder she caught June's delighted smile, as if to say, 'There, what were you worrying about?'

Pym was TV material at its best, accomplished enough

to look natural. He took them on a tour of the centre, the camera tracking him like a faithful dog. Kate realised how cleverly the centre had been done out. Several of the old rooms were decorated as they might have been in the eighteen seventies, with a ship's captain's room full of charts and instruments, and a captain's wife's boudoir, and a little nursery.

'But . . .' and Pym stressed this, 'it is not a museum. It's a Tourist Centre. Here we have an information room, complete with books, videos and even a computer with CD-ROM showing shipping lines and courses, and buried treasure to amuse the children. Now, let's go back this way.' He managed to be both nimble and elegant as he steered his bulky frame through the corridors of the old house, followed by Jerry, the camera still on. Pym paused, then said, 'I think you can stop rolling now, Andy.' De Salas smiled back cosily, pleased rather than threatened by Pym's TV knowledge.

'Good,' the big man went on, 'and if we buy your film, Andy, this is of course where it will play, for the thousands of visitors who want to know about this fascinating area with its nautical history.'

Kate was not the only listener to catch the word 'if' and then to catch her breath. She caught the alarm which whipped between de Salas and June.

'And now let's go into the conservatory for morning coffee,' Pym was saying. 'Do you know, this is a genuine Victorian conservatory, though we have enlarged it on one side to provide seating for about twenty. Our fare is delicious, all made locally and featuring delicacies like Cumberland shortbread, ginger scones and rum butter. Interesting how so many west coast recipes feature ingredients from the New World, isn't it? Britain's first trade with the Americas was not from Liverpool but from Whitehaven, of course. It seems to be the fate of the west coast to decline by one port a century.' But his guests were no longer riveted by such speculation.

'Paul,' Andy de Salas was practically scampering after him, his smooth handsome features working like dough. 'Paul, we really did understand that you were virtually committed to the Rural Rides project.'

'Do sit down, Andy, and June and Kate, of course. Do sit by the window, Kate, and get the view over the sea. Breathtaking, isn't it? Now here's someone to take our orders. Coffee all round? And will you try some scones? Lovely.'

'So, just to go over what you said earlier, Paul,' de Salas gabbled. 'Can we be clear that you will definitely be buying a copy of the film for the Centre?'

'We'd be delighted to, Andy, you know that.'

De Salas leaned forward and put his hand tentatively on Pym's arm. 'Paul, you did indicate that we could expect some contribution towards the film. After all, if you're going to have rights to show it here . . .'

'Of course, Andy. And we've allowed you to film today, without a facility fee . . .'

'Yes, but while we're very grateful for that, there's no way such a generous gesture alone will substantially help funding.'

'No, no, I understand. I'm not playing games, Andy. We are sincerely interested in contributing sizeably towards your film. But I still have to make sure the arrangement is endorsed by our board, which meets next week. We have to be sure the film is what they want. One detail which might stand in your way is the possibility of this controversial new theme park being opened.'

'And where do you stand on that?' Kate was openly listening now.

'In principle, I am personally opposed to the theme park. I think we do a good enough job here of describing the history of the area. But it seems that Malcolm Hodgson, the councillor who has been suggesting this, and who intends to vandalise fascinating local buildings like Skirlbeck Barn, just to make a leisure site, is gaining ground. If his proposal wins the day, your video will be outdated.'

De Salas looked horrified. 'But, Paul . . .'

'Of course, if you can guarantee me that any film you produce will be utterly positive about the area, ignore any crazy plans, and include the Tourist Centre . . .'

'I don't think we can do that,' Kate said, her own voice seeming loud enough to stop the clinking of cups and saucers. 'We need some editorial control. We can't have any local group dictating what we film.'

'Oh, Kate,' de Salas sounded appalled. 'That's all very well in theory. But in practice, Paul, I think we should come back next week and get even more shots of the Tourist Centre. And perhaps a few "pieces to camera" with you. In fact, maybe you should introduce the film . . .'

'Steady on!' Pym seemed to be laughing kindly at the younger man.

Kate said nothing more to de Salas, although she was quietly horrified at the thought of yet more footage of the Tourist Centre, and the transparent way Andy was trying to appeal to Paul Pym's vanity. If Andy intended to make nothing more than a promotional video to show at the

Tourist Centre and to sell at the mill, it didn't matter who was featured on the film, or what their motives were, or even what they paid. But if Rural Rides wanted to win a slot for the film on proper TV, it was vital that they were not 'bought' by any vested interest. And to fund a film like this, a broadcast slot was vital.

She thought perhaps Pym understood more than de Salas. He seemed amused. He caught her eye with a benevolent smile, and she thought of her meeting the next day with Channel Four. She had promised Ruscroft violence and dark rural activities – and she had promised herself a good programme, with an objective look at an area which fascinated her. There was no way that would square with these latest developments. She felt like running away from the whole complicated mess, until she saw from the window the fresh blue sky beating back the clouds, and the hill rolling down to the town.

'Let's pop out for a little walk,' she said to de Salas, after Pym had suddenly leapt up to greet a large lady in a tweed coat who seemed to be something to do with the local art group. 'It's clearing up.'

The changeable west coast weather was blowing the grey pad of clouds away, and more stone-washed strips of blue sky were appearing. De Salas followed Kate to the edge of the paved terrace at the back of the house, where the view was not so dramatic, looking into the back streets of the town beneath them. Rather than tackle de Salas head on, Kate tried the non-confrontational tactics he appeared to favour. She said gently, 'Did June tell you I want tomorrow off, to go back to London?'

'Yes, she did. I'm not thrilled about it, but we'll manage.' Kate controlled her annoyance, thinking that de Salas could hardly object after disappearing for a day himself. But she resisted the temptation to be provocative, and said instead, 'Thanks, Andy. I'll be back on Saturday anyway. My boyfriend is coming for the weekend so I hope we'll travel up together. Did June tell you why I was going back to London tomorrow?'

'No, but then we haven't had much time to talk.' I bet not, if you've been in bed two nights running with my friend Liz, thought Kate, glancing speculatively at his less than perfectly shaved face, and his haggard, handsome eyes.

'Andy, I've managed to get an audience with an acting commissioning editor at Channel Four. Don't build your hopes up, but he's quite interested in the film.'

'What?' De Salas turned away from the view to stare her in the face. His eyes were sparkling and she could see colour coming into his cheeks. 'Really? A real TV slot? Oh, that's excellent. Excellent. That's the sort of thing Ben could pull off. When are you going there?'

'Tomorrow at eleven thirty. But don't expect too much, Andy. Remember, the days are gone when Channel Four bought anything just because it sounded different, at the whim of the commissioner. The chap I'm seeing is called Hugh Ruscroft . . .' the name clearly meant nothing to de Salas, ' . . . and there's just one proviso.' She tried as clearly and calmly as she could to indicate that Ruscroft's interest depended on the inclusion of some element of the dark and violent. 'He only got excited when I mentioned that there were some facets of country life that weren't from the diary of an Edwardian lady. And I think he's got a point, though I didn't like his salaciousness. I mean, there *is* a dark side to all this.' De Salas's brow was wrinkled; he was genuinely perplexed.

'What?'

'Well, there are rumours about dogfighting – have you heard about this? Illegal rings of sadistic gamblers?'

'I'm sorry, Kate, I haven't. Doesn't sound likely to me. And anyway, what would that have to do with rural regeneration?'

'Not much, on the face of it. But if it gets Ruscroft interested . . .'

'But it's not what the film is about, is it?'

Kate sighed. How could she explain to him that his film would be monumentally boring if all he did was interview people about their own achievements? He went on, 'Anyway, Kate, even if what you say is true, and we did put in touches of the dark side of country life, as you call it, then Paul Pym won't even look at it, and we need his money.'

'No, but it might be a more honest film.'

'How can you say that! I've already told you, this is going to be a real examination of how a semi-rural society rallies in recession. That should be enough for anyone.'

'Oh, come off it, Andy. In this day and age? People want more than a few sepia shots of basket weaving.'

He turned away from her to look at the streets below. Even on a bright Thursday morning, the rainswept, shiny pavements of the town were hardly bustling. It would take more than tea shops and woollen mills, commendable as they were, to revive it.

'Anyway,' de Salas said crossly, 'how would we do it?'

'Well, I've met a local clergyman who might help . . . and perhaps someone who knows about the dogfights would be interviewed anonymously . . .' she had a vision for a moment of Malcolm on TV, back to camera and silhouetted, telling his son's story.

'It's ridiculous Kate. Lady Marshall would pull out.'

'Well, at least consider making a film about the dark side of life here, a sort of antidote to the usual country idyll . . .'

'I can't, Kate. It isn't what I want to do. I appreciate your help, and I want you to see Ruscroft and try to sell the idea to him. I know we need the funding. But I'm not prepared to spoil my film. My film is about rural regeneration.'

'Look, Andy, don't be too hasty. Everyone in TV has to compromise. You aren't John Pilger. This isn't some major work of art. Think about it, when you're not so tired.'

'And what the hell do you mean by that?' De Salas turned back angrily.

'Nothing. You just look tired, that's all.' She realised, suddenly, where his anxiety was coming from. 'I'm sorry, Andy, I wasn't making knowing remarks about you and Liz.'

'I beg your pardon?' Instead of irritation his whole manner now stiffened into wary hostility. Oh God, thought Kate, he didn't know I knew! I've done what I promised Liz I wouldn't do!

'It might be best for everyone, Kate Wilkinson, if you minded your own business.' The juvenility of the phrase did nothing to lessen the aggression she sensed like heat, as he leaned towards her. Then he seemed to realise what he was doing, and stepped back, shaking his head like a confused dog. He paused a moment, expecting Kate to react with equal anger then, when she didn't, went on, 'Look, I'm grateful you're seeing Ruscroft, don't get me wrong. But I don't see how we can make what he wants.' He plunged his hands into his pockets and took a few steps nearer the edge, as if assessing the drop below them. 'As for Lizzie and me, we'll sort things out. I suspected you knew. Did she tell you?'

'No,' replied Kate, truthfully.

'You worked it out?'

'I saw her in your car.'

'Oh. Did you talk to her about it?'

'Yes, a bit.'

'Did she tell you about what happened?'

'Yes.' Kate was slightly puzzled, looking at de Salas's twisted features and wondered for a moment if he meant something more than an affair. But he was saying, 'I'm sorry for being so rude. I really didn't mean to snap.' But you might snap in another sense, thought Kate. For a second she was tempted to reach out and stroke his arm. He seemed now like a baffled boy, with all of these conflicting pressures piling up on him.

'Come on,' Kate said cheerfully, 'let's go back in. I know you'll get some lovely shots of that conservatory. Now the sun's out, there's some stained glass showing up beautifully. I think it must be original, it's over in the far corner. Did you spot it? It will look really pretty now.'

'Oh, I'm not sure it would work.' De Salas was too proud to accept her suggestion, but Kate could tell he was intrigued. He loved the images, Kate thought, but couldn't bind them together. She followed him back to the house, where the sunlight, dappled in gold and scarlet on the conservatory floor, was as beautiful and unfocused as he was.

At lunchtime, she walked outside again, drawn by the sunshine which was bright and wintry and strong now, but still very shiny on the lingering wet puddles in the stone work of the terrace. It really was a beautiful location. She had been looking over the sea when she sensed someone beside her and had been astonished to see, out of the corner of her eye, that it was Pym.

'Gorgeous, isn't it?' he said conversationally. 'I imagine the sea captain, when he grew old, looking out here at the white sails beating down to Whitehaven. Once, all of Britain was linked more effectively by coastal shipping than by any planes or railways. Years ago, I even met an old lady from Workington, who remembered going Christmas shopping in Liverpool by packet boat, before the first world war. What price motorways!' What he said was fascinating, but Kate was more interested in why he was saying it.

'Did you want to speak to me about anything in particular, Paul? I thought you seem to be producing yourself very effectively this morning.'

'You're very direct, Kate.'

'I hope so.'

'Well, I really came out here to congratulate you. De Salas is a very febrile young man, talented but diffused, you know, and when Ben Lowe was injured I'm sure several people were wary about Andy being able to cope. I really did think he needed a father figure. But you've got him working well.'

'I'm surprised you say that. I hardly feel as if I have done anything.'

'You've made him discipline himself, Kate. And you probably don't realise how much you keep him moving along. When he came to recce this place last week, we spent all morning just in the chartroom.'

'All I do is look at the location plans and the notes on the interviewees the night before, and then organise the order and the content.' And some times, I don't even do that very well, she thought, remembering the overnight distraction she had experienced recently, thanks to a mixture of Malcolm Hodgson and the twins' domestic drama.

'Well, take it from me, it's going better than many people would have thought. The key thing though, Kate, is to get the tone right. We need to be positive about the area. There has been too much downbeat, defeatist rubbish written and broadcast about it. We have to talk it up.' That's fair enough, Kate thought. She smiled back at Pym, who seemed almost youthful with his hair blowing across his face. He was looking at her with real attention.

'Why don't you pop over to the Centre for lunch one day next week, without Andy? I'd love to talk the message of the film through with you. I can see your point you know. I'm not really narrow minded.' He leaned down and patted her hand with a soft, smooth touch, and Kate knew she was feeling flattered despite herself. Yet Pym had the air of bestowing a secret favour on her which made her feel a completely new and surprising loyalty to de Salas.

'Thanks,' she replied, hoping she didn't sound ungracious. But the possibility of her refusing had obviously not occurred to him. He nodded and turned away, then paused.

'I've just remembered what I came out for! A Sally Dodds has called you. My secretary has the number.'

'Great.' Kate felt her smile broaden. Sally, the luscious girlfriend of Clifford Thompson, the media lecturer and farmer's wife-to-be, was good news. She walked briskly up to the house, and the phone.

Kate would have loved to have seen Sally for a drink that night as Sally suggested, if she hadn't been so desperate to get back to London. Another evening in the company of Malcolm Hodgson might take her too far. But an evening in West Cumbria without him, wondering whether or not he would phone, would be torture.

That morning Kate had listened to the twins making final preparations for the following day's funeral, which she would not be able to attend. Kate felt they were masking their concern over their mother's death with frenetic discussions about vol-au-vents and sherry supplies. Fond as she had become of them, she was glad she would miss the intensity of the funeral day. She had asked them if she could bring John Maple back with her on Friday night. After all, she had arranged a weekend in Cumbria with John, and she was still committed to the plan. They were thrilled and excited, giving her a tiny window of attention between arguing about whether to serve gateaux with pouring or double cream, and if mints with coffee would be too 'gay' for the occasion. She smiled at their choice of words and wondered what John would make of them.

So when she phoned Sally Dodds back, she was sure there was no way she would find time for them to meet. 'I'm going straight over to Newcastle airport this evening, to catch the seven thirty shuttle, Sally. I'm leaving here a bit early, just before five.'

'So you'll be coming through Carlisle?'

'I suppose so.'

'Are you getting a taxi over?'

'Yes. It's costly, but June, our production manager insists. She's thrilled because I've got a meeting tomorrow with Channel Four to see if they might buy our film.'

'Oh, well done.' But Sally was clearly thinking of something else. 'I was wondering, Kate, why not get your taxi to drop you at the station? If you like, I'll pick you up and drive you over.'

'That's very kind. Listen, I don't want to be rude, Sally, but why are you going to such trouble?'

'To be honest, it's because I want some professional advice. And before you ring off, I'm not after a job. I just want to talk something through . . .'

Kate had only met Sally once. But she had been impressed with the young woman's relaxed confidence and sense of belonging. Sally had seemed to her to be the perfect example of someone at home in her own world. Now, though, she sounded dislocated.

'Well, OK, that would be nice. I hope I can help you.'

'Even if you can't, I'd like to talk to you.'

'OK, see you about five fifteen. But you must be there, Sally. I can't afford to miss this plane.'

John Maple would be meeting her at the airport. She had phoned him to say she was coming home. She had been unsure whether he was pleased, or vexed at having to reorganise his Thursday evening. He had not sounded warm. But he had promised to be there to pick her up.

At four forty five that afternoon, Kate tiptoed away from the shoot, taking just enough time to signal goodbye to June. 'I'll call you to let you know how I get on at Channel Four,' she whispered, and then she stepped out into the dusk. She felt as if she was on the run, as the taxi with its silent driver sped to Carlisle.

Sally was waiting at the station. She was still a glowing picture of health, but she was frowning anxiously, peering at the cars as they drove into the forecourt.

'Hi,' she said, as if they had been friends for years. 'Hop in to my Volkswagen.'

It took Sally about ten minutes of concentration to drive through Carlisle, over the River Eden Bridge and on to instant country roads, along what Kate thought must be the locals' route towards Newcastle. They were at the Brampton by-pass before Sally really started to talk, and Kate thought wryly that here was another fraught trip across the Pennines. But while Sally was as tense as de Salas had been on that first journey from hell, her driving was a model of calm.

'So what is it that you wanted my advice on, Sally?'

'It's a technical matter, really.'

'Technical? I hope I can help. Producing at my level isn't really a very technical job. It's more like organisation, linked with a sort of theoretical knowledge of what's technically possible. But I'm not up to speed with things like computer editing and digital recording.'

'Hold on a minute, that's light years ahead of me! Probably anyone with a bit of operational know-how could help me, but the reason I want to talk to you is that I don't want to discuss it with anyone locally.'

'What's your problem?'

'Well, a neighbour of ours died recently. Last night, I went over to his farm with my mam, and Cliff's mam, to help sort things out.'

'You wouldn't mean Tom Flint, would you?'

'Yes, that's right. Oh, yes, of course, you were there when we first heard about it, weren't you? Well, me and mam went over there to help out, as you do.'

Do you? thought Kate.

'Anyway,' Sally went on, 'we did all the usual bits, sorting out clothes and things, and then Mary asked me if I would look at the video machines. Plural. You see, normally anything like that would be taken care of by the menfolk, but as far as Mary Flint is concerned, I do men's work, in TV. Anyway, she asked me to have a look. And I couldn't understand it. You see, I thought Tom knew nothing about media. Once he wanted to get a satellite dish. He was a bit of an innocent in some ways, old Tom, and he'd heard about the cartoon network. He loved the idea of it. But I couldn't get it into his head that the dish wasn't a satellite, and that he needed a decoder and a smartcard. And here in the old still room next to the milking parlour, were two video machines and a monitor. And one VHS tape. When I picked it up, it wasn't like an ordinary VHS tape. It had like a sort of square section in it where normally the reel would be.'

'Well, there's no mystery about that. You can buy those from lots of electrical suppliers. Loads of people who have video cameras have them. You can put the tape from the camcorder into the VHS tape case, into the square bit where the ordinary reel of tape would have gone in. Then you play it like an ordinary video tape. And you can dub from this on to another VHS tape. That's how people make copies at home. Your friend Flint must have been dubbing off versions of his holiday video.'

'Old Tom Flint never took a holiday. More to the point, he didn't have a camcorder.'

'I see. Strange.'

'Yes. I mean, you have to be keen to go in for that sort of thing, don't you? I mean, I know we have a camcorder at college and the students make their own films, but we have an operations assistant who dubs the tapes on to professional standard beta tape and then we cut them the conventional way.'

'So you never have to deal with domestic VHS, the sort

most people with video cameras use?'

'No. Why should I? That's why I hadn't a clue what this set-up was for. Well, I did have a clue, in that I guessed it was for some sort of reproduction. But I wasn't sure.'

'Well, maybe old Flint was pirating copies of Snow White. Or maybe he had a nice line in duplicating off-colour movies.'

'Then why the tape holder for tape shot on a video camera? I doubt Tom Flint would be *shooting* blue movies. He wouldn't know one end of the camera from the other . . . nor one end of the participants from the other, if I know Tom.'

'Well, wouldn't Cliff know what was going on?'

Sally went quiet. 'That's my problem. I'm not sure whether or not Cliff does know something . . . or suspects something . . . but he's not telling me. It's really wrecking things between us. And I'm frightened. Say they are all involved in some sort of pornography?'

'Well, you know these people, Sally. Is it very likely? Be realistic. You can hire soft porn from a video shop anywhere. Can you imagine the farmers of Skirlbeck being into something more sexually sophisticated than the sort of thing you can buy openly? I mean, what would Tom Flint know about, that some sleazy London porno director wouldn't?'

'You've got a point. But then what the hell's going on? You're sure that these video playback tapes for camcorders are common? And with two machines you'd assume that they were making copies of tapes?'

'Yes. I mean, I'm not a technocrat, but I know one or two people who work in TV facilities, and I've heard about this. The only explanation seems to be that Flint *was* making copies of something, something shot by a camcorder locally.'

'Or that Flint was letting someone else do it. You see Kate, that was the other strange thing. I rang Mary Flint this morning to say that the college would buy the video machines off her. She already had their normal video under the telly in the parlour like everybody else, and she hardly ever used it, so she wanted rid of the other two. She had no idea why Tom had them. But when I called, she went over to the outbuildings to look at them to tell me the specifications, and they'd gone.'

'Gone?'

'Yes. The old still room was part of the buildings rather than part of the farm house, and you could get through to it from the milking parlour. And you could get into the milking parlour from the yard. Their dog died in the summer, and for some reason Tom didn't get another, so no dog would bark if someone just walked in and took the machines away. Perhaps they thought Mary would never know the machines were there. I mean, she only went into the still room, because when we were sorting out the old clothes she couldn't find Tom's cap.'

'Pardon?'

'His cloth cap. Mary was going mad about it, the way people do about trivial things in the middle of a major crisis. Tom always wore a cloth cap and Mary couldn't find it. She was frantic. She said that even if Tom was going to shoot himself, he would have come in and hung his cap on the peg in the hall. Mary had been in Cockermouth shopping when it happened and when she got back the police and the ambulance were already there, and she had been completely flustered, but afterwards she was demented about the cap. Mam and I just listened. But then she said Tom had been in the still room a lot lately and she was going down there to check. And that's when she saw the video machines.'

'Well, whatever it's all about, Sally, your best bet surely is to have another go at Cliff. If you tell him you're just curious, instead of being uptight . . .'

'Yep. And now I'm sure in my own mind what it was for, I'll put it to him straight. You see, when I suspected that some of the lads were duplicating films – blue films – it made me sick to think Cliff was involved in that. But you're right, they must have been filming something themselves, and I can't think what that could possibly be. Perhaps it had nothing to do with old Tom; perhaps he just lent them his buildings. But then why is Cliff so touchy? And the machines disappearing . . . that strikes me as odd.'

'Me too. But I can't throw any light on that.'

'Hey, I don't expect it. I can't tell you how relieved I am just to talk about this with someone who isn't going to spread it all round Carlisle Auction Mart. I'll get the truth out of Cliffie this weekend. If he doesn't tell me, sexy films may be the nearest he gets to the real thing!'

Kate smiled. But on the plane to Heathrow, she realised that Sally knew nothing about Tom Flint's more sinister hobby. There was no way Kate could have broken her promise to Malcolm and repeated the story. But she thought of the way Flint's dog had died, and shuddered.

John Maple was smiling as she came down the escalator into an arrivals lounge at Heathrow which was teeming and boiling with hundreds of people. Kate felt that the sheer anonymity of it was like liberation. She pushed past a family of Hindus, was elbowed out of the way by three Essex girls back from Las Palmas, and tripped over the briefcases of a group of supersmart business men, but she could have kissed them all. Instead she kissed John. He was wearing his clerical collar, which always made her feel uncomfortable, but she clung to him, more to make sure she wasn't swept aside by the human tide than out of love.

'You look shattered,' he said kindly. But, even as she held him, she was aware that he smelt different from Malcolm Hodgson. The thought made her guilty and guilt made her irritable.

'I'm fine.'

'You look as if you haven't been sleeping too well, Kate. I hope you're coping.'

'What's that supposed to mean?'

'Nothing. Calm down.'

'Don't you be so bloody patronising. I *am* calm.'

'Sorry.' He had taken her bag and trudged a little in front of her. He looked sad rather than cross. She caught him up.

'I'm sorry too, John, and you're right, I'm tired. It's good to see you.' He didn't reply, being parted from her for a moment by a family of half term holidaymakers squawking and flapping past like a flock of bright parrots. She saw him on the other side of them, drab in his navy coat, the white collar peeping coyly through from under his scarf. He was tall, nice looking in a gentle way, with his brown wavy hair, and his face was still healthy with smile lines etched round his mouth.

He had been a golden boy in his youth, the grammar school scholar destined for great things, a rugby player and local hero who, even when he had entered the church, had been treated like a star. But his wife had left him, after ten years of feeling she was being tugged in his wake. John had described his own state just before this trauma as a mixture of complacency over his wife's support, and growing confusion over his role as a clergyman. He had wanted to do something dramatic to affirm his faith and when he had suggested taking a parish in Central London, caring for the homeless, to his astonishment, his wife had left.

He had been stricken with guilt over taking her co-operation for granted. He had been agonising over his own soul without even granting her the status of a soul in her own right, and not only had his pride and his domestic peace been shattered, he realised that his love for her had been no better than proprietorial. When he had met Kate, it was her independence that he treasured. He loved the sudden, unexpected moments of companionship despite their varying views, like the moments when they came home to a dark house and he turned on the light and saw her there; their smiles over a cup of coffee; or when she spontaneously took his arm in the street, or they both burst out laughing. They had laughed a lot when they had first met, but these days he sensed she was disappointed in him.

And he was becoming angrier. What was he supposed to do? Sometimes he felt Kate was taking a stance just to goad him, and what was the point in that? The last thing he wanted was to row, to be seen as trying to impose his views on her. It was essential to his view of himself as a good guy that Kate felt no pressure to be his.

He looked at her starting to move through the crowds towards the airport doors. She had not caught his eye. For the first time since they had met, he did not feel a reassuring sense of delighted surprise that they were in a select club of two. There had been times when his chief source of joy was Kate's evident amazement that they had anything in common at all, those moments when she would look at him and beam or wink, communicating the secret knowledge that this unlikely couple really worked.

'Kate?' he called.

She turned round, startled and hopeful. But he didn't know what he was supposed to say.

'We'll need to get a cab. They're over there. There's a long queue.'

'And I suppose you need to jet back for Bible class or something?'

'No. Actually I've booked my long weekend from tonight. I thought you might like an Indian take-away and a bottle of wine.'

'Great.' But Kate was wondering if Sally's information meant she should contact Malcolm Hodgson. And even as she realised, with a twist of weakness and guilt that her motive was not to help Sally, but to find an excuse for ringing Malcolm, she was saved from eye contact with John by his rooting distractedly through his pockets to find his diary.

'Kate, I'm really sorry. You reminded me. I *should* call in on one of the kids who comes to the youth club. I'd forgotten I said I would. She's got problems with her stepfather. I'll just get the cab to drop me off. They just live round the corner and it will only take an hour. You order the food. I'll be back by ten.'

'Fine.' Of course it was. You would have to be a truly selfish bitch, Kate thought, to resent a priest's visit to a teenager with problems. But she was working on it.

By the time John came back at twenty past ten, she had talked herself up into a fine state of grievance. She knew her tetchi- ness was also owing to the fact that she had phoned Malcolm Hodgson, her stomach churning at this first call to his home, and that he had not answered. She wondered where he was, as the phone rang out. But then she heard John's key in the door, and put the phone down with a flutter of panic which made her annoyed with herself. There was no reason why she shouldn't tell John at least *something* about Malcolm. After all, it was an interesting story and John might even have helpful ideas.

But it was too easy to talk lightly about other things. And within minutes her hesitation hardened into concealment. It was the first evening they had ever had where Kate felt uninvolved. She no longer cared about winning John's attention back from the preoccupations of his parish, and she was surprised at how easy it was to hide her real thoughts under a layer of small talk. They talked desultorily about the last week without saying anything. And then it was time to go to bed.

She found the same strategy worked there too. It meant no great tide of passion, in fact her own climax was non-existent. But John fondled her a little, and then made love to her, and it seemed to work for him, as if he was too tired and harassed by his own job to worry whether Kate was there in body rather than spirit. And did he even realise? She doubted it. For Kate, the last memory of the day was the North West Cumbria Tourist Centre, white but stark, its Victorian battlements fretted against the grey clouds. She rolled around a little, uncomfortable, before falling deeply asleep.

John lay there, neither pretending to be asleep nor

wishing to communicate. He was not insensitive, and he too thought about a house. It was his own and he felt as if he had come home and all the lights had stayed off. It was the darkest night he had had for a long time.

Chapter Eight

Kate looked out of the window and thought that London reminded her of the sandwich she had seen stuck to the pavement when she got out of the taxi the night before. The area had a squashed look and the sky was like the off-white bread, with the crowded roofs and dirty bits of foliage reminiscent of the greasy, flattened centre which had been oozing out. She turned round and looked at John's bedroom. He was renting the house while he was helping Father Marcus and had done nothing to enhance it. Last night's Indian meal hung indigestibly somewhere around her ribs, which was why food was on her mind. She had slept, but not well. John, who usually woke early, had drifted off in the small hours and now lay asleep, but with a tense, unhappy face. She realised she dreaded him opening his eyes. She wanted to talk, yet she couldn't bear the dull, unnatural chat of the night before.

Kate turned and looked out in the other direction, down a crack between a block of flats and a garage, towards the high street's encrusted Edwardian façades, crammed against the modern, glossy, impermanent offices. Today was Jean Robinson's funeral. And the second day of the shoot with Paul Pym at the Tourist Centre. In Cumbria, events would go on, whether she was there or not. Of course the fact she was a novelty character, arriving from outside into a circumscribed world explained her feeling of centrality. But now she was back 'down south' she wondered if perhaps she had been imagining her own importance. She tried to recapture the sense of escape she had felt arriving at Heathrow airport, but it had gone. For all its fears, everything stimulating about her life seemed to be up in Cumbria.

John stirred and woke, and then instantly set his face into the sort of neutral expression she realised he'd been wearing since her arrival. He said nothing.

'John, are you still coming back up to Skirlbeck with me this afternoon?'

He heaved himself up, one naked shoulder rising from the duvet. She had used to feel instantly attracted to his shoulders, which were broad but thin. She still felt an almost objective pleasure at his body, which had none of Hodgson's overt heavy strength, but which was both lithe and protective, the flat span of his chest with its ridge of tiny hairs as welcoming as ever. Then she remembered the night before and the sex by numbers they had had for the first time, and deliberately looked for the bad things. She noticed the beginning of creases in his skin and thought of Liz's joke about the wrinkly peach. Liz's graphic description of sex with an older man made Kate draw depressing comparisons. John reached for his glasses to read the alarm clock.

'Hold on a sec, Katy, I'm just coming round. Good morning. Will you make the tea or shall I?'

'I will. In a minute. But I've got to get dressed and get out soon. I still want you to come to Cumbria with me. We really do need to get away for a few days. You do think it's a good idea, don't you?'

'Yes . . . Yes, I do. But only if you want me to, of course.'

'What's that supposed to mean?'

'Nothing Kate. I'm looking forward to it. But I don't want to get in your way.'

'I hope that's what you mean. And not that you've suddenly remembered a pressing engagement with another lame duck.'

'That's unkind Kate. You're letting yourself down, saying something like that.'

'But it's true, isn't it?'

'Not really. But I don't want to argue about it. Can you put some toast on? I need to shower and get to the church school for a PTA meeting at ten.'

She left him and mooched into the cold little kitchen. Half an hour later, on the Tube, she realised they had hardly spoken since, other than to arrange to meet at Euston in good time for the train. John had refused to fly north on grounds of expense, but Kate felt she could hardly bear the tedium of a five hour rail journey, sitting next to him, saying nothing.

She had not been entirely honest with John earlier that morning. There had been no rush to get to the Channel Four building in Horseferry Road. She left the Underground at St. James's Park and wandered down towards the river. Then she found a typical London coffee shop, utterly cosmopolitan and un-British, and went in, looking at the enormous array of fabulous filled rolls and ciabatta bread with every imaginable filling piled against the glass. They were all crispy fresh but she remembered the dead sandwich of the night before and felt slightly sick, overwhelmed by the cornucopia spilling over in the cabinet. She took her cappuccino from the swarthy man in the waistcoat behind the counter, aware that she hadn't seen anyone even vaguely foreign looking in the last week, and sat at the little table against the wall in the narrow corridor three feet from the counter that formed the cafe. She wondered how someone like Hodgson would feel there – probably no more out of place than she did. For the first time she experienced a sense of disorientation, although she had lived in London all her working life. She felt that she had suddenly been lifted out of a film in which she had a key role, and plonked down as an extra in someone else's production. The streets looked out of focus, and in contrast her thoughts of Skirlbeck were crisp and sharp, but jumbled like slides in a box. She tried to order them in a mental presentation.

What had really happened to Jean Robinson? Had her sons left her to die on that empty shore? And then there was poor, unstable Andy de Salas, too serious and naive to make sense of his tangled affair with Liz Jones, who was herself tortured over her desire to love him, love her family, and love herself. Kate still couldn't work out why de Salas had been so hysterical after their minor car accident. And what about the lack of money for Andy's film? Hopefully, she would help resolve all that if she was successful with Hugh Ruscroft at Channel Four. She glanced at her watch. She had three quarters of an hour to fill.

But to impress Ruscroft, she had to talk about the dog fights. Would she be able to communicate to a Channel Four sophisticate some of Hodgson's horror? Should she be trying? And where did Tom Flint and his video copying come into it? She remembered Sally's anxious face and resolved to talk to Malcolm about it.

Malcolm. What on earth was she going to do about him? It was a dilemma, and yet she knew that if the dilemma dissolved she would feel far, far worse. After the incident in the car, and his anger at seeing the dog fight gang tramp through the night bloated with aggression, his charm had vanished. He had been curt when he had dropped her back at the Skirlbeck Bridge Hotel.

The feeling that perhaps he did not desire her after all chilled her like the cold, drab wind from the river. How many opportunities would she have to sleep with someone like Malcolm? She tried to quash the treacherous little thought but it was as pervasive as the fetid wind from the Embankment.

'Kate! Kate Wilkinson! Fancy meeting you here!'

'Felix! Hi!'

Kate had hoped to bump into him. Felix Smart was one of Kate's oldest friends, though 'friend' was perhaps rather a strong word for the easy acquaintanceship they both valued more than they would admit. When she had first met Felix he had been almost too dashing for her to approach, a bright intellectual producer in current affairs with an Oxbridge education, but also boasting two years' apprenticeship on a newspaper, and a soft northern accent on top – the perfect wunderkind of the seventies. As time went on Felix had become much more of a style guru, abandoning journalism *and* his accent, firstly for the managing directorship of a largish independent TV production company and then for a very smart and lucrative job with a firm of City consultants. Yet he had always been honest, and Kate admired him for it. In return, he liked Kate and had stood by her through the ups and downs of her career. She knew he frequented the coffee bar. And suddenly, seeing him, her world slipped back into place.

'Oh, Felix, it's brilliant to bump into you!'

'Really? Steady on. I haven't met with so much enthusiasm since I ran into Dickie Attenborough in a traffic hold-up on Twickenham Bridge.'

'Felix! You didn't!'

'Right again. But you almost believed me.'

'Of course I didn't, you idiot. How are you? You look great! I'm just on my way to Channel Four.'

'Groovy. I never thought you'd become one of the Grade-style groupies angling for a commission. What happened to your lovely job in cable?'

'Still there, but resting for a month, so I'm working on a film for an independent company up in Cumbria.'

'Oh, yes, the project that pal of Liz Jones was doing. Is it OK?'

'OK? Well, yes, it is OK actually.'

Felix's laid back manner made Kate refocus. The Skirlbeck project was 'OK' . . . and that was all. She had an urge to hug Felix, then remembered that he might be able to help her unravel things, as well as put them back into perspective.

'Felix, I suppose you're busy at lunchtime today?'

'Yes, of course I am.'

'Oh well then . . .'

'Unless you've got lots of juicy gossip, Kate?'

'Not really. I'm on my way to see an acting commissioning editor about trying to get a slot for the film I'm working on. I've got pretty tied up in it. Too tied up really. But you might be able to help me with some background information.'

'Me?'

'Yes. I've met someone up there whom I think you know. In fact you put Liz Jones on to him. Paul Pym. Remember him?'

'Pym! Do you know, I'd forgotten he existed till Liz came to see me all of a tiswas and asked for contacts 'oop north'. Did that chap she was working with get hold of him? They say he used to be a bit of an operator.'

'Was he, Felix? Can you tell me more?'

'I don't know, but I'll try. I'm rather pushed right now. So you want to "do lunch"?'

'Yes,' she said bluntly. 'Though I have to be at Euston for three.'

'Fine,' Felix laughed. 'I see you're playing hard to get as always! Seeing as it's you, I'll change my appointments at huge personal inconvenience and book Shepherd's for one o'clock, and we'll see if we can spot any VIPs. Must dash.'

And as always he darted out of Kate's orbit in search of brighter stars. But that was Felix, she thought affectionately as he dodged between cars, smiling at the irate drivers as if bestowing an award for consideration. For an absurd moment he reminded her of Sally Dodd, so sure of himself in his own environment.

She stood at the bottom of Horseferry Road, watching the traffic, and thought for the first time of the real possibility of making a fool of herself with Hugh Ruscroft. There were too many uncertainties about the project. It would need sharpening up, and extending; and even if she was successful, and gained Rural Rides a Channel Four commission, the thought of battling with de Salas about his concept, while he constantly invoked Celia Marshall like a plump rural Muse, horrified her. A taxi went by with its yellow light vivid against the purply sky and the flat, cold, draughty embankment seemed bleaker than the west Cumbrian shore. She had a crazy desire to hail the cab and ask to be taken to Marks and Spencer's, Marble Arch, which was about as different from Skirlbeck as she could imagine. She felt exhausted, confused, drained at the thought of the interview ahead, and stupid and impulsive for fixing it up.

Perhaps there was no real reason to go ahead with it. De Salas's solvency was his own concern. Perhaps she should abandon the idea. Ruscroft would probably breathe a sigh of relief to be free of another supplicant claiming a great idea to revitalise British TV. And who knows, it might all be all right anyway. De Salas could go on making his comfy little movie, and maybe he might just get enough money from Paul Pym and Lady Marshall. Then if he was lucky he could see his project run on a loop in the technology room at the North West Cumbrian Tourist Centre. And Kate could work her contract out, forget Malcolm Hodgson's chilling stories and warm body, and come back to London. Then she could face up to the fact that she was going to spend the rest of her life with a vicar who could not talk to her for fear of fracturing their intellectual truce, and who preferred to spend his time in the safety of other people's problems.

The disembodied trilling of her mobile phone sent her first into a sort of freeze, and then scrabbling in her bag for the little instrument.

'Hello,' she breathed.

'Kate!'

'Yes?'

'It's me. June.'

'I'm sorry, there's some crackle on the line. Who is it?'

'June. June Ridley. Oh, Kate, can you talk?'

'June! Where are you?'

'In Paul Pym's office at the North West Cumbrian Tourist Centre.'

A truck veered close to where Kate was standing and splashed her shoes with filthy water as it belched past. The thought of June looking out of Pym's window over the shore made Kate long for the fresh tang of the sea. June was saying, 'I asked him if I could use the phone. But I didn't tell him why. Oh Kate, I don't know what to do.'

'Hold on, let me walk into this doorway so I can hear you properly. That's better. What's wrong?'

'It's Andy. He had a blazing row with Jerry about half an hour ago and he's walked off the shoot.'

'Andy? He's done what?'

'Walked off the shoot. I can't believe it, Kate. I just don't know what to do next. I'm sure it happened because you weren't there. You've no idea how much calmer he was when you were there to take responsibility too. Now we've no producer, no director and a cameraman breathing fire. I left Jerry taking GVs of the house from the front and came in here. I knew you'd be sensible enough to keep the mobile phone on so I could get you.'

Not quite, thought Kate, who had switched the thing off on the plane and could only assume it had turned itself on again, bumping around in her bag. At least that meant the batteries were still full of life. But she didn't enlighten June, who needed to believe Kate was coolly in command.

'Yes, well, I suppose that's what mobile phones are for.'

'And as you're the producer, I wanted to tell you before I did anything else.'

'Yes. You're right. Let me get my breath back. Look, June, don't panic. I'm sure you can manage the shoot this morning. The difficult bit was done yesterday and this is just a continuation. When is Andy likely to come back? I mean, what was it all about?'

'Nothing, really. Some stupid idea abut getting shots of light through the stained glass of the conservatory.' Kate smiled despite the drama. So de Salas had bought her idea after all.

'And what happened?'

'Jerry said it was far too dark a day and he should have done it yesterday when the sun was shining. Andy went berserk. He really did seem at the end of his tether.'

'Seriously?'

'Absolutely. This wasn't half an hour's histrionics, this was the real thing. I'm worried about him.'

'I'm more worried about the shoot. Has he abandoned it completely?'

'Well, that's what he said.'

Kate felt herself grow colder. She had not expected de Salas seriously to desert the project. Now she was shocked.

'That's ridiculous, June. Even if this film has been a pig to get together, there's been so much money and time invested in it already, de Salas must be out of his mind.' The words hung in the air, and Kate imagined them slow and heavy with implication, flapping like black ponderous birds. She wished she hadn't said 'out of his mind'.

'What are we going to do?' June's voice was trembling and Kate remembered the PA telling her how much she needed the money.

'Well, June, the director may have slung his hook and the cameraman may be behaving like a five-year-old, but there are two solid, experienced professionals on this shoot.'

'Pardon?'

'You and me, June. I'm the producer and theoretically in charge. And you're a bloody good PA, more than capable of holding the fort. We're not giving up on this film, June. You owe it to Ben Lowe and I owe it to myself.' And despite the mess Liz Jones seemed to be in, Kate owed it to her too. That meant saving de Salas from the consequences of his actions, but Kate was prepared to do that for the sake of her friend. And even as she was thinking it through, it occurred to her that de Salas's tantrum might be the answer to her own dilemma. 'Listen, June, you never know, if Andy wants to walk away from the film, we might be able to make something even better. I'll need to rake over the budget. And I think we should find out exactly what Ben Lowe knows, in his hospital bed. Let's get started.' Kate outlined to June what she thought that morning's agenda should be. 'And don't let Jerry and that blonde pixie he's married to think that the project is falling apart. Make sure they know where we're setting up on Monday and don't so much as allow a *hint* that things may be called off.'

'But where *are* we going to shoot on Monday, Kate?' June sounded fraught, but then controlled her shaking voice. 'I'm sorry, Kate, but I didn't know where to turn. I can't tell you how glad I am I've caught you.'

Kate felt a rush of adrenalin, as if the project was suddenly coming together in her hands. 'Come to my hotel at eight o'clock on Monday morning. We'll take it from there. And I'll have the people I'm staying with lay on coffee for all four of us while we pick up the pieces. By then, we might have heard what Andy's really playing at. My hotel is called the Skirlbeck Bridge. And June . . .'

'Yes?'

' . . . there's a man called Hodgson. Councillor Malcolm Hodgson.' She groped again for her Filofax. 'Here's his number.' She hoped June would never ask why she had it. 'Call him, officially, from Rural Rides and ask him to ring me on my mobile phone about possibly taking part in the film.' Personal feelings apart, the film would only work if Hodgson could be persuaded to talk.

'Fine, Kate, will do.'

'And most of all, June, keep your nerve.'

'Yes. Yes, of course. When will we see you, Kate?'

'I'll be back tonight. I'll phone you this afternoon anyway, to check out what's happening. You never know, Andy might turn up again, all smiles, once he's calmed down.'

'I don't think so. Not this time.'

Good, Kate thought suddenly, aware of a strange elation, as if she didn't want de Salas to change his mind. If he really had wilfully and destructively walked out on the project in that unprofessional way, it would be her film now, hers and June's, and she could put up a finger at Paul Pym and Celia Marshall, perhaps make something better than any of them had dreamed of.

'OK, June, I'll talk to you once I'm on the train. Keep going. It'll be all right.' Kate punched the phone into submission, and then turned and walked with new vigour up towards Channel Four.

It took her a few awkward turns to find the building which was even more startling when she came across it. It rose like a plastic package from the pavement with a phallic drawbridge suspended half erect across an impractical moat. Exterior lifts buzzed up and down, exposed occupants still shrinking in their coats, looking colder than the people outside. It was like a cross between the Pompidou Centre in Paris and the Lloyds building in the City, and like both of these the exterior revealed the privileged lives of those inside like an alien spaceship grounded in a hostile environment. Kate smiled at the multi-faceted shine of it, remembering the Scott Fitzgerald description of the wedding present for the bitchy lady – a cut-glass dish which was classy, expensive and as easy to see through as the bride.

She had never been entirely at ease at Channel Four. Even in its old headquarters up near Oxford Street, she had felt intimidated by the 'right on' receptionists and defeated by the queue of intellectual hopefuls waiting for an audience with a commissioning editor. Years ago, stories of their whims had been legion. Kate knew of one ITV producer who had been asked to sell a programme idea to a man whose pet rabbit was roaming round the room. She knew many submissions had to be made and few chosen, but so many were offered that the whole process was a demeaning lottery, and there were times when commissioning editors behaved like demigods in a world where their own judgment was the only criterion. She wondered what Ruscroft would be like, because despite all that, here she was, ready to pitch.

'Yes, through the turnstile and up to the first floor,' the receptionist said pleasantly, making Kate feel guilty for her resentful thoughts. She wriggled her way through the electronic gate, and into the lift, watching it rise above the dreary streets below. She emerged into a grey corridor, where a smiling woman waited.

'Kate Wilkinson? Follow me. Hugh's waiting for you. Tea or coffee?'

Kate's spirits rose further. The whole tone of the encounter looked as if it would be different from the dreary pleading session she had imagined. With luck she would be able to busk her way through, knowing now that she had a decent concept for Ruscroft, which could be tailored for Channel Four and unhampered by de Salas's precious vision. At the back of her mind she thought she ought to visit Ben Lowe in the Cumberland Infirmary and talk it through with him before making a final commitment, but she was sure that the older, wiser partner in Rural Rides would be delighted with what she was doing.

She strode into Ruscroft's office with new enthusiasm and for a moment she sensed the man's surprise at her confidence. But the moment passed as they focused on each other and took stock of what they saw. As she recognised him, Kate thought how odd it was that you remembered people for irrational reasons to do with the cast of their eyes or the shape of their jaw, something totally individual to that person. Of course she knew Hugh Ruscroft. He still had a funny little curl to his mouth, and the arrogant tilt of the head was the same, even though the hair had receded and the face was overlaid with jowls. He had been one of the older generation of news producers when she had started at LondonVision, but he had not been there for long after Kate joined, because to everyone's surprise he had left to take up an administrative post with the ITV Association. But before he went he had impressed a much younger Kate as one of the band of intellectuals who had gathered round the bar each night to put the world to rights, tolerating the occasional beautiful well-spoken woman and pretending to be David Frost.

'Little Katy!' he said expansively, rising from the desk, holding out one hand to grasp hers, and with the other raking his thinning, suspiciously dark crest of hair. 'It was only after your call I put two and two together and really remembered all about you.' Strange, thought Kate. She had only been a very minor, not so beautiful woman, a little awestruck at the edge of the crowd with half a pint of cider and a full measure of insecurity. And there had been no hint of personal reminiscence when Ruscroft had spoken to her on the phone. But she hadn't really remembered him either, she had just heard a bell tinkling weakly in her mind. And memories do come back. It was possible Ruscroft had thought about her, and then been able to place her. Twenty years in the same industry meant that what went round came round.

'Now do sit down, Kate, and outline this great idea for me.'

It was amazing, Kate thought, what a little bit of insider camaraderie did for you in the TV business. He was happy now because he could see they had the right sort of background in common. Heaven help anybody with a brilliant idea in Wakefield or Dudley, or Skirlbeck for that matter, who could not claim passing acquaintance with some courtier in the metropolitan in-crowd. She almost began to feel sorry for de Salas again.

'I've been working on something I think has amazing potential, Hugh. How would you feel about a film which showed a rural community dotted with small towns, deeply confused by its own identity, to the extent of a whole subculture reverting to the seventeenth century level of barbarism for its pleasure?'

Ruscroft nodded sagely, clearly impressed by her socio-babble. Then he licked his thin lips, smiled knowingly and said, 'And the barbarism?' It was reassuring to know these guardians of integrity were as salacious as anyone else. Kate smiled back, and began to tell him Malcolm's story, being careful to mention no names. As she built up the story, cosmopolitan Westminster began to fade around them and she knew she was using all her narrative powers to draw him. He leaned towards her, his mouth slightly open.

Yet there was something about Ruscroft's bated breath she found disturbing. Much as she wanted to intrigue him, the concentration he brought to bear was mildly disgusting. But there was no doubt he was interested. She paused at the most gruesome part of the story, almost for the mischievous pleasure of hearing him say eagerly, 'And what happened?' before having to rein himself back to his proper stance of reserved, objective interest. When she finished he said breathlessly, 'Fascinating, Kate. And just how would you fit this into your film?'

The phrase 'your film' gave her no cause for concern. From what June had just told her, that was exactly what it now was.

'We might need an extra week to shoot the whole project, but we've already got some very visually beautiful material showing the area with its mix of rural, small urban and coastal cultures. What I need now is a concentrated effort to get the right people talking to me about the dogfighting. I probably need a slightly larger budget to include a researcher.' She thought of Liz Jones or, if Andy's problems meant Liz was out of the equation, there was Sally Dodd. Suddenly the whole thing looked utterly achievable and she couldn't hide her excitement. 'We need to infiltrate a little more. I'm convinced we could perhaps even get some shots at a dogfight meeting.' Even as she was talking she was convincing and converting herself. Sally's Cliff would surely know something about the dogfight ring, even if he wasn't really involved (and for Sally's sake, Kate hoped he wasn't). Up in Skirlbeck, with the personal acceptance Kate thought she had won from everyone from the Robinson boys to Malcolm Hodgson, she was sure she could get the material. Ruscroft was leaning over the desk, and for a moment she suspected she could see a shining blob of spittle on his chin.

Then suddenly, abruptly, he stood up, pushing his modern metal chair back so it scraped horribly on the hi-tech floor. He turned away from her to the window, and she could have sworn he was actually getting his breath back. She knew her rendering had been exciting, but she was surprised at Ruscroft's violent reaction. As she watched his back she felt the tingle of triumph. He was going to buy it, she was sure. It was her turn to wait, but as she did, her imagination had already started planning the rest of the shoot. For at least thirty seconds he said nothing. Then, still with his back to her, he murmured, 'Well, Kate, I have to say it's an absolutely fascinating idea. But quite frankly . . .' he turned to smile at her now, looking more vital and enthusiastic than ever, but with a cruel sort of enthusiasm, the enthusiasm for his own power, ' . . . I don't think it would work. There just hasn't been enough research done for me to even think of commissioning it.'

'Sorry?'

'I'm not convinced, Kate.'

'But, Hugh, it isn't the sort of project you can go away

and research and then walk back into. For God's sake, I was just lucky enough to stumble on this when I was sitting in the area with a film crew. If I don't do it now, it won't happen. In a few weeks' time, I'll be back at my real job and my contacts will have disappeared. You can't turn it down just because I haven't brought you a beautifully typed treatment and sponsorship from Pedigree Pet Foods!'

'Now, Kate, you're being hasty. Look at it from my point of view. There just isn't any guarantee this will work.'

'I'm not asking you for twenty thousand pounds in a Tesco's bag *now*. I don't need a firm commitment immediately, and quite frankly I didn't expect one. I realise you have no idea that what I'm telling you is true, never mind obtainable on video tape and broadcastable. But all you need to do is say that you're really interested and that will give me the confidence to convince everyone else. You *know* it's a brilliant idea. And it's not just me. Channel Four has taken plenty of material from Ben Lowe before, and I'll be liaising with him as soon as I get back.'

'I'm sorry too, Kate.' He was treating her now with a sort of superior blankness, determined not to react to her arguments. It riled her even more than his rejection of her idea.

'Look, Hugh, with all due respect I'm very surprised, and I must say I'm very suspicious. You couldn't possibly be considering putting some of your own chums up to doing this, could you, now I've spilt the beans?'

'Kate! That's an outrageous suggestion. That reflects on the whole of Channel Four and if I thought you meant it I would ask you to leave now. In any event, I do have to move on. I have hundreds of ideas to look at.'

Kate felt herself rising to her feet. 'OK, but as soon as

Chrissia is out of hospital I'm going to tell her about this. You've missed out on something which could have been national news, *and* cleaned up a despicable trade in low grade terror. For God's sake, Hugh, on the most venal level look how cruelty to animals is a growing concern. Remember Shoreham? It's become fashionable now, for Christ's sake. Isn't that right up Channel Four's lift shaft, even if a decent reaction to a good idea is too simple for you? But if you don't want to know, there's nothing I can say.' As she spoke, she was aware that Ruscroft's eyeline had shifted slightly and that his expression had moved from exasperation through a cold stare of frozen horror at her impudence, to a sheepish look over her shoulder.

Kate turned to follow his glance. In the doorway, rather pale, and wound up in a heavy coat, scarf, and fur hat, was Chrissia Cohen, Channel Four commissioning editor for news features. She leaned a little dramatically against the wall, removed her heavy glasses, rubbed her eyes, happily conscious that everyone else's were on her, and said, 'Kate Wilkinson, as I live and breathe! If I do live and breathe after getting out of St. Thomas's! And Hughie, looking less cool than I've seen him since the time he danced with Magenta de Vine at the Christmas party. Let me unwind this scarf from round my ears so I can hear what's going on. Tell me, Kate, what are you doing here? No, don't answer; get me something to sit on. I feel as if my internal organs are about to leak all over the floor.' With a burst of raucous laughter she sank her bulk into the chair and went on, 'Christ, that's better! They called it a little scrape but it was more like a decoke. Embarrassed, Hughie? Gynaecology not your strong suit? Let's get some coffee.'

Ninety minutes later, in Shepherd's at lunchtime, Kate

sipped her very dry white wine and, pink with excitement told Felix how Chrissia had insisted on hearing the whole submission all over again.

'And, Felix, she loved it! You should have seen Ruscroft's face!'

'Well done, Katie. He was probably too scared of commissioning anything more adventurous than a straightforward war story with the requisite quota of bodies. Good old Chrissia. Now what would you like to eat?'

'Smoked salmon followed by fishcakes and sorrel, please.'

'I say, you must need to build your strength up. Or are you in training for a diet of tatie-pot and black pudding?'

Kate remembered Felix's mother lived in the north and gave him a cross look.

'Not at all, Felix. Don't be such an old snob. The food at the hotel where I'm staying would pass muster with any of you precious foodies. It's just that I'm into comfort eating at the moment.'

'I can see that. You look about as comfy as an old armchair, Kate Wilkinson, with the shape to match.'

'Felix! Don't be awful.'

'I'm not being awful. I'm your good friend and I'm telling you you look as if two weeks eating lettuce in a health farm would do you the world of good. I can see by your face that you're stressed out. Now tell Uncle Felix all about it.'

So Kate did. She said little about her relationship with John, although she did annoy herself by hinting to Felix that all was not well, but she said a lot more about Andy de Salas. And that took her on to the subject of Paul Pym.

'Felix, I seem to be bumping into an awful lot of ex-

LondonVision people, Hugh Ruscroft this morning, and then this chap Paul Pym.'

'Yes, but you must remember that thousands of people have worked at LondonVision over the last thirty years. Paul Pym must have been there a good ten years ahead of Ruscroft, who must be at least five years older than you. Pym was there in the thrusting investigative reporter days of early ITV, the first "World in Action", that sort of thing. He was a bit of a legend. On the other hand, I overlapped with Hugh Ruscroft but I don't remember him very well myself. He was part of that stale current affairs group in the eighties who harked back to earlier glory but never quite did anything as good. By your time, LV were making some decent programmes again, even if they were going out disguised as knitting manuals.' He was referring to the daytime programming where Kate had made her name. She was used to the disparaging way men referred to it, but at least Felix was bright enough to see its value.

'Thanks, Felix,' she said, not entirely sarcastically.

'In fact,' he went on, 'I would say Ruscroft is mid-forties maximum, and Pym must be getting towards his late fifties. The LondonVision Pym was at, and your LondonVision were very different.'

'Yes, but you're right about Pym's generation. He told me he was on "Inside Scope", so he can't have been a bad producer.'

'Quite the reverse. In fact I understand no-one ever knew quite why Pym disappeared from the scene.'

'Some sort of scandal?' Kate hoped she didn't sound eager.

'No, I don't think so. Or at least nothing very public. If I'm right, he inherited some family money and went off to be a squire somewhere. Or something like that. I never met Pym, but he was a bit of a legend. I heard all about him. We all did, although I never associated him with the north. But when Liz was getting worked up about her toy boy's project, I remembered reading about him in the LV newsletter. It said that Pym was doing something or other very worthy and local in the Lake District. So I suggested they got in touch with him.'

'Hang on, Felix, what did you mean by calling Andy de Salas Liz's toy boy.'

'Oh, come on Kate, it was obvious. She couldn't look me in the eye and she was all red-faced. And the last time I bumped into her and Steve it was like meeting a star and one of his researchers. I mean, Steve was so difficult and demanding. I couldn't see Liz putting up with that for much longer. She always had quite a lot of spirit. I almost used to fancy her myself. But then my heart always belonged to you, Kate.'

'Oh, Felix, pullease!' But Kate liked the flattery and the comfort of flirting harmlessly with an old friend. She had felt both pressurised and uncertain about her relationship with Malcolm Hodgson, and deeply unhappy at being taken for granted by John. So to have Felix wink elegantly at her over the cut glass brought a little more of a glow to her face.

'That's better,' said her friend. 'Now let me tell you all about this marvellous girl I've met. Do you think it matters that she's only twenty-eight?'

Kate laughed, at herself ruefully and at Felix for his incorrigible optimism. And they clinked glasses to something, though she wasn't sure what.

But in the taxi to the station she remembered another

incident she had forgotten to tell Felix, which made her little triumph at Channel Four even more worth savouring. Chrissia had hauled herself into the lift beside Kate, announcing that she had just popped in to see 'Hughie', who winced, before leaving to lunch with 'Michael' – at which Ruscroft winced even more – and would travel downstairs with Kate to see her out. Once in the sliding glass bubble, Chrissia used the opportunity for a good moan about Ruscroft.

'He wasn't really up to it, but I had to go in for the op rather suddenly and he was all I could get. And he has done it before.' She hooted with laughter again. 'Last time he commissioned that awful tedious rubbish on Bosnia, do you remember? Not a very original thinker, poor Hugh. But sound enough in a crisis.' The lift slid into the ground floor and Chrissia, walking with a melodramatic lurch but looking very spry, led Kate into the foyer. But, though Chrissia was a big woman in every sense, she was quite capable of exploiting her own status.

'Oh, shit! Oh, no! Kate, I've left my glasses upstairs. I don't want to hike back up there in my condition. I want to go straight on to meet Michael Grade at Bibendum – that's why I just *had* to get out of hospital today – and anyway I can't face traipsing upstairs and listening to Hugh bleat on about how he didn't mean to really turn you down. Would you be a sweetheart and pop back for me? I'll sink into a sofa in reception and nurse my ovaries.' Kate laughed, and turned back into the lift. She felt mildly embarrassed about bumping into Ruscroft again. But if Chrissia sent her for her glasses, then off she would jolly well go. A commission almost in the hand was worth it.

Upstairs, confused in the badly labelled ubiquitous grey

glass corridors that reminded her of being trapped in some sort of giant scientific phial, she took a wrong turn and found she was approaching Ruscroft's office from the other side, not through his secretary's room. The door was open. She stood there, looking at Ruscroft's back as he spoke heatedly into the telephone.

'And then she just walked back in, rabbiting about her bloody operation, and I gather she does mean bloody, when I'm right in the middle of the interview!' The person at the other end obviously interrupted to sympathise, then Ruscroft went on, 'Yes, well, she is a bit above herself, stupid cow. And you're right, it probably will pall. I'll have another go at her this afternoon when the other woman is out of the way . . .'

'Hugh?' Kate said softly. He spun round like a guilty lover. 'I've come back for Chrissia's specs. They're there, on her desk.' He put down the phone slowly, saying nothing to the person on the other end, and his mouth formed a perfect little pink O in his pale and puffy face.

Kate went on, 'It *will* be her desk again now, won't it? And I'll mention to her that you think she'll change her mind about my idea, when you talk to her. I'm sure she'll appreciate knowing that your good judgement will put her right.'

'Now look here, Kate, I didn't mean . . . I mean, I wasn't . . . I wasn't talking about you, actually. Which doesn't mean I think you should be prowling round listening to private conversations.'

'Fair point, except that you left the door open.'

Ruscroft collapsed into Chrissia's chair. 'Katy, I always thought your idea was a good idea. You know that. For goodness sake, it was me who invited you here this

212

morning. All I said was I needed more evidence. That was hardly asking too much was it? And it wasn't you I was talking about. This department does have other submissions coming in you know, and sometimes Chrissia takes irrational likings to very strange ideas. I've had a very fraught time trying to keep the place going for the last two weeks. Chrissia has a horrible habit of ringing from the operating table to check up on me, and she can change her mind like the wind. That was what I meant. But you *know* I liked your idea. And I'd like you to make sure she realises that. I have a feeling we would have got there in the end even if she hadn't turned up. So, no hard feelings, hey?' He smiled the smile she was sure he believed charmed the knickers off scores of Sloanes, and held out his hand. Kate looked at him, sighed, and shook it. There was no point in having a row about the situation now it had turned out so well, although she was sure Ruscroft had just been using her to exercise his petty little bit of power in the last few days before giving it back.

'OK, Hugh,' she smiled at his visible relief. 'Now I'll take the specs and go. And wish me luck with the film.'

'Er . . . good luck,' he said feebly, taking a tissue from his trouser pocket to wipe the sweat from his temples.

At Euston, John was waiting with her bag, and he made a huge effort to grin at her and hold out his arms.

'I really am looking forward to this, Kate,' he said. 'I'm sorry if I've been a little bit distant lately. Let's try and have a nice time together. And I promise my work won't intrude.'

'Yours mightn't.' Kate kissed him on the cheek with more enthusiasm than she had brought to their whole love-making the night before. 'But mine might!'

'What?' Did he look a tiny bit disappointed? She hoped so. And then he smiled and spontaneously let his finger drift over her lips.

'You're incorrigible, Kate Wilkinson.'

'What do you mean?'

'This morning you looked like a piece of cold Spam and now you're buzzing like nobody's business. I can always tell when you're excited.'

She laughed and pinched him on the arm. 'That too if you're lucky!'

He smiled and leaned forward, whispering conspiratorially so the two old ladies behind couldn't hear, 'I do want you, Kate. I'm going to try and forget all about work this weekend, and then perhaps things will be better in every way. I've been feeling harassed and preoccupied. Marcus has been so . . .'

'Useless, demanding, a pain in the bum?' she suggested. He laughed and shrugged at the same time, so that she realised he was reluctant to criticise another priest, but inclined to agree with her. He went on, 'I do realise I've been wrapped up in the parish, not given you enough time, been too involved . . .' Kate looked back at him questioningly. It wasn't the time spent at work that she minded. Most people became tied up at work at sometime or another. But John's work was his faith and his faith was his life. Not talking about his work meant not talking about his soul. It was different from accepting that marriage to a brain surgeon meant that you couldn't share major operations.

'Oh, John, I'm not intolerant of your work. How could I be? After all, I realise that I demand equal freedom myself. It's just that . . .'

'What?'

But she couldn't explain that because he chose not to argue with her, she was unconvinced of his need for her. It seemed truculent to say that if he really cared, he would discuss everything with her, passionately, instead of this cool, uncaring acceptance that they agree to differ.

Still, at least this weekend his tolerance could be put to good use as her own commitments were crowding in on them. And he had come as near as he ever had to trying to explain. For a moment she suspended judgement and pretended they were still as close as they had once been.

'At least because of that, John, I know you'll be good about the mess I've just found myself in.' He nodded, eyes on her, waiting. So she told him all about de Salas, the shoot, the weird relationship with Liz, all in a rush of enthusiasm, contrived at first and then becoming real. And John didn't let her down, smiling, nodding, pushing squidgy cartons of thick scummy coffee into her hand, and above all listening. She even mentioned the dogfighting business to him in a hushed voice as they stood on the concourse waiting for the barrier to be raised. It was like a boil bursting, she thought. And for a few minutes they were like they used to be, she chatty, laughing, telling him everything at once and he sympathetic and shrewd, thrilled by her enthusiasm and lit up by her companionship. Then her mobile phone rang again.

'This is Malcolm.'

'Oh. Yes. Hello.'

John felt her shift from him, physically and mentally. She took two paces backwards, and then looked awkwardly over her shoulder at him. He moved away too, aware that something was happening to ruffle the atmosphere he had just worked so hard to restore. But he could tell by the angle of Kate's jaw that without starting a fight, which he was absolutely determined never to do, there was nothing he could say. He trudged towards the train. Kate, for her part, felt hot with embarrassment and furious with frustration. She could hardly talk naturally to Malcolm Hodgson with John only yards away, and she was also convinced, irrationally, that John could hear everything Malcolm said, although her mobile phone was plastered to her ear. Guilt! she thought, at the same time desperately trying to catch what Malcolm was saying.

'A woman from your film crew rang me. She said you wanted to talk to me about your work.'

'Yes, thanks for ringing. Look, er, Malcolm . . .' she was whispering his name, but John had walked ahead, carrying the bags ' . . . I don't know if you would want to get involved, but I'm trying to change the nature of this weak little film we've been making. I wonder if you'd consider letting me use the dogfight story.'

'What?'

'Interview you, or someone, about the dogfighting.'

She realised as she was saying it that she was speaking too soon, that their friendship was far too fragile for what she was asking. She should have made an arrangement to see him formally, like she would have done with any other potential interviewee, and taken things far more slowly. The coolness between her and John had made her overestimate her closeness to Hodgson. How easily intimacy could dissolve, and how often it was a fantasy anyway! With the feeling that she had charged in and wrecked everything, she tried madly to remedy the situation.

'Please, Malcolm. Look, we need to talk about the theme park plans too. I've been left having to remake the film, and I want to broaden it out from an accolade to Celia Marshall.'

'But it's the dogfighting you really want to talk about, isn't it?'

Kate wondered whether to lie. She saw John, yards ahead, signalling her to get on the train. How much deceit could she cope with?

'Yes, you're right, it is the dogfighting I'm interested in.'

'For Christ's sake!'

'Now don't blow up, Malcolm. Think about it. All the information in the film could be from an anonymous source, and surely it would stop them? They'd be ashamed to show their faces if the business was aired on TV. It's perhaps the best way of getting to them.'

'But it would come straight back to me. You must think I'm a fool.' She could hear the harsh, surprised irritation in his voice, and knew he suspected her of violating his trust.

'Malcolm, listen, I haven't mentioned this to anyone and I know it isn't just you who suspects. There's someone else who's involved on the fringes too. Clifford Thompson. His girlfriend Sally has talked to me . . .'

'What do you mean?'

'Sally thinks Cliff's mixed up in it as well. Or mixed up in something. She doesn't know what.'

'Did you dare to tell her what I told you?'

'No, I just said that I didn't. You know I wouldn't.'

'Do I?'

'Yes! Malcolm, don't misunderstand me. Sally only knows that something strange was going on at Tom Flint's.' Kate realised she had not told Malcolm about the video equipment, but this was hardly the time to start explaining technical operations. John was waving at her more frantically from the open train door.

'Malcolm, I'm going to have to ring off shortly. Can I call you tomorrow?'

'I'm out tomorrow.'

'Listen, Malcolm, think about this. Don't just get angry. This is a way you could get even. No-one would ever know who spilt the beans, and the bastards who are doing it would be forced to stop.'

'How?'

'Because they'll be exposed on TV.'

'And you'll look like a clever little reporter, at my expense. Who do you think you are? Roger Cook?'

'Malcolm! That's not fair. You said yourself you wanted an answer. Couldn't this be it?'

'Having you poking your nose into the region's cesspit and telling the rest of the country what you've found floating there?'

'But, Malcolm, you said yourself this was just an aberration, in a fantastic place.'

'But that's not how it will come over, is it? This is where I live, remember? We don't want outsiders coming up here and muckraking.'

Kate paused. A prickly sensation of heat crept up on the back of her neck. Hodgson was right. She cringed inside as she thought of the way she had portrayed the area which she was growing to love and where she had accepted so much hospitality, with the avid gluttony for scandal that had aroused Ruscroft's prurient interest. Malcolm went on angrily, 'You're just one of those tabloid journalist bitches, aren't you? I should never have talked to you.'

'No, Malcolm, listen . . .'

But the phone had gone dead. Numbly she walked towards John who was standing with one foot inside the train.

'Hurry up, Kate!' he yelled. For a moment she felt like turning and running away and forgetting about the journey, escaping from him, from Malcolm, and from her own dishonesty. But John put his arm out to yank her into the carriage, and pulled her on board. The train shook, grumbled, and slowly eased its way forward, away from the platform, away from London, and on its way north.

Chapter Nine

At the Skirlbeck Bridge Hotel, Terry and Bill Robinson
looked with satisfaction at the wreckage of their buffet.

'Not bad.'

'No, not bad at all.'

With the peculiar synchronisation neither they nor any
one else could fully explain, they turned to each other at
precisely the same second and raised glasses of brandy
with an air of triumph. There was still, as always at these
gatherings, a spray of stragglers festooned round the
fireplace, people linked aimlessly in conversation who were
drifting towards going home with no real motivation, or
nodding sleepily in front of the fire. Ada, their mother's
friend and rival, nodded in dozy contentment with her teeth
dislodged in her slack jaw, deep in the big chair by the
hearth, the winner of the contest to live longest, as yet
unaware of the loneliness of her laurels. Two farmers who
had long since forgotten why they were there smoked,
scattered ash on the smouldering logs and discussed
fatstock prices. One of the Skirlbeck girls who helped out
as a waitress when there was a 'do' idly ate crisps from a
glass dish and stood on one foot then the other, her sweet
face twisted in the calculation of how to get half a smoked

salmon mousse into her carrier bag and home to her husband. The funeral was finished successfully, and Bill Robinson felt a surge in the veins of his temples, like a headache stopping, which meant the tension was over. The wave passed, and the tiredness followed. As always, he turned to acknowledge that his brother felt the same and, by the sudden look of release on Terry's face, the dropping of the cheekbones and the drooping of the eyelids, he knew they had made it through, together.

'Shall we get the girls to clear?' he murmured.

'Aye,' said Terry like a sleepy gnome. 'I'll call them. Good do, Bill?'

'I think so Terry. I think we can safely say that, now it's over.' And he smiled, not his usual smile, but with a relief completely at odds with grief.

It was nine o'clock. They'd come back from the crematorium at Carlisle at five. The initial stiffness, with the men in unfamiliar suits and stringy black ties hopping from foot to foot before the first dram, the women with hushed voices in little clusters, had relaxed into the inevitable exchange of nostalgia, and from there into the gossip about the present. By seven o'clock most mourners – guests, as the twins called them – had been relaxed enough to laugh without suddenly coughing to cover the embarrassment of a faux pas, and by eight the atmosphere of a party was in full swing. The twins were used to Skirlbeck funerals. But there had been an air of release about this one which was not due solely to the endless supplies of alcohol from the hotel bar.

At eight thirty Cliff Thompson's mother and father had left to go back to Gillfoot where their son was holding the fort and, like a breach in a dam, others had trickled after them until only the sediment was left. Now, Bill even felt relaxed enough to motion to Terry that they should park their bottoms on the bar stools, an almost unheard of informality for the Robinson brothers.

The banging at the door was enough to make Bill stumble from his perch, and Terry freeze. The noise had an urgency reminiscent of the night the police had called with the news of their mother's death. It made old Ada sit up, her eyes starting as if the last trumpet had sounded for her too. Even the farmers broke their chat for a few seconds.

'I'll go,' said Bill, but his twin followed him like a fair shadow through the hall. The door was on the latch, and Bill silently pulled it open.

'Reverend!' exclaimed Terry, looking over his brother's shoulder and out into the cold night with the droplets of mist as heavy as pearls in the misty air.

'Good grief!' Bill opened the door wider, although the man framed in the archway seemed shrunken, like a leaf blown against the step. 'Come in.'

George Goff almost fell into the hotel, his left hand inside the lapel of his old-fashioned mac and his right hand clutching his waist, his body hunched over as if he were cuddling into himself for more than warmth in the raw air. Behind him, twice as big, his wife Eileen stumbled forward, her handbag slung over her shoulder and a debonair Barbour rainhat leaning over one eye. Yet her expression was fierce. She spoke for her husband.

'Bill, Terry what can we say? George is devastated. We only heard about your mother when we got back from the retreat.' She was clearly younger and seemed infinitely bigger and taller, straighter and stronger than her husband, who was leaning against the wall. She looked at him anxiously.

'Retreat?' Bill said blankly.

'It doesn't matter.' George Goff had aged ten years. He spoke with uncharacteristic brusqueness and then with real weariness he crept quietly into the bar area like a tired lizard. Ada drooped again, and the two farmers paused to say, 'Howdo, vicar.' and went on talking.

'A drink, Reverend?' breathed Terry.

'Get him a whisky,' said Mrs Goff quietly. 'We're so sorry. George is very shocked. We had no idea until half an hour ago when we got back, and called in at the neighbours to collect the spare key.'

'Nor should you have,' said Bill, voice firm with reassurance. 'She was cremated today at Carlisle. We would have liked you to do it, but you were away. Once the coroner sorted things out we wanted to get it over with as soon as possible.'

George hadn't spoken. He looked white. He sat in the chair opposite the comatose Ada, without loosening his overcoat. Then he took the whisky Terry provided. 'How did she die?' he rasped.

Bill told him, his voice with its lilting accent rising and falling with the right cadences for the sad story.

'Oh, God,' said George Goff, and meant it. He put his head in his hands. His wife leaned forward.

'George,' she said. 'Tell me. What is it?'

She wasn't sure, but she thought she heard him say, 'I need a priest.'

The Reverend John Maple had sat with his eyes closed as the train sped through Milton Keynes and Rugby, then he read for a little while, before sleeping again. Kate, eyes wide but unseeing, went over and over her phone conversation with Malcolm Hodgson.

There had been something in Hodgson's voice which had hurt her more than his words. Like all TV producers she had been accused of using people before, sometimes rightly. But she had rarely heard such intense resentment. It was something she couldn't place, unsure whether it came from Malcolm's fear that he had betrayed his background, or that she might repeat his dis-closures. Or then again, perhaps it came from something else – anger that their friendship had just been a front for her opportunism. Whatever its cause, the thought twisted her breath so her chest hurt.

When her mobile phone rang again she almost dropped it in her urgent need to answer it, but it wasn't Malcolm Hodgson; it was June Ridley, much happier and more confident, full of renewed enthusiasm and ready to discuss the next week. De Salas had not come back to the shoot, but June had contacted the Summerlake Hall Hotel, and he hadn't checked out either.

'He probably needs a good talking to from you, Kate,' she said, with more certainty than Kate herself could muster. 'I'll try and have a word with him when I get back tonight. Then perhaps he'll pull himself together for Monday. And if he doesn't, it's his hard luck, as you said. You need to talk to Ben Lowe about taking over. He's the senior partner in Rural Rides after all, and you need his blessing. How did you get on at Channel Four?'

Kate wiped the misty window and saw the sharp dissected fields. They were into stonewall country.

'Kate? Can you hear me?'

Kate repeated what Chrissia Cohen had said.

'That's wonderful.' June sounded infinitely more enthusiastic than Kate did. 'If there's any chance at all of getting this film on Channel Four . . .'

Kate sighed, 'Yes, June, it is wonderful, but it's not simple. It's going to be a lot of work and I need your support. We need to get Rural Rides to agree to a change of theme, and only Ben can do that. But he might, if you speak to him first. And if you *do* manage to dig Andy out from under the duvet, where he's probably sulking, tell him I'll phone him when we get in tonight. I still think he should explain himself to me, and I'd feel better if he formally handed over. We expect to be back at our hotel about ten o'clock. That won't be too late for me to call.'

'Who's "we"?' June asked archly.

'My boyfriend's with me.'

'Oh, how nice for you.'

'Yes, well, thanks.'

'You must let us meet him on Monday.'

'Oh, I should think he will have gone by then.' Kate rang off. For a few minutes she sat and thought about the responsibility of the film. But there was no reason why she couldn't do it. Even so, the thought of the men and the dogs made her shiver. It was getting colder, and the carriage was emptier now they had passed Preston. But that meant there was no-one else to hear them. John Maple opened one eye and looked at her.

'You didn't sound too enthusiastic.'

'What about?'

'Me being with you.'

'Well, you haven't spoken for hours.'

'Kate, you got so involved in that phone call when we

were on the platform you nearly missed the train, despite the fact that it was you who made all the fuss about going up to Cumbria in the first place.'

She didn't deny it but turned to watch narrowboats manoeuvre their way slowly along a remote and rambling canal, slicing the bright water under the low, grey dusk as the train bounced past.

'What's wrong, Kate?'

'I should ask you that. I hardly see you and when I do, you never talk to me about anything that matters.'

'That's not true!'

'Anything that matters to you, I mean.'

'Of course I do. I ask your advice about everything.'

'Oh yes, on the level of which suit to wear and what brand of soap powder to buy. But what about real issues?'

'But I don't want us to argue. I know you have different views on a lot of things from me, and I understand that. It's your right. I admire you for it.' It was a point of view she couldn't attack. How could it be wrong of him to respect her opinions? She sighed and turned away again.

'Look Kate, I haven't been sleeping; I've been thinking. We need to resolve things. Father Marcus is getting better, and to be honest I think that if I left now and he had to get on with it, he'd probably recover a lot more quickly. How do you feel about being the tower of strength behind a prison chaplain, or a priest in industry? Or if I went back to working with the homeless? Would that make you happier?'

'Oh, come on, John, Marcus has got you running that parish like clockwork. You're brilliant at it. Look at you, out every night at some activity or other, and steering people through weddings and christenings and God knows what.

'I expect She does.'

It was an old joke that used to make them both laugh, but this time Kate shook her head in irritation.

'Be serious, John. The congregation must have doubled since you went there.'

'Well, yes, it has grown. But there are other ways of working as a priest, and I want to keep you happy too.'

'So I'm another obligation?'

'No! Or rather, yes, but one I want. Look Kate, we need to make this work.'

Kate looked away. Outside the window it was dark now. Lights from a farmhouse punctured the rubbery sheet of darkness. John was saying what she had longed to hear a week ago. Yet he had said, 'we *need* to make this work,' as if she were a duty, and she thought contrarily of Malcolm Hodgson, and the desire between them that had nothing to do with obligation.

'Kate, look at me. Wouldn't it make things better?'

'Of course it would.' She turned to him, thinking that she should be ecstatic and wondering why she felt nothing at all. In a panic she wondered if their love really had died away in the last few months, withering now he had regained self confidence and self-esteem. To her own surprise she heard herself asking, 'Will you explain your faith to me one day?'

John's smile dissolved until his face was devoid of expression, except for the wariness around the eyes which she remembered from the night before. He was deliberately still.

'I don't expect you to get involved,' he said flatly. 'I don't want to trap you into religion. Just let me get Marcus sorted out, Kate, and then I'm off the hook. There'll be no more lame ducks. I can look for something that suits us both.'

She said nothing for a moment, then whispered, 'Thanks.' She wanted to believe John, to be gratified and delighted, to feel that everything had come right, even though she knew she still hadn't got to the heart of him. And then she drifted into an uncomfortable sleep until he woke her to see the lights of Carlisle sliding past.

As they stood in the station forecourt Kate imagined that the air smelt completely different to the recycled breath of London. It had the slightest tang of woodsmoke, and seemed familiar and challenging at once. They took a taxi to the west coast, a major expenditure about which John felt uneasy, but Kate paid with reckless cheerfulness. The further west the minicab travelled the more excited she became. She suspected that it was for the wrong reasons, but she concentrated on attempting to give John some insight into the place itself. And he seemed to understand, though how much of the atmosphere he could really gauge, looking out into the black hedgerows, and only barely aware of the sea, she couldn't tell. By the time they approached Skirlbeck she felt more like a demented tour guide than a real enthusiast for West Cumbria.

But when they left the cab and staggered up the gravel sweep to the stone hotel, buffeted by the wind, he paused and took a deep breath and said, 'Yes, I think I see. When you're in London it's hard to remember anywhere so wild exists in Britain.'

'Well, that might be overdoing it, John; it's hardly that isolated. What about the Western Isles, or Snowdonia?' But even as she said it, she looked out over the low stone wall to where there was just the road between them and the

Solway Firth, and had to agree with him. There had been only the occasional warm light of a farm in the darkness, or the sudden cluster of stone houses in towns that would hardly be hamlets in the Home Counties. On a moonless night, after a half-hour taxi ride, it must seem astonishingly remote to someone who had spent the last year without leaving the London perimeter.

'Come here,' he said, and put the bags down on the gravel, to grab her. She had forgotten how strong John was, and how restrained for most of the time. This time he pulled her towards him so forcefully he took her breath away as she collapsed on to his chest. Then with great enthusiasm he kissed her smackingly on the lips, laughing at the same time. 'You look great, all windblown,' he whispered, his lips icy on the rim of her ear. 'I'm so glad we had that chat on the train. It's going to be all right, isn't it, Kate?'

'I think so. Oh, of course it is. Come on, let's get out of the cold.'

She rang the bell, ignoring the solid cast iron knocker, and John's remark that the building was like a miniature mansion from Edgar Allen Poe. The door swung open to show Bill and Terry in the hallway, even more strikingly alike in the white shirts and black ties the day dictated.

'Kate!' they said in unison. Bill went on, 'And in time to have a bite and a drink. We've just had two more visitors, so the buffet is still laid! Come in.'

'And your, er . . . young man,' murmured Terry.

'Not so young, unfortunately,' Kate said cheerily. 'Bill, Terry, this is John.'

The handshaking went on in the hallway, and then, glancing through the door into the bar, Kate saw the last few mourners, the remains of the buffet, and George Goff's bowed head.

'There's your friend the vicar,' she said. 'We must have a word with him after we've taken the bags upstairs.'

John was looking bemused as one of the farmers cracked an incomprehensible joke to the other and grunts of laughter echoed from the bar round the Victorian hallway. Curious, he did not immediately follow Kate to the stairs, but turned to look into the bar area. At that moment George Goff glanced up and his face widened in astonishment before it broke, in what looked to Kate like some sort of relief.

'John. John Maple!' Goff leapt to his feet with the alacrity of a much younger man. 'Oh, thank God.'

'George! I never expected to see you tonight. How nice. Kate and I have just arrived.'

The older clergyman had come forward and almost fallen on to John's arm.

'Maple, I need to talk to you.' As if suddenly remembering himself, he turned and looked at Kate and she saw the frightening struggle he had to recognise her, and pull himself back from whatever terrifying journey his mind had been taking.

'Of course. Kate. I'm so sorry. I wasn't making the right connections. My dear, this is my wife, Eileen.' The big, rather queenly-looking woman behind him nodded, but her eyes were on her husband. Kate felt some surprise. Eileen Goff was at least ten years younger than she had expected, with a Junoesque build and a great deal of dark, intense authority. But she wasn't interested in Kate. She too was now looking desperately at John.

'Has everything gone well?' Kate whispered to the twins,

while the two clergymen patted each other's arms, and George staggered back to the bar.

'Very well,' said Bill. 'Except for the Reverend. He's taken it terribly.' They watched George Goff reeling into his armchair. John was helping him.

'John,' she called, trying to attract his attention. 'Let me show you our room.' He murmured something reassuring to the elderly clergyman, then followed her. But on the landing he said, 'George is in a bad way.'

'Yes. What's up, do you think?'

'I don't know. Let's dump the bags and get back to him. He looked a lot older than I remembered. In fact, he didn't look well at all.'

Kate had hoped as they walked up the windy path to the hotel, that in the privacy of the pink room, she would draw the heavy curtains on the cold dark world and John would hold her with renewed enthusiasm. His embrace outside had reminded her of their first heady, passionate encounters that had left her bruised and breathless. Instead, he flung down the bags, left his coat over the chair, and said, 'I'm just going to the loo, and then I think we'd better hurry back.'

In the bar, George Goff seemed better. He had loosened his macintosh, and Eileen Goff had taken her coat off, as well as her hat. Now, she looked less like a Valkyrie and more like a big and surprisingly attractive woman with clouds of dark greying hair and large, anxious eyes. John immediately sat opposite George, with Eileen perched on the arm of her husband's chair, looking down at him protectively. There was no room for Kate. She withdrew to the bar and stood by Terry and Bill.

'By the way,' Bill said, 'one of the waitresses who came

up from Skirlbeck to help out took a phone call for you about an hour ago, Kate. Someone called June Ridley, staying at the Summerlake Hall Hotel?'

'Of course.' Kate put down the glass of malt whisky that Terry had pressed into her hand. 'I'd better return her call. I'll pop up to the bedroom, Bill. Tell John that's where I am.' Though he may not even notice I've gone, she thought, glancing back to where John and George Goff had their heads together.

In the warm room, she sat on the bed and dialled the Summerlake. June was in her bedroom, and picked up the phone at once.

'Kate? Good. Your journey OK? Look, I've tried to speak to Andy de Salas, but there's no-one answering the phone in his room. He and . . .' She paused.

'I know about his girlfriend, June.'

'Good, that saves me having to be discreet! Anyway, they must have gone out to dinner or something, I don't know. They certainly haven't checked out. But they're not here, and it's getting late. I want to go to bed.'

'Listen, June, just put a note under his door. Tell him that I'm back and I propose that we all meet here, at the Skirlbeck Bridge Hotel, on Monday at eight. Write to him that if he isn't going to be there, I'd like to know. Have you got that? The Skirlbeck Bridge. In the meantime, June, you get home if you can and see your family. It will all be fine.'

'Thanks, Kate. I will. I'll push this note under Andy's door. No doubt he'll be in touch.' No doubt, thought Kate raising an eyebrow. But she said nothing except, 'Thank you too, June. It was you who kept everything going today. Goodnight.'

Kate went downstairs again where, to her relief, the Goffs

were leaving. George was a better colour, and Eileen, though hovering protectively, was smiling in a tense sort of way.

'Goodnight, John,' she was saying. 'And you have our address, don't you?'

John nodded and then turned apprehensively to Kate. 'George and Eileen have asked us over for dinner tomorrow night,' he said, his smile set and his eyes scanning hers worriedly. Kate grimaced back, feeling as if her smile was as fake as gilt on a cold white plate. 'Lovely,' she said, teeth just unclenched.

The little group split up in the hallway. When the heavy Edwardian door swung shut behind the Goffs, Kate turned angrily to John, regardless of the twins.

'John, how could you! This was supposed to be our weekend together. What's going on?'

'George has got problems, Kate. I'll tell you upstairs.'

Bill intervened anxiously. 'Take some coffee up, Kate. I'll make it for you.'

Kate waited in the hallway for the tray and then staggered to their room. When John came out of the bathroom in his dressing gown, she poured him a cup, and tried to wait patiently for his explanation. But he said nothing, turning instead to look out over the sea. So much for closing the curtains and taking her into his arms. Finally Kate spoke.

'Did you *have* to arrange to see the Goffs tomorrow?'

'Yes,' said John shortly.

'Why?'

'George has a professional problem. He's a lonely man, Kate. His bishop is miles away, and he's never been an ordinary routine clergyman. There was all that business with Eileen . . .'

234

'What business?'

'She'll probably tell you herself. The point is that he's different. That's why we stayed friends. I was one of his students and he was marvellous to me. Now he needs me. I'm not sure why, but that doesn't matter. George is someone I owe. I need to chat to him alone. You'll be all right with Eileen tomorrow won't you?'

'What do you mean, all right with Eileen?'

'Before dinner. You can chat with her while I talk to George?'

'No, I bloody well can't!' John winced.

'Look John, for Christ's sake . . .'

He winced again and she heard her voice rising: 'I *mean* for Christ's sake, please talk to me. Explain. This is just like Father Marcus. Only a few hours ago you told me you wouldn't let it happen again.'

'Kate! It's not – not really. You must understand.'

'I'm never given the chance to understand. Anything of any significance and I'm out in the cold.'

She stormed into the bathroom and slammed the door. She could hardly wash, she was so angry, and when she tried to clean her teeth the brush shook too much to go into her mouth. She wanted to go out and confront John, yet this time she felt he was really determined not to talk. She left the bathroom, to see that John was already in bed, and turned away from her. She stood, breathing the cold night air like ice through her lungs, determined not to speak if he didn't, and sensing the estrangement between them like a solid block, no longer a suspected gap she had just to reach across, but a wall he wanted to build.

She undressed silently, crawled into bed, and put out the light.

* * *

Walking gingerly on the grey boulders of the beach late the next afternoon, Kate felt as if the whole day had been a series of delicate manoeuvres over stony ground. She and John had been woken (theoretically, anyway; she suspected they had both been lying awake) by Terry with a pot of tea, and forced cheerfulness which she was sure hid the shrewd little man's assessment of the atmosphere. John had been fulsomely pleasant, at his most interesting, chatting with practised professional ease over breakfast and delighting the twins with his keen interest in everything local. Kate had to admit he had absorbed far more than she realised, and despite herself she was impressed with his warmth.

After that, he had found people to engage in conversation wherever they went, at the bus stop, on the country bus to Keswick, in the coffee shop in the lovely monochrome Lakeland town, and on the bus back, where he was particularly engaging, exchanging anecdotes with a small boy about computers. It all saved him having to talk to her. Kate suggested they get off the bus and walk back along the windswept beach, and even here he found a couple to whom he could chat with real delight about the habits of Yorkshire terriers.

And then suddenly they were on their own. For a few minutes the charade continued, with John jumping ahead on the stones and pretending to have a lovely time, until Kate made an unexpected effort and caught up with him, tugging at his jacket.

'Hang on, Kate, you'll have me tumbling,' he laughed.

Kate stood still. 'Stop this farce,' she said sharply.

'Kate?'

'Oh, for God's sake, you know what I mean. Tell me

what went on with you and George Goff last night.'

John looked out to the stainless steel sea, and said nothing.

'Oh, that's it, is it?' Kate felt her fury boiling after the fruitless, stupid waste of a day. 'You won't discuss anything with me, will you? That's at the root of our problems.' She grabbed his jacket by the lapels with a fierce violence she hated, but she wanted to shake him until he looked at her properly, not with the evasive eyes of a man she no longer knew.

'Katy, please. Let's get through this evening with the Goffs without an atmosphere between us.'

'That's all you care about, isn't it? Making sure everything is fine so you look like the knight on a white charger. Woe betide anyone who makes John Maple, crutch of the crippled cleric, look less than saintly. Well, don't worry, I'll do the little wife act tonight. But don't expect it again. Ever!'

'Kate, that's not fair!' His voice disappeared in the soup of birds and sea and crunching pebbles. Livid, she tried to stride back up the beach, only succeeding in wobbling on the rocks so her ankles twisted and tears came to her eyes. She hobbled along the shore and then up over the hummocks of scoured grass to the road, and the glow of the hotel.

George and Eileen Goff lived in a bungalow on the other side of the village, with a windswept garden of smooth, short grass that backed on to the shoreline like a crew cut. The curtains weren't drawn and Kate could see flickering firelight deep in the low-lying house. It had to be sheer bad luck, Kate thought tetchily, that George Goff, who had been such an inspiration to John at theological college, should be here, the village she had chosen for their escape. But that was a double-edged thought. If George had not been there to rescue her on her first night in Cumbria, who knows what would have flared up between her and Andy de Salas before twenty-four hours were up. And then the film she wanted to make would have had no chance at all.

It was only now she realised how much she wanted to make that film – not the de Salas version, but the Kate Wilkinson version, a real, honest, concerned look at the area. That made her remember Malcolm Hodgson for the first time that day, and she traced a smear amongst the wriggling worms of rain on the misted taxi window and watched it grow fuzzy and fade.

Eileen Goff welcomed them, with George hovering behind her. On the outside, their bungalow looked conventional, but inside, for subtle reasons to do with space and colour, it seemed like the ideal setting for the large, peculiar woman who was Mrs Goff. The bungalow was low and long, with one great room ending in a huge stone fireplace. There was a lovely wooden table with pretty crimson glasses and a bowl of leaves and berries in the centre, and a blazing fire which caught the red glass and filled the room with reflections. It was Scandinavian in tone, and not a bit like the sort of cluttered living room with ornaments and photos that Kate had imagined. Eileen was wearing a purply woollen jumper over leggings that suggested very good legs indeed. She poured them drinks, motioned them to a beanbag and a shapeless cushiony seat and settled George in his Parker Knoll style armchair, the one standard piece of furniture. Then Eileen curled up on the parquet floor by the hearth like a large cat.

But with a sort of jerky impatience, after ten minutes of small talk largely provided by Kate and John, George suddenly stood up.

'We have to go,' he said to his wife, looking in passing at Kate as if she, too, would be sure to understand.

'All right.' His wife looked concerned for the first time. 'Don't be long. It's cold in church.'

John stood up too without speaking to Kate, unravelling his long legs from the low squashy chair by the fireside, and the two clergymen quietly left. Eileen Goff didn't move from where she was sitting on the floor in front of the fire. She sipped her whisky reflectively, and turned to look at Kate, who felt the silence lengthen. In typical Kate fashion she wanted to fill the conversational vacuum, and to get to the point. But she found herself silenced by Eileen's stare. The other woman said, 'You've been trying really hard to be chatty, haven't you? I appreciate that. But something is eating away at you.'

Kate looked at her, surprised. She had thought her worry was hidden, and she was both alarmed and impressed by Eileen's words. The vicar's wife was right. It wasn't just that she was angry with John. The situation was 'eating away at her'. She remembered the fat worm-shaped dribble of rain on the window.

'Eileen, what's all this about?'

Eileen shrugged and stayed irritatingly quiet. Then she said, still staring at the flames, 'I don't know. I know George is worried and I know he desperately wanted to talk to another clergyman.'

'But why John Maple?' Kate heard her own voice like a cross between a plea and a whine. Eileen looked sharply at her. 'You have a problem with this, don't you?'

239

'I'm sorry?'

'You have a problem. You don't like George leaning on John.'

Kate felt instantly embarrassed that her resentment had shown. But Eileen Goff was looking at her without rancour. Her steady gaze broke through Kate's social skin.

'No, Eileen, I bloody well don't. I suppose you think it's selfish of me, but for the last six months I've put up with John being at the beck and call of the neurotic vicar he's working for, and I had hoped that this weekend . . .' Kate stopped, listening to her own tactlessness.

'Hoped, or hoped and prayed?' Eileen flashed her a smart look, full of surprising good humour. She was unfazed by Kate's outburst, but seemed to want a real answer to her question.

'No, OK, I didn't pray. But then, I'm not one of you lot.'

'Us lot? Anglicans, you mean?'

'Well, believers of any sort, to be honest. I'm not one of any description.'

'Neither was I till I met George,' said Eileen with an air of significance.

'Really?' Kate knew she was being invited to ask more. And Eileen Goff intrigued her despite her own anger. 'So what were you?'

'Oh, I still am. I'm a medium.'

'What?'

'A medium. A spiritualist's medium. Don't laugh. I can see you want to. I don't practise now, in case it compromises my husband. But you can't stop being a medium; it's a state, not a belief. George tells me I never talked to the dead, because their souls are with God. But he does accept that I was in touch with something – people's feelings, perhaps.

240

I know for certain I'm a psychic. Our affair caused quite an upset round here.'

'I can imagine!' For a minute a stunned Kate forgot her own complications. This explained the outwardly conventional George's alienation from his colleagues, and subsequent dependence on John. Kate shuddered. She would not wish to be classed like Eileen as a 'difficult' wife. She would rather not be a wife at all. She tried to smile sociably.

'Your husband mentioned the night we met that the Robinson twins went to spiritualist meetings.'

'Yes, they do. Sunday nights. I never go now. I do the odd psychic consultation, though George doesn't really approve. But all the controversy has blown over. I'm good at being a vicar's wife. There's nothing I can't organise and the fact some people think I'm a bit of a witch helps.'

Kate had a sudden insane vision of Eileen Goff being the gypsy palmist at the Church Christmas Fair, and then quelled the thought, just in case Eileen could read it.

'Another drink, Kate?'

'Yes, please.'

As the other woman rose to go to the pine cabinet where she kept the drinks, Kate noticed a picture on the top showing a much younger George with a woman clearly of his own generation. The two had their arms around each other and were laughing to the camera. George had an open-necked shirt and the woman a floral frock and cardigan. It looked like a fifties or sixties trip to the seaside, and far more the sort of partnership she had expected. Eileen saw her looking, and in her dramatic fashion said, 'That's George and his wife.'

'Sorry?'

'George and his wife. Oh, I know I'm his wife but we're such an odd couple I always think of Beryl as the real wife and me as some sort of strange addiction.'

'Really?'

'Mmm. Beryl died of cancer about fifteen years ago, when George was teaching at the college where he met John. He was very fond of John, you know. I think John was a star pupil. George was upset when he heard that he'd given up parish work. He's pleased now, and says John's a lot more confident. That must be thanks to you, Kate.'

'I doubt it. Sometimes I think I'm just there as a frame for his picture of godliness.' Eileen laughed for the first time, a jolly sound that Kate could imagine genuinely enlivening a thousand whist drives and bring-and-buy sales, minus her crystal ball. For the first time she could imagine Eileen as a vicar's wife.

'I know, dear,' Eileen said. 'Isn't it hell sometimes? And the hardest bit is not asking.'

'You feel that too?'

'Oh, yes. I just have to let George get on with it, and I'm always here with the whisky and the sympathy. I never thought I would, but I love being his wife. We're both keen on spiritual things, I suppose.' Kate smiled, a little embarrassed, but Eileen Goff didn't notice. 'I was a divorcée and I moved up here to take care of my mother who had been mad enough to retire to Skirlbeck. I was completely wretched. George fell for me the first time I took mother to Communion. I sat at the back thinking what a lot of unnecessary nonsense it was. Now, sometimes I'm first in the queue.' She laughed again.

'So how do you cope, with living your own life, I mean?'

Kate wanted to know the practical details with a new urgency. This was the first time she had met anyone married to one of John's friends. 'Do you go to work, Eileen?'

'Work? Oh, yes. I teach part time. French.' That figures, thought Kate. 'I'm at the local comprehensive. We've been busy lately. But this weekend's the start of half term, so I can relax.' Kate remembered Liz Jones saying that Steve was taking the children on holiday for half term, and nodded. 'Of course.'

Eileen went on, 'I'm not sure if I'll be able to keep the work load up, if George is going to go through a wobbly patch. They all do, dear.'

'Do you find it stressful?'

'Only at times like this, when it's unresolved. And because George is getting on now, he needs practical looking after. He's always in the clouds. The locals laugh at him, the way he ambles along the lanes, his mind on higher things and his feet all over the road. Yesterday he was so distracted he was nearly hit by a car outside. He came in covered in mud. I told him not to walk down the lane at dusk, but he didn't listen to me. I find that side of things worrying and tiring.'

'Yes, I can see that.'

'And, of course, lately I've been so much in demand at school. The other French teacher left over a year ago. Susan Hodgson. You might have come across her husband. Malcolm's into everything around here. And everybody!'

'Malcolm? Councillor Malcolm Hodgson?' Kate felt her face grow pink and hoped Eileen would put it down to the whisky.

'That's right. Nice chap but a bit of a ladies' man. Regular enough churchgoer, though. Still, I suppose he just attends because he thinks it's the right sort of thing for a councillor to do. Have you come across him?'

'Yes, we have met.'

'He's quite attractive . . .' Eileen Goff looked Kate squarely in the eyes and Kate wondered what she was going to say with some trepidation.

They were interrupted by the front door swinging open to let in a blast of cold wet air that raced through the long, low house. George was booming cheerfully about the weather and ushered John in. For a moment Kate caught the whiteness of John's face before a revived George began asking about his dinner. Eileen cheerfully uncoiled herself from the floor and left for the kitchen, ignoring Kate's routine offer of help. It was just as well. Eileen Goff had said enough to leave Kate with plenty to think about over the remains of her drink.

She glanced at the two men, George visibly reassured and back to his capable self, and John, in the background now, looking into the flames to avoid her face in case it should be tilted questioningly towards him. But it wasn't. Kate was looking away, pondering Eileen's remarks about keeping her distance from her husband's affairs.

To everyone's surprise, against all the odds, it was a dinner party that worked. The food was obscure but delightful, with local ingredients and lots of imagination, and neither George nor Eileen made strenuous efforts to be anything other than quietly welcoming. It was as if some sort of tension had passed from George into John. John failed to meet Kate's eye, and was much quieter, but she was used to him wearing himself out solving other people's problems, and George seemed much happier. He told them stories that made them laugh, but never gave the impression, unlike so many clergymen, that he was patronising his parishioners. Eileen said little, content to back him up.

'Do you know,' George was saying, 'the best moments of my life – and I've never told anybody this – have been when the people you least expect show signs of faith. Like that time the gypsies at Workington turned up to get their baby baptised.'

'Or when Tom Flint asked you to say a few words over the grave of his dog!' Eileen supplied.

Kate felt the hair on the back of her neck stand up. She wasn't sure whether George knew Tom Flint was dead, and it was not for her to tell him. She heard George's cheery laughter and shuddered. That must have been the dog Malcolm's son saw destroyed. After a pause which she hoped no-one noticed, she said, 'After just a week in the area I'm astonished about how close people are.'

'Yes,' George said reflectively. 'Once you accept it, it's the most wonderful area in the world.'

An hour later, standing on the step breathing the sea air and looking down over the sleeping village as they said goodbye, she felt she could believe him. Eileen leaned forward to kiss her and murmured, 'You'll make it if you want to, you and John.' Kate felt mild irritation at her intrusion, though she kissed her back affectionately enough. But she suspected, with a chill that had nothing to do with the cold night air, that Eileen might be wrong.

On the way home she and John were silent. It was almost a relief to be hailed on the doorstep by the twins who insisted they both stay up for yet another nightcap. After some subdued chat, with John more uncommunicative than usual, Kate literally swayed upstairs and any heavy discussion was postponed by both of them as they clambered drunkenly into bed.

'Did you like the Goffs?' John murmured.

'Yes. They were OK.' Kate was sleepily noncommittal.

'Did Eileen talk to you?'

'Mmm.'

'Did she tell you about what she did until George found her?'

'Yes, she did, as a matter of fact. And you're being rather condescending.'

'I just meant that she was an unconventional vicar's wife. It is possible.'

But only if you keep on separate tracks, and are content to see yourselves as the spiritual version of the Odd Couple, Kate thought. On top of that she had a feeling that Eileen Goff rather enjoyed the melodrama of their situation. That was not for Kate, for all she liked Eileen.

John turned restlessly, without touching her. She knew he wanted her to reach out to him and tell him it was fine, that she understood. But it wasn't and she didn't. Equally, she wanted him to turn to her, and hold her tight and explain. But he was silent. They both lay in the dark watching the room spin round, pretending to sleep. Kate thought again about two of Eileen's remarks. Firstly, could she, Kate, ever become an unquestioning support to John, as Eileen was to George? And secondly, just how much of a womaniser was Malcolm Hodgson? And the thought pursued her into sleep.

At six am she woke to see John sitting in the chair by the window.

'What is it, John?'

'I think I need to go back to George.'

'*What?* I thought you sorted all that out last night! He seemed completely restored after your mysterious little chat in the church.'

'Look, Kate ... oh, you wouldn't understand. But last night I thought I could leave him to it. Now I think I have to go back.'

Hurt more by his remark that she wouldn't understand than by his decision to go out so early, she shouted, 'What do you mean? It's only half past six!'

'That's right.' He spoke with determined softness. 'George takes an early eucharist at eight. I'd like to be there.'

He stood up decisively and Kate felt she couldn't bear it. It was as if the whole of her life was to be lived around someone who was forever walking away from her.

She sat up in bed. 'If you go now, John, you risk going for good. I can't stand being jerked about like this. Unless we have the time to sort out what is wrong, you might as well walk out.'

'But Kate, just let me help George. He really does need me. Then we'll have all the time we want.'

Like a firework Kate could not control the resentment of the last six months flaring.

'It's *your* need that really matters, John. Your need to be a hero. So go and talk to someone else about important issues. Confide in some nice insecure clergyman who'll lap up your views without questioning! You don't want an equal relationship with a real partner, so sod off!"

'Kate, that's crude, and cruel, and untrue. And I haven't time for it.'

'Time? You're talking about time? OK, then, I'll give you time! Here's a deadline. If you love me, come back here at lunchtime. Give me one afternoon, take an extra day away from your Father Marcus and leave George Goff on his own, go home tomorrow instead of on the sleeper tonight. Just give me one afternoon of your precious time. We'll use it to get to the bottom of this. I'll wait here till one o'clock. If you want to talk to me, to explain where you're coming from, I'll be here till then. If you don't turn up, I'll know I'm not one of your priorities. You can spend as long as you like with these other people if you just give me those hours, and vow to talk to me truthfully. If you can't do that, God help us. Both.'

'But you might not like what I have to say.'

'Then let me be the judge of that. I'm a grown-up, for Christ's sake.'

John looked at her with a sadness that shocked her more than his decision to go to George Goff.

'OK,' he said. 'Done.'

He swung himself out of bed and walked to the bathroom, leaving Kate icy in the warm soft bed.

Chapter Ten

It had been ten years at least since the Marshalls had moved into separate bedrooms. He had complained of her restlessness, which she put down to sciatica. But the truth was that they no longer wanted the burden of discussing intimacy. He could not admit to his lack of libido and she could not face her lack of desirability. This led them to tortured ways of asserting their viability. Sir Michael waged constant terrorist action against his wife, totting up in his head the number of direct hits he scored against her self-esteem each day, but it always bounced back like one of those metal man-shaped targets he remembered from a brief stint in the Territorials in the fifties. He had avoided national service – just – because of the business, but he felt he knew about guerrilla warfare, living with Celia.

On Sunday morning at ten to eight, he went along to the freezing little church in Skirlbeck, irritated at Celia's adamant refusal to join him. He had left her munching toast, crumbs on her chin and her face in *The Mail on Sunday*, with the central heating 'cracking the flags', as he put it grumpily. He went to early Communion because he liked the 1662 service, or so he said, but the truth was that it finished quickly and there was no sermon. It also gave him a sense of virtue. That morning he noticed that George Goff had a strapping looking fellow serving with him, and the size and good health of the new man pointed up the vicar's frailty. Goff seemed very old, and the thought made Sir Michael whistle triumphantly as he strode back through the village, still expecting the odd bit of forelock tugging from the few elderly men up and about, although most now wore Pringle sweaters and lightweight anoraks and had small dogs on leads as they walked out for copies of the *Sunday Express*, rather than the crusty cloth capped labourers of Marshall's youth. He was made aware that Goff had raced through the service even more quickly than usual when he realised that villagers he usually saw at the newsagents were still walking down the road, and that the morning sun was still struggling against a ridge of cloud bouncing over the felltops.

He felt pleased to be up early, and especially pleased that he would be back ahead of schedule and probably able to surprise Cee as she smeared jam on the newspaper or committed some other satisfactory little domestic felony. He practised his reproachful look and imagined her surprise and annoyance at his early return as he swept his stick across some of the dying autumn weeds which fringed his driveway.

It was essential that he enter the house quickly by the kitchen garden, and creep along past his 'office' so that she would be caught unawares. He sidled down the passageway, hoping his joints would not creak, and then at the last minute turned smartly into the breakfast room in the noisy act of unbuttoning his stiff waxed jacket so she could not accuse him of sneaking up on her unawares. *The Mail on Sunday* was lying, jam-smeared, on the table, with crumbs on top, but there was no-one to scold. Doubly irritated Sir Michael walked up two threadbare stairs and into his black-and-white flagged hallway. His brogues clattered across to the drawing room, where he hoped to find his wife guiltily engaged in watching TV or, worse still, tidying his books and pipes. But the high, flock-papered lounge held only dusty sunbeams. He stood and listened. There was no sound of Radio Cumbria or busybody footsteps, the two other things most likely to enrage him. He felt suddenly lacking, aware of something adrift in his life. There were no irritations, which irritated him in itself.

'Cee,' he called out despite himself. He listened, hoping for her breathless reply. There was nothing. He clattered back down to the breakfast room, wondering if somehow he had failed to see her. But the room was still empty – suffocatingly warm, but empty. He scurried down the scabby, damp passage to his office and looked inside. There was no-one there, and the curled papers from his abandoned attempts at accounts lay untouched on his rolltop desk.

'Cee,' he called again, surprised to hear how panicky his voice sounded.

It suddenly occurred to him that perhaps she had gone back to bed, but he felt an urgency to know. He scampered up the stairs with a strange lack of dignity and went, for no reason, to his own room first. It was just as he had left it, masculine, largely grey through grime and taste, and empty. Then he hurried to her room, a room he hardly entered except on her birthday and Christmas morning. The door was swinging open as if she had just left, but he knew that wasn't possible. His heart was pounding. He fended off his thoughts as he pushed his way into the jumbled room enhanced by woolly cushions, chewed paperbacks, patent medicine bottles of every type and a woven bedspread of hideous knotted design which for some reason was on the floor, not on the bed which was across the far side of the room.

His first thought was that the room was even messier than usual, then he realised what the mess was. His wife's body, fully dressed and shod, lay over the bed in a desperate doll-like position, her arms flung out and her legs, rarely still, sticking out stiffly from her homespun skirt. Her face was purply and blotched and although he knew at once she was dead, there was a warmth from her that made him fling himself on to her and try to pummel life into her. But she was completely flaccid.

'Cee, Cee!' he screamed at her in a final orgy of irritation, aware that this was the most infuriating thing she had ever done. 'For goodness sake, Cee, come round.' But for once she did not rise to the bait. As he shook her, he was aware even in his panic, of something rolling from her clenched hand. It was a bloodstained man's cap.

'What are you doing with that, Cee?' he asked her, dazed. When she did not answer he fell to the floor and shouted with rage, clinging to her grey stockinged calf, until his anger turned into the horrified certainty that there would never again be busybody footsteps and the stern injunction to, 'Stop that, Michael!' The reason for keeping going was gone, and Sir Michael Marshall lay at his wife's feet, and wailed.

Kate Wilkinson stood looking out of the window of her bedroom at the Skirlbeck Bridge Hotel, and then went back to the desk and chair, which were both pretty and functional. She had spread her papers across them, and it looked efficient enough, with an agenda for the Monday and Tuesday of the following week neatly written out, along with a synopsis of the new programme, and a list of possible interviewees. Councillor Malcolm Hodgson's name was shaky, but none of it was written with particular confidence. Kate looked at her watch. It was ten to one. She had managed her morning through sheer self discipline. Now, even ahead of the hour, she had a sickening certainty that John would not come back on time. And if he didn't, she was left with her useless ultimatum. She stood up again and went into the bathroom where she used the loo and washed her hands. Twelve fifty five.

The phone suddenly shrieked and she leapt across at it. The voice at the other end failed to register for a moment. 'Who is it?' she said vacantly.

'Kate, it's me, Liz. I just thought you ought to know about Andy.'

'Andy?' It took Kate a moment to gather her thoughts. 'What about Andy? I was leaving him to sort himself out over the weekend.'

'He's left. Gone back to London.'

'What?'

'He's gone. Actually checked out and gone. He doesn't want to make the film any more. He went this morning. I've been lying here in bed since he left, drinking tea and feeling miserable, but then thought I'd better call you.'

'Well, I can't say I'm surprised. June told me about Friday's row. But I'm annoyed. Does he expect me to take over?'

'He thought you were doing that anyway. That was part of the trouble.'

'Liz! Be fair! The wretched programme was underfunded

and badly thought out. What was I supposed to do?'

'It's all right, Kate, I can imagine what happened. I haven't got any illusions about Andy's organisational ability, believe me. But I thought you were managing him so well!'

'Obviously not. Why haven't you gone with him?'

'To London? How could I? He's gone to stay with his parents. They'd hardly want me in the circumstances. He says he needs space to think about everything, including us. And there's no point in me dashing back to Hammersmith to sit on my own feeling even more guilty. It's half term and Steve's taken the kids to Alton Towers, remember?'

'So does this mean you and Andy have split up?'

'No! But I had to let him get his act together. He just needs time. Everything has got on top of him. He knows he's acted irresponsibly, Kate.'

'Clearly, if he's just walked out on you, and the film. Not a very impressive way to behave, is it?'

'Don't be hard on him, Kate.'

'I'm not in the mood to be soft to men at the moment. You're not the only one with problems. John and I have had a bust-up too. He's supposed to be staying here with me. We'd planned a weekend together, but he's got involved with the local vicar, who seems to have a problem which is too sensitive to explain to a philistine like me, and I haven't seen him since eight o'clock this morning.'

'Oh, God, that's bad.' But Liz sounded noticeably cheered.

'Bad? It's awful, worse than you think. Listen, Liz, get out of bed and pull yourself together. Then you can pull me together too. I need a shoulder to cry on even more than you do, so if you can get yourself round here we can commiserate over a bottle of wine for lunch.'

'That sounds like the sort of therapy I need. Gimme half an hour.'

'Done.' For a second Kate wondered why the word gave her a sense of doom, then she remembered John's grim agreement to come back and talk, or to stay away. He too had said, 'Done.' And he had kept to the agreement by not coming back.

'Liz,' she said, her voice breaking.

'I'll be there.'

They sat in the bar of the Skirlbeck with a few other locals who had come in now the mourning was officially over, and drank a bottle of Chardonnay, looking at the weather through the bay window. The weak early sun had been defeated by strips of mottled grey cloud. It was Liz who saw the ambulance go careering past at the end of the drive towards the village, but Kate was too sunk in self pity to take much notice.

'I've had enough,' she was saying. 'You know how much I cared for John. I thought he was the love of my life. But you can't be in love when there are pieces missing. It's like never finishing a jigsaw.'

'Oh, come on, Kate, you knew he was a priest when you fell for him, and you didn't mind.'

'No. In fact I thought it was interesting. I still find it odd that he wanted me, despite the fact I have no religious feelings at all. And I admired his tolerance. But now he's so busy leaving me my free will that he never talks to me about anything that matters. I'd love to have a good old row with him about women priests or gay clergy, or abortion. I've got a secret feeling that he thinks women priests are unnatural, gay clerics a pain in the bum, and that abortion is child murder.' She laughed weakly. 'But he would never do me the honour of discussing it with me.' Then she stopped, aware that Liz's bright attempt at sophistication was fading like a torch with low batteries. And her friend's eyes were suddenly full of tears. Liz wiped them with the back of her hand and smeared mascara over her wrist. She sniffed too, a great snorting sob-like sound completely at odds with her brittle nonchalance.

'Liz, are you all right?' But Liz had slumped forward a little in her chair, and her face had lost its colour. She blinked away the tears and her eyes met Kate's and in the silence between them Kate raked over her last words, wondering what had triggered Liz's desperate expression.

'Liz, what have I said? You look white as a sheet.' Staring at her friend, she remembered the greyness of Liz's face the time they had met in the pub, her tortured self-justification and the desperation when she had talked about her children. And earlier that first day, when Kate had phoned her at the Summerlake, Liz had seemed on the verge of further explanation, but had stopped in mid-sentence.

'Liz, why did you really come here?'

'Can't you guess?' Liz's voice was bleak.

Kate put her hand over her friend's.

'Please tell me.'

'I was pregnant,' Liz said abruptly, then added, with a flash of her old style, 'but not for long.'

'Oh, no!'

'Yes, unfortunately,' Liz said harshly.

'Oh, God, I'm sorry.'

'Don't be. I'm not. It had hardly started. But I knew I

256

didn't want another child. That wouldn't be the way to sort things out, and I've got Lily and Tom to think of. And Steve's feelings, though that might surprise you.'

'And what about Andy?'

'I was sure he wouldn't be able to face it, and I was terrified he would think I was trying to force the issue. It was a complete accident, a total mistake, the traditional broken condom story. I hoped and prayed that I wouldn't get caught. I should have gone for the morning-after pill, but I couldn't believe I could be so unlucky. I made the decision alone, but Andy had to know. He was desperate to try and be supportive. I came up here the first time to tell him, and that nearly drove him off the rails, but he insisted that I come up again to recover. If I'd gone home Steve might have guessed.'

Kate nodded. It explained why Liz, usually so active, had been staying in bed all day, with darkened eyes, and de Salas's air of exhausted preoccupation. Kate leaned forward. 'If there's anything I can do . . . ?'

'That old cliché. Well, there is. Don't mention it again. Ever. As far as I'm concerned, it's been a minor op and I'm OK now.'

'But you mustn't go home on your own.'

'Oh, rubbish. If I had to, I'd be fine.'

'But, Liz, you don't have to. Book in here, at the Skirlbeck. You could . . .' She was about to say 'get over it here', but caught Liz's defensive glance and said, 'You could get involved with the film.'

Liz blinked in surprise. 'You think it still has a chance, this film? Andy said he was going to phone Ben and tell him that unless you could save it, it would have to be cancelled. He said you had some hare-brained idea of getting money from Channel Four, but he didn't hold out much hope.'

'He lost heart because he knew he was on the wrong track. I agree he's visually very talented, Liz. But he needs someone to control the content. I suppose that was why Ben and Andy worked together so well. You can't make a film these days about pretty country crafts, with no proper thesis. But there is a possibility for something different . . .'

'What?'

Kate wondered, for a split second, how Liz would react to her changing Andy's theme. She leaned forward confidentially and began to tell Liz about the programme she really wanted to make.

It took ten minutes to explain it all, from the initial revelations of the vicious brutality Malcolm Hodgson's son had witnessed, to Sally Dodd discovering that someone had been reproducing videos in Tom Flint's barn. As she talked, Liz became more involved, the misery lifting from her face. 'And you see,' Kate finished, 'you could stay here for a week like you originally planned, and help me do it. Maybe Sally could help too. You'd like her. We could still use a lot of Andy's footage – maybe you could even persuade him to come back on that basis. And we'd have a film that was really worth making.'

Liz Jones looked away and in the hard light through the window Kate saw the new lines that had dug into her friend's face.

'Go on, Liz; it'll be well worth it.'

The other woman paused to think.

'What about Rural Rides?'

'As far as I'm concerned it's still their project, if they want it. But we need to talk to Ben Lowe.'

The colour was coming back into Liz's face. 'Well, I can help there straight away.'

'How?'

'I know Ben Lowe quite well, through Andy. He was the one person Andy confided in. He tells Ben most things. I think we should go to the hospital to see him, as soon as possible. What about this afternoon?'

Kate thought for a minute about John. But he had made no attempt to contact her.

'Great idea. And you'll move in here, and stay on?'

Liz nodded, already thinking about the film.

While Liz went back to the Summerlake Hall Hotel to fetch her things, Kate booked her a room with the delighted twins and then shut the door of her own room and sat in the armchair to think. She was distressed for Liz, but she knew how important it was to her friend not to make a fuss. Kate could imagine how desperately difficult the decision had been for Liz, despite her protestations, particularly as she had Lily and Tom, her children, as living, much-loved, examples of what pregnancy could produce. And it all went some way to explain de Salas's neurotic behaviour. But not far enough. After all, in her usual organised way Liz had solved the problem, however drastically, and had left herself with just one baby to care for, in the shape of de Salas himself.

The person Kate wanted most in the world to talk this over with was John. She had no idea how he would react to Liz's story, and the idea of putting it to him fascinated her. She remembered the envelope she had found, with George Goff's name scrawled on it and the anti-abortion campaign address on the back. Kate had been in the same position as Liz, fifteen years earlier. She rarely thought of it now and had only regretted the abortion when she had miscarried, during her brief marriage. She had mentioned this once to John and he had merely hugged her. Now, she wondered how he would react to Liz's story. If they hadn't argued that morning, this might have been the perfect opportunity to discuss the things they disagreed about.

Kate rang downstairs to check for the second time that there had been no message. But Terry Robinson assured her no-one had called.

So, brushing her hair and changing into the sort of business-like clothes she felt would be right for the hospital visit, she made herself think about the film. She still had no interviewee who would supply the information which she had promised Channel Four. Once she was ready to go out, she dialled Malcolm Hodgson's number, quickly, as if it didn't really matter. There was no reply. She was not sure whether she was relieved or sorry. But she would have to try again later. Then her fingers hovered over the numbers, and she wondered whether to ring the Goffs and try to speak to John. But she stopped herself. She had asked him to come back, and he hadn't. Once again he had let her down.

She stood up sharply and looked out at the crisp fells on the Scottish horizon, and felt a sudden quickening of her resolve. If John failed her, and Malcolm didn't want her – what the hell? She still had herself. And while she was still wondering at this new and sudden surge of strength, she heard the sound of Liz's cab outside and grabbed her bag to join her friend on the trip to the Cumberland Infirmary.

Ben Lowe was in a small ward which caught the westerly light. He had been in the hospital long enough to give the little area around his bed a sense of being his own territory. Some of his books lay on his locker, with a plant still in a paper wrapper and a clay mug balanced next to it.

Ben himself was a small wiry man in his forties with a mass of bushy brown hair and glasses mended at one side with Elastoplast. Kate wondered if they had been damaged in the accident which smashed his leg. The leg in question was propped on a footstool with a complicated dressing round it, not the plaster Kate had imagined. Liz strode forward and bestowed extravagant and inappropriate media kisses on Ben's still weather-beaten cheeks. He looked surprised to see her, but with the muted astonishment of someone who was so removed from everyday routine that anything and everything surprised him equally.

'Liz, fancy seeing you here.' He smiled at her. 'Where's Andy?' Kate moved forward. 'I'm Kate Wilkinson, Ben,' she said. 'I'm sorry to tell you this isn't just a social visit. Let me fill you in on the latest developments.'

But Ben Lowe was better informed than she had expected, principally thanks to nightly phone calls from the efficient June Ridley. He knew the background to everything that was going on, and he listened with intelligence, asking bright practical questions. He was obviously the mature and sensible side of Rural Rides, and for the first time Kate could see how the partnership had worked.

She felt she had managed to gloss over Andy's departure when Ben Lowe said sharply, 'You mean that neither Paul Pym's Tourist Centre, nor any broadcasters are committed to funding the film? After Pym's promises and Andy's efforts?'

'No.'

261

'Shit! And has Andy just buggered off?' Kate looked at Liz. 'More or less,' she said lamely.

'For Christ's sake, Liz! Couldn't you stop him?'

'How could I, Ben? You know what he's like when he gets worked up.'

'You're damn right I do. I always said he should be careful. With his history, I can't see why he wanted to get so involved in this film at all . . .'

'What history?'

'The accident. He must have told you about it.'

Even if de Salas had never mentioned any accident, Liz could never admit it. She nodded sharply and said, 'The one involving the woman?'

'That's right. Well, apparently she was from Cumbria and the whole mess happened not far from here. I knew, of course. Andy told me years ago. That was why I couldn't understand how keen he was to film up here.'

He was stopped in mid-explanation by a woman with a trolley from the Friends of the Hospital, and the proceedings were held up while Liz was despatched to purchase twenty Silk Cut from the trolley.

'Look,' he said when she came back after two attempts to get the right brand, and had sorted out the change, 'I think taking the film down this new route sounds excellent. But it's going to cost more.'

'I'm prepared to do a deal on that.' Kate sounded as if she had worked it all out a great deal more clearly than she had. 'I'll stay on until the shooting is over, and if Liz helps me and we can revise the schedule now, instead of wasting days on schmoozing with the Tourist Centre, we won't need much more time. Plus, I'm prepared to post-produce in an edit house in London after we've finished.

And I'm really confident about the commission from Chrissia and the advance arriving as soon as possible, as long as we can organise the evidence.'

'But Andy did say we had a sum of money already promised. You'll have to check with June.'

'Possibly. But it may not be from the right source. We don't want to be under obligation to anyone.'

'Good point. No local businesses should have a hold over us. This could be a really hard hitting documentary. I've made programmes for Chrissia Cohen before. She's good, and she knows what makes a riveting story. I think you're on to something here. But you'll need at least one interview with someone who has real experience of this dogfighting, and you'll need some sort of footage. Christ, I wish I could get up and about. Perhaps by the end of the week . . .'

'Don't worry.' Kate felt better now Ben Lowe was firmly on her side. 'I'll get something.' Again, she knew she would have to ring Malcolm. In the distance she heard the hospital clock striking four.

'We have to go.' Liz sprang up and was suddenly her old self, scarves and bags flying, face alert with interest. 'Thank you so much, Ben,' she said, swooping down on him. 'We've got a lot of work to do. And I want to try phoning Andy. He'll be back in London by now.'

As Liz bustled away towards the door, Kate turned and caught Ben's glance. He raised his eyebrows and shifted his leg uncomfortably, then said softly, out of Liz's earshot, 'Andy de Salas may be a poor little rich kid, but if she can handle it, it could be the making of both of them, you know.' Kate stared back in surprise. She had not envisaged the relationship between her friend and de Salas as anything less than a disaster for both of them.

* * *

As they headed west under a high grey sky, Kate's mind ticked over the conversation. Eventually she asked, 'Liz, what was the accident Ben was talking about?'

'It was something that happened to Andy when he was really young. Seventeen. It was always on his mind. I think it must have undermined his confidence right at the outset. I know he seems so brash when you first meet him. But he's insecure underneath.' And that's why you love him, thought Kate. Liz was going on, 'But since meeting Ben, he's got better and better. From what I gather, before Rural Rides, he was a bit of a mess.' Unlike now? Kate thought drily, but she said nothing and let Liz explain.

Ben Lowe had been a talented producer in the BBC in the eighties, who had taken the minimal risk usually known as a 'sweetheart deal' and left to form his own independent production company at a time when the Thatcher government had been screaming for the break-up of the monopolising TV networks. It was all very fashionable and very lucrative and the new businesses could usually get started with the huge redundancy cheques they had to invest, and with commissions from their former companies.

But Ben had been more intrepid. He had wanted to make films about rural Britain, which was not the current flavour of the month. So he had been honourable and had resigned, with no cash, and had set up his own company and advertised for a production manager. Andy de Salas had applied.

But Andy's credentials were minimal. He had been a mediocre student of Media at a college in the north, and had then become a runner for a production company in Soho, making coffee and distributing tape stock. The one thing he had was the one thing Ben Lowe needed – money. Andy de Salas was a very rich young man in his own right.

'His parents have a house in Chelsea and another place like a sort of stately home with chunky bits on . . .'

'You mean battlements?'

'Yes, something like that. In Sussex. And Andy is their only child.'

'So he can have anything money can buy?'

'Yes . . . which counts out common sense. I know his flaws. I love him dearly, Kate, but I can see that.'

'So what is it that you love?'

'He tries so hard, it makes my heart turn over. And he wants me so much. You know what I told you about Steve's domestic bullying? Well, Andy is exactly the opposite. He needs people. Me and Ben for that matter.'

Kate could see that.

'And Ben was doing a marvellous job of training Andy. Andy has got fantastic artistic ability, but no organisational or journalistic sense at all. Ben realised that, and he was working on turning Andy into a first class pictorial director. You said yourself that some of his film work was excellent.'

'True.'

'So Andy's confidence was building; that's why his cracking up this weekend was such a shock and a shame. But he's never been terribly stable. And part of that is because of the accident. He told me that when he had been very young, he had injured someone badly in a smash. He wouldn't tell me more, except that his father had helped him pay the damages. It had happened when he was at college, in his first term, and he had been in a desperate hurry to get to see some friends – Oxbridge friends, I think – who were in the area on holiday. He left college on the

Friday night, but he had been drinking. His parents had bought him a car to learn in, and he hadn't much experience. He lost control coming down a steep hill in the dark, and then he hit another car with a woman driver who had been pulling out of a pub car park. He said he was distracted by the lights of the pub. It was virtually a vertical drop down into this valley and it was a very dark night.' She paused. 'Kate, why are you staring at me?' Kate physically strained to move her eyes off her friend. There was no need, she knew, to distress Liz by telling her about that ghastly Pennine drive. But the story sounded terrifyingly familiar.

'Liz, this accident years ago, it couldn't have happened on the road from Newcastle, could it?'

'Well, that's where Andy was at college. Didn't I tell you that?'

Kate knew then that Andy de Salas had been reliving a terrible moment when he had catapulted the Porsche down the bank towards the pub on her journey from hell. And her mind was racing faster than his car. Sometime in the last week she had heard about a woman involved in an accident, on that same road, seventeen years earlier. She furrowed her eyebrows. And then with a feeling of bile in her mouth she remembered. Jean Robinson.

'How old is Andy?'

'What? He's thirty-four. A lot younger than me I know, but . . .' Liz went on about the age gap, but that was not what interested Kate.

'You've gone quiet, Kate.'

'Have I? Sorry. I'm thinking about John.' But, for once, she wasn't.

* * *

266

But John Maple was thinking about her. He knew that he should have been trying to pray with the same intensity as George Goff, whose head was bowed in the pew next to him, but John was asking Kate's forgiveness rather than God's.

John knew he should have been back at one o'clock to reassure Kate, and he could see through the silly drama of her ultimatum to the real insecurity beneath. But one o'clock had found him at the Goffs' bungalow, with George more distraught even than the night before.

They had returned to the church after a stressful lunch, and now John watched George pray and realised from the movement of the old man's lips that he was relying on saying by rote, again and again, the Prayer for Grace. John sighed. George was in a mess, but in John's opinion he was making it worse by not coming clean to anyone other than the Almighty. The younger clergyman touched his shoulder and George looked up as if shot.

'George, tell me again. There must be a way through this moral morass.'

George looked down at his white hands, still clasped together.

'I've told you all I can. Someone came and confided a huge fear to me, but did so because I was a clergyman. She needed to unburden herself in God's presence.'

'She?'

'John, forget the pronoun. I couldn't give this person absolution and anyway, she didn't ask for it. But she told me another person was hounding her. They both had been equally blameworthy in a guilty endeavour, but while my . . . parishioner . . . felt some remorse, the other person felt none. I was begged, begged in the name of God, not to reveal who was involved.'

'But you think you know who it is.'

'Yes.'

'And what are you going to do next?'

'I must contact this person again. If what my original informant said was true, the man is in need of help. He's a regular communicant, John. I'm frightened for his immortal soul, and I'm frightened for myself. You know I invited you here because I wanted to pray with you, and to tell you as much as my conscience allowed.'

'But there's little I can do, George. I can stay with you for a while, but I can't watch over you all the time. If you won't tell me who the people are or what offence they are supposed to have committed, I can do little more than pray with and for you.'

'That should be enough. At least, as another priest, you understand my constraints. And, you see, the whole thing is so unlikely I can't be sure. John, you have to just support me while I try and get to the centre of this. Maybe I will be able to invoke the spirit of Christ . . .'

'Oh, come on, George. I believe in Christ, you believe in Christ, but we both know God doesn't act like bleach. You won't be breaking any ecclesiastical confidence if you *tell* me, and at least I can help you deal with these people.'

'I can't – it's so incredible. If I tell you it will mean I suspect that it's true. And I promised . . .' George began to moan.

'But can't you go back to the woman who spilt the beans to you and ask permission to tackle the madman at the centre of this? If there *is* a madman at the centre of this?'

'No.' George's voice rose to a wail. 'I can't. Don't you see? She's dead!'

* * *

It was an hour later when Kate and Liz arrived back at the Skirlbeck Bridge Hotel. Kate had sat in the taxi from the Cumberland Infirmary absorbed in thoughts that generated their own progress, even when she tried to stop them. The evening dropped and darkened over the bright westerly sky. It seemed crazy on one level, and utterly possible on another, to imagine that Andy de Salas, years ago, had been involved in a car accident which had crippled Jean Robinson. It could explain why de Salas had wanted to be in the area in the first place.

On the other hand, what was to stop him travelling up any weekend if he wanted to visit West Cumbria and meet a woman whose life he had blighted so many years ago?

But say he had no idea where Jean Robinson now lived, and he wanted to find out? He would have needed time, and some reasonable pretext to be in the area for a protracted period, so he could find her, and approach her. Why? Kate remembered what the twins had revealed about their mother's financial affairs, sitting on the bed that night surrounded by her dockets and cash books. The 'bad old bitch' of Hodgson's vernacular could have been bleeding Andy for years for all she could get. Perhaps, now, he had needed to settle something with her.

Like a lot of crazy notions, the more Kate tried to dismiss it the more it stuck. She glanced at Liz who was staring with a sort of exhausted fixation out of the cab window towards the sea. Could Liz be involved with a homicidal maniac? Kate put the thought in those terms to show herself how laughable her theory was. But looking at Liz's face, years older and sadder than before this trip to Cumbria, Kate wondered if her wild ideas could actually be true. In fact, putting them into words made them more, rather than less, likely to be fact.

Kate wanted John desperately, with the need for a comradeship she had undervalued. His common sense, his refusal to overreact or get into heated argument, suddenly seemed to her the most attractive traits in the world. But then her pride reasserted itself. John had had every chance to come back and explain things to her, but he hadn't.

In the hotel Kate asked for any messages. Yes, said the girl who was still on duty, there had actually been two. One was from a Miss Sally Dodd, wondering if she and Kate could meet the next day. And the other was from Malcolm Hodgson. Trembling, Kate picked up the message pad and stared at Malcolm's number. He had not left anything else. She was amazed at the strength of her own reaction. She needed Malcolm, professionally, and perhaps personally, and their conversation on the mobile phone had shaken her more than she had admitted to herself. Kate said nothing to Liz, but folded the paper and stuffed it in her bag. They parted to tidy up before dinner, and Kate hurried to her room. The phone was ringing as she walked in the door.

'Kate, it's John. I owe you an apology.' She felt a sudden burst of relief, then the hardening of her heart, because John sounded harassed rather than sorry. He went on, 'I'm still here with George. I can't leave him.'

'If you say so,' she said coldly.

'Kate, you have to believe me that this is serious.'

'I'm sure it is. Too serious for me.' There was a silence before Kate spoke again. 'You were supposed to be travelling back on the sleeper tonight. Are you going home, or coming back to the Skirlbeck? Or staying with George?

And what about London and Father Marcus? How on earth will they be able to manage without you?' He ignored her sarcastic tone.

'I must take care of George. I'm going to tell Marcus I need to stay up here for a couple of days.'

'So now you've found another dependent. Although I wonder who needs whom most?'

'That was nasty, Kate.'

'But true, I suspect? I'm tired of being understanding, especially as I'm not allowed to know what I'm supposed to understand.'

'Look, I couldn't leave George to get back to you for one o'clock. You have to understand that. And tonight Eileen is making a meal for us before she goes out. But when we've eaten, and George's settled, it'll be safe to leave him. Can you give me another chance? I desperately want to talk to you.'

Kate's voice softened. 'OK,' she said. 'If you mean that, come and see me later. After supper.'

'All right. Thanks.'

But it was an unsatisfactory call, limping to goodbyes.

Then Kate rang Malcolm Hodgson back. But yet again, there was no reply, giving her a little more time to think. She had to work out carefully what to say to him. She was desperate to convince him that she was not just a southern muckraker out for sensation. And more important than any sexual desire between them was the need to get Malcolm to agree to be in the film. The more she repeated his story to other people the more the horror of it struck home. She remembered the incident in the little Renault when they were surrounded by louts with dogs, not because of her furtive passion, but because of the fear and disgust the mob

271

outside had engendered. Malcolm Hodgson had to be persuaded to tell the story. And she would need no persuading to ring him again.

That left Sally Dodd. Kate dialled the number and heard the younger woman's cheery voice at the other end.

'Kate. Great of you to phone back. Look, this may be a crazy idea, but it's half term this week and I get a few days' break. Cliff's up to his neck in it, literally, on the farm. Could I come and join you on your shoot? I want to talk to you, anyway.'

'Great minds think alike, Sally,' Kate smiled. 'We could actually use you and I was working along these lines myself. We've got a lot to do. It looks like we might have a commission for this programme after all.'

'Brilliant!' Sally sounded enthused. 'When can I join you?'

'Why not breakfast with us at eight tomorrow? We plan to have a production meeting then, and if you really want to do this seriously you should join us.'

'Done.' That word again.

Kate said goodbye. She had half an hour before dinner. She took off her clothes and walked into the little bathroom, running the shower until it was steaming. The water was a purge of stinging rods that hit her like red hot hailstones, and she scrubbed at her skin with a desire to expunge all the murky mess around her. Unexpectedly, it made her remember a steamy session with John, when he had come into the shower after her, and she had been pink and scrubbed and languorous with the effort of washing. They had started making love as a joke, the sort of fun thing they had both read about. But John had turned off the water because it was making them giggle and he wanted her with fierceness now, not fun. He had massaged her breasts with violent intensity, and then lifted her up, so that with her feet on the low shelf round the shower tray and his legs between hers, he could push into her from an angle they had never tried before. Their bodies had been wet and hot and slippery with soap, and Kate had clung to him half in fear she would slide down the tiles and half with the sheer pleasure of his thrust. The pressure had brought them together for a climax that had stunned her and left the imprint of the soap dish in her back for hours. John had laughed at her waddling out of the shower, bow legged and blotchy thanks to him, and she had moaned because in books the couple were immediately cloaked in immaculate bathrobes and sipping champagne by the fire, while she had a half cold cup of coffee dripping by the basin, and a grey-green towel draped over the toilet lid! But they had been so happy. It had been one of those Sunday evenings before every hour of John's time was pencilled in with meetings and masses. As she shampooed her hair she remembered later Sundays, when she had been reduced to walking round the muddy little park near the house on her own, filling in time waiting for him on some errand he chose not to explain.

The seeds of their problems had always been there. She wondered if perhaps, fundamentally, a love affair between a priest and an agnostic had no chance at all, but was as much a mirage as the faith he thought sustained him. She and John had experienced a great rapport, which was more to do with a shared sense of humour, and sex, and a sense of trying to do the right thing in a wrong world, than any common ideology. But it had not been enough.

And then there was Malcolm Hodgson. There was no doubt Kate desired him, but she wondered if perhaps that was just because he had been the first man for a long time who had shown signs of desiring her. She had been too wrapped up in John to even notice other men before, and now the distancing he had put between them made her far more susceptible to attention from others. Like most normal, vulnerable human beings, she wanted to think herself desirable. And Malcolm made her feel attractive, even if it was just with the practised habits of an inveterate womaniser.

She paced the room. She knew she had been over dramatic that morning, but the result was that for the first time she had given John an ultimatum, and he knew it. And surprisingly, the unexpected burst of confidence she had felt earlier that afternoon – probably because she saw her vision of the film working out for the first time – had given her the guts to tackle him honestly.

Honesty. She thought again about Liz and de Salas, and shuddered. It made her see her own situation with greater clarity than ever before. If what she suspected was true, Liz was in an unbelievable mess.

But Kate's suspicions needed verifying. And if it were true, how could she possibly tell Liz, who was already in such a vulnerable state: hey, you think your lover is cracking up because you've had an abortion, well, now for the bad news! He was actually responsible for maiming a woman who was a well known blackmailer, and now she's been found dead, and your lover has disappeared. What do you make of that!

Kate shook her head, and moved back from the window, drawing the curtains as if to shut out her own dark thoughts. But they stayed with her as surely as if they had seeped through the keyhole.

She dried her hair and went downstairs to meet Liz, who looked better now, more relaxed.

'Did you get Andy on the phone?' Kate asked, knowing the answer.

'No, but I spoke to his mother.' Liz seemed fragile but bright. 'It was the first time we've spoken and she actually sounded very nice.' Kate could see this meant a significant advance to Liz. 'She said Andy had arrived home safely but had gone out for a walk. I took a risk, and asked how he was. She knew what I meant. She said he was thoughtful, but not too miserable. And he'd left a message saying that if I called to send me his love! Wasn't that nice!'

'Mmm. So will he be getting in touch?'

'I don't see any reason why not. But his mother said he was fine.' And that's the most important thing, thought Kate, raising her eyebrow. She was becoming more and more convinced that de Salas was on the run. But from what, she was unsure. She said nothing and ordered a mineral water.

It was Liz who drove the conversation through dinner. She had been thinking about the film and was filled with enthusiasm. It was Kate who was distracted. Over the coffee, Kate heard the door of the hotel being opened and Bill greeting someone with his usual bonhomie.

'John,' she called out, leaping up. John Maple stood in the doorway.

'Don't give me this crap about not caring about him.' Liz laughed. 'Look at you!' But Kate wasn't listening. She had left the table and walked into the hall and was looking at John. He seemed older and more tired, his tall frame more stooped, and his manner impatient. He said, 'Let's go straight to our room. We need to talk. Make an excuse with Liz. She won't mind. And ask those landlord chaps to let us have some tea upstairs.'

It seemed an age before she had organised tea, and John had taken off his coat and settled in the armchair in their bedroom. Kate sat opposite him and raised her cup to her lips at the same time John put his head in his hands.

'You start, Kate.'

'All right. But I'd like to know what's happening with George Goff. As much as anything, because I like him too!'

'It's a nightmare. He's as obsessed about confidentiality as I am, if not worse. I'll tell you a little, but you must promise me faithfully not to repeat this to anyone. Anyone, you understand?'

'Of course.'

John outlined for Kate what George Goff had told him about his parishioner's revelations, and the old priest's obvious terror.

Kate listened intently then said, 'It's clear the woman was Jean Robinson.'

'The strange twins' mother? I think you must be right. But who the other person is, I don't know.'

'Does George think this man killed her?'

'He doesn't know. He's terribly distressed. He knows that if he so much as voices the name of the person, he smashes a whole rural structure. He can't face that.'

'But if he doesn't, he may leave a murderer on the loose.'

'Quite!'

Kate sat back in the chair and sipped more tea. Then she leaned forward and said, 'I think George's fears might be completely unfounded. Everyone now suspects Jean Robinson was helped to her death. But she had so many enemies! I've got a different theory about who did it.' Slowly, carefully, she went through all the things that had happened since she arrived in Skirlbeck, and which pointed to Andy de Salas's guilt. John listened intently.

'Kate, this is incredible. And terrible. Even more terrible than George's scenario.'

'For us, yes, because of Liz. And she's already wretched enough.'

'Wretched enough?'

'Yes. She's recovering from an abortion.'

John face twisted in what Kate could only think of as spontaneous disgust. He tried to cover it, but she had seen it. She waited, but he said nothing. Then she took a deep breath.

'Let's put all the Skirlbeck drama to one side, John. We need to talk about what is happening to us – you and me. I think there's more to our problems than you spending time with Marcus, who sounds like a loathsome self-obsessed creep, and George, who is a lovely man with genuine worries. Your face just said it all.' She paused. 'There is a real gulf between us on some things, isn't there? That's why you're frightened of talking. It's not just a question of my not believing in God. It's deeper than that!' She said the last few words to make him smile, because she knew nothing mattered more to him than belief in God, but he did not smile back. Instead he looked up, anguished.

'You're right. There are things that divide us.'

'And abortion is one of them?' suggested Kate.

'Yes, it's a real problem for me. It was a big issue when I was young and I campaigned against it. I didn't want you to know that.'

'But isn't it better to discuss it, John, than pretend it doesn't matter?'

'But, Kate, I want to respect your beliefs. I don't want to argue. If we do, it could lead to us . . .'

'Splitting up? Well, if we did, wouldn't that be better than living with a time bomb?'

'But it wouldn't be a time bomb. It would be something that we chose not to talk about.'

'So how does that leave you with my past?'

'Your past is yours, not mine.'

'But say I told you that I would do exactly the same again?'

'That wouldn't happen, Kate.'

'It might. Say I had an affair with someone?'

'You wouldn't do that!'

'How do you know? You've paid me so little attention lately I might easily. But that's not the point. I'm asking you about what you would think, if now, like Liz, I chose an abortion?'

'I would hate it.'

'So how do you cope with the fact that I did it once before?'

'Because I can understand someone being driven to it. And as long as you're sorry . . .'

'Sorry! Sorry! How can you sit there and say that? As a matter of fact, I'm *not* sorry. I regret it had to happen, but I'm glad, really glad, that I had the choice. Otherwise I'd have been left with a monster for a husband and a life of misery. Why should I have to face that, and you not? You can't tell me every time you've had sex, it's been in responsible circumstances. For heaven's sake, John, we've even taken risks ourselves, and our relationship is by no means settled!'

'I accept what you say, Kate, but what I feel is what I

feel. This is why these rows are so damaging. We're not discussing things, we're throwing our love at walls.'

'But I'd rather do that than pretend the walls aren't there!'

'Would you? Can't you accept that there are some things we must agree to differ on?'

'But, John, you can't fail to understand. It's a woman's body and she knows that it isn't wicked. It isn't right or desirable, but it isn't a fundamental human crime either. If it were, women just couldn't do it. Look at it from Liz's point of view . . .'

'Kate, this is exactly what I mean. You've opened a wound and our relationship will haemorrhage to death.'

'Because you won't see sense?'

'Because you won't let things be!'

'OK, then let it bleed!'

She stood up so sharply the tea splashed over into the saucer. She clattered her cup down on to the desk. 'I can't live like that, John. I'm not Eileen Goff, happy to see my views as weird and there to be humoured and sidelined. I need a relationship with another adult who can talk to me . . .'

'You don't want to talk, Kate. You want to convince.'

She was silent. He had hit a nerve. But she too had fired some pretty damaging shots.

'So where does that leave us?'

'Nowhere. It won't work.'

'No. I think you're right.' The coldness in his voice stunned her more than any of his arguments, and she saw that their discussion had cut him to the quick. But there was no going back. Suddenly she felt enraged with him. They had had so much potential together, but it was all a stillborn mess. Abortion! How ironic!

'Well then, leave, John. Go where you really want to be. With George Goff. Pack your bag, and stay with him. I suspect you planned to do that anyway.'

He was silent and in cold fury she realised that her throwaway line was actually true. John had been meaning to go back to the Goffs' all along. Her voice raised to a shout.

'That was what you planned, wasn't it? Going back to your precious clerical friend whose views won't upset you. You hypocritical bastard. Get out of my room. I can do without you, John. I'll sort out the rest of my things from the flat when I get back to London.'

'You're saying terrible things, Kate. It doesn't have to end like this.' He was shouting too now, still controlled, but pale and shaking as if the effort was almost too much.

'Don't patronise me, John. I need a better partnership than that.' She strode to the window and drew back the curtains, looking out over the dark sea as if its breadth would give her some sort of comfort.

'OK, Katy,' he said, suddenly and surprisingly quiet. 'I understand. I can't give you what you need. So perhaps we should go our separate ways.'

When she turned back from the window, the door was shutting behind him.

Chapter Eleven

Kate looked at the excited group in front of her around the main table in the Skirlbeck Bridge dining room, eating scrambled eggs, smoked salmon and home-made croissants. Jerry the cameraman and his truculent partner – still resembling a cropped blond pixie – sat slightly apart from the rest of the team. But Jerry was looking intently over his coffee cup with a mixture of apprehension and admiration at Liz Jones. In turn she was deep in animated conversation with Sally Dodd. Next to them sat June Ridley, looking quietly satisfied as she made notes about the day ahead.

Kate had spent the lonely misery of the night before working out what she was going to say and do at this, her first production meeting. She had the taut, alert sensation that comes from lack of sleep and stress. But she knew that it was only by focusing every nerve on the details of the work ahead that she could live with the great empty ache with which she had woken. It had not been a question of opening her eyes and remembering that John had left, more a sensation of loss even before she woke.

She looked at Liz, who was still talking with Sally. To Kate her best friend seemed to be in a fools' paradise, still convinced that de Salas was merely needing 'space', and sure that he would suddenly phone, contrite and charming, ready to start again. Kate wondered which was worse, to be happily duped like Liz, or tortured by the need to take everything to its ultimate conclusion as she was. In her pain it was only her pride that made her support the latter option.

'Kate?' Liz was calling. 'Isn't it time you talked us through the next stage of the plan?'

'Yes, absolutely. Has everyone had enough to eat, and refilled their coffee cup? The way I'd like to organise things is like this: Liz, could you work as director with Jerry? Sally Dodd, who's local to Skirlbeck, will act as our researcher. And June will be the PA as before. This week, we were going to film at an aromatherapy centre and possibly the sailing school. I'd like to go ahead with both, but for shorter shoots. One thing, before I go any further. I need to rely on absolute confidentiality.' She looked at Jerry in particular as she said this. He was the one in the group she felt she knew least. He nodded almost imperceptibly. 'Right,' she said.

Quietly, she outlined the new shape for the film. Realising that Sally knew nothing, Kate tried to describe what she planned in unemotional terms, but she saw her grow pale. For a moment she wondered whether she should have sprung it on Sally in quite this way, but reminded herself the younger woman had asked to join them rather than the other way around, and for the sake of speed and solidarity, it was better to go through everything with the whole group.

'There is one person I can't mention at this stage who would make a superb interviewee on this. But as yet he won't play ball, though I intend to suggest it again to him.'

Liz raised an eyebrow which Kate ignored. 'And, Sally, whilst we wouldn't expect you to make the approaches, you might have the local contacts to help.'

'It's a shock to me,' Sally said but looked at the group without flinching. 'I've never heard of anything like it, have you, Jerry?' The cameraman shook his head for a fraction of a second, and then seemed to think better of it. 'Actually,' he said, hesitantly and without his usual slightly bolshie tone, 'I *have* heard about something like this dogfighting. It's the sort of thing that gets mentioned sometimes in pubs. The Castle Arms down on the coast and places like that. But it wasn't my scene.'

Kate, surprised but heartened by this new evidence, nodded at him gratefully. 'We still want to cover the new commercial ventures in the area, and look at how this corner of West Cumbria is adapting to change, but we will use that as a backdrop to the main story. Today, Liz and Jerry should proceed down to the aromatherapy centre with June, and Sally and I will start making some calls and follow on. We'll all meet up at lunchtime and I'd like to invite everyone back here for dinner tonight, to talk over the day's progress. I understand if you want to get away, Jerry, but if you could spare us an evening I'd appreciate it.'

'Glad to,' said Jerry gruffly, to her surprise.

They left in a clatter of chat and equipment which seemed to Kate to be the proper state of professional bustle, and she felt another surge of confidence. Then she and Sally were left alone at the big table.

'What did Cliff tell you last night?'

'Precious little, to be honest. I certainly never knew . . .' Sally shook her head, trying to look more knowing and less stunned.

'Look, Sally, I'm sure it's the predictable minority of people who actually take part in this cruelty. But the more I think about it, the more I'm sure that the video reproduction must have been for the dogfights.'

'I think you're right. Things haven't been the same between Cliff and me since this all blew up, but one thing he *did* say was that it was nothing to do with him, and if I was so damn interested I could find out about it in the local pubs. Cliff's not involved, but he knows who's behind it all, I'm sure.'

'You mean there's one person setting this up?'

'I think so. Cliff said that he didn't like what was happening but that he "couldn't take them on". Last night was the first night we've sat and watched TV with the old folks rather than sneaking off on our own. He couldn't face me. If we get to the bottom of all of this, it won't be thanks to Cliff. But we've got to try.'

'A woman after my own heart.' Kate smiled, but the pain of being reminded of her own new independence made the smile twisted, and she turned away in case her eyes filled up.

She left Sally reading about the sailing centre from the leaflets June had provided, and moved over to use the phone on the big oak sideboard at the side of the dining room. Kate knew that ringing Malcolm Hodgson was on her agenda, and the thought made her tired throat feel dry and her stomach churn. But next, it had to be Paul Pym.

His secretary answered and put her through after a deferential pause, saying obsequiously, 'Mr Pym, director of the Centre, is on the line for you now.'

'Hello, Paul. Kate Wilkinson here. Producer of the project for Rural Rides Revisited.'

'Kate! Delighted. What can I do for you?'

'I'm calling to let you know that things have changed slightly. Andy de Salas has left us to go back to London so I've taken over the filming, strictly in accordance with the wishes of Andy, and Ben Lowe his partner.'

'Really? I do hope Andy has no serious problem?'

'Not at all. We're hoping he'll rejoin us before the end of the week. But the nature of the programme has changed too, Paul. I know Andy was talking about even more filming at the Centre. But that won't be necessary now.'

Pym paused momentarily and then said, 'That's actually very good news, Kate. I assume you have a broadcaster interested?' She admired his ability to master the situation. Perhaps he had found de Salas's dependency cloying. His voice seemed genuinely warm and encouraging.

'Yes, we have. Channel Four.' She could sense his surprise.

'Goodness, you really have hooked a big fish.' His voice was a compelling mixture of encouragement and astonishment which made her want to impress him. She remembered Malcolm Hodgson telling her that everyone wanted to make their mark on Paul Pym, and she knew that she was feeling the same. He went on, 'I'm surprised a commissioning editor took the bait.'

'Well, fortunately for us an old colleague of mine whom I think I mentioned to you – Chrissia Cohen – is very keen. But of course we are having to change the nature of the film a little.'

'I should think so. Tell me how you hope to develop it?'

'We have some evidence about other rural interests being revived as well as the crafts. Bloodsports of a sort.'

'You can't mean the rumours one hears about in local

hostelries? Oh, surely that's just gossip.' A slightly huffy note entered his voice, making Kate keener to placate him than any aggression would have done.

'Oh, please don't feel let down, Paul. Perhaps we can re-edit something for the Tourist Centre. But this Channel Four opportunity cannot be ignored.'

'I suppose not. Although obviously this is a minor disappointment to us. Not that anything was guaranteed, of course. Out of interest, though, how are you getting this other information you need? I wouldn't have thought you had too many local contacts.'

'Oh, we're doing better than you might think. As a matter of fact, the local vicar, George Goff, is a friend of a friend and may well help us . . .'

'Really? What a small world. He's a nice old chap, but I can't see him in some sort of "World in Action"-type investigation.'

'You never know.'

'Well, you're the expert. And, of course, you've been taken up by Councillor Malcolm Hodgson haven't you?'

It was on the tip of Kate's twisted tongue to mumble, 'How did you know . . . ?' and then she remembered the night at the Summerlake Hall Hotel and how she had looked out of Malcolm's Range Rover window and into Pym's disgusted face.

'Not exactly.' Kate tried to avoid the embarrassment creeping into her voice. The implication that Malcolm had actively tried to insinuate himself worried her. 'But yes, Councillor Hodgson has been helpful.'

'Dangerous chappie, nonetheless. Got a reputation for being on the make.' Kate remembered Malcolm's confession about Pym's secretary. Perhaps it was the woman whose saccharine voice had put her through earlier. Pym was saying, 'Do watch him.' Kate wondered whether he meant personally or professionally. She recalled Malcolm Hodgson's discussion with the twins about a catering contract for the theme park. A little local government venality was perhaps inevitable, but it did undermine Malcolm's integrity. But she had promised him her discretion.

'Paul, it's fair to say Councillor Hodgson is not involved in this film at all.' At this stage, she added mentally.

'That's a shame. Sounds like you have quite a job on your hands. The area is harder to penetrate than you think. Just when you believe you're accepted, you find you're right back on the perimeter.' He sighed. 'You know, the Tourist Centre might not be central to your new concept, but I do think you should think carefully before falling prey to an idea which could be merely sensational and which could do a great deal of harm to the district.'

His point silenced her for a minute. 'Look, Kate, why not come over to the Centre today? I'd like to try and change your mind for you. Channel Four money isn't everything.'

'I'm sorry, Paul, but I can't. I've got masses to do, as well as some researching at the local paper offices.'

'Really? Which one?' he asked.

'*West Cumbria Informer*.'

'First class paper. I'll call one of my contacts, the chief reporter, and let him know you're going over.'

Her heart sank. She was hoist now, forced to spend at least part of the afternoon looking up things she hardly needed to know, just because something about Paul Pym made it impossible to say 'get lost'.

'Thank you. In the circumstances, you've been very kind.'

'Anything I can do to help the cause of quality TV.' He was ruefully warm now. 'Perhaps your film can be re-run six times on cable! No, that was really just a joke, Kate. I hope you see now that I'm not the old stick in the mud you thought me! And despite your change of direction, do let me know if there's anything we can do to help. I'd like to try and influence you to make sure the area doesn't appear all bad in your film.'

'Paul, it wouldn't! The place has really got under my skin.'

'Well, don't forget; we're here to help you make it look as wonderful as possible. Although I can see that light and shade might make for a more stunning product, nevertheless.' His voice had an intelligence Kate had not appreciated. Surprised at his generous attitude, she put down the phone.

It remained to telephone Malcolm Hodgson. However confident she tried to be, without his input there was little likelihood of the film really happening. The phone rang out again at his home, but once again there was no reply. She put it down and chewed her lip. If Malcolm really couldn't be involved, she had to find other people. George Goff?

She went over the conversation she'd had with the elderly priest the night she arrived in Skirlbeck. She remembered his distraction as they stood on the step to say goodbye, and how she thought he had flinched from her London-style kisses. But George had flinched because a dog had barked. She remembered how he had tensed and how a group of men had passed the end of the Skirlbeck Bridge's drive with a dog. Now she was more in tune with the area she realised how odd that was. Why would men and dogs be traipsing through the lane at eleven o'clock at night? Skirlbeck was just a village. How many mysteries could it contain? Was George's anxiety linked to the dogfighting too? Her fingers flickered over the phone keypad. And she dialled the Goffs.

Eileen answered. From the breathlessness of her tone Kate knew the formidable Mrs Goff was distressed. Eileen Goff wore her emotions like designer clothes.

'Eileen. Hello. It's Kate Wilkinson.'

Before she could carry on Eileen said, 'John's not here at the moment, Kate. He and George are up at Skirlbeck House because of Celia Marshall.'

'Sorry?'

Eileen's agitated breath could be heard and her voice was rising. She was an unusual blend of capability and self dramatisation, and the latter was gaining the upper hand.

'Celia Marshall. She had a heart attack yesterday morning. I'm afraid she's . . . It's quite dreadful. Sir Michael is in an appalling state. He stayed with her on his own for hours. I *knew* there was something going on myself; George may joke about my gift, but I do *know*. I was drawn back to the meeting last night, I know I was . . .'

'Hold on, Eileen. You're saying Celia Marshall is dead?'

'Yes.'

'When did you find out?'

'This morning.' Eileen's voice was calmer now. 'Apparently it happened early yesterday but Sir Michael didn't even call an ambulance until two o'clock. Then they took her to Carlisle. He had to be treated for shock and the police brought him home this morning. The first person he contacted was George. As if George didn't have enough to worry about. And then there was the message . . .'

Eileen's voice was rising again.

'Eileen, I'm so sorry. You've obviously got plenty to get on with, without me. Look, forget I called. I'll ring later.'

Eileen was so harassed she almost put the phone down without a breathy goodbye. Kate rose from the chair by the sideboard where she had commandeered the phone, and made for the door at the back of the dining room.

In the kitchen Terry Robinson was dressed in his usual pinny, a sensible white apron which somehow on him had the look of a French maid's frill, and was absolutely intent on rolling pastry to within a millimetre of its life. In the background, Kate caught Bill watching him. She was suddenly made acutely aware of the differences in the twins. Bill was fractionally bigger, and his features were slightly coarser, so that Terry had the look of an ageing cherub while Bill was like the blueprint that hadn't quite worked. Bill was watching his brother with protectiveness and Kate was made aware of the strength in his folded arms, and the concentration in his features. She remembered Cliff Thompson's mother saying, 'Bill wanted to go to London or Manchester, and take Terry, but his mother wouldn't hear of it.' As she watched, Bill turned to rip a piece of kitchen roll from its holder on the wall. He leaned forward and mopped his brother's brow, then dropped the paper into the bin, all in one swift movement. Kate had never noticed the muscles in his arms, or the quiet power of his manner.

'Bill,' she said, adding 'Terry' as an afterthought. The younger twin looked up surprised and stopped rolling. Bill moved forward.

'Kate?'

'I came through to ask if you had heard about Lady Marshall.'

'No, what's she up to now?'

'Nothing. She isn't up to anything, Terry. I'm afraid she has had a heart attack. I understand she's dead.'

'Oh, good Lord.' Terry sat down heavily on the hoop-backed kitchen chair, and Bill moved in to hold him lightly on the shoulders.

'Who could believe it?' whispered Terry. 'She was so fit, and busy and sort of bustly . . .'

'Quite. I only met her once, but she made an impression. I just thought I'd tell you. I needed to ring the Goffs and Eileen Goff told me. It seemed wrong, me knowing and not you.'

'Well,' Terry said after shaking his head ruefully, 'no wonder there was such a strange atmosphere at the meeting last night.'

Kate looked at him curiously. 'What meeting?'

'Our meeting. The Spiritualists. We must have told you that we go religiously!'

He smiled up at his brother over his own joke. 'It's something we find interesting, Kate,' he said warily, but Bill was not smiling back.

'But after your mother . . .' Kate knew she was being intrusive, but she would have thought that the idea of contacting the late Mrs Jean Robinson would have killed the twins' enthusiasm for spiritualism deader than a bucket of ectoplasm. 'I mean, do you really believe in it?'

Terry was mildly outraged. 'We certainly do,' he said.

'That was one of the reasons we went last night.' Bill looked apologetic. 'We just wondered if perhaps we might get a clue – you know, about mother – and when Eileen turned up, Mrs Goff as she is now, we thought that perhaps there really would be a message for us.'

'And was there?'

'Yes. Well, sort of,' Terry said agitatedly. 'Eileen told us there was death in the air, didn't she, Bill? And that Mother wasn't yet at peace but soon would be.' Bill was still looking at him and again nodded encouragingly, as if this was something Terry had needed to hear. Then Bill rushed on, 'But she did say that our mother's death had something to do with a castle, and of course our mother used to go to the Castle Arms down on the coast and so it all added up. And we felt happy with that, didn't we, Terry? After all, if Mother is soon to be at peace . . .'

'Anyway . . .' Terry was looking longingly at the pastry, 'back to work. Thank you for telling us about Lady Marshall, Kate.'

She was about to say 'a pleasure' when the inappropriateness of the remark stopped her. She looked back at them.

'I hope you don't mind me asking,' she said, 'but when did your mother have her accident?'

'The twenty first of October, seventeen years ago.' Terry said it so quickly she knew it had been on his mind.

'So it was the anniversary the night I arrived?'

'Yes.' Bill was looking at her with unusual reserve. 'Why do you ask?'

'I'm sorry. I was just curious.'

She smiled, but awkwardly, and turned to go back into the dining room.

Sally was waiting for Kate. She had pushed the sailing school brochure to one side.

'Is that fixed up?' Kate gestured towards it and Sally nodded back. 'Yeah, I just phoned them. We can go straight there tomorrow morning.'

Kate grabbed her bag and led the way out to yet another hire car, delivered that morning. Driving into the watery sun her eyes ached with the effort of focusing and she and Sally said little.

The aromatherapy shop and clinic, bizarrely called Fells and Smells and run by an unbearably folksy couple with strong London accents, had obviously been chosen by Andy de Salas for its visual strength rather than any claims to revitalise the area. Most of the clients seemed to travel from Manchester or Newcastle and pay enormous amounts for the home-distilled oils which glowed from a disorganised crowd of attractive bottles along the pinewood shelves. It was all rather jolly, but of even less local significance than Kenny the jeweller's bronzed kneecap brooches.

At a convenient moment Kate pulled June to one side. The PA was infinitely happier this Monday morning than the week before, when Kate had met her and de Salas in the mill car park. Kate remembered the vibrant Celia Marshall bouncing out of her little red car, and shuddered.

'June,' she whispered. 'Have you heard about Lady Marshall?'

'What about her?'

'She's dead.'

'*What?*'

'She died. Heart attack. Yesterday.'

June was standing staring at Kate with her mouth open, and the colour dissolving from her face to leave a pale waxy mask.

'I didn't mean to shock you. Good heavens, June, you look as if you're going to faint. Sit down.'

'Oh, God.' June lurched towards a spongy chaise longue

in one corner of the bric-a-brac laden consulting room, redolent of some sweet and unusual unguent.

'What is it, June?'

'Oh, Kate . . .'

'Tell me.'

'The money. The money Andy got for the film. It was from her.'

'Who? Oh, you can't mean Lady Marshall?'

'Yes. There's a confidential letter she wrote to Andy confirming that she was prepared to support Rural Rides on his project with a donation of several thousand pounds.'

'But you can't do that. If the film was ever to get on to ITV or Channel Four it would be against the rules, because we feature her mill and shop.'

'I know.' June's voice sounded like agony.

'So how was he going to square that with the regulations?'

'You know how confusing all so-called guidelines are. I think Andy was hoping no-one would ever spot it. Lady Marshall apparently had another business and the cheque was to be drawn on that, so no-one would ever be able to say she'd paid for the mill to be featured on TV.'

'And was her contribution going to pay for the hotel, and the crew?'

'Yes.'

'So what about paying Jerry and the pixie?'

'Well, obviously Andy thought he would have a cheque from her before the end of the shoot.'

Kate sighed. The minefield of regulations covering TV programme funding drove her and most other producers mad.

'How could Andy have been so stupid?'

'Oh, Kate, you know lots of people do things like that now.'

'But whatever the rights and wrongs, there's no money?'

'There's probably enough in Rural Rides' general account to pay Jerry and the hotel bills. But until we get an advance from Channel Four, there's no more for anything else.'

'Not for me? Or you? Or the bill for editing this, or the voice-over? Or making title sequences, or title music?'

'Nothing.'

Kate leaned against the wall and looked at June's pale face. Then she said briskly, 'OK. Well, that's that. If we get a Channel Four acceptance, Celia Marshall's money will be neither here nor there. But we won't get that go-ahead unless we turn in something worth seeing. So we'd better get a grip here . . .'

'Yes. Yes, I'll get back to Jerry.'

'Fine. Let's carry on shooting those gorgeous little glass containers over there.'

Kate tried hard to keep her worries to herself over lunch. She had enjoyed watching Liz and Jerry establish a slow but secure professional relationship, and had been impressed with the way Liz had tactfully included Jerry's funny pixie partner, minimising the potential resentment. And after she had drunk a black coffee with her plastic ploughman's, she asked June what Celia Marshall's other company had been called.

'Oh, something to do with cartoons . . . I can't quite remember. Yes, I do. Flintstones.'

'Flintstones?'

'Yes, weird isn't it? You would imagine Lady Marshall calling a business something far more homespun.'

'Mmm.' But all the way to the local paper offices in the town, beneath the crag where the Tourist Centre sat like the focus of a wedding breakfast, Kate wondered about the mesh of strange coincidences weaving a net around something she could not quite catch.

The newspaper offices were plain, red brick and solid, and the pleasant and efficient receptionist informed Kate that the archive departments could be visited, for a fee, between two and four each day. There was a small, bright room to one side, and a clerical-looking woman bustled through and asked Kate whether she wanted microfiche or real copies. 'Real copies take longer to find and the fee's higher,' she explained apologetically. Kate opted for the microfiche, and commented on the size and efficiency of the place. The woman shook her head. 'This used to be a family concern,' she said. 'But we have new owners now, some local newspaper group based down south. It's not the same. The editor's been retired and we have one or two bright sparks who want to change things. I suppose it's like that everywhere these days.' Kate tried to look noncommittal, and succeeded only in seeing the woman shake her head miserably as she left her. An hour later, with tired eyes and a feeling of frustration, Kate stepped outside into the charcoal dusk, the first winds of winter whipping round her jacket. She had discovered that Kenny the jeweller had been welcomed to the district five years ago as 'a major Scottish craftsman', that the sailing school had been hailed as a 'watersports palace and the start of a new marina lifestyle on our coast', and that the theme park plans had been the subject of hot debate for about two years. But she had taken the chance to look further back, for another local story. And there had been no reference, in any editions the whole of the relevant October, to a local woman being involved in a serious car crash. She stood for a moment blinking on the steps, when a cheery voice said, 'Excuse me, are you Kate Wilson?'

She turned to see a smart man in his thirties smiling brightly at her. He had a neat little face, split by a thin lipped but wide mouth. His hair was greased and stood up in rather disarming spears, and she noticed the faint scar from a pierced ear. Despite the greenish suit and narrow tasteful tie, he had obviously had a racier past. He grinned at her, and she was caught by his look of cheeky supplication.

'Well, I'm Kate Wilkinson, not Wilson.'

'Darren Jackson. Chief reporter. We heard from our esteemed Tourist Centre chief that you were visiting. Did you get everything you wanted?'

'Yes, thanks.'

'And what do you think of the area? Bit of a weird mix, isn't it?'

Kate laughed. 'Well, you could say that.'

'So what's this film you're working on?'

'Oh, it's just a look at the new industries growing up here.'

'God, yes; we need them, don't we? The place could be a real dump otherwise. You've got the glorious Lakes only five miles away and the glorious Scottish hills across the water and our little strip of decay like the tide mark of the North washed up along the coast.'

Kate blinked. 'It's not like that at all,' she said. 'But I suppose you could look at it that way. We're trying to show something a bit more interesting though.'

'Well, good luck to you.' Suddenly he seemed impatient

to be off. 'Well, nice to have met you, Miss Wilson.'

She didn't bother to correct him, which was just as well, because he was already swinging through the doors to the right, into what seemed like the hub of the offices.

She drove over the darkening hills to Skirlbeck trying not to think about anything except how to cope with the shadowy roads and the vagaries of another strange car. It worked. She had a splitting headache when she arrived back at the aromatherapy centre, but she had not thought about anything more disturbing than a rabbit caught in her headlights.

She rejoined the crew to finish off the filming and had to admit that de Salas's choice of venue was certainly visually gripping. With the evening darkening outside the big glass windows and the bottles glowing like medieval alembics, the aromatherapy centre seemed a rich, intriguing mix of gothic fantasy and modern aspirations. But Kate was struck again, as they packed up to go, by its lack of relevance to any theme de Salas should have been developing.

When the team returned to the hotel and sat down to dinner, the only person who did not appear before seven thirty was Sally Dodd, but as she'd had to go back to Gillfoot, Kate expected her to be late. There was a healthy feeling about the rest of them. Kate noticed that Jerry was now actually joking with Liz, while June was once again the quiet, organised, reliable support she must have been for Ben Lowe.

It was nearly half past eight when Sally came through the front door, calling to the twins that she was the late-comer and entering the dining room as if it was another warm and welcoming farmhouse kitchen. She reminded Kate of the first time she had seen her, incandescent with health in her creamy blush pink jumper and smart suit. With the onset of the bad weather Sally was wearing a cream quilted anorak with a soft brown fur-edged hood which would have made most women look like a cross between a Michelin man and a weasel, but had the effect of turning Sally into a soft, beautifully huggable specimen of elegant femininity, like a supermodel in a bathrobe. She flung this expensive accessory on to a chair at an adjacent table and sat down with a jangle of bracelets.

'*Now* you can call me a researcher,' she said dramatically, then flung her head round in a tidal wave of soft shiny hair to check all the doors were closed behind her.

'What have you got for us?' Kate felt like an elder stateswoman, trying to be calm and sensible in the babble of excitement that Sally's entrance had caused.

'For a start . . .' Sally was gleaming with delight, 'I'm sure now this dogfighting business has nothing to do with Cliff.'

'Really?'

'Yes. Because there's going to be one on Wednesday night. And on Wednesday, Cliff and his dad are going to stay over in Hexham to look at some new machinery.'

'How do you know about this?' Kate's heart rate was up. She felt her face flush and took another mouthful of the Skirlbeck's best red wine.

'He told me. Cliff did. He came in after feeding the calves and the old folks weren't around. And he said, "You were asking about what old Tom was mixed up in. Well, it weren't old Tom, understand? He was just a gullible old fool".' The others were smiling at Sally's gruff, affectionate imitation of her fiancé's terse way of talking. Then he said, "I don't like womenfolk being mixed up in this either" . . . because you've got to remember my Cliff is a man of his times . . .'

Liz guffawed sympathetically, feeding Sally's need for an audience. 'And he went on, "There's summat goin' on at the old barn at Skirlbeck on Wednesday. You can tell that to your interfering southern friends".'

Only then did Sally look slightly discomfited, but she soon got over this in the triumph of seeing the others break out in gasps and quick questions.

'Where's this barn?' Liz asked.

'Down by the coast. It's derelict now, because they're planning to put the theme park on the site – if it gets planning permission, of course.'

Then the chattering stopped. They were suddenly as silent as naughty children in the presence of the headteacher the moment Bill opened the dining room door. Standing there, a huge tray in his hands and an expression of suspicion on his face at being met by silence, he looked momentarily forbidding framed in the doorway. Then he smiled his best 'mine host' smile, and the party relaxed.

But when he had gone, the atmosphere changed. People had had time to digest Sally's information, even if their food lay untouched. Kate drank another gulp of wine, aware that she was entering the zone where tiredness threatened to supercede judgement, but she could hardly eat the chicken and sauce on her plate.

'We need a strategy,' she said to the table at large. 'Someone needs to be at this . . . thing . . . on Wednesday night.'

'What sort of equipment could we take?' Liz asked. She was the one person for whom the dogfight story in all its horror distracted from her own personal mess. Her eyes were bright. Kate looked to Jerry.

'Well,' he said cautiously, 'there is a very small Hi-8 camera we could use. But I would need to go to Manchester tomorrow to get one. We'd need to put it in a shoulder bag, and shoot the pictures through some sort of hole in the side. It's not impossible but it's not easy, and we'd have to hire it.'

'Do it.' Kate knew her face was as red as her wine. June Ridley said quietly, 'Kate, think of the cost . . .'

'I'll take the risk, June. It's not much. Can you operate the camera tomorrow so that Jerry can have the day off?' Kate said to the truculent blond pixie. The woman looked at her with saucerlike eyes.

'Well, can you?'

'S'pose so,' said the pixie, and looked quickly to Jerry for approval. It was the first time Kate had seen her anything less than sulky. Jerry puffed out his chest. 'Of course she can do it,' he said, upholding Kate's long-held theory that any man would become a feminist if his pet woman was threatened.

'That's that, then,' Kate said. 'We go ahead at the sailing school tomorrow as planned. And Wednesday, we plan to shoot the dogfight in the barn. OK?'

Various degrees of 'Yes' came back to her from the table.

Suddenly Kate felt tired and remembered that later, in bed, there would be no-one to talk to about the day's events. Part of her was devastated that John had made no attempt to contact her, even though she had sensed their row was final. It was a mistake, she knew, to try and pretend that she could go on living the same life without him, but for the time being she had no option.

She had to face the huge void, which threatened to reveal itself at night and at the times when she thought to herself,

'Oh, I must tell John that . . .', and then had to remind herself she couldn't. And even if she could cope with the loss, her work – which should provide a consolation – was really an almighty headache. Even with footage – if she and Jerry were lucky enough to get it – could the film cope without some sort of witness interview? For that she needed Malcolm Hodgson.

The wine and the misery told her she needed him for more than that, but he too seemed to have gone when she wanted him. She traced lines on the white table cloth with her fork. The prongs showed parallels, neat little furrows mocking her.

On their own, after everyone else had left, Liz kissed Kate on her brow and announced she too was ready for bed. But Kate felt the need to sit up a little longer, finish her drink and work out how to persuade Malcolm Hodgson to talk. Liz left her to her reverie. Then Kate drifted into a half dream, slumped over the table.

The sound of the phone had her waking with strained and startled eyes. Bill was standing in the dining room doorway, his face pink with drama.

'Phone, Kate,' he said. Kate leapt up and raced towards him but when she placed the receiver to her ear, there was only the dialling tone.

'Who was it, Bill?' she demanded, trying to sober up.

'Just a man. I'm really sorry, I couldn't say who . . .'

'Was it John? You know John. Was it him?'

'I'm sorry,' Bill seemed as bothered as she was. 'I really don't know.'

'What did he say?'

'He said something about passing by the Skirlbeck. Kate, wait . . .'

But she had swung away from him out of the hall, pushing open the huge front doors and racing out into the path where the cold, wet, newly wintry air hit her like freezing wet towels. She stood alone on the gravel path and, with the enforced sensitivity of the slightly drunk, she heard the splashing of the little waves on the stony shore and the wind in the gorse bushes. There was no-one there.

She turned, more frozen with disappointment than with cold, back towards the house.

Only then did she see it. It was badly decomposed, with strips of flesh and hair, and because of that it held no fear for her until she worked out what it was. Then, as she pieced it together in her mind, she saw where its eyes should have been. The dead dog's sockets looked back at her and its rictus jawline seemed to gape in an attitude both frightening and desperately sad. Kate had once had a dog, as a child. It had been a spaniel-labrador cross with silly short legs and a labrador's loping body and sleek head. She had loved it. For a moment she could see her own pet's face looking back at her from this dead travesty. She knew she was screaming but she wasn't sure why, and then she ran hugging her body, into the arched doorway of the Skirlbeck Bridge.

The hallway was empty. Whatever *her* crisis, something else had lured Bill back to the kitchen. She scrambled upstairs to her room and slammed the door, sinking to the bed in a trembling fit.

And then she rang the only person she knew who would understand. The phone rang out again and again and she found herself begging for a response.

And a voice said gruffly, 'Hello?'

'Oh, God,' she said. 'Thank God you're there. It's Kate. And whatever has happened between us I've got to see you. There's been another dead dog. I need you, Malcolm.'

Chapter Twelve

It was hardly twenty minutes later when Hodgson's Range Rover drew up in a surf of gravel outside the door. Kate had not left her room but had been sitting on her bed, shivering, frozen to the core. She heard him talking loudly in the hallway, and then he called her.

He was standing next to Bill and Terry Robinson who looked frightened, and Kate could see why. Hodgson was a big man and his face was florid with rage.

'You're coming with me!' he said.

'What?'

'It's for the best. The Robinsons understand.' Kate wasn't so sure about that. Terry looked overwhelmed, his eyes round and flicking from Hodgson to his brother, and then to Kate. But Bill Robinson looked angry.

'Really, Councillor Hodgson, Kate is quite safe with us, whatever is going on,' he said, his voice deeper than Kate had ever heard it before.

'I'm not criticising your hospitality or your security, Bill, but Miss Wilkinson called me, and she's upset. I'd like her to come and stay with me.'

'I don't know what can have upset her . . .'

Kate moved forward. Malcolm had seen her coming

down the stairs, and she could see from his warning glance that he did not want her to say much to the twins.

'It's all right, Bill,' she said quietly. 'It's really no reflection on the Skirlbeck Bridge. I've just had rather a nasty . . . er . . . encounter to do with my work, and I would like to go with Councillor Hodgson. We need to talk. Now.' She glanced at Hodgson, who looked back and nodded.

Bill shrugged, then said, 'Of course, Kate. But we don't want you to move out. We have our reputation as hosts to think of.'

Kate nodded but she suddenly felt lightheaded. She gripped the bannister post, then sat heavily on the stairs.

'Christ, you look awful. Get her a whisky,' said Hodgson, and Terry scrambled into the bar. 'What do you need?' Hodgson went on gruffly.

'My case,' Kate said faintly. As he strode past her up the stairs she felt his leg brush her shoulder. Two minutes later Kate was gulping the whisky down, and Hodgson was back. The hidden agenda was so near the surface Kate could not look him in the eye, and she could sense by the way his huge fingers nearly touched her, and the tension in her own skin every time he gestured near her, that there had been no lessening of desire despite their disagreement. If anything, it had been heightened.

Kate looked at him. The thing in the drive, the murkiness of Jean Robinson's death, the fact that John had left her and was helping someone else less than a mile away while she suffered alone, all conspired to make her want to go. But her real motive alarmed her. Under her fear and reaction, Hodgson's presence was like an electric fire in the hallway, his big frame within yards of hers like a signal to her tired neglected body, by-passing her brain. The desire for him was hardening her nipples and moistening her even as she sat shaking on the stairs. Her fear seemed to heighten her lust, as if her skin was stretched and her mind was on red alert, but all focused in one direction: Malcolm Hodgson. She put on her jacket in a dream, grabbed her briefcase, and felt the heat between her thighs as they went out into the freezing night.

She walked down the drive without feeling the soft rain, but Hodgson stopped.

'Where is it?' he asked.

She pointed to a small, dark, insignificant looking bundle to the left of the main sweep. Hodgson strode over to it and kicked it into the stunted, skinny shrubs which clustered for shelter near the low stone wall.

In the Range Rover he said, 'I had to get you out of there. I've been wondering if it could be them.'

'*What*?'

'Bill Robinson is pretty forceful underneath that quiet exterior. It was Bill who told you someone was on the phone, wasn't it?' She nodded. She had garbled her version of events to Malcolm, the facts tumbling over each other, before he'd said, 'Don't say any more, I'll be there.' And she had found herself crying with relief into the phone. Now in his car, the horror of what he was suggesting hit her.

'You mean the twins are behind the dogfighting?'

'Not the twins. Just the big one. Bill.'

'Oh, no, surely not!' But Hodgson's words slotted like another jigsaw piece in her mind.

'You're safe now,' he said, and changed gear with his left hand, hitting the clutch with his left leg, the muscles taut, the strength of his thigh flexing through his trousers, and Kate felt uncomfortable with desire. She turned to stare out of the window, fascinated by the straightforward physical response of her body while her mind told her this was all a mistake.

'Where do you live?' she asked in a shaky voice.

'The west side of Bassenthwaite Lake, just a mile out of the National Park. But to me it's as picturesque, if not more so. It's bleaker and less dramatic, but I like the feeling that the sea is a stone's throw away. And my house is beautiful, if I do say so myself!'

She laughed shakily as they turned into the gates leading to another, bigger, more imposing Georgian farm than Gillfoot where the Thompsons lived. Hodgson had two pots containing manicured bay trees at the side of the steps up to the brass-laden front door, and Kate could see a small terraced garden drop down the fell. In the distance she sensed the bottom of the valley and the deep darkness of the lake, blacker than the sky which had cleared and was dotted with stars.

Hodgson held the door open for her and she went in. But once in the door, he snapped on the light and the atmosphere changed. His home was covered in dust and dog hairs. A smelly and ancient collie dog waddled up to her and for a minute, as his tail wagged laboriously and his nose probed her trousers, she wondered if the dog could smell the desire from her. It ebbed immediately. She and Malcolm looked at each other awkwardly.

'The front of the house is from about 1812,' he said, 'but the back's older. Look.' He motioned her through an archway under the elegant stairs to where stone flags took over. The passage to his kitchen wound in front of them, and then on her left a low beam signalled where another much older and less symmetrical staircase bumped over them. In the kitchen, thick beams supported bouquets of herbs and copper pans, all once hung there to render the place fit for a colour supplement. But the dust and grease gave everything the same fried smell and slimy appearance.

Kate could not keep the look of surprise and disgust from her face. Malcolm seemed so smooth, but behind closed doors his wife's departure had clearly hit him hard. Dirty clothes lay in piles on the floor and three or four newspapers were strewn about. There were two empty milk bottles on the table, and a plate with grease caked like white frost all round it.

'I keep the front nice because of the business,' he said glumly. 'But since Susan went I don't bother so much inside.'

'So I see.'

'I'd make you a coffee but I've no clean cups, so have another drink.' He seemed to find two glasses among a mass of letters, papers, pens, a comb, scissors, two batteries, crocodile clips and a collection of screwdrivers on the workbench.

'What did your girlfriends think of this mess?' Kate asked.

'Actually, I never brought them back here. They always had nice little flats with central heating.'

Kate laughed, but sympathised. Malcolm's beautiful old house was freezing cold. She took half a tumbler of whisky from him and her teeth chattered against the glass. He was busy with his back to her, lighting the gas stove. At first the smell was sickly, then she heard him swear quietly before the soft roar of the blue-flamed jets reassured her. Within seconds the kitchen was warmer, but she realised that for the last ten minutes Hodgson had not looked at her. She sensed he was embarrassed by the mess. She was surprised that he had let the house get into such a state, but it was a timely reminder that Hodgson had a background where the womenfolk looked after that sort of thing. It was quite different from the neat self sufficiency of her New Men friends in London.

'Thanks for coming to get me,' she said simply.

He looked round at her and took a gulp of his drink.

'I was fucking furious with you when I spoke to you on your cellphone,' he said. 'I couldn't believe that you were seriously thinking of making what I had told you into a TV programme. And then I thought about it and I realised you might be right. But I never rush into things. I called you and left a message on Sunday and I was going to call you tomorrow. But the bastards got to you first. But how did they know?'

'If you're making a programme you can't keep it secret. Anyone could find out. I tried my best, but obviously someone leaked it.'

'Who?'

'God, it could have been anyone.' The warmth, whisky and fear were leaving her limp and floppy. She sat down heavily on a kitchen chair laden with old magazines, and a woolly jumper which gave off a sweaty smell she suddenly found irresistible. He walked over to where she sat.

'Now you're here . . .' he said coolly, and paused. Then he put his hands on her shoulders and looked down at her.

'How about it?' she added lightly, watching the surprise on his face. Then he knelt in front of her, his big face on a level with hers and the whisky on his breath as intoxicating as the whisky she had drunk.

'I'm not allowed to say things like that,' he whispered. 'I have to tell you that you're beautiful, and that I can't control myself because you are so lovely, and that I want you, and that it isn't just sex.'

'But it is just sex, Malcolm. That's what I want. I want you to want me. I've had enough of love. The truth is that I want sex until I'm too shattered to move.' The drink, the horrible mess he had made of his lovely house, the unmistakable bulge in his trousers and the lust in his red-rimmed eyes left Kate with no need to be anything other than basic, and that was freedom in itself. She was aware now of little more than the hot animal desire to be penetrated. This event had no meaning for her other than the desperation of the moment, but the delight of being with someone who wanted her so fiercely, and in circumstances where it didn't matter how she looked or what she thought, excited her. Malcolm was still inches away from her, looking at her as if unsure what move to make. She put her hand out and found the hardness between his thighs. He groaned slightly and moved in her hand so she felt him grow, suddenly flexing to his full extent.

'Christ, that's uncomfortable,' he breathed. She said nothing, but intent on what she was doing, she found the metal zip tag and pulled it down. He sprang out through the vent into her open hand, and she gasped as she held him. He was enormous. He was pushing his hands up under her jumper and massaging her breasts with a ferocity just short of violence.

'Get your clothes off!' he ordered her.

'I'm a feminist. Get your own bloody clothes off,' she said, listening to the thickness in her own voice. While she held him he pulled his jumper over his head and then unbuttoned his shirt.

'You're beautiful,' said Kate. 'You're beautiful and I want you. I can't control myself. You have to let me,' and she rubbed rhythmically up and down on his penis while he laughed back at the irony of it. 'You're just using me,' he said, joking and gasping at the same time. 'Yes,' she said, leaving hold of him just long enough to take off her own jumper so he could lean forward and lick her breasts. She had to stand up to take off her jeans and knickers, while Malcolm fumbled with the condom he just happened to have in his pocket, his prick lurching wildly out of his trousers like a pole. Then he undid the clasp at his waist, and pulled his pants down, gasping as they rode over him. Kate pulled at his shorts till they dropped too, and then she could see how wonderful he looked, with his massive erection, the tangles of dark brown pubic hair and the power of his muscular hips. Then Malcolm lifted her on to the kitchen table and she instinctively spread her legs for him so that he immediately went into her with her legs astride him and her bottom perched among the dirty cups and discarded magazines. He was so big she felt fiercely tight around him and she looked down and saw him going in and out of her with enormous power. The action caught her just where it mattered and he thrust so hard Kate felt she would explode. To her own surprise her orgasm built as soon as he was in her. She came shudderingly, with the whole kitchen table shaking, but realised the minute afterwards that Malcolm was still going strong.

'Lie on the floor,' he said. Cushioned by the mounds of clothes flung on to the flags, she realised her head was on a level with the base of the washing machine and was about to laugh at the fact when her body started responding again, and she was coming in waves, her feet scrabbling at the sweaty washing underneath her. Malcolm was an experienced lover who explored every inch of her body and who wouldn't let her stop, moving her as soon as she had come from one place to another.

By the time Hodgson carried her to bed, they'd had sex in every corner of the kitchen and then on the stairs. Kate, shattered, lay on the bed and heard him snore. It had been a marathon, but only she knew that after the fourth time, she'd had enough. She remembered Malcolm groaning inside her, pushing her up against the kitchen wall, and her body climaxing for the last time. She'd opened her eyes and had seen his screwed-up face and the desperation of his thrusting, and suddenly realised that for her it was as dramatically and suddenly over as for the least sensitive of the men she had ever had. She went along with their final copulations, longing for Malcolm to come, and was so relieved when he did her sighs could have been taken for satisfaction. When it was finally done he had staggered with her up the last of the flight of Elizabethan stairs. He had been too tired to speak. And now she lay next to him, horrified by what she had done, sore and sleepless and disgusted.

At last she did sleep, but not well, and in the first steely light of dawn she woke with a headache and a feeling of thick grey fur in her mouth. Malcolm lay on his back, his fantastic chest exposed and his mouth open emitting another giant snore. His bedroom was a tip. The bed was magnificent, a huge ancient oak platform. If they'd had the patience to wait, it would have been like having sex on a stage. The big sash windows were curtainless, or at least one was. The other had a curtain pole with one drape hanging in big baggy loops. She tried to doze but it was no use. So she gingerly turned her head. In a mass of aspirin boxes, books, cassettes and half eaten biscuits, she saw a cordless phone and a clock saying ten past eight.

She sat bolt upright, and grabbed for the phone, not caring whether or not she disturbed the comatose giant beside her. It rang out at the Skirlbeck Bridge Hotel and Bill Robinson answered.

'Bill? It's Kate. Yes, I'm fine, thank you. Can you tell Liz Jones I'm having a breakfast meeting, and I'll see her at the sailing school? No, please don't go and disturb her.'

She was aware as she spoke that Bill seemed even cooler than on the previous night. 'Is there anything wrong, Bill?' she asked. 'No,' he replied, leaving her with the clear impression that there was. She sighed as she clicked the phone off. She may have been tactless leaving the hotel the night before but even so it was odd for Bill to be so rude.

She put the phone down and looked at Malcolm, still crashed out. Her only feeling was that she wanted to escape back to Skirlbeck, dead dogs, dead mothers and missing film directors notwithstanding. She knew it would take her days to evaluate what she had done, but at that moment she knew that anything more meaningful with Malcolm Hodgson wouldn't work. He needed the sort of woman he had always known, the farmer's wife-type with just a bit more bite than the traditional helpmate, who would clean up this awful mess for him, and jolly him along and have the deep satisfaction of knowing that without her he was rather pathetic. A sort of Sally Dodd, in fact. And she was

ure he would find one. For a moment she developed a
fantasy where Malcolm became her friend and came down
to London and was introduced to some of the women she
knew who really wanted a good, straightforward man. She
even allowed herself to smile, before realising the tears
were streaming down her face.

She stood up and went to the window and looked out
over the terraced garden. It wasn't a picture postcard view
because she could only see the lake if she looked hard to
one side. But she could see why Malcolm thought it was
beautiful. She had an absurd desire to nudge John Maple,
here and then, in his bony ribs and say, 'Look, what a nice
view.' But the thought of that camaraderie now being gone
for ever made the tears worse, although she knew that was
what they had been for in the first place.

She looked back at Malcolm. He was certainly a big man
in the community, she thought, trying to josh herself out
of her misery.

Kate had covered herself with a woolly blanket lying on
top of Hodgson's duvet for her walk to the window. Now
she realised she would have to creep naked down the stairs
to get her clothes. She felt ridiculous, fat and ungainly and
downright stupid, manoeuvring down the narrow Tudor
stairwell and into the kitchen where the big old dog seemed
to be struggling to its feet with undue haste to lick at her
large, naked bottom. She found her pants and her jeans in
one tangled mess, and her jumper which had ended up on
the other side of the room. Her bra was more of a problem
until she discovered a fat black and white cat was sitting
on it. She drank some tap water and then found the phone
book. She rang the same cab company as before, and while
she was waiting for them she found a downstairs cloakroom

and washed herself from top to toe. There was no hot water
and Malcolm's towels all seemed about ten years old and
as thin as grey, much-washed nappies, but she managed
When the cab arrived she emerged into the morning light
with a face so well-scrubbed she felt she had been over it
with a Brillo pad, and there were other parts of her body
which had had the same treatment.

She braved the driver's raised eyebrows. 'Skirlbeck
Sailing School,' she said. 'Can I use the mirror to put some
makeup on?'

'Go ahead, lass,' said the driver, and fifteen minutes later
she was able to wait on the steps of the sailing school
clubhouse and look suitably superior, if inwardly exhausted
when the rest of her team turned up a little late.

But she was unprepared for the awkwardness of the
meeting. Sally, who arrived first in her own car, was
distinctly embarrassed. Then the crew car turned up and
the blond pixie scarcely spoke to her. When Liz and June
arrived, the atmosphere could be cut with a knife.

'Liz, what's wrong?' Kate asked, almost before her friend
had got out of the car.

'What's wrong? Oh, I suppose you haven't see this.' Liz
thrust a copy of the *West Cumbria Informer* into her hand
'After all you've said to us, Kate, I don't know how you
could have been so stupid!'

Kate looked down at the paper, and saw a small inset
picture of the Skirlbeck Bridge Hotel in the bottom left
hand corner. Then she saw the caption. ' *"We'll transform
dump" says TV Woman. See inside.'*

'What the hell is this?' Kate barked at Liz.

'Read it. Then you'll know. I just hope Ben Lowe doesn'
get this in Carlisle.'

Kate read the copy in front of her. A busy strap headline said 'Gossip Page'. Bylined 'Darren Jackson', the copy read: *A TV crew is currently based at the Skirlbeck Bridge Hotel (see left), making a film about West Cumbrian crafts. Producer Kate Wilson says, "The area is pretty mixed. It could be seen as a real dump between the Lakes and the Scottish Lowlands. But our film is going to try and look on the bright side." Miss Wilson's comments have already been criticised by Head of News at Border TV Neil Graham who said, "It isn't a good idea for outsiders to make this sort of swingeing criticism. Border has not yet been approached to show this film, but it doesn't sound like our sort of programme." '*

'Oh, God,' said Kate. 'Liz, you don't believe I said this do you?'

'It's in the paper.'

'Well, I bloody well didn't. I've been set up by some little creep.'

'Well you must have said something, Kate.'

'All I did was agree with him, to be polite.'

'That was obviously enough! How could you have been so daft? This might well stop local people helping us.'

'God, I hope not!' Kate looked ashen, and Liz softened. 'Oh, who knows; perhaps people know this rag is unreliable. What about your councillor? Has he seen this? Was it him you were meeting for breakfast?'

'Sort of. Actually, my meeting went well.' She knew she was now blushing, her features going from cold to hot. 'Malcolm will understand that I was misquoted. At least I hope so, because I'm pretty sure he'll be interviewed now.'

'Oooh, what did you do for him?' Liz started to smile until she saw Kate's face. 'Oh, poor Katy. You do look upset. I should have realised you'd been shafted by the paper.

317

Never mind. It'll probably be a nine days' wonder, even here.' Liz, always kind after her temper had blown away, linked Kate's arm and went with her into the sailing school, where Kate had to concentrate on the arrange ments.

But at coffee time Kate brought the team together to explain what had happened to her on the steps of the *West Cumbria Informer*. Her self confidence returned slightly as each person expressed their sympathy.

'That paper's been crap lately,' said the blond pixie succinctly. She was taking to camerawork so well Kate wondered if Jerry would have to look to his laurels. June seemed unconcerned about the misquotation once she had established that the paper's circulation was pretty local and unlikely to reach Ben Lowe. And Sally, who had most reason to be upset, just said, 'Well, I was sure you would never have said something so tactless, Kate, but a lot of people *think* it. And a lot more people want someone else to say it! Some folks just love being victimised.'

Half an hour later Kate was summoned from the shore where she had been trying to make sense of some strange manoeuvres by people in wet suits with little Topper dinghies, back into the clubhouse to take a phone call. It was Malcolm. For a moment his voice embarrassed her but within seconds the fact that her desire was dead made the call surprisingly friendly.

'Where the fuck did you go, Kate?'

'Oh, the table, the floor, the wall, the fridge, the stairs.'

'Yeah, well . . .' he sounded sheepishly flattered. 'That's not what I meant.'

'You were dead to the world. I had to leave.'

'Oh, fair enough.' She sensed that for him too, the heat

was gone. It was strange how some lust was regenerated while some was exhausted, by exactly the same act. 'Malcolm, have you seen the *West Cumbria Informer*?'

'What?'

'The paper. There's some crap in there that's supposed to be quotes from me about the area. It's awful.'

'Did you say it?'

'*No!*'

'Well, then, I'll get the editor to print an apology. Don't underestimate local clout. That rag's been going downhill ever since that southern lot bought it.'

'Malcolm, that would be great!'

'Well, I owe you a favour.'

'No, you don't, absolutely not. But if you think you do, there is one thing.'

'What?' There was a hint of hopefulness in his voice that was more to do with pride than passion, but even so she felt mean.

'Malcolm, when will you be interviewed?'

He took a deep breath. 'OK, you've got me. And I did say I would, didn't I?'

'Not in so many words, but pretty well.'

'All right. Tomorrow night?'

Kate thought of the arrangement to go to the dogfight. She had obeyed her own instructions to the letter, telling no-one, not even Malcolm.

'OK, about eight, at the Skirlbeck Bridge Hotel.'

'No, Kate, not there. I still think there's something weird about Bill Robinson. I don't want to be interviewed there. Come over here to the farm.'

'All right, then, but only if you tidy up.'

'If I must!'

She breathed out with relief at the laughter in his voice, and replaced the phone.

Then she walked back to the shore, where Liz was watching the crew take pictures of the yachts. 'We've got the key interview!' Kate whispered.

'Your councillor will play?'

'Yep.'

'What did you have to do for that, then?'

'I didn't have to do anything, Liz. He did it for me!'

'What?'

'You shouldn't assume the woman does the giving. I spent the night with Malcolm Hodgson, but I made all the running. I've never wanted a man so much, or got over it so quickly. So I owe him, rather than the other way round.'

Her friend was still looking at her in astonishment when the sailing school receptionist who, like her boss, did not seem to have yet received the *West Cumbria Informer*, trotted over. 'Another phone call,' she said sweetly. Kate followed her back inside and picked up the receiver.

'Kate,' said a voice that for a moment she could not place. 'Paul Pym here.' He was speaking with funereal solemnity.

'Paul! What can I do for you?'

'I was wondering if I could do something for you. I read the *Informer* this morning and I really am very, very sorry. I do hope this won't lead to you cancelling your film.'

'Why on earth should it?'

'But, Kate! You mustn't underestimate the strength of public opinion. This really is very damaging and I can't apologise enough!'

'You?'

'It's kind of you to sound so surprised. I was sure you

would blame me for alerting Darren Jackson to your arrival at the newspaper offices.'

'No, Paul, not at all. I realised I had been badly misquoted and he had probably set me up in advance, but I really don't see how you could be to blame.'

'I'm so glad you see it that way! After all, it may become well nigh impossible for you now . . .'

'I don't see why. We already have a lot of material in the can.'

'Well, I'm glad you're optimistic. But don't underestimate the trouble this sort of thing can cause. Please don't hesitate to call me if there's anything I can do.'

'Well, I suppose you could contact the paper and ask them to print a retraction.'

'Kate, I've already called Darren and he swears you said those things. I find it hard to believe, but there seems little that can be done.'

'Paul, please don't worry. I'm sure the people I know personally like the Robinsons, and George Goff, would never believe this rubbish.'

'I hope not.'

'Well, thanks for calling.' Paul's remarks were worrying. The last thing she wanted was to alienate people, and she had been lulled by the sympathy of her team into thinking the newspaper article might be ignored.

She went back up to the waterfront and watched the team at work. The sailing school was ingeniously built with a large, conservatory-style extension to a traditional boathouse design at the estuary, where the long suffering river flowed out of the town and into the sea. A small breakwater had been constructed across the opening so that a lagoon was framed in which all sorts of beginners' sailing classes could be held, with more advanced sailors making for the open sea. The late morning had calmed down so that there was little activity in the lagoon. Sally had done the routine interviews with the owners and now Liz was organising the overlay – the covering shots to enhance the interview – on the edge of the breakwater looking to sea. Kate stood with the last trace of wind blowing through her short hair. The sailing school was reflected in its still water. She was admiring the glass structure, which looked like a set of gleaming steel battlements and which suddenly and incongruously reminded her of the glass and steel structure of the Channel Four building with its moat and drawbridge.

She was interrupted by the little receptionist, her arms akimbo against the cold. 'Another call,' she whispered into the wind.

'I am sorry. I'll come straight away.' Kate went back into the office at the clubhouse and picked up the phone.

'Kate! Chrissia Cohen here! I've been trying and trying to get you on your mobile but the damn batteries must be flat. Good job this shoot is well organised. Your PA faxed us a copy of your new itinerary.' Good old June, thought Kate.

'Well, I'm glad I've tracked you down,' Chrissia was going on. 'Look, I don't quite understand why we've got a copy but Hugh has just been brandishing a fax at me showing a local newspaper cutting.'

' Sorry?'

'Yes, no wonder you're surprised. But Hughie seems to have lost the top sheet so we don't know who's sent it. Probably somebody malicious, but even so, I can't afford to ignore it.'

'Chrissia, that newspaper article is pure garbage. I never said stupid, tactless things like that! There are plenty of people here who don't want this film made. You have to believe me that I've been set up.'

'I'm inclined to do so, Kate. But I would like to see some sort of retraction in the paper as a defence in the future. We can't afford to have the regulators on our backs over bias. I think we may need that before we clear the advance. This film could be dynamite, you know.'

'I'll make sure that happens.' Kate thought with desperate gratitude of Malcolm's promise.

'Jolly good. I told Hugh he was overreacting. How's it going?'

'Fine, except for that bit of vicious journalism. It's causing quite a bit of local upset already. I've even had the director of the Tourist Centre on the phone commiserating this morning. Paul Pym, ex-LondonVision. Do you remember him, Chrissia?'

'Paul Pym. Good grief, is that where he's ended up? I thought he came from a very moneyed background. Some sort of estate in posh Gloucestershire somewhere.'

'Well, he's still rather like the local squire, even up here. But not so rich that he doesn't need to work. Did you know him well?'

'Know him? I was his secretary just before he left LondonVision. It was like working for the Duke of Edinburgh.'

'That's just it! *Noblesse oblige.* He's a pillar of the community.'

'That follows. He would have a position to keep up. He certainly got through masses of dosh when I knew him. That was why he had to go, of course. Mind you I was always too insignificant for him to notice. I was just a secretary. A secretary with a first in PPE, can you believe it these days? But Pym and his crowd thought women with brains were witches, I can tell you.'

'Why did he leave, Chrissia?'

'Ah, well, it takes an ancient old crone like me to remember. Actually it was really very funny. In the days before snorting coke, fiddling exes and breaking the ludicrous ITC codes got you the sack, we had our own moral agenda.'

'Pym was sacked?'

'Oh, yes. Though it was never called that. And Pymmie was fortunate enough to have inherited masses of money so he could go on living in the style to which he'd become accustomed. Yes, he was asked to leave when they found out he'd blown the film float on betting.'

'Betting?'

'Oh, yes, but the high class country sort, don't you know? They couldn't get him away from point to points. Horses were his weakness. He got through mountains of LondonVision money.'

'Unbelievable!'

'Not really. We used to have our bad boys even then. Well, must go, Kate. Let me see the follow up in the local rag as soon as possible.'

And she rang off.

Kate mooched back thoughtfully to see how Liz was going on, and then the crew broke for lunch. The rest of the day went slowly for Kate because she was agonising over her return to the Skirlbeck Bridge Hotel. She knew that Bill and Terry would be devastated by the article and the fact the hotel was featured on the front page.

On top of that, every time her mind took a break from the difficulties at work, her emotional emptiness came rushing in like a negative force, a sort of draught through her life. She was glad when in the afternoon a cold wind blew up for real and everyone got wet and chilly, and she had to stand and hold the boom for the blonde pixie. She needed something difficult, alien and completely demanding to do, and holding the rod with the fuzzy microphone on the end, her ears encased in headphones, her eyes glued to the meter, and the wind catching her off balance, was just right.

She was numb when they finished, and huddled into the car, with Liz as a passenger.

'What a day!' Liz said, glowing with the effort. 'I have to say, it's not easy working in the wind and rain.'

'Beats the office. How much useful footage did we get?'

'Oh, it will probably edit into about five minutes!'

'Not bad, eh?'

The two laughed. It was a quiet if companionable journey home. But as Kate drove down the coast road towards Skirlbeck, she felt apprehensive. Liz was leaning forward.

'I don't want to worry you,' she said, 'but I don't think you're going to be able to get a car parking space.'

'What?'

'Well, maybe I'm exaggerating slightly, but it's a lot fuller than it was.'

Kate indicated, and looked to where Liz was craning to see. She was right. There were about six cars in the normally deserted hotel car park, with a seventh turning in. Kate pulled into the drive, and found that by really trying she could squeeze the hired car into a little gap near the arched gateway to the kitchen door. The two women got out and walked against the wind to the doorway. They were aware of the babble from the bar. Bill Robinson came bouncing out to greet them.

'Kate,' he said expansively, 'you must have been so distressed by that rubbish in the paper. And we're very sorry for being a little brisk with you last night. If only Councillor Hodgson had told us that it was the press who had upset you! Of course, you wanted to get away, if reporters were after you!'

Kate blinked at him but said nothing. Sometimes Bill's mixture of naivety and knowledge was startling. He had rationalised her disappearance with Hodgson to his own satisfaction, and looking at his happy face, she was glad for him. She was sure Hodgson was absolutely wrong and that the Robinsons were far too innocent to be involved in the dogfighting. Bill was chattering on again. 'Of course, we were horrified when we first read it, Terry particularly. He thought it might mean you'd be hounded out! Silly boy. But then Councillor Hodgson telephoned to tell us that you had been completely misquoted and were thinking of suing. He's here now, with a reporter from the *Cumberland News* in Carlisle. They're rivals to the *Informer*, and they're following it up! I have to say, it's our busiest Tuesday night for months.'

Beaming he led her through the bar like a celebrity, with Liz in her wake.

'Fine.' Kate was dazzled. She saw Malcolm across the bar, already deep in conversation with a svelte young woman she took to be the reporter from the *Cumberland News*. Kate felt a stab of jealousy, acutely aware of her own tired face and crumpled jacket and then thought, what the hell, and reminded herself that earlier that morning she

326

had been desperate to get away from Malcolm's greasy, dusty house with his snores shaking the Tudor beams. But despite all that she was pleased when he stood up to greet her.

'Quite a stir you've caused,' he said smiling.

'Quite a stir who's caused?' she laughed. 'It's you rather than me who's got this lot going, Malcolm.'

He smiled back. 'This lady is from the Carlisle paper. I've been telling her how you were misrepresented.'

The reporter smiled and eyed Kate's dishevelled appearance with a wry smile, then took Kate over to the only table left, in the window, to interview her. Afterwards Kate grabbed a moment to check if John Maple had left a message, but there was nothing for her.

She went slowly upstairs to shower and change. Malcolm was still in the bar, in his element in every sense, and she was sure he had hardly noticed her departure as he locked into conversation with the Carlisle journalist. And Liz had been called to the phone.

It took ages for Kate to get the knots out of her hair, and another bath before she felt the night with Malcolm recede to a regretful memory. An hour later she joined her team in the dining room. The atmosphere was highly charged, particularly now Jerry had arrived back from Manchester with the other camera. Kate kept the dining room door shut as Jerry demonstrated.

'Look, it's a straightforward Hi-8 video camera, just like the new best quality domestic ones, but I had this bag made for it.' He pulled on to the table a large leather bag, like a woman's handbag. On closer inspection, it was a woman's handbag, with a section cut from the panel at the side, so that flung over someone's shoulder, it would look just like a normal bag, but the lens would be peeping straight ahead.

'All you have to do is press the right buttons, and hold the bag carefully so no one can nudge you and affect them. And of course you have to be pointing it in the right direction.'

'All that, and you've got to look absolutely natural at the same time,' laughed Liz.

'Yeah. Piece of cake,' said Jerry. 'There's only one problem.'

'What's that?' asked Sally.

'Well, I'm damned if I'm going to a dogfight carrying a ladies' handbag.'

For a moment the room fell silent. Then Kate said, 'I'll take it of course, no question.'

'Are you sure, boss?' Jerry said, giving Kate a silent burst of professional happiness.

'Yes,' she said.

There was a token protest from Liz and Sally, but both knew she was right. Kate thanked her lucky stars there had been no picture of her in the paper, and she reckoned that with an anorak and hood borrowed from the blond pixie, and Liz's squashy hat, she could pass unremarked.

'Is it just men?' Liz asked.

Jerry had shaken his head. 'Mostly men, so I understand. But some women go along. And it's quite dark and busy. The usual form, I gather is for people to meet at the Castle Arms, and then the word gets passed around. The Castle on the coast is one of the most popular pubs for miles, everyone goes there, and not everyone is involved in this business, of course, so they let you know by word of mouth about the time and the place.'

'But thanks to Sally's contacts, we know that it's the barn?' Kate confirmed.

'Yeah. I'll go with you. You'll need some help. In case the camera goes wrong,' he added hastily. But Kate knew he was thinking about possible violence.

They ate after that in near silence. June produced the agenda and shotlist for the next day, which would just comprise a few hours picking up GVs of the locality. The climax would be the evening interview with Malcolm Hodgson, and the undercover visit to the fight.

'We'll have a late start,' said Kate. 'We'll meet at half nine here tomorrow morning. OK?'

The team nodded, and quietly drifted away. Kate squeezed Liz on the shoulder before leaving for bed.

'Any news?' she asked softly.

Liz shrugged, 'Well, Andy's mother says he left again this afternoon, but she doesn't know where he's gone.' For the first time Liz seemed defeated.

'Don't worry, I'm sure you'll hear from him,' Kate lied.

Undressing, Kate was aware of tiredness stretching her limbs. She huddled into the dressing gown the twins had provided, a sort of large, white towelling affair that made her feel like a boxer. She heard knocking at the door downstairs, and for a moment her heart leapt and she wondered if it might be John. But then the hotel fell quiet, and she dismissed the thought. A few minutes later she finished cleaning her teeth and turned off the noisy flow of ice cold water. It was then she heard the tapping, and with complete assurance she flew to her door, knowing John would be on the other side.

It was Liz. But she looked stunned. Her face was white and her eyes were wide.

'Kate, come downstairs.'

'Yes, of course. What's the matter.'

'It's Andy.'

'Oh, God, what's happened?'

'No, you don't realise. He's here.'

'Here? Oh, Liz, I'm so pleased for you.'

'Pleased? Oh no . . .' Liz collapsed against the door frame, her shoulders hunched. She seemed to have aged years. 'Kate, I don't understand. He's hardly spoken to me. He's not here for me at all. He's come to speak to the twins. Listen.'

Kate walked on to the landing. She could hear raised voices from the dining room.

De Salas was yelling, 'But you have to listen to me. Stop saying that I don't know what happened. Of course I know.'

Kate inched closer, and strained to hear.

'I know what sort of woman Jean Robinson was.'

Kate signalled to Liz to keep quiet, and then took her best friend's trembling hand and led her down the stairs. Liz followed.

' . . . but it was through my criminal stupidity Jean Robinson was injured seventeen years ago and I should have come clean about it then. I ruined her life.'

Kate led Liz by the hand down the stairs, drawn to the dining room. As the two women approached the doorway they heard a voice ring out.

'No!' The voice came from Bill as if from some demon inside. Kate saw him rise from the table, his muscular arms clutching at the cloth and his face livid with emotion. 'No,' he said again hoarsely. Terry Robinson was white, and put out a hand to his brother who clasped it almost without seeing it. 'No. I don't know who you are, but I've expected

330

this for seventeen years. It's us who should come clean to you. Jean Robinson wasn't injured at all.'

Bill's declaration was met by complete silence, the sort of silence that rarely happens in real life, when the air seems to be cold and sinking and the shock on people's faces will always be remembered. It was Terry who, holding his brother's hand, punctured the tension with a funny little practical voice saying, 'Tell them, Bill, it'll do you good,' as if urging his brother to take an aspirin.

Bill put his head in his hands. 'I always wondered who . . .' His voice broke up. They all waited until he started again. 'I always wondered who it was. Month after month the payments came in, through the bank at Carlisle.' De Salas was watching him as if hypnotised, as Bill talked on one note. 'But I knew that one day the poor young man she was squeezing for the money would turn up . . .'

'So she wasn't injured?' de Salas repeated, stunned.

'But what difference was that to you?' said Terry. 'You left her lying by the road, didn't you, with the mini smashed on the driver's side?' Kate saw that tears were running down de Salas's face. 'You left her. You pulled the car over. Your car. It was a Lotus. She'd crawled out and she lay on the grass. You walked over and you thought she was unconscious, but she grabbed your wrist.'

'Yes.' De Salas's voice was high pitched again and his face was immobile, his eyes like black buttons on a white pad. 'Christ, it was terrifying. I thought she might be dead and this hand came out and grabbed me.'

'But you'd thought you could leave her . . .'

'No! No, I swear to God I never thought that.'

'And she said "Help me . . ." '

'No. She said "You drunken maniac. You've wrecked

331

my car." And I said "It was your fault as much as mine. You pulled out." But I had been going far too fast. I knew that. And she started to scream at me about insurance. And like a fool I said "What insurance?" And I swear she knew. She said "How old are you?" I was in shock, but she wasn't. I said "Seventeen" and she said "When did you pass your test?" She was a witch, she really was, because she knew . . .'

'No.' Bill was calmer now, and to Kate's surprise he leaned across and put his hand on de Salas's arm. The younger man did not move. 'No,' said Bill. 'I can believe you, now, though I believed her then. You need to know something about Mother. All her life she had this . . . knack. She knew as soon as look at you what your weakness was.' For a second his eyes flickered over his younger brother. 'She could sniff out anyone's Achilles' heel. You were easy meat. She laughed about you when she told us. She said it was as clear as dammit that you hadn't got a licence. And when you panicked it was easy for her. You wrote your name and address for her. Then you heard the men coming from the pub. They'd finally decided to investigate. And she told you to go, that she'd contact you later.'

Andy was sobbing now. 'And like a fool I went. And for the next seventeen years I paid for it.' He looked across the table at Bill. 'So who was the solicitor?'

'There was no solicitor. I wrote the letter. At the time I was just doing what my mother wanted. Later I wanted to take Terry and go to Manchester. But she had a hold over me then.'

For the first time, Andy turned to Liz. 'Like any kid, I tried to forget it. I told myself that the woman wasn't really hurt, and that it would all go away. I told my dad I'd hit a

332

wall driving by myself, that I'd been stupid, and he paid for the Lotus to be repaired without any questions. And then the letter came. It said she had been seriously injured, that she had collapsed after the accident. They asked me for a payment out of court. I was too young and scared and stupid to question. I had a trust fund, and I paid their mother whatever she asked for. The so-called solicitor did not give me her name, just an address for the payments. I was so naive, and just bloody grateful not to be in court. And financially, it didn't make much difference. For a while I even took it in my stride, like a loan to pay off. Then I met Ben Lowe, my partner in Rural Rides. And I realised that here was something I wanted to put all my money into. Getting the money for programme producing is a nightmare now. We need more investment. My father put in thousands, but this time I'd found something I wanted to be mine.' He paused and then turned to Liz with the miserable pleading face of a frightened child, but at least he now looked alive.

'And then I found something else I wanted to be mine. I'd had girlfriends – nice, pretty ones – but they were like the cars. I had plenty of those too. But if I was going to marry someone like Liz I needed more money, money for our future, money for the kids' education, money for our own kids if we were lucky enough to have any, and money for even more programme-making so Liz could come and work with us. And over the years I had realised I was being blackmailed.'

'So how did you find her?' Liz's voice was soft with love.

'I read about Celia Marshall's mill in a magazine. It gave me the perfect opportunity. You see, afterwards, when I remembered the accident I could see the mini clearly in my mind's eye, and there was a sticker in the back saying 'Skirlbeck Garage'. I've always been good at seeing pictures. It's the only thing I can do. And there were piles of disposable tablecloths in the back of the car, obscuring her rear window. I knew that meant she was in catering. I only had to ask around a bit, for a woman who had been injured years ago, and her name cropped up, along with all sorts of remarks! She could have covered her tracks a lot more efficiently but I guess she didn't care. The point about blackmail is that you have the victim under control. But I was all set to face her. And then Liz had ... then Liz suddenly had to come up to see me, and that delayed me. I was going to face Jean Robinson this weekend but the tension was getting too much for me.'

'So you had that stupid row with Jerry?' Kate whispered. De Salas nodded. 'Then I got a note on Friday night saying you were staying at this hotel, Kate. I couldn't believe the bad luck. You see . . .' he turned to the others, 'June and I had only communicated with Kate by mobile phone. We had no idea where she was staying. The Skirlbeck Bridge Hotel, of all places! There was no way I could come to see Jean Robinson without risking bumping into Kate. Kate seemed to be always on my back. When I had brought her over from Newcastle, I pranged the Porsche because the accident had been on my mind. It was the anniversary. And Kate had been chattering on about possibly featuring a small hotel in the film. Do you remember, Kate?'

'Yes. I'm sure that didn't help, but I didn't know.'

'No. And it was stupid of me to overreact. I'm afraid it's my stock in trade. Last weekend, when I realised you were staying here, it seemed like you had been sent to thwart me. I panicked. I couldn't cope any more. I knew the film was a complete mess and I knew Ben would suss out that it had just been a front, with that silly mill woman's money. So on Sunday, I buggered off. I've done that all my bloody life.' He put his head down.

Very softly, Kate said, 'But Andy, why were you planning to face Jean Robinson *this* weekend. She was already dead?'

'But I didn't know that, did I? How was I supposed to know she was dead? I'd booked us into the biggest hotel in the western Lakes, miles away from Skirlbeck, hoping it would give me somewhere to run for cover if things got tough, so I was hardly likely to hear Skirlbeck gossip!'

'So how did you find out?'

'Well, that was the bloody irony! Of course all the gossip spreads, but I found out too late! I called Liz at our hotel. But she'd moved on here. I couldn't believe it. The receptionist at the Summerlake Hall chatted on while I was still reeling, saying how lucky Liz was to get a room here because the place was shut owing to the owner's death! And I knew then I could come back.'

Bill spoke. 'Because it would all be over now she was dead.'

Kate leaned forward. 'It's none of my business, I know,' she said softly, 'but if your mother wasn't really disabled, why didn't she walk back from the shore the day she died?'

Bill laughed, but it was a sour sound.

'After seventeen years, she could hardly move without help. It was self-fulfilling. I carried her around the house towards the end because she liked it that way. She loved being an invalid. The accident seventeen years ago was perfect for her. That night, she must have tried to get back up the shore, but she hadn't the strength any more. I got to the stage when I started to wonder if perhaps she really had been injured, something in her mind perhaps . . .' He too was crying.

Later, Liz and Kate made tea in the big quiet kitchen. They said little, except when Kate whispered, 'What about the money, Liz?'

'You mean, will Andy want it back? How could he get it? After all, he was driving without a licence, and drunk. What if it had gone to court, even if it was her fault? And money wasn't really what motivated him. I think that he wanted his life under his own control, for the first time.'

'But it all seems so astonishing. Me being here, and Andy being involved with the twins' mother.'

'Not really.' Liz was always practical. 'Look at it from the other end. We're *only* here because Andy was involved with the twins' mother. The single coincidence in the whole scenario is you, staying at the Skirlbeck. And even that isn't so surprising, to anyone who knows your independent nature. It was odds-on you wouldn't want to be organised by June, and how many other hotels are there on the coast?'

'No, I suppose you're right.'

'It had to happen. I always thought Andy was burdened with something. Perhaps now he might grow up. I mean, look at the things he said in there. About the future, and about us, even about having children.' She stopped for a second, and Kate caught the pain in her eyes. 'You can imagine how it happened, can't you, Kate? Andy must have been denying it mentally for years, and so he went on paying. We all do things when we're young that come back to haunt us.'

Kate nodded. For a moment, irrationally, she thought of John, and then she realised why. Her own abortion, in her early twenties, had been like Andy's denial of some terrible mistake, and here she was, paying for that too. But unlike Andy, no confession would heal her because she wasn't sorry and the price was her life with John.

'Hey, you're dreaming,' Liz laughed. 'I can't tell you how much better I feel.'

Kate said nothing more. But there was another question left hanging in the air, which the others seemed to have forgotten.

If Andy de Salas hadn't wheeled Jean Robinson on to the shore to die, who had?

Chapter Thirteen

Kate crept downstairs in the early morning and for the first time the Skirlbeck Bridge Hotel looked less than pristine. In the bar, the remains of snacks lay congealed in the seventies-style baskets, the debris of various drinks and meals scattered horribly across the tables with no hint of the pleasure they had given the night before. In the dining room the tables were still pushed together for the film crew, and a beautiful cut-glass tumbler of half-drunk pale peaty liquid sat there, patently bottom-heavy, as if Andy de Salas had just put it down. But Kate was aware of another person somewhere in the vicinity. She identified a faint, tuneless humming. She tiptoed towards the kitchen. There, in his pinny, was little Terry Robinson, wiping out a huge black iron frying pan, a box of eggs at the ready.

'Kate.' He stopped singing to himself and looked at her brightly. 'Life goes on. Smoked salmon and scrambled eggs?'

She laughed back at him, but for a second felt a frisson of discomfort. It was odd that Terry seemed sublimely unaffected by the revelations the previous night.

'Is Bill OK?' she asked.

'I think he'll be fine.' Terry almost looked surprised. 'It's all a shock, of course. But Bill and mother were always a bit at odds.' He shook his head.

Kate withdrew, surprised. She had sensed that Bill, the stronger brother, was the one most likely to be irked by their mother's dominance, but she had never thought that Terry might see this as disloyalty.

And then Bill himself came into the dining room. Unlike Terry he looked dreadful, red-eyed, unshaven and distracted.

But he said, 'Good morning,' cheerfully enough.

'Bill . . . how are you?'

'Fine, surprisingly. Sleepless, of course. I got up at six and took another look at mother's papers. You remember how upset we were by them last week. You can see the money listed coming in from that poor young man. But here are two other payments I don't understand.'

'Oh, Kate doesn't want to hear all this.' Terry was smiling in his usual unworldly way. 'Come along, get everyone down for breakfast. I don't know why, but I feel we should have Buck's Fizz.'

It was the sort of insanely inappropriate suggestion that instantly works. Kate had imagined that Liz and de Salas would be unlikely to emerge from the bedroom, because of embarrassment, but she was wrong. They came in to breakfast, and before long there was an air, not of celebration, but of release about the Skirlbeck Bridge. Kate was sipping Buck's Fizz with her slippered feet on a chair, and Liz and Andy were holding hands in the window seat, the whole scene blessed by a sweet frail golden sunlight lapping through the bay window and catching the colours of the dahlias and Michaelmas daisies in the flower arrangements.

Kate thought about John again. She had a desperate urge to call him just to say, 'Guess what . . . ?' and tell him about de Salas's story. And it might have some bearing on George Goff's fear. But the finality of John's last few words to her echoed in her mind. Since then he had made it clear he didn't need her and the thought made her feel wretched. She shifted her slippers off the chair and announced she was going to get dressed.

By nine thirty the Skirlbeck Bridge Hotel seemed back to normal. Sally Dodd arrived, looking flushed, followed by the now sprightly June Ridley, just as burdened with administration but now looking busy rather than harassed. June was delighted to see de Salas. There was no doubt Andy was much more relaxed. His voice lacked that upper class hectoring tone on which he had previously relied, and he seemed able to listen as well as talk. Jerry and his pixie wife arrived last, seeming calm despite the difficulties of the day ahead, and they accepted de Salas's return with no comment. They were clearly used to the vagaries of media luvvies. De Salas, to his credit, murmured, 'Jerry, before I left we had a difference of opinion. Well, you were right.' Jerry raised his eyebrows, then shrugged and nodded with a silent gruffness that was better than contempt. De Salas wisely said nothing more and Kate, for the first time, was impressed by him.

There was little really to be done, and there was an atmosphere of unnatural quiet. Jerry left to take some sweeping panoramas of the village from the fellside, accompanied by the pixie who was actually offering him advice, and by June who was shotlisting. Liz and Andy left for a walk along the shore. Sally and Kate stayed behind in the dining room and talked yet again through the arrangements for the evening. But Sally was not her usual happy-go-lucky self. When the conversation faltered, she stooped to dredge in a large leather holdall. She said, 'Cliff and his dad have already left for Hexham. I know Cliff isn't really involved in all this, but . . .'

'But what?'

'I went through the videos in the parlour at Gillfoot. I don't know how Cliff got this, and I don't want to know. It hasn't been opened or played – I do know that – so I'm reassured. It probably came from old Tom's. Or mebbe someone gave it to Cliff. It had an elastic band round it and it had been rewound to the colour bars, you know, the line-up colours at the beginning. Cliff never bothers to rewind things properly. That's how I know he hadn't used it. But it's sick.' Sally could not look Kate in the eye as she passed over a VHS cassette. Kate took it off her, then went to find the twins.

'Bill?'

'Yes?'

'Do you have a video machine? We want to play back some footage.'

'Yes, use the one in the bar.' He went in there himself, and started polishing glasses.

But Kate waited by the bay window until he had finished, watching for Liz and de Salas to reappear along the road. A few minutes later she caught sight of them and ran to the door and called to de Salas.

'Can you help me?' she asked. He blushed with pleasure.

A few minutes later they sat on the floor of the bar, watching a badly shot video of a dogfight. Or that was what they thought it was. It was in such soft focus it could hardly be distinguished, but occasionally the camera operator managed to sharpen up the picture, at moments of irrelevance, suddenly revealing with superb clarity the outlines of a door, or the back of a flat cap. There was little to shock. Sally, standing behind Kate said dully, 'That's Skirlbeck barn. It ought to be demolished.'

'Tonight's venue?'

The younger woman nodded.

'But who's filming this?'

Sally said, 'Christ knows.' They watched the shots settle and try to focus.

'This can't be the finished article,' Kate said crossly, trying not to look at the snarling grey mass that had to represent two dogs locked by the jaws. If she distanced herself she could imagine it was just a canine street corner brawl seen on any council estate. It was a blur, and then the recording deteriorated to snash – the snowy effect on the screen – and finally to more colour bars and then more interference.

'Looks like an attempt that didn't quite work,' said de Salas.

'Yes,' Kate agreed. 'But Andy, you're a director. Working backwards from the camera angles, can you tell me where the person who filmed this was standing?'

'That's a bit of a tall order.' But de Salas smiled confidently. It was the sort of question he could answer. Ignoring the subject matter, playing the video through again and again, de Salas said, 'I would hazard a guess that the cameras . . .'

'Cameras plural?' Kate interrupted. 'Are you sure?'

'Yes. Look how they show virtually the same bit of activity from different positions. You couldn't move one camera to another viewpoint fast enough. I think we're talking about someone who either has a mobile mixer desk . . .'

'Unlikely,' Kate murmured.

' . . . or who has a two machine edit facility,' Kate caught Sally's eye, both remembering Tom Flint's still-room. De Salas went on, 'The director must be working the camera angles from behind the crowd and at a considerably raised height, looking down. Perhaps it's being filmed from a gallery?'

'Is there a gallery at Skirlbeck barn, Sally?'

'Well, of sorts. All barns have a hay loft round here.'

Andy was peering at the monitor. 'Looks nasty. But what is it that they're trying to show, Kate? I can't really see what's happening.'

'It's dogfighting, Andy. Illegal, cruel and, in this case, very badly filmed.'

De Salas smiled. 'You can say that again. It's been done by operators who can't even pull focus. Where did you get this?'

'I found it at a local farm,' Sally said noncommittally, her red blotched and pinched face revealing her embarrassment to Kate at least.

'Well, I would say that the people filming are up several feet from the ground floor, looking down, with two VHS cameras and that what we have here is a first rough edit. Does that help?'

'Yes, Andy, it does.'

Liz, who had been standing behind Andy, avoided Kate's eyes and said, 'There's another dogfight tonight and Kate and Jerry are going to film.' Kate said nothing. It was too late for de Salas to have any views that mattered on the subject. He had abdicated. But strangely, now he had no ownership in the film at all, she wanted him to approve. Out of the corner of her eye, to her surprise, she caught sight of him nodding, and he looked back at Kate.

'Could I go with you?'

'I thought this wasn't the film you wanted to make?'

'Kate, the truth about me is that I don't really know how to make a film. I just see pictures, beautiful pictures, not programmes. But you see the whole story and I admire you for it. If I can help tonight, with you and Jerry, I'd like to be there.' He was looking at Kate beseechingly, but his pleading eyes were nothing compared to Liz's.

'That's really nice of you, Andy.' Kate gulped her coffee, and swallowed her reservations. 'I'd love you to come along.'

Later that morning she went out by herself and walked up the path at the back of the hotel, away from the sea, ostensibly to join Jerry at the brow of the hill. It was a rare windless day. She took the long way round, first up through sweet-smelling gorse, and then as the path grew steeper, winding between boulders and crumbly red brown earth. The hill at the back of the hotel was smooth and undemanding compared to the fells further inland, but it still left Kate breathless. When she reached the ridge, she could see the wide sweep of Skirlbeck Bay, with the village clustered in the curve, the church standing slightly to one side, squat and sandstone built, with no spire or tower, just a solid gable end, because frills would not withstand the weather. The Skirlbeck Bridge Hotel was definable at the other end of the village. In between was a gaggle of pretty early Victorian terraced houses, some with Dickensian bay windows and all with running roofs of different colours. Most of the buildings were colour washed now, so that they had the pastel arbitrary variety of a toy village, but some were still grey concrete, and others just the sandstone blocks of the original builders. She thought she could see the Goffs' bungalow, low and cosy down by the shore. Near the church was a tall Victorian house, the nearest the village came to elegance, which was now holiday flats, and which Kate guessed must have been the original vicarage. The beautiful but weak sunshine of the early morning was ailing and there was a dull wintry touch to the clouds massing inland. Kate remembered the roaring fire at the Goffs' and wondered how Eileen managed to keep that going. She obviously wasn't bothering this morning. Despite the chill, there was no curling smoke from the bungalow, unlike the other cottages. For some reason this gave Kate a prickly sense of insecurity, but she told herself tiredness and other people's excitement was making her over-sensitive.

She chatted for a while with Jerry, both of them acutely aware of the evening's work ahead, but neither mentioning it. Then Kate lifted up her collar against the breeze just coming in from the hills, and slowly walked back to the hotel.

There was nothing to do but wait and have lunch. She wondered how she would get through the empty afternoon. She stood in the bay window, a glass of mineral water in her hand and thought about how things were coming together now, for everyone but her. As she watched, Malcolm Hodgson's Range Rover swung into the drive. She tested her feelings in the same way as you test your limbs after a fall. There was no reaction. He stepped down from the car, and she thought, 'What a nice looking man,' in the same way as she might have admired a horse or a picture.

Her equanimity saddened her. Splitting up with John had provided a sort of negative thrill at first, and of course her lust for Malcolm had been lurking. Now she had no emotional excitement and it was hard to see a point in anything, except the film, and by tomorrow that would be done.

She heard Malcolm come in and speak to Bill, who was flitting between bar, hall and dining room. Then Malcolm came into the bar and ordered his usual malt whisky. One day, she thought, he would be breathalysed, but he would probably be related to the magistrate, or be prepared to seduce her. Kate laughed to herself, and turned around.

'Hello, Malcolm, what are you doing here?'

'Just passing.' He smiled at her. 'I didn't see you there. Quiet day?'

'Yes. Well, until later. You're organised for our interview tonight?'

There was no-one in the bar. Terry had served Malcolm and left to rush down to the village shop for something for Bill's lunch menu. Bill was back on form in the kitchen, but the emotional exhaustion meant that he was caught out over little things – like running out of butter. The bar was deserted, but even so the councillor glanced round. Only when he was sure no-one was in earshot did he speak.

'Yes. And you're right. I think I ought to tell the full story.'

'You should. It really matters, Malcolm.' There was a short silence while they both mulled over the significance of what he had said. Then to lighten the atmosphere she added, 'And have you cleaned up for us?'

'Mmm. I've even mopped the kitchen.' He gave her a conspiratorial and friendly glance and she remembered his flagged floor at eye level and wondered how something so overwhelming at the time had been reduced to a private joke. But at least she sensed that Hodgson would keep it private. Companionably she moved next to him and leaned against the bar.

'Why don't you have a malt?' he asked.

'Oh, I have to keep a clear head. I can't drink and drive like you seem to.'

'Oh, come on, Kate! It's only one, and a weak one at that! Anyway, it isn't the drunks you have to watch out for on the roads round here, it's the mad pedestrians. Shame about the vicar, isn't it?'

'Sorry?'

'Poor old George Goff. Do you know him? They say things come in threes, don't they?'

'Malcolm, what are you talking about?'

'George Goff. Knocked down by a car this morning on his way back from the church.'

'Oh, my God!' Kate felt her knees give. She clutched Malcolm's arm and he looked down at her hand in surprise. 'What's this, Kate? Another onset of passion?' But her face, panic stricken, made his joke catch in his throat.

'Tell me what happened to George.'

'Hey, I don't know the details. The woman in the newsagent's told me. It seems Eileen heard the noise and rushed out of the bungalow and put George and the other man in the car and took them to Carlisle.'

'What other man?'

'The one who took the brunt of the hit-and-run. That's why the vicar wasn't killed. Look, here's Terry. He's just been down to the village, he'll know more. Christ, Kate, you look as if you've seen another dead dog.' But Kate had run out of the bar to the hall.

'Terry, what's happened to George Goff?'

'Kate, hold still.' The little twin fended her off as he unwound his scarf. 'He's been taken to the Cumberland Infirmary. He was knocked down by a car this morning.'

'And John? Was John with him?'

'John? Oh, John! Of course, that must have been who it was. They say there was another chap who pushed George out of the way. He's the one that's badly hurt.'

Kate felt as if she had been hit herself. Her chest seemed to cave in with a physical pain and her face froze as if her blood had stopped. She could hear a wailing noise that must have been coming from her own mouth. Terry was standing staring at her, and even at that moment, she saw the way he looked at her as if what had happened to John and the vicar had happened to people he didn't know. It was Malcolm who was holding her by the elbow, saying, 'What is it, Kate?'

'Malcolm.' She turned to him. 'If you're a friend, get me to Carlisle now. Please!'

'OK,' he said and his unconditional, matter-of-fact kindness suddenly relaxed her so that she felt her arms and legs again. 'I don't know what the hell has upset you, but it must have been bloody awful. Get in the Range Rover and tell me on the way.' She was running out to the car now, but he was behind her and again she felt his hand on her arm as she stumbled.

The Range Rover was unlocked and he pushed her up into the seat, hurrying round to the driver's side. 'Thank God for you, Malcolm,' she said, and to her own surprise she meant it. He turned the ignition key.

'You'd better tell me what this is about,' he said as the Range Rover engaged the gravel.

And in the half hour journey she did, tears pouring down her face until Malcolm, at the traffic lights in Wigton, said calmly, 'So this man whom you don't love, and who never talks to you about real issues and who disagrees with you on certain things which are key to his faith, is lying ill in a hospital twenty-five miles away, and you happily hijack another lover's car, with the lover inside, to get to see him? This man you don't love?'

'Yes. No . . . Oh, Malcolm, nothing's that simple.'

'It seems simple enough to me. Now look, keep calm. If either your boyfriend or the vicar had snuffed it, or been anywhere near snuffing it, the jungle drums would have beaten out the news by now. This happened after the early service. George Goff always liked playing at being a saint, so he probably went off to church and then got hit on his way back after a little too much communion wine.' Kate was about to remonstrate that George wasn't like that until she realised that Malcolm, his mind really on performing like a rally driver, was using his heavy handed irreverence to try to make her laugh. 'So,' he went on, 'it's now just gone one o'clock and if either of your vicars were at death's door, Eileen would have been on the phone to her mother or her neighbour, and the village would know all about it.' This time she did laugh, relieved.

'There,' said Malcolm. 'You're looking better. Trust me, I'll get you to the hospital as soon as I can. My God, whatever you say, I've never seen a face like yours when you heard about the boyfriend being knocked down. You must really care.'

'I do. At least I think I do. But that doesn't mean it will all work out.'

'No, but you should give it your best shot.' For a second, she heard real sadness in his voice, and she leaned over and touched his arm.

'What about you, Malcolm?'

He laughed, and pushed the gear lever into fifth for the long straight road past Thursby to Carlisle.

'Me? Well, it's a good job I like casual sex.' Momentarily ashamed, Kate turned to look out of the window, until Malcolm leaned over and squeezed her hand and said, 'The hospital is just down here. I'll drop you there. I'll go and see some people I need to see in Carlisle, and I'll come back for you later. I think you might want a lift back to Skirlbeck then. Or if not, leave a message for me. And stop worrying!'

It was an impossible order, but his confidence helped. At the hospital, Kate spent fifteen minutes ascertaining where John was, only to arrive at his ward to be told that moments before, he had been taken away, and was now being prepared for the anaesthetic. Kate felt a wave of anger and frustration which made her spin around, looking for someone in authority to intercept. A calm, condescending but kindly sister took her to one side, and described John's condition. Knowing she was crying, feeling stupid and yet recognising that the nurse must face people in a similar state everyday, Kate tried to listen. After the third attempt the details sank in. John had a blood clot . . . an extradural haematoma. It had only been identified by the CT scan, the nurse was saying to Kate's glassy eyes.

'But will he be all right?'

'Probably. He was lucky to be brought in here, apparently

with an old chap who had a broken ankle from the same accident. Your friend seemed dazed, but we brought him up here to the neurosurgical ward for observation and he deteriorated pretty quickly. But he never lost consciousness for more than a few seconds so he should make a full recovery. He's gone down now for craniotomy. He could well be back to normal by tomorrow, but he could easily have died.'

'But he's going to be fine?'

'There's every chance. You mustn't worry.'

'What can I do?'

'There really is nothing. To be frank there's no point you being here, and you look shattered yourself. Have a rest and call us later on.' The sister clearly had other things to do.

'But will you make sure he knows I've been?' pleaded Kate.

'Look, he won't be in a fit state to take in anything until tomorrow. Why don't you just make sure you're here yourself when he comes round?' said the nurse helpfully.

'When would that be?'

'Tomorrow morning, at about nine?' suggested the nurse.

If she could get a lift, or re-book the hire car from Skirlbeck Garage, Kate could be there. Liz could look after the crew and work out what final shots were needed for the film. The nurse watched Kate's face furrow as she worked out the logistics.

'Don't worry,' she said helpfully. 'Whether you can get back or not, he's in good hands.'

Kate involuntarily looked down at the strong, white hands of the sister. They were beautifully shaped with clean, perfect-shaped nails unlike her own which had been chewed on the journey and which were stained with biro, and grimy from Malcolm's car door. The nurse was smiling with the calm patronage of one long used to hysterical relatives, her thoughts actually on the next round of medications.

'I'm sorry to keep you,' Kate said, floundering inadequately. The nurse continued to smile. Suddenly Kate felt drained. Her head slumped. She felt her shoulders give as if someone had cut her strings. What more could she do? Would John really want her there in the morning? Hadn't he made it clear that he wanted to escape, to get away from their endless bickering? She had an insane vision of herself at the end of John's bed, standing like some sort of arbiter of his right to consciousness, upbraiding him as soon as he opened his eyes with a few well chosen questions on abortion, or the apostolic succession. She realised she was laughing irrationally, and the nurse, sympathetic, but only to a point, was getting ready to stand up.

'Well, be here if you can,' the woman patted Kate on the shoulder. 'But if you can't, he'll be fine.'

That just about sums it up, Kate thought. She really would try her hardest to get there in the morning, but she was unsure whether it would matter as much to John as it would to her. She only had him, whereas he had his faith. She wondered if he had prayed about her as much as he had about the demanding Father Marcus or the desperate George Goff, and in a moment of contrariness she made her own vow. If John relied on a God who had decreed that, after all her efforts, she arrived at the hospital only to miss him by minutes, she would do no more. Trying was obviously not enough, and the world was full of strong, straightforward nurses who would be there for John if he didn't want her!

She left the corridor outside the ward and trudged back to reception to try and trace George Goff. George had a broken ankle, cuts and bruises and was suffering from shock. Kate wasn't allowed to see him, but she found Eileen dominating the Friends of the Hospital shop.

'Kate.' Eileen swooped on her. 'How marvellous.' She was oblivious to the bleakness in Kate's face, as if her own drama had blocked the reception of any messages to her other senses, psychic or not. And she bore Kate off to a corridor with a collection of plastic chairs where in a loud and dramatic voice she regaled Kate and all the passers-by with what had happened. It had been quite simple. The two priests had gone to celebrate Communion at eight o'clock, the regular midweek early service. It was Hallowe'en, she explained to Kate, not a festival in the Church, and the next day was All Saints' Day, when George intended to celebrate early Communion again. Eileen thought it was too much to do two early communions in a week, but as always she hadn't argued. And Hallowe'en this year seemed to be giving George the willies. She got up with him, to insist he drank some hot water, all he would take before officiating, despite her protests that he was getting too old for such devotion. Normally, she would have stayed in bed. But after George and John had left, she sat in the kitchen, eating toast. Then at twenty to nine, she had heard the sound of a car in the lane, unusual in itself, and even more unusual because of the speed she sensed it was doing. She had heard the squeal of tyres and the thwack of a body, but no screech of brakes and when she'd reached the door, she had run outside to find George crawling in the mud, and John, on his hands and knees at the side. She hadn't realised then that John was badly hurt, concentrating instead on getting George into her car before she thought about helping John, who only seemed dazed. But she heard him say over and over again, 'I couldn't see him. But he could see us. He meant it. He meant it.'

'What was he talking about?' Kate asked desperately.

'I think he was talking about the driver.'

'What?'

Despite her sense of the melodramatic, Eileen Goff dropped her voice. 'Perhaps John didn't know what he was saying,' she murmured. 'But the tyre marks in the mud showed whoever was driving made straight for George. I'm not stupid. I didn't hear a skid. I think someone was trying to hit him.'

'But you said yourself George was doddery on the road.'

'Not that doddery. He didn't fall under that car. The car drove towards him. And remember John saw this. No-one would have expected John to be there. And anyway, my gift tells me that someone has been wishing death on the village.'

'Oh, come on, Eileen.'

'You may skit at me if you like, Kate. But you don't have to believe. I know it's true. And I know there's a lot more than just this going wrong in Skirlbeck. Believe me, Kate, it's all linked. Ask yourself: why do John and George get knocked down today? Jean Robinson died last Sunday. Tom Flint died in the week. Then Celia Marshall at the weekend. And now George has been attacked. I *have* got a gift, Kate. I know something is linking them all.'

A gift, or just a dramatic sense of intuition, Kate thought. They sat for a minute in silence. Then Eileen, with her astounding ability to swing from the other-worldly to the strictly practical, announced she was desperate for a cup of tea. In the café, with other people surviving other crises, it all seemed to diminish into the nasty hit-and-run accident it surely was, except for Eileen's dark frown. As they sipped, she tended to become even more wrapped up in her theory, giving Kate a full résumé. It was a relief for Kate to take her mind off her own crisis and to indulge Eileen in her rambling.

'So you believe that your . . . spirit guide . . . gives you warnings?' Kate enquired.

'Yes! Just like George's Holy Ghost or intercessionary saints. It's not so crazy.'

'So why didn't you know in advance that someone was going to drive into George?'

'Because it isn't always clear like that.'

'No, you can say that again. It all seems a bit deliberately mysterious to me.' She remembered Terry and Bill and their messages about their mother. 'The Robinson twins were telling me that you knew their mother drank in the Castle Arms, because you got a message about it from the other side.'

'What? Oh no! No, they've got it wrong. Yes, I did get a message that their mother's death was to do with a castle, but I didn't mean a pub. Definitely not. No, this was a big, very elaborate building; a modern castle, I called it, sort of fortified, and all shiny. But it was just a message. Sometimes I can't make much out of them myself. Funny things, spirits.'

For the first time at the hospital Kate smiled. Even at her maddest, there was something sane about Eileen.

'What are you going to do?' she asked the vicar's wife.

'Oh, I shall stay here. I've friends in Carlisle. And you?'

'I have to go back. I've got work to do tonight. But I'm going to try and be here in the morning for when John comes round.' And who knows what good that will do? she thought. She wondered for a minute if she should have been more understanding. Yet it all came back to the same old issue, whether it was John's views on controversial matters, or his need to make space for his colleagues. If he wouldn't talk to her about it, then how would she know when to keep silent?

She met Malcolm in the hospital foyer, and was grateful but quiet on the journey back. She felt dislocated from life with tiredness and shock. The decision just to let it be with John, to stop trying and to let go, knowing that he was in someone else's care and truly beyond her help, gave her a sort of exhausted peace. The dash to the hospital seemed to have worn her to breaking point as far as he was concerned.

When Malcolm dropped her at the hotel, she kissed him on the cheek with a new, negative sort of calm, feeling his skin as cool as a brother's. She had noticed that he too had become quieter, obviously worrying about the interview that evening. She knew he was putting his local loyalty on the line, and although she had never felt an equivalent sense of belonging, she could recognise it, and the conflict that it caused.

The film was now the main matter of the hours ahead.

She was scared, in a quiet consistent way, of what the evening would bring, but more scared that after all this, the material would not be there. And the key thread in the material was Malcolm Hodgson's story.

In one way she was looking forward to questioning Malcolm on film. The formality and the presence of the crew would close one chapter for her personally, and yet at the same time be the opening they needed for the programme. If he was nearly as compelling on camera as he was when he talked to her in the glimmering gas firelight of the old pub, it would be riveting.

She had an hour to fill. She tried to nap before changing into her sloppiest clothes, jeans and a shapeless pullover. She didn't want to eat but found she couldn't sleep either. She went over what she had to do. Malcolm had to tell the story of his son, in the most moving way. She was worried that when it came to it, he would be halting, or try to wrap the whole thing up in matter of fact machismo which would leave the viewer with no sense at all of the horror. And on top of that, only *she* could get the shots that they really needed to bring home to people what it was they were talking about. That was the real editorial dilemma, faced by the best producers on every programme: walking the fine line between gratuitous, or even perverted, pleasure in violence, and the proper need to show the terrible pictures, to drive home the facts.

Liz and Andy had been out for the afternoon, but Liz came back to join the crew. Sally turned up at seven thirty, and in an air of tension they all drove in two cars over to Bassenthwaite. On the road, Kate told Liz about John's accident. Her friend was horrified. Then she said, 'It really is too much of a coincidence for one village.' Kate nodded. Perhaps Eileen Goff was right. But if that was the case, the evening's dogfight might be the focus for far more than a mere sporting scandal. Liz leant over and squeezed Kate's hand. 'Keep smiling,' she said. 'At least John's safe now.' Kate turned and looked out of the window. Yes, John was safe. But who else was in danger? She had to physically grip the car door to force herself not to shake. Then she turned back to Liz, and made herself smile.

They arrived at Malcolm's brass-decked front door at eight o'clock.

'What a gorgeous house!' breathed Liz in an aside to her friend. 'If you'd played your cards right, Kate, you could have had all this to polish!' Kate laughed, hearing the sound in surprise as if someone else was making the noise. 'Wait till you see inside,' she murmured, thinking with some trepidation of the mess and hoping Liz wouldn't be too appalled by the interior. She felt a shiver of embarrassment when Malcolm opened the door, but now events of the night before last seemed a century away. And Malcolm really had tidied up. There was even a faint scent of floor cleaner.

Malcolm was ready for them, eager to get the interview over with a nervousness which troubled Kate. Jerry set up in Malcolm's office, a room which Kate could not remember from any angle and which had a suitably businesslike air. But as soon as the camera was rolling, she realised that she need not have been concerned about Malcolm's performance. His nervousness came from the strength of his emotions, and the strain of his decision to talk. The slight tremor in his voice added to the sense that he was something special. He had the ability which reminded her of Paul Pym to grasp the subject matter clearly and put it to camera. But Malcolm had something Pym did not, a real integrity and belief in what he was saying. She hardly needed to question him, and the feeling he brought to the subject had the rest of the crew intense with concentration. He finished by describing his son's alienation, so that Kate caught Liz's face and the horror on it.

'Cut,' said Liz, moments later, and they all exhaled.

'Shit!' Jerry was surprisingly forthcoming. 'That's quite a story, mate.'

Malcolm sat, exhausted, head in hands.

They packed up quietly, Kate and Jerry tense about the work to come, the others quiet and reflective, Malcolm still sitting, looking into the popping gas fire. Kate felt her heart beating in sympathy with the guttering flames, like a trapped bird. In less than half an hour, they would be on their way to Skirlbeck Barn. Malcolm stirred.

'Would any of you like a coffee?' he asked.

'Thanks, mate,' Jerry said. Malcolm got up to go to the kitchen, then signalled to Kate to follow him. The room, newly tidy, hardly registered with her as the scene of their passion. As she stood and watched Malcolm with the cafetière on the newly scrubbed surface, she heard the sound of de Salas's Porsche pull up outside.

'I know what you're planning,' Malcolm said quietly. 'I heard the cameraman talking about it, just now while he was packing up and you were going over the shots – is that what you call them? – with that director woman. Look, I'm very worried about you going there tonight.'

'Oh, Malcolm, why?'

'I really think that you could be putting yourself in danger. Whoever left the dead dog outside the Skirlbeck Bridge Hotel knows you're on to them. If you insist it isn't the Robinsons, then who could it be? There's more than just a cruel sport involved here. I've made another decision – I'm going to call the police and get them out tonight. Where is the fight?'

'I can't tell you, Malcolm. Somebody told me, and I can't pass it on.'

'Who was it?' For a moment he seemed threatening. Kate hesitated.

'This is a bit dramatic, Malcolm.'

'I can still remember my son's face. I should have tried to stop it before. Tell me the venue, Kate, even if you can't tell me who told you.'

'But if you call the police, that could ruin everything.'

'So it's more important for you to get the pictures than for these despicable people to be stopped?'

It was the same difficult line to walk which she had been thinking about earlier. If the dogfights could be stopped without the film, which would she opt for?

'If I get the pictures, Malcolm, it'll be much harder evidence. One police raid may stop things for a while. National publicity might stop it for good, not just here, but in other places too.'

'And make you a bloody good programme?'

'Yes. What's wrong with that?'

To her surprise, he laughed softly, 'Well, you're honest, I'll say that for you. But I've made up my mind. I should have faced facts and done it months ago. You'll still have your interview with me.'

'But that's not enough, Malcolm.'

'You mean, people really need to *see* this?'

'Believe me, Malcolm it will have twice the effect.'

'I don't like it, Kate.'

'Please!'

'All right. I'll wait and give you time. But it seems a funny sort of reporting to me that will let these animals suffer for pictures when we could stop it now.'

'You've agreed a deal, Malcolm.'

'OK, fair enough. Now tell me where it's happening?'

She murmured, 'It's in Skirlbeck Barn.'

'Skirlbeck Barn? Just there? Fucking hell. That's why it's been the centre of the planning row . . .'

She heard what he said, but her mind was on what was about to happen. The other members of the crew had come quietly into the kitchen, anxious and preoccupied, drinking Malcolm's coffee and thanking him in thin small voices.

And then it was time to go. Liz gave Kate and Andy her usual media kiss, yet it seemed to actually mean something this time, and to Kate's surprise Sally and the pixie followed suit. Furtively Sally whispered something to Jerry. She caught Kate's glance and looked away.

'It'll help you get into the barn,' she murmured shamefacedly, and Kate guessed then that Cliff had known what was happening, and how to get in, and had chosen to do nothing about it, like Malcolm before she had pressured him. It made her feel vindicated, though more frightened than ever. Outside in the biting wind off the fells, she and Andy got into the battered estate car Jerry had brought for the purpose, and she thought she could smell her own fear. Without speaking Andy drove down the dark lanes, the headlights dipped. She noticed before they got to the barn how cars were parked at random, dotted in strange places as if a flock of courting couples were out.

But around the barn itself was complete emptiness. She wondered for a minute if they had got it wrong. But Jerry had done his homework, asking in the Castle Arms, expressing a new and prurient interest. Jerry was local which helped, but Kate was sure it was Sally's tip-off that gave him the password to get inside. No-one even looked at Kate. Women in tow were too insignificant to need a password.

The barn had a door at the rear. Inside, there was a corridor of old hay bales, then it widened out. There must have been about thirty people, in the dark and dusty atmosphere. Kate noticed the men had hats pulled down and collars pulled up. One or two had ordinary dogs on leads which seemed to sense something unnatural. They were strained and whining. There were one or two blobby shapes that could have been women. But the dark of the audience was made thicker by the TV-style filming lights focused on a clear space in the middle of the barn, surrounded by hay bales which gave off a sickly, stale smell. Furtively, she groped in the shoulder bag to press the right buttons on the Hi-8 camera. In the barn, there was hardly any conversation but Kate heard the harsher notes of Geordie and Scots. A man with a leering face half hidden by an anorak hood seemed to be taking money. Jerry had withdrawn, and Andy, wearing a parka and scarf and stooping, mumbled something and Kate saw notes change hands. The man ignored her. Women obviously played no part in the business of the night. The small crowd was gathering behind her, and she realised that in the crush she had become separated from her colleagues. She was aware of feeling real, bone-crumbling fear, as if her legs would give way. But she didn't have long to dwell on the reasons, before fear of the alien hardened into something even more terrifying. Suddenly the crowd pushed forward. Her greatest sensation was of smell, a vile, rank sweaty smell, and then the crowd started a low, throaty roar. She could hardly see, crushed up against a man's harsh waxed jacket on one side, and pressed fiercely from behind by another fat, greasy man in a soft gaberdine-style raincoat. She felt his leg against hers, and a stiffness from his body,

pressed right against her buttocks. She heard hersel
retching, but the heaving of her body just brought hir
closer. The crowd roared again and she heard yelping, bu
she couldn't see, caught between the big rank bodies. Sh
had no idea where Andy had gone, and while the part c
her brain which was still functioning registered concer
that she might not be getting any shots, her instinct wa
ordering her to keep her head down, shut her eyes, preten
to be anywhere else and pray for this to be over. The sme
of animals thickened. She could feel the crowd's tensio:
now, like a corporate erection and through a chink in th
bodies in front of her she saw the dogs in the light. To he
they were nightmare versions of ordinary dogs, with twiste
mad faces, snapping jaws and saliva that hung in shinin,
loops. The snarl was primeval as one leapt at the othe
fastening its teeth into the flesh and pulling with an almos
slow-motion violence so the crowd exhaled in a soft
orgasmic 'aaaah'.

Then there was a shocking, sharp snapping and snarlin;
of such speed Kate was left as breathless as the men nex
to her, and before she could close her eyes, one dog wa
clenched around the other. The dog which was being tor:
had the strained shock in its eyes that you only see i:
animals, the recognition of what is happening coming slowl
but without imagination, only certainty. Kate could see th
bubbles of blood now, out of its razored throat, and th
dominant dog's teeth still in position as its victim, slowl
twisting, ripped its own flesh. Then suddenly the submissiv
dog wrenched its huge head from side to side and tore o:
a piece of its own throat to rid itself of the monster latche
on to its neck. The dominant dog shot backwards, and th
roles were reversed. The pit bull with the gouged throa

leapt forward and snapped its huge jaws around its opponent, bringing it to the ground with a sickening crack.

The crowd was panting now, the disgusting excitement mounting. Kate was suddenly so sickened she didn't care any more about the project. She knew now what Malcolm had meant. No film was worth this. She twisted against the man behind her but found only that his face was right up against hers and his loathsome intrusive body ramming her. 'Don't you like it, missy?' he said. 'Well, you're going to have to take it.' She remembered then what had happened to Malcolm's son, and in terror wondered if there was more, far worse, than he had ever told his father.

'No!' she screamed.

And then Kate heard the voice. It took a moment for the crowd to turn from the hideous spectacle in the ring, but she knew at once what was happening. Andy de Salas was yelling 'Stop! You bastards stop this!' She could see him, standing on the steps leading up to the trapdoor to the hay loft. With him was Jerry, and Jerry too was shouting, 'You bastards!' Kate knew what Andy had done. He had worked out that the cameras were in the loft and he was going for them. Jerry was behind him, pushing him up the ladder.

With an agility Kate didn't know she possessed, she turned round in one fierce movement, beating her elbows against the heaving men. As she did so, she brought her knee up into the engorged groin of the vicious man behind her. He screamed and fell back, his bulk pressing the crowd away from her for just a few seconds, enough time for her to clamber over limbs and bodies with flailing arms to join Andy and Jerry on the stairs. They were climbing up now, despite a few hands that tried to stop them. But the crowd had gone silent as de Salas thumped open the hayloft door.

He clambered in, pulling Kate after him, with Jerry behind

'What the fuck's going on?' Paul Pym stood there, looking like an eighteenth century Squire, his face florid with drink and exhilaration. There were two VHS cameras, on either side of the wide loft, one peeping down through the floor directly on to the ring below, another at the back, on the other side of the square trap door de Salas had beaten open. The greasy Roy, Pym's assistant, was behind one camera his excitement evident and probably accounting for his inability to focus. Piles of ten and twenty pound notes lay next to Pym on a flimsy trestle table burdened with equipment.

Sophisticated video monitors and a computer terminal crowded for room with bottles of brandy and long-hand ledger books like some crazed combination of past and present.

'You bastard!' de Salas was yelling. 'You fucking hypocritical bastard. We'll get you for this!'

'Oh, yes?' Pym advanced on de Salas and suddenly almost lazily, slapped him on the face, so that Andy reeled back against the wall.

De Salas rallied and made to hit out at Pym, who was stooped now, ready to swipe back with the aim of a drunken yob. But his voice, slurred with drink, still had the cut glass tones Kate remembered from the ghastly dinner party when he first let his prejudices show.

'Don't hit out at me, you nobody.' Pym flung another blow at de Salas, so the younger man, though fitter, was subdued by the fleshy man's sheer weight. 'So you call me hypocritical, you talentless little creep. Well, you belong to a culture that lets kids watch "Gladiators" on TV and roar for blood every Saturday night. That's mob rule, not sport.

He hit at Andy again, who fell back nearer to the trap door opening. 'And you belong to a culture which agonises over whether live executions can be shown on video, with the excuse that it will turn people against capital punishment. Oh, yes, I've heard all those fucking hypocritical arguments. Well, we're not voyeurs here. We're in it for the sport.' He hit de Salas again. 'Real sport. Real blood sport. The best beast winning. That's what life's about. So keep your sanctimonious townie views to yourself!'

'We'll expose you . . .' de Salas was saying, spluttering now. 'We've got film of this.'

It was that which enraged Pym. 'You've got film have you? And your snotty friends at Channel Four will show it, will they? You must be mad. They won't show anything unless it's guaranteed to have the chattering classes writing it up in *The Guardian*. Who cares about a few yokels and their sport, hey? They were the people who didn't want the likes of me, de Salas. They wouldn't know real television if it hit them in the face. Don't kid yourself. Maybe the best thing you could do is sell the footage for late night viewing. They'd buy anything that turned the masses on.' He advanced on Andy to hit him again, and then saw Kate. His words had stung her, but she clutched her handbag to her chest even as he advanced. She knew and he knew that however many creeps might get a thrill from the shots she had managed to take, there were enough decent people out there who would clamour for Pym and all those like him to be stopped, and shamed into never indulging their gross pleasures again. For every ounce of his cynicism, she felt in the balance her faith in the decent people, like Sally and Cliff and – thank God for him – Malcolm. She thought of his determination to ring the police and was so grateful she felt the wetness of tears on her face in the heat of the hayloft.

'Don't come near me, Pym,' she said. 'You may be the Lord-of-all-you-survey here, but outside your little world, we'll expose you to people who will make sure you never get a chance to exploit suffering like this again in your life.'

For some reason her words stopped him.

'Me?' he said, and there was a twisted smile on his face now. 'Me? Lord-of-all-I-survey. Oh, no, my dear. You've got that all wrong.'

'What?' She was aware, now, of someone behind her. De Salas was looking over her shoulder, and she heard the creaking floorboards as someone approached. There was a soft sensation on the back of her neck that she knew instinctively meant new danger. It was someone's breath. And then there was a tiny, sharp pinprick. She gasped, clutching her bag to her chest for safety but the attack came so sharply from behind she hardly heard de Salas shout, 'Watch out, Kate!'

Suddenly Kate felt a pain which knocked the breath from her windpipe and she realised that an iron-strong arm had clenched her around her neck so that she was held in the crook of an elbow. Her head was rigidly pinioned to someone's chest. The grip slackened just enough to allow her to breathe in her panic. She stood stockstill as her writhing calmed. In front of her Jerry, Andy de Salas, Paul Pym and his assistant stared, transfixed not by her, but by the six-inch blade held against her throat. Very slowly she let her eyes swivel round keeping her face straight ahead. And her mouth snapped shut, as the clasp tightened terrifyingly around her neck, in the moment of recognition. But she could not be sure.

'Oh, Miss Wilkinson – or should I say Miz . . . I think that's how you modern ladies like it, isn't it? – how wrong you are about everything.'

'Bill?' she gasped, unable to speak properly because her jaw was forced up by the steel-hard force of his arm.

'Bill? Oh dear me, no. Brother Bill wouldn't get involved in this sort of thing, Miss Wilkinson. He just likes playing at being a waiter.' Terry Robinson was grimacing, inches away from her, like an insane cherub. 'Mother and I knew we could do a whole lot more than that. Our only mistake was using the fool Pym. Now, let's be practical. We need to get this film of yours, don't we? Because there really is no need for a load of offcomers and southerners to upset themselves about all this. Tell them to give me the film, Miss Wilkinson.' Even in her fear, Kate realised Terry had no idea the video tape was actually in the handbag she was still clutching. 'How funny,' he was saying. 'No-one's making a move to save you. I'm not surprised. But *you'll* be surprised at how your posh friends fade away when the going gets tough. And what will you do when there's no evidence? That lot will soon give up. Mr de Salas hasn't got a very good track record for integrity, has he? And Jerry is a local joke, he's in so much debt keeping his little wifie happy that he won't be saying much. You really haven't got a leg to stand on.' And in a grotesque parody of humour he swung Kate off her feet by her neck, still jammed in the crook of his arm, so she felt she was choking and for a moment a curtain of blood filled inside her eyelids. Then she was back on the ground, her head pounding, but conscious again. Malcolm, she thought, for Christ's sake, Malcolm, where are the police?

But even as she was coming round she heard the shouts from the room downstairs.

'There's someone out there!' a Geordie voice was shouting. 'Get the fuck out of here.' The grip tightened again around her throat. But she could feel Terry's breathing in great gulps as his chest rose and fell against her back. Pym had backed up against the hay bales, as far away from the trapdoor as he could, as if the space would keep the police away from him. She felt Terry move and eased herself slightly out of the rock-hard grip whispering, 'Terry. Let me go.'

It was as if the sound of her voice, hoarse and cracked like an old woman's, shook him.

'Do you know what night it is?' his voice was sibilant in her ear. 'It's All Hallows' Eve, when the spirits come back. You thought it was all rubbish, didn't you, Miss Snooty Wilkinson? But it's not. Mother is still with us, you know. Bill said she was a wicked woman. That means she would burn in Hell. But she's not there. She's here.'

Paul Pym was still staring. With heightened awareness Kate tried somehow to signal to Andy with her eyes that Terry was tiring. His voice had become singsong, like the tuneless humming she had heard in the kitchen that morning. Downstairs, she could hear the rumpus of barking animals and shouting men. But her own consciousness was slipping now. The pressure on her throat was consistent. Terry was cutting off just enough oxygen for her to see the world beyond his grasp fade and die. Even then, she was aware of how stupid she had been trying to persuade Malcolm Hodgson to delay calling the police. No pictures were worth dying for, not even by the animals she had condemned by asking him to wait.

'We had a good system, Mother and I,' Terry was whispering to Kate. 'I like strong women. That's why I liked you at first. But you can't trust southerners. Look at Pym. Mother thought he was rubbish really. Silly, self-indulgent rubbish. It would be good if Pym burnt instead of her, wouldn't it?' he said, almost conversationally.

'Pohleece!' screeched a voice downstairs.

Swiftly, hardly loosening his grip, as if he had always expected this chaos, Terry Robinson shot his foot out and kicked the trestle table which wobbled and fell, the computer screen and video monitor crashing to the floor. But so did the big TV light which had been illuminating the dim loft. The bulbs burst on to the hay, along with a smashed bottle of Pym's brandy. In the dark Kate saw the fire start, and it seemed in minutes the loft was full of burning acrid smoke. Robinson let go of her to cough, as suddenly as he had grabbed her, and the knife slithered to the floor. She saw it gleam in the firelight with blood on it, her own blood. She fell forward on her hands and knees to where de Salas was coughing too, but with his hand out for her. He slithered back down through the trap door and then there was nothing but a black square. She stumbled towards it and fell, scared of Terry behind her, and Pym sprawled to one side, winded and making choking sounds. Feeling her fingers scrape on the wood, the scratch on her face from a piece of splintered table leg and the terrifying invasion in her lungs of the coils of smoke, Kate began to crawl to the opening, aware now of vicious stinging in her eyes and her throat.

Then, like a mirage, she saw through the greyness that Liz was there, straining for her arms, and she willed herself towards the opening. She wriggled with all her might into her friend's arms and backwards down the stepladder into the barn. But as she looked back through the smoke, she saw Terry Robinson stretch up in a last lurch, his arms forward as if to run to someone waiting for him. The flame went up in a sheet and she fell backwards to the barn floor.

She fought desperately against losing consciousness as she was pulled past the hay bales and out into the cold, starry night. She knew she was coughing her lungs out, but it was as if the pain was searing someone else's chest. Her eyes were sticky and sore, the eyelids clinging to each other then suddenly popping open as if in surprise, giving her sudden crazed glimpses of the sky, and making her feel absurdly as if someone had superglued the soft bits of her face. And there was a thin searing pain round her neck as if a wire was tied too tightly so she wanted to put her hands up and clutch the nuisancy thing away, but her hands wouldn't move.

She lost consciousness for a minute, but was not aware of fear. The coming and going of reality seemed to have a rocking rhythm. She knew Liz was beside her and could hear her friend crying but as Kate came and went more frequently, she started to wonder why Liz was so distressed. A little later she came round again, and her eyes cracked open. Instead of the stars there were orange lights waving overhead as if she was washed up under a lighthouse.

'Bad case of shock, flesh wound to the neck, some breathing problems and some scorching,' a matter of fact voice was saying. Who's got that? Kate wondered, as the trolley lurched into the ambulance. The voice, distant now, was saying, 'There are two more in there, but they're past help. One badly burnt, the other seems to have suffocated.' A further voice seemed to ask a question; Kate tried to understand, but then the answer boomed out from the paramedic beside her. She looked down to see the man attaching something to her wrist. Funny, what are these tubes for? she thought, as his voice rang out. 'Yes. Terry Robinson. Everyone knows the Robinsons. You can just about see it's him. His brother's here. Creepy how alike they are. I mean, how alike they were – one's well cooked now! The twin brother ran all the way, but the other one was gone long before he got here. And the Pym chap is dead too. I would say his breath was enough to start a fire from the smell of him. Stinks of drink. Missed the flames by miles, but choked, I would say.' Kate lay, in a world of tubes and red blankets and noise and complete lack of responsibility. But she knew if she tried she could speak, now.

'Where are you taking me?' To her, the noise from her throat was like a mighty roar, but the paramedic strained to hear her.

'Shush, don't speak.' She was aware now of something cold and stinging round her throat, like a wet scarf.

'Please,' she strained again. 'Where are you taking me?'

'West Cumbria Hospital at Whitehaven, sweetheart.'

'Whitehaven?' The paramedic hardly heard her as she shut her eyes. She heard the engine start and felt the ambulance swaying to move out of the rutted track.

Whitehaven. More than fifty miles from where John Maple would come round in the morning. She fought unconsciousness this time. There was absolutely no way she could be there when he woke. The God he believed in had it all worked out. As the vehicle lurched and she felt the restraining straps keeping her to the stretcher, she found herself laughing, a hoarse, silly, bitter sound which worried the ambulanceman sitting over her. She thought of what John had said to her the night he had left.

And then the injection the paramedic had hurried to give her on hearing the rattling from her throat took over. But her last thought was that now she and John had literally gone their separate ways.

Chapter Fourteen

'You can use the phone on the trolley, dear; I'll just have to wheel it over to you,' said the orderly. 'Have you got the right coins?'

'Coins?'

Kate was sitting up in bed. The cloth screens were still around her, but she had been tidied up, and had drunk a very weak cup of tea. The woman in the pale green overall had been passing the bed with a dustpan and brush when Kate had demanded the phone. Fifteen minutes earlier Kate had listened in a daze to a very young doctor tell her she was recovering from shock and had slept for fourteen hours. It was two o'clock in the afternoon. She had a flesh wound to her neck, he said, and her face had been singed. 'But really, not much worse than putting your face too close to the oven when you get the roast out,' he had joked. Kate had felt a sudden lurch of nausea, thinking about what had happened to Terry Robinson, but the young doctor was unaware of his insensitivity and grinned cheerily. She had smiled back weakly. He obviously put her in the same bracket as his mum. She hadn't the heart to tell him that she would never want to make a roast dinner again.

Then he and the sister had left her, and she had drunk

the tea, and stared at the sunlight on the pale green pleats of the cloth screen, feeling quite aware of everything that had happened but completely incapable of doing anything other than wonder at it all, until suddenly she had sat bolt upright, spilling the tea into the saucer, and had thought of John. She wanted to ring him. She needed to know how he was, even if that was all. But the phone business now seemed unbearably complicated. Her shoulders ached to relax back onto the pillow, and then they did, without her permission.

It was an hour later when she awoke again. This time she saw things with the clarity of a frosty day – crisp, clear, but cold and unusual.

'My bag,' she called out in panic to a passing nurse whose silhouette appeared on the screen. A cheerful face popped around it.

'Your bag, dear? I don't know about that. But here's a friend to see you. Doctor says it's OK.'

Liz Jones tiptoed slowly around the screen, then rushed over to hug Kate, who winced and shuddered, but Liz still embraced her with enthusiasm.

'The tapes, Liz. Where's the bag with the camera in?' Kate yelped.

'Hey, calm down, we got that all right. You were clutching it.'

Kate leant back and shut her eyes in relief, before snapping them open and sitting up again.

'John,' she said.

'He's all right too. Keep calm.'

'Tell me, Liz.'

'OK, OK, you're supposed to be still half stupefied, for goodness' sake. John's fine, but not great. He managed to talk to the police this morning and after that they let me see him, but he's desperately tired. It looks as if it was Paul Pym's car which ran them down. John said George the old vicar knew about the dogfighting all along, but he was too terrified to talk about it. What a place! George was notoriously short-sighted and Pym rarely used his car, so he must have thought he'd get away with a hit-and-run, even if George wasn't killed instantly. Pym probably didn't see John until he stepped out and pushed the old man to one side. John was able to give a good description of the BMW. Not that it matters now, with Pym being . . .' She stopped as if she had been tactless.

'Dead. I know that, Liz. I heard the ambulancemen talking. Did John ask after me? Can I phone him?'

'Tomorrow, perhaps?' Liz looked away. 'Kate, have you got some Lucozade? You'll be in here for at least another day, so should we make a list of things you might need?'

'Lucozade? What are you talking about? I was asking you about John. Liz, why won't you look at me? Did he give you a message for me?'

'No . . . no, not really, Kate. He's still really very weak. But he did say that you mustn't worry.'

'Oh. Did he? Was that all?'

Liz nodded. Kate lay back again, feeling a stinging on her scorched eyelids which cut through the stickiness of the hospital's cream. If she wiped her eyes, she wiped away the medication, so she had no option but to let the tears run.

Liz leant forward. 'I'm going to take you back to London as soon as possible, Kate. You've had a terrible experience. You can stay with Jodie,' one of their mutual friends, 'and then I'll come back here to Andy and sort things out. But you need to get away and rest.'

'And John?' Kate had said again, weakly.

'Call him tomorrow.' Liz stroked her friend's hand as Kate once again drifted into the drugged sleep which had given her some release. Liz sighed. She had not been entirely honest and that bothered her. That morning she had been shocked by John Maple's cold detachment. The ward sister had warned her that because of the blood clot John had sustained, as well as the effects of the general anaesthetic, he would be lethargic and still dazed. But John seemed too remote even to talk, as if he was in his own bubble of misery like a fish in a bowl, unable to communicate other than with sad, shallow eyes. He told her, drearily, that he had heard from the police about what had happened to Kate, and then he had said bleakly, 'Kate doesn't want me.' Liz was too astute to make some palliative remark. She had said nothing. And John had turned away bitterly to face yet another policeman wielding a notebook.

A month later, Liz arrived at Kate's flat bearing a bottle of Chardonnay and a big smile. She had seen Kate several times since the drama at Skirlbeck, but tonight was the first time Kate had been fit enough to do the entertaining.

'How are you?' she said as Kate opened the door.

'Much better. Still a bit sore around the neck, but the eyelashes are growing back. And longer!' Kate fluttered her bald lids at Liz. 'Come in.'

Liz followed her into the little flat, wondering why it looked different, until she realised it was crammed now with things Kate had retrieved from John's place. John himself was still in Cumbria, part recuperating and part helping George Goff restore some stability to his shocked and brutalised parish.

Liz sighed. She felt she had a serious purpose, but she made easy conversation to begin with. It was at least a week since they had last met, and in the meantime Liz had been back up to Skirlbeck. Now Kate needed to be filled in on the way de Salas had wound up the film project. He and Liz had taken Jerry and the pixie, and Sally and Cliff, out for a quiet dinner at the Summerlake two nights earlier. Jerry had a new assignment on a fisheries vessel for BBC Scotland, a venture which would gross him enough cash to solve some of his problems, and Sally and Cliff had finally named the day for the Skirlbeck wedding of the year. It would help folk put things behind them, Sally said.

It was now Monday, and Liz was back at LondonVision. Kate had been in an edit suite all weekend putting the finishing touches to the film. It looked good, and Chrissia was pleased and wanted to get a slot for it before Christmas, especially as there was to be no court case.

'And how's Bill? Have you seen him?' Kate asked.

'Bill? He's OK. The hotel is open again of course. But shouldn't you be asking about John, Kate, rather than Bill?'

'John? Well, I know he's fine. I've telephoned him twice at the Goffs'. The first time he was so cold . . . and after that, I needed to speak to him about logistics.'

'But you must know that with his sort of injury he would hardly be in sparkling conversational form.'

'Yes, but that's not the point. Our affair was over before all this tragedy happened. Just because we were both injured doesn't mean everything's going to end happily ever after.'

'But you obviously wanted to speak to him?'

'Oh, yes. I had to tell him I was going to let myself into the flat, to get my stuff. That was what we agreed.' Kate turned her back abruptly on her friend and went to get the glasses from the kitchen.

Liz said no more until they had drunk the wine and relaxed over Kate's expert selection of Marks and Spencer's pre-cooked cuisine. Then she said tentatively, 'Actually, I went to see John at the Goffs' on Saturday.'

'Really?' Kate got up to clear the plates, but Liz followed her.

'Look, Kate, he really misses you.'

'Does he? That's not what he tells me.'

'Kate! You know what John is like. He's terrifed of pressuring you. It's really important to him that people are free to make up their own minds.'

'Oh. Is it? And how would you know that, Liz.'

'I'll tell you, Kate, if you'll listen to me instead of banging around with a red face and a pile of dirty dishes in your hand. You remember the reason I went up to Cumbria in the first place, the incident you promised never to mention again?'

Kate turned and nodded. It was Liz who was red-faced now.

'Well, I swore I would never talk about it to anyone, Kate, not even you, but I spent a whole afternoon on Saturday with John and I found myself talking about it then. He asked me about . . . abortion . . .' the word hurt Liz, 'in a general way. I didn't tell him about me, at first. He said it was a subject you two had quarelled about and he wanted to understand.'

Thank goodness for John's discretion, Kate breathed. However embittered she was about him, she was at least grateful for his tact. Liz was going on, 'And he must have sensed that it had some personal relevance for me because he just let me talk. It was bliss to find someone who would listen while I went over it all for my own benefit. You see Kate, I was absolutely sure I had done the right thing, and absolutely terrified of what other people would say. I couldn't discuss the rights and wrongs of it even with you. At the back of my mind I feared that it might really be a heinous crime. But when I was explaining myself to John, I began to see I couldn't be a heinous criminal. I made my own choice about my own body. You know deep in yourself that all the theorising is so much rubbish and it's only about you! And that's what no-one else can understand. My guilt wasn't the corrosive guilt of having committed an appalling moral crime, but the social guilt of worrying what others thought.'

Mmm, Kate thought, remembering her own row on the subject with John; at least something she had said had made an impression.

'And,' Liz was going on, 'if you'd ever told me I'd have even discussed the matter with a middle-aged clergyman, never mind get some comfort from it, I'd have told you I was more likely to tell the pompous old fart to go to hell, but it wasn't like that with John. He was wonderful.'

'Oh, he's always wonderful at being superior and helping people through their dilemmas.'

'No! Kate, you've got that all wrong. I talked *him* through it, and helped myself in the process. John's a good listener, and he's not frightened to admit it when he's unsure and wants to know more.'

'Oh, come on! He was never like that with me. He closed the door in my face every time anything even remotely controversial came up.'

'Well, perhaps you were always goading him for his

views, when you should have had the confidence to explain your own! He certainly listened to me.'

'Well, thanks for your homespun philosophy, Liz.'

'OK, no need to be snide. I can see you're thinking that I've got no right to lecture you about relationships. Fair enough. But Andy and I are going to give it every chance and at least we're not hung up on pride.'

Liz flounced away to the tiny lounge.

'I'm sorry, Liz. What's happening with you and Andy?' Kate followed with the coffee.

Mollified, Liz explained how she was going to approach Steve for a divorce, and how she and Andy, among other plans, wanted a cottage on the Solway Firth where they could watch the sunsets together. Kate raised her singed eyebrow at this romantic vision.

'And the children?'

'We'll work it out. And that's another thing, Kate. It's obvious John doesn't like the idea of Steve and me getting divorced, but we still had a good discussion about it, without John making me feel like a moral defective. He's good at making you think.'

'Oh, yes. He's very good at that. He let me think myself right out of loving him, and he never tried to win me back.'

'Oh, for Christ's sake, Kate . . .'

'Look, Liz, when John was in the hit-and-run accident I took the most appalling liberties to get to Carlisle to see him. I missed him by minutes. They'd just wheeled him away to the theatre. And I suddenly felt: what the hell? He's always had God to fall back on and perhaps this is the result of his prayers. I really wondered if someone somewhere was trying to tell me something. I still planned to go back and see him in the morning, of course, because

I still cared for him. But I was sick of struggling any more about our so-called relationship. And then that night, when the ambulance took me miles in the other direction it was almost funny. I thought it was conclusive. It was almost a relief.'

'A relief? Sick of trying? You? Kate Wilkinson! What utter tosh. Since when did you stop making your own fate? That's passive rubbish. For the last two years you've had all your confidence back and you've come through. A lot of that has been down to John Maple . . . and a lot more has been down to you never giving up! You can't turn your back on your life with John. All this business about him not wanting to face controversial issues is so much rubbish. He was just frightened of you getting on your high horse – and that's what you did! So if you're half the feminist you think you are, take your so-called fate in your own hands, and do the running. Since when has a mere man stopped you!'

Kate's face was so sore that twisting it in anger and flashing her eyes made her squeal in pain. Liz leant across from her chair and grabbed her hand.

'I didn't mean to hurt your feelings, Kate. But John is really wretched.' Kate looked back at her friend, the misery on her own face made both touching and comic because of the perpetually startled look caused by half her eyebrows being missing. Liz giggled, and Kate looked down at her coffee and took a reflective sip. Her friend leant back, knowing there was no more she could say on the subject.

'Anyway,' Liz went on, 'forget all that and look at this.' She rooted in her bag, and pulled out a crumpled magazine which she waved at Kate.

'What's that?'

'It's the LondonVision newsletter, largely for people who

haven't got a life and who are stuck in a career timewarp. It's full of the doings of ex shop stewards and producers who made one good show in 1983, people who hit one heyday and can't let go.'

Kate picked up the magazine, which Liz had opened at the appropriate page. 'So?'

'Look at that feature at the bottom of the page. "LVV – LondonVision Veterans." When I was trying to get help for Andy, I asked Felix Smart, and he pointed me in the direction of Paul Pym . . .'

'Yes, Felix told me that he found out about Pym being up in the Lakes from the LV magazine.'

'Right. Well, I was tidying up at home yesterday,' Liz blushed slightly. The fact that she was tidying up prior to moving out bothered her as well as Kate. 'Anyway,' she rushed on, 'I found the mag that Felix had passed on to me, and spotted this. Look.'

Under the section about Pym, written in glowing prose, and referring throughout to 'my personal inspiration', who was 'still a close friend', was the byline Hugh Ruscroft.

The wind was whipping up the waves so that they rolled on to the stony beach and frothed and crumpled before collapsing with the effort of travelling in through the wide flat Solway Firth. The same wind lifted the Christmas lights outside the village shop, the bright bulbs rippling along the frontage, the only dabs of colour in the street at four o'clock in the afternoon. The houses huddled together for warmth, occasional glimpses of light through netted windows emphasising the bleakness of the day outside. A few hardy visitors walked on the shore, or sat in parked cars drinking hot tea from flasks, watching the weather.

Eileen Goff wondered about drawing the curtains, as she looked out of her bungalow at the muddy track meandering to the sea. Behind her, the fire was drawing nicely despite the wind.

'Cup of tea, George?' she called, but there was no answer from the frail old man sitting in the easy chair, his bad leg balanced on a low stool. She sighed. George was drained these days.

Then, to make a liar of her, he looked up suddenly, more alarmed than alert, and said, 'Where's John?'

'He's up at Skirlbeck House seeing Sir Michael. He told you he was going.'

'Oh, yes.'

Eileen sighed. George didn't seem to register what was happening half the time, and the other half he was so tense and tetchy. For lack of something to do she drew the curtains. Before too long it would be late enough to have a drink, so that would be all right. She went into the kitchen to play at cooking, but the evening meal was already well prepared.

'Eileen . . . ?' George's voice had that new, peremptory quality which drove her mad. 'Eileen, there's a knock at the door.'

'Are you sure?' George wasn't himself. She wondered if he was imagining it. Eileen was experienced enough as the vicar's wife in Skirlbeck to know that no-one would come knocking on the door at four o'clock on a wet Friday afternoon the first week in December, when they could telephone instead.

'Eileen, please answer the door, will you?' Tutting, she strode through the long, low room into the narrow hallway, and opened the front door expecting to see nothing but the wind in the gorse bushes. But an apologetic woman stood on the step, her short auburn hair blown back in spikes, and her face pink with exertion and embarrassment.

'Kate!'

'Eileen. How are you? Do you mind me calling?'

'Mind you calling . . . ridiculous! Come in.'

Kate followed her into the living room, where George, clearly delighted, seemed on the point of actually trying to get up.

'No, don't do that.' Kate hurried over and hugged him. This time the old man did not flinch when she kissed him. She was aware of Eileen taking her coat and pushing forward one of her squashy chairs, right by the roaring fire.

'John's not here; he's up at Skirlbeck House,' Eileen was saying.

'Perhaps that's just as well,' Kate said, surprised at the tremble in her own voice. 'I'm not sure how he'll feel about me turning up, and anyway, I wanted to see you two as well.'

'How are you, my dear?' George asked.

Kate felt the crusty scratch on her cheek, and unconsciously moved her head. The gash from Terry Robinson's knife had left a fresh pink scar the medics said would soon fade. She still found herself coughing, sometimes for no other reason than her imagination, and though she appreciated the Goffs' roaring fire she edged the chair further from it than Eileen would have liked. But all these little gestures were as nothing compared to the relief of being alive.

'I'm fine,' she smiled at the Goffs. 'And you?' But she could tell George was different. His mouth had a petulant turn, and Eileen looked strained. She left them to pour drinks, almost with relief, Kate thought, and she wondered just how much stress the Goffs were under.

'And John?' she asked, awkwardly.

'Much, much better. But you have spoken to him on the phone, haven't you?' The mention of John was the first time George Goff's face relaxed back into its old, cheerful form.

'Yes, but . . .'

'Things aren't quite right?' George leaned forward now, suddenly more like the wise and sprightly man she had first met.

'That's true, George.'

'Well my dear, it has all been a terrible shock for both of you. And you had to go back to London while John was still in hospital.'

'Yes. I had to go back to work and I needed to convalesce myself. So I went to London to some friends, and Liz and Andy stayed here to tidy things up.'

She sat for a minute, unhappy to look directly into the fire, but seeing its light play round the glass which Eileen was pressing into her hand. She sipped, silently aware that George had relapsed into deep thought, until suddenly he started to move.

He was struggling to stand up. Eileen Goff turned round to him. 'George, what are you doing?'

'I'd like a walk. I'm sure Kate will come with me.'

'What? George, you must be mad. You haven't been out all day, and it's stormy. The doctor said . . .'

'The doctor said I needed to try and take an interest in life again, didn't he?'

'George! When did you hear him say that?'

'Oh, you've all been treating me like a dozy old fool. But

my ears are sharp enough. My trouble has been that I've been preoccupied. We've had more trouble in this village in the past two months than in the last ten years, though . . .' he paused for a minute, 'I suppose it was incubating all that time. And I know Kate can help me piece things together. There are things even now that I don't understand.' He shook his head dispiritedly. 'Do you fancy popping down to the shore, Kate? Just to get the colour back into my cheeks?'

'Well, only if Eileen thinks it would be a good idea?'

Eileen was nodding, 'Oh, you go ahead. It's the first thing George has bothered getting worked up about for weeks. I'll need to sort out some more food anyway. You will stay to dinner, Kate, won't you?'

Kate wondered how John would feel about that, but Eileen was looking genuinely keen, as if relieved at the prospect of something to do.

'Thanks, Eileen; I'd love to.'

'I'll get your coat, George,' said his wife. 'But do remember the doctor said you mustn't overdo things and you mustn't get upset.'

'Oh, to hell with the doctor!' said George, with such expletive force that Eileen actually laughed. 'And I don't say things like that lightly.' George was laughing too, a rusty sort of sound. He limped into the hallway, and began to fuss, looking for his wellingtons.

'Well, that's a turn up for the books!' Eileen said to Kate. 'That's the first time he's shown any signs of enthusiasm since Terry Robinson's funeral. It's been a dreadful business, but the rest of the village is getting over it. Even Michael Marshall has been seen out and about. But George is going downhill. He talks to John, of course, but it's still as if something was on his mind.'

Kate heard the vicar calling her and grabbed her own coat to join him. He slammed the front door behind them, and they made their way laboriously down the track. Kate walked slowly by his side, not sure whether to offer an arm and risk rebuff, the wind thumping both of them and making talking impossible. Finally the track widened and dissolved, delta-like, on to the beach.

George stood and looked out to sea.

'They must have come this way, that day,' he said bleakly.

'Who must, George?'

'Jean Robinson and the person who killed her. She was wheeled down here, and left over there.' He pointed to where a flock of oyster-catchers scurried along a sand bar. Kate said nothing, but followed his eyes along the stony beach. They were sheltered now by the slightest rise of a tussocky dune behind them, and George could be heard.

'You know, Kate, if I'd acted sooner, she might not have been killed. Nor Tom Flint. And Celia Marshall might not have died. I blame myself. And as for Maple, who was completely innocent, being injured so badly . . .'

'Oh, George, how can you take the blame?'

'Easily. I've spent the last four weeks going over and over and over it. It must have been my fault.'

'It's funny you should say that George, because I tend to think it was *my* fault. I should have realised long before we went to the dogfight that Paul Pym was involved. I don't think I would ever have guessed that Terry Robinson was the godfather figure, but if I'd had half a brain, I'd have realised that Hugh Ruscroft at Channel Four was in contact with Pym from the start. Of course I can't prove it. But I've told Chrissia my suspicions. Channel Four is pretty

scrupulous and I don't think Ruscroft will ever work there
again. I think he and Pym tried planting an article against
me in the local paper and before that, Ruscroft turned down
my idea for the film. I'm sure he even tipped Pym off.'

'Did he, my dear? How do you know?'

'Because I should have listened to my own ears. I had to
go back to the office for the commissioning editor's glasses
– she had left them on her desk – and I heard Ruscroft on
the phone. He referred to someone as a stupid cow – me,
of course – and said the programme idea probably would
pall. Or at least I thought he meant that. But what he must
have really said was: "It probably would, Paul!" P.A.U.L . . .
don't you see?'

'Oh, Kate, you can hardly blame yourself for not spotting
that!'

'But I can blame myself for telling Pym about you.'

'What?'

'Well, you see, I was so busy trying to justify the change
of theme in the film to Pym – you know that authoritarian
way he had of making you try and impress him – that I
implied to him that you were helping me. I'm sure that was
why you were attacked.'

George Goff was silent, deep in thought. Then he
murmured, 'Is that true Kate?'

'Yes, it is. If I hadn't said anything, there was no way
Pym would ever have associated you with the threat of
exposure. But in a desperate attempt to prove I had some
evidence for the film, I hinted that you were helping me,
and he assumed far more than I meant.'

'So you believe that was why he tried to run me down?'

'Oh, yes. I think he believed that if you were killed, I
would lose a key contact, be scared off filming, and you

would be safely out of the way unable to talk to anyone. And people had been saying you were a danger on the road, walking round with your head in the clouds, so a hit-and-run accident was perfect!' She smiled. 'But he didn't think of John.'

'He certainly didn't. My dear, I can't thank you enough for telling me that. I feel as if a weight has been lifted from me. You're a Godsend, literally. I've been torturing myself with the suspicion that I must somehow have indicated to Pym that I knew about his nefarious activity, although I had been sworn to absolute secrecy. The person who confided in me knew Pym was lethal, and warned me against even hinting that I had been told. But if Pym thought I was passing information on to you, then I can see why I was attacked!'

'But it wasn't you giving the game away that was to blame at all. It was me and my big mouth.' Kate turned. 'Come on, let's go back. It's maudlin standing here, George, looking at the place where Jean Robinson died. By the summer it will just be someone's picnic spot.'

'You're right, m'dear. You know, with Jean, Terry and Pym all being dead, no-one will ever know for sure, but I believe it must have been Pym who pushed Jean Robinson down here. It had to be one of her blackmail victims, someone she might initially trust or feel enough contempt for to be unconcerned. She must have left her friend Ada's and arranged to meet her victim. Then she became the victim in turn.'

'So was she really blackmailing more people than poor Andy de Salas? Was that what all those payments were in her cashbooks? How many people was she extorting money from?'

'Plenty. What a lot of questions you have. Look, let's get back to the bungalow and have another drink. I can't tell you how much better I feel, being able to talk about it. I'd like to go through my theories with you.'

They slowly retraced their steps up the rutted lane, although Kate fancied that now George was firmer on his feet. In the bungalow it took Kate the best part of half an hour to slowly get the story and to sort out the facts. But George's realisation that he had not been to blame for the hit-and-run attack seemed to cheer and strengthen him, so he could voice his speculation for the first time.

After the fire in the barn which killed Terry and Paul Pym – one rushing into the flames with the joy of a madman, the other too inebriated to save himself – the police had charged a few outsiders with possession of dangerous dogs, and one local man with illicit bookmaking. That was all. The question of Jean Robinson's murder, and others, would never be raised. But the answers had all been laboriously worked out by George, as he had languished, lost in guilt, by his fireside.

After her fake accident seventeen years ago, it was clear the twins' mother had acquired the Skirlbeck Bridge Hotel on the basis of a small deposit which had come from Andy de Salas. And from there she had started a reign of silent terror over Skirlbeck. Most people in the village patronised the hotel and nearly all had confided at some time or other in the cute little woman, so frail, yet so bright eyed and cheerful in her fraudulent infirmity, only to find out later that she had the strength of a demon. She had a finger in every pie, and had accumulated secrets about everybody. After his brother's death, Bill Robinson had ceremoniously burnt his mother's documents in front of John Maple and the Reverend Goff. Bill had never realised the full extent of her blackmailing activities, although he had known about her first victim without ever knowing his name – Andy de Salas. But the elder twin's disgust had meant he was kept out of her future ventures. Terry, the favoured younger son, had probably always supported her. Bill had wanted to destroy all the evidence, but not before they had worked out that she had been extorting money from Tom Flint, Celia Marshall, and Paul Pym, as well as Andy.

'I think that she tried it on with Malcolm Hodgson too,' Bill had told the two priests, 'but he was the only person to call her bluff, even though it caused his wife to leave him. Mother phoned Susan Hodgson about Malcolm and his other women.'

So that was why Malcolm had been so emphatic about Jean Robinson being a bad old bitch! Kate looked at the carpet when she heard this, and said nothing, but she had a feeling that George Goff guessed what she was thinking about. He resumed the explanation.

Jean Robinson had always masterminded the odd bit of gambling and wasn't above encouraging a little cockfighting in time honoured tradition, but when Pym arrived in the area, it hadn't taken her long to discover his obsession. And with Terry she had begun a much bigger and more frightening business.

Pym was a technophile, still embittered after his enforced departure from TV, and working his way through his family's money, bet by bet. She encouraged him to develop the dogfighting ring into a video business, using Tom Flint's remote and rundown farm for his editing, and she had organised the events.

'But where did Celia Marshall come in?' asked Kate.

'Ah,' said George, 'that was one of my many mistakes. You see, I couldn't bring myself to reveal to anyone, not even Maple, all I had been told. So I let John assume from what you said that it was Jean Robinson who had come to see me, to tell me of the criminal activity in Skirlbeck. But it wasn't at all. That old witch wouldn't know the meaning of the word remorse. It was Celia Marshall who came to me!'

'Celia Marshall?' Kate was astonished.

'Yes. She wanted to confide and confess. She and old Tom Flint had got together – a most unlikely combination – and they were making extra copies of the dogfighting videos, to sell. Celia was just a greedy old woman who was desperate to get more money into her mill venture. She had heard her husband talk endlessly about the money to be made in new technology, but he's a very tightfisted old so-and-so and really has no initiative, so she went ahead, and then got herself caught up in something she couldn't cope with. She just believed that anything to do with media was a goldmine.'

'So that was why she invested in Andy's film,' muttered Kate.

'Did she? Well, that adds up. But apparently she and Tom set up another company, to process the money from the dog videos.'

' "Flintstones"! Of course. Tom loved cartoons and Celia loved TV!' Kate whispered to herself. 'But how did she know Tom Flint in the first place?'

'Well, of course everyone knows everyone around Skirlbeck. But I know what you mean, they were hardly from the same stratum of society, though the Flints were very wealthy in their own way. No, she really teamed up with him when they both lobbied against the theme park. One of the reasons Flint, Pym, and even Jean Robinson, didn't want it, was because it would mean knocking down the old barn. And without the barn, they were short on places to hold the dogfights.'

'Of course. But how did you work all this out?'

'Celia told me about it. She came into church after Family Communion on that Sunday before I first met you, Kate, the morning of the day Jean Robinson died. She told me how Jean Robinson had blackmailed her with the threat of telling her husband she was involved in something illegal. Sir Michael would have been apoplectic! Celia hated and loathed Jean, but it wasn't Jean who made her frightened for her life. It was Pym!'

'But why?'

'Because Celia Marshall believed that if Jean Robinson was blackmailing her, she was sure to be blackmailing Pym too, and Pym was getting nasty. Mrs Robinson made no secret of her contempt for offcomers, and the tension was making Pym violent. But it was poor old Tom Flint who pushed Pym over the edge. Tom had been getting more and more unstable and untrustworthy from Pym's point of view, since his dog died. Celia wasn't sure why the dog's death upset Tom so much . . .'

'But I know why!' Kate breathed. 'You say Celia never went to the dogfights?'

'No.'

'Well, she wouldn't have known that Tom Flint's dog was killed by these bastards, for pleasure.'

'Then no wonder Tom was becoming very shaky, and getting the sharp edge of Pym's temper. Celia told me that she had seen Pym threaten Flint, and that she feared Pym would turn on them all, Jean Robinson included! But you know, Celia was a brave woman in her own foolish way. She told me that day in church that she was going to tackle Pym, and threaten to expose him if he did anything to Flint.'

'So Celia told you that Pym was a threat to all three of them, her, Flint, and Jean Robinson?'

'Yes! But Jean was too arrogant to take it seriously. She had lived a charmed life in Skirlbeck.'

'And did you believe Celia?'

'My dear, I wasn't sure. Pym was such a decent chap, as far as I was concerned. He was director of the Tourist Centre, and a regular communicant. And as she seemed prepared to tackle him herself, I advised her to do just that. But it must have been my advice that led to her death.' The old man put his head in his hands, and his wife got up restlessly, looked at him in concern mixed with frustration, and walked over to pour him another drink.

'Surely not,' Kate was trying to be comforting. 'Lady Marshall died of a heart attack, nothing more.'

'But don't you see, Kate? Something must have caused it! Sir Michael told me he found her with a man's bloodstained cap in her hand. I think she faced Pym with evidence that he had killed Tom Flint, and in the row that ensued, she started her heart attack.'

'But that's not your fault. It was a whole week after she confessed to you. And in that time, we all heard that Jean Robinson and Tom Flint were dead. Celia had plenty of warning that Pym might be a murderer.'

'Did she? I suppose so. My dear, you're so right. You know, Kate, I've spent the last four weeks agonising over all this, not wanting to talk to Maple because he hasn't been well himself, and not wanting to talk to Eileen because she felt she should have foreseen more. But talking to you is putting so much of it into perspective.'

George still blamed himself for going away on his retreat, as planned, after listening to Celia Marshall's allegations, but as Kate pointed out to him, at that time speculation against one of his staunchest church members was all there was to go on. But George had worked out that on that very day Pym had arranged to meet the overconfident Jean Robinson, and had wheeled her to the shore to die. It was an almost perfect crime, in a silent village on a deserted Sunday evening. Even if he had been seen, he could have said that she had asked him to do it, and had assured him that she could get back alone. But with Jean and her extortion – and contempt – out of the way, Flint was still a problem for Pym. George believed he had given in to the bloodlust which up until that moment he had contained in voyeurism and had gone up to Flint's farm and shot him, probably in pleasure. But Celia Marshall must have been there just afterwards and taken Flint's bloodstained cap. She would know that no local man would leave his cap on to sit at his kitchen table, even if he was planning to shoot himself. Kate smiled, though it was hardly funny.

But then poor Lady Marshall had worried more and more about Pym's next move. She had wanted to tackle him, yet had needed to find her moment. She probably felt it was safest to confront Pym in her own home, which would be difficult because her husband rarely went out. But he always went to early Communion on a Sunday. Normally, so did Pym – George had wanted John Maple at early Communion with him in case Pym was there! But that morning Pym had not been at the service. George believed Celia Marshall had asked Pym to Skirlbeck House.

'So you think Pym killed Jean Robinson, then Tom Flint, and then went to Celia on the Sunday morning, and caused her seizure?'

'I'm sure so. When I came back from the retreat and found Jean Robinson was dead, I was becoming frighteningly sure Celia's fears had been well founded. But I was terrified of doing anything about it in case I was wrong. The human ecology of a village is very fragile. The man she was indicting to me, strictly in confidence, was a pillar of the community and a churchgoer! I needed another priest to talk to. Then when Celia died the next morning, I went into a state of complete anxiety. You see, Sir Michael rang me and told me before he even called the ambulance. I knew she was dead by midday on Sunday, and I was paralysed with fear. I don't know what I would have done without John . . .'

Kate remembered her ultimatum to John to leave George and come back to her, and felt a wave of guilt. No wonder he had not reappeared at one o'clock that Sunday. Kate shuddered despite the fire. If only John had told her! George Goff was tiring now. Kate was looking into her glass, thinking of all the evil that had been stalking Skirlbeck for years. But the glass reminded her of something.

'But what about your spirit messages, Eileen? Where did the castle fit in?'

'I don't know,' Eileen looked depressed. 'George tells me I've just been stupid and histrionic.'

'Now, Eileen darling, that's not fair,' her husband interjected, looking as miserable as she did once more. 'I never said you were histrionic, and not stupid either. I never ever demean your gift, although you know I can't believe in spirits. But I'm sure you have perception denied to most of us. Though in this case I can't see how your vision has any relevance at all.'

'It doesn't look like it, Eileen.' Kate stretched her legs in front of the fire. Even the flames seemed safe in the Goffs' house.

'You're probably right,' Eileen admitted sadly. 'I suppose all that's left now is to watch your film. When will it be on Channel Four, Kate?'

Channel Four. Kate looked into her whisky tumbler with its cut-glass indentations, and remembered what she had thought when she had seen the Channel Four building. It had looked like a glass fortress, with its moat and drawbridge. A castle, with Ruscroft inside. She felt a funny shiver from her neck to her ankles.

'Eileen,' she said, 'your message may not have been so daft after all . . .'

It was at least another half hour before she and the Goffs had finished mulling it all over. George finally took his last sip of the whisky which had lain forgotten on the hearth. He was beaming now, holding Eileen's hand as she sat at his feet, his faith in himself, and his secret faith in her, restored.

'My dear,' he said to Kate, 'you are here for supper, aren't you? Where are you staying?'

Kate smiled. 'The Skirlbeck Bridge, of course. But just bed and breakfast!'

'My goodness! You're actually staying there! Doesn't that upset you?'

'No, funnily enough, it doesn't. It was lovely to see Bill again. He seems different now, bigger and more normal, as if he can be himself. He must always have known about his mother, but he must have suspected, and protected, Terry too.'

'You're so right. How is he? With my bad leg, I've not been down there since the funeral.'

'You won't believe it, but he seems wonderfully well. He's already got a rather camp young man in to manage the place, and who knows . . . ?'

They laughed. Then Kate suddenly thought of the time, and her heart lurched into her mouth. She heard her voice say hollowly, 'When will John be back?'

'Oh, soon.' Eileen looked at her watch. 'I'll leave you two chatting on, and pop to the shop. I think we need a bottle of wine tonight.'

'Marvellous idea.' George grinned delightedly as she bustled away.

'And now,' he said, more seriously when Eileen had gone. 'What do you intend to do about my friend Maple?'

'Oh, God, George, I don't know. I still feel guilty about the accident. I should never have mentioned you to Pym . . .'

'Kate, any guilt you feel has been more than expunged by the relief you have given me in being so honest. And the accident is only a peripheral matter. What do you think is really the problem between you and John?'

'I think the problem is that he won't really talk to me. He's terrified of rowing. He wants us to pretend everything is fine, all the time.'

'And you can't do that?'

'No. Why should I? And – I hope you don't mind me saying this – meeting you and Eileen *should* have helped, but it hasn't.'

'Really? Why not?'

'I think John thought that I should see you as rôle models. You know, the way Eileen is able to live her life, with her very different approach, and you yours. But much as I admire you both, I couldn't be like that. I'd want to fight it out. George, why are you laughing?'

'Because it's funny. Kate, see that picture over there?'

'Oh, yes . . . you and your first wife, isn't it?'

'Yes. Beryl. This is a difficult thing to explain, but much as I love Eileen, and I do love her very much, Beryl and I were married twenty-six years and 'til she passed away she really was the love of my life. I thought I would die when she did. And there wasn't a day of our lives when we didn't row about something. We did the lot. We fought about theology, politics, ethics, news, everything. And when she died I felt as if my brain had been amputated. Eileen and I have a different way of life. But it isn't the only way, or the best way.'

Kate looked at George in astonishment. 'Do you think John could handle that?'

'Of course he could. He's just scared of losing you, that's all.'

Kate looked at the elderly vicar. She was aware of a new warmth, more delicious than the whisky, coursing through her. George had given her a sip of hope, but almost as soon as she tasted it, it turned to bile. How could she even think about making things work with John, after what had happened with Malcolm Hodgson? The next morning, in Malcolm's bedroom, she had looked down the fell to the lake and known she would never have John's easy companionship again.

'George, there's something else I'd like to tell you. Confidentially.'

'Of course, my dear. What's that?'

'During the time John and I have been apart, there's been someone else.'

'Aah.' If George guessed who, which would not have been difficult, he said nothing.

'But it didn't work. At least . . .' she blushed, 'it didn't work emotionally.' George smiled. Kate went on. 'And I feel so bad about it. How can I go back to John with that between us? And if I tell him, he'll be hurt, I know he will, but he won't say so. So I can't clear the air. It will hang between us like a cloud.'

George took another sip of his drink. 'I know you're not a Christian, Kate, but if you were I'd tell you you're already forgiven, if indeed it was a sin at all, because you're so sorry. But there's no need to hurt John by telling him. Perhaps, if you do consider this a misjudgement – a sin, even, in my terms – then the price you have to pay is keeping it to yourself. Confession usually takes the burden off one person and on to another, that's the whole concept. Don't put the burden on poor John. Carry it yourself.'

Kate looked into her own glass. There was a wisdom in what George was saying.

She said softly, 'But I was horrified at myself.'

'Oh, come now, Kate, it can't have been so dreadful. Listen, I think you feel deep down that somehow John's faith makes him better than you. Well, it doesn't. Remember the Ash Wednesday prayer, "Almighty God, who hatest nothing that thou hast made . . ." Especially not the wonderful Kate Wilkinson!'

Kate turned to stare at him in amazement, then in a rush of grateful enthusiasm she leapt over to the old armchair and flung her arms round George's neck. The front door opened so she and George sprang apart like guilty lovers. John and Eileen had met on the path outside and came in together, to catch John's former mistress and Eileen's husband in their embrace. It was a great way to overcome the awkwardness and when the laughing had stopped, Eileen opened the bottle of champagne she had bought.

But despite the air of reconciliation, John looked dreadful to Kate, stressed, too thin, older and almost stooped. He still had a dressing across the side of his head, and he was pale. He kept catching her eye. At first she looked away, and then slowly, she found herself nodding, then smiling, then laughing with him. She felt that something more than their injuries was healing, but that any sudden emotional shift might open the wounds.

Not much later, they all sat down to dinner. It was an interesting meal, with the conversation going over and over the Skirlbeck murders, but never dwelling too much on the final gruesome tragedy and dwelling more on the relationships and chronology.

'But there was one point which interested me,' Kate said, in the middle of this. 'Once, I thought about accusing John of always wanting the director's cut. You know, the uncommercial, one-off version of a film, with no discussion. And so many people in this mess were directors, I mean people in charge. There was Andy de Salas, film director; and there was Paul Pym, director of the Tourist Centre. Celia Marshall was a director of the mill; and they say her husband was obsessed with becoming a director of Border TV . . .'

'You could even argue that I was a spiritual director,' John contributed.

'And actually . . .' Kate's voice was low, 'Terry and Bill Robinson were directors of the Skirlbeck Bridge Hotel. They had a partnership agreement. The director's cut . . .' she fingered the scar on her neck, and shivered.

'Time for dessert,' said Eileen Goff firmly.

At ten thirty, John offered to drive Kate back to the hotel. Even in the car they said nothing significant, except that Kate was hoping to see Sally Dodd and Cliff Thompson for Sunday lunch.

'And tomorrow?' asked John.

Kate looked away, embarrassed, then remembered what George had said. She would have to bear her guilt. 'Tomorrow morning I'm hoping to see Malcolm Hodgson, the councillor who alerted me to the dogfighting in the first place. I have a cassette of the programme for him.'

'And in the afternoon?'

'I haven't thought that far.'

'Could we go out together? I could pick you up at about two o'clock?'

It was on the tip of her tongue to snap, 'Are you sure you have time? Won't someone else more worthy need you?' But she didn't.

'I'd love that,' she said.

At two o'clock the following day, Kate stood in the bay window of the Skirlbeck's bar, waiting for John and wondering why she had been surprised that morning when she had taken the bus to Malcolm's house, to find the door being opened by a drowsy-looking woman. It had taken Kate a few minutes to recognise her as the attractive reporter from the *Cumberland News*, wearing what was clearly one of Malcolm's shirts. Malcolm had loomed behind her, saying, 'Kate! Good Lord, I'd forgotten you were coming.' He looked different too, smaller, rather older, and more relaxed. 'The theme park's been passed,' he said cheerfully. 'We've been celebrating.'

'I was doing the story,' the reporter said with some embarrassment. And that's not all, thought Kate, looking at the debris of wine bottles and cigarette ash in Malcolm's kitchen. He caught her eye and they exchanged a glance of good-humoured understanding. Malcolm seemed delighted with the tape of the programme, and they had stood on the doorstep prior to parting, exchanging mutual invitations to visit, like two old, familiar friends.

'How's the boyfriend?' he had said, just as she turned away to walk down the drive.

'Fine,' Kate said noncommittally.

'Give it your best shot,' Malcolm had said again, winking.

And here she was, prepared to do that. Her heart turned over as the Goffs' car drew up, with John driving. For an awful moment she thought he might have brought George and Eileen too, but John was alone.

'Hi,' he said softly. They didn't kiss, but Kate ached with the desire just to be next to him, and as she sat down in the car, the mere proximity of his shoulder warmed and soothed her.

'Do you remember the first day we went out together?' John asked, and she nodded. They had driven over the hills between Yorkshire and Lancashire, at Easter. 'Well, this countryside is different. Much more dramatic, but in a strangely accessible way. I'm going to take you to the most beautiful place in England.'

'Where's that?'

'It's called Watendlath. It's just above Derwentwater.'

He turned with the ease of someone who now knew the area well, down the narrow lanes.

'I'm going to miss this when I get back to London,' he remarked. Kate said nothing. She hadn't been sure what

John's plans were, and she knew that they were no longer her business, but she felt an irrational delight that he would be coming back.

It took them about half an hour to get to the lake, and on the way they chatted a little, but not too intensely, about Jean Robinson, Andy and Liz, Paul Pym, and the tragedy of Terry Robinson.

'It's all about whether other life can be dispensed with for convenience,' said John. 'That was where I was coming from, over Liz and the abortion, until you made me see it was different. But someone like Paul Pym used the deaths of those animals for pleasure, and it can't be too great a step from that to using the deaths of people for convenience. And in a way Jean Robinson was worse. She didn't revert to murder because she didn't have to. She took on more of the powers of God than anyone, even Pym. Her son inherited that form of madness.'

They said little more. But as they drove through the Lakes, Kate found herself enjoying the place's beauty. The trees were largely bare now and the water was as slate-coloured as the slab-like rock above, but it was gorgeous in a way that was too comforting to be magnificent, but too dramatic to be pretty.

They crawled up the bleakly challenging Honister Pass, and down into Seathwaite, past the thick, solid, wind clean cottages and the much nurtured scraps of trees and gardens, and down past the flatness of Manesty at the head of the lake, to where the water lapped the road. Then John turned dramatically right, up the hairpin bend towards the village, over Ashness Bridge, which was utterly satisfying in its stony symmetry, and along the straight narrow, upper valley road which reminded Kate of childhood readings of

Lorna Doone, into a clearing with a semi-circle of low white and slate farmhouses.

'You've probably never read Hugh Walpole, but this is where he set his books,' John said. 'My parents came up here on a motorbike, before the war, and once after that when we were children and they had enough money for a holiday, we came here and stayed at the farm. Everyone else went to Blackpool, but my dad took us for bed and breakfast in the Lakes and the neighbours thought we were mad. I was transfixed. We had the fells at home, but nothing as remote and wonderful as this. I thought when I was a boy that one day I'd come back, with someone special. Then time goes on, and you forget. But suddenly, today, there was a chance to get here.' He said nothing more, and she stood by him, looking with him at the ring of hills around them.

As they watched, a man hurried down the path from the tarn, which lay further up the mountain beyond the houses, his iron rimmed clogs clattering and rivalling the splashing of the river which cascaded down to the hamlet, a little bunch of ducks, white Aylesburys and brown mallards, bustling in front of him.

' 'Owdo,' he said, tipping his cap. 'Bad weather for just standing.'

'Quite right,' said John. 'Come on, Kate. Let's walk up to the tarn.'

The little lake gathered like a giant tear in the bowl of the hills. Kate stood on the bank, looking down at the cosy circle of houses. She felt John's hand on her shoulder and her whole body reacted. It wasn't lust. It was more and better than that. She turned into him instinctively without thinking too much of the significance.

'I've missed you!' he said.

'I've missed you too.'

'I'm so sorry, Kate. Lying in hospital, I realised how maddening I must have been, avoiding arguments and tiptoeing round issues. Not only that, I should have trusted you and told you about George's fears from the beginning. But I thought you would just laugh at him, and I couldn't bear that.'

'And I thought you thought I wasn't good enough!'

'Oh, no, not at all; I was just scared of the fierce blast of your common sense. Funnily enough, when we had our discussion about abortion I realised you had convictions too, which could be seen as just as irrational as mine, but which you passionately believed. It made me love you more at the very time I feared you loved me less! And I realised I had been unfair to you. We need to have discussions, I know we do; and if you blow up, well, that's you! And then look at what happened in that barn. I heard all about it. You were so brave. I felt really bad about the silly way I tried to protect us both from nothing worse than rows, when you had the courage to take on a horde of men like that.'

'But I understand too,' she whispered back. 'You don't argue for the sake of it, like me. It all matters so much to you. And I know I can fly off the handle, and that I always want to win. I can't say I won't want to persuade you, John, but I promise to try not to make an issue out of *everything*.'

'Don't worry, Kate, you've just got to be you.'

Almighty God, who hatest nothing that thou hast made . . . Perhaps some elements of John's faith weren't so bad.

'And you have to be you too, John. But I will try.'

'Not too hard. I love you as you are.'

'Do you? Oh, John, I love you too, I really do. I've been so lonely, me and my principles. And you can't argue with yourself.'

'Not even you?'

'Not even me.'

'Well, here's a real issue to struggle with. Kate, how do you feel about the principle of love and fidelity, for life?'

She did not really take in what he was saying. The word fidelity made her glance away from him. For a minute her eyes looked west, across the tarn and over the fells and down towards Malcolm Hodgson's house with its secrets. Thank God for George Goff's advice. She breathed deeply. 'Love and fidelity for life sounds like bliss,' she said lightly.

'Then will you marry me?'

'What?'

'Will you marry me? Forget God and the bishop and the sacrament and my faith. They're what's in it for me. What I can offer *you* is just love and fidelity for life. That's it. Is it what you want?'

Kate moved her own hand up towards his where it lay on her shoulder. She felt the tension in his fingers.

'Yes,' she said. John's hand twitched, then scrabbled to enclose hers, with a grip that made her squeal. His silence was solid. She knew he was astonished that she wasn't arguing.

'Just yes?' he said at last, in a whisper of surprise and near apprehension. 'You mean you don't want to talk about it?'

'No, I don't,' she smiled. 'The answer's yes. You're right. We're already there. It's not a controversial issue. No argument necessary.'

She heard him laughing as she turned to him and kissed

him. When she opened her eyes, she was aware of the dusk dropping round them like a gentle blanket.

'We'd better go,' said John. 'We'll need another bottle of champagne tonight.'

He turned to walk down the path, suddenly running like a little boy with his arms outstretched, aeroplane style. She watched him with complete, uncompromising joy as he jumped over the stones, and waited for her near the flat wooden bridge.

'Hey, Kate,' he called, a mischievous grin on his face. 'All this talk of life and death has made me think. We're not too old for children are we? At least, you're not.'

'What?' she said again, stopping to make sure she had heard him correctly.

'A baby,' he said. 'Or more than one.'

'A baby. For us? At my age. But, John . . . !' He was laughing and running away, so she had to scramble after him.

'Wait, John. Wait!' she called. She felt the wind in her face, and the stones under her feet. Everything around her seemed clearer, subtler, richer, from the growing grey darkness in the west, to the lights from the farmhouses glowing on the cushion of the night in the east.

'John, hang on; you can't just throw that one at me!' But he was running on now, his long legs always striding just too far for her to catch him. 'John, listen to me. We need to discuss this . . .' He turned to laugh at her. 'John, it isn't funny. That *is* a controversial issue. Hey . . . !' And, feeling more alive than ever before, she ran after him to start the very first argument of their new life.